Charlie felt more than good.
Charlie felt like God.

Metal shrieked. A thin, wailing scream, human
perhaps, rose above the forges of destruction.
The sky itself shattered, iron thunder, and the
rain that fell was a rain of hot steel. The ground
shook as the helicopter burst to shards. A fragment of its blade whipped over the ditch; Charlie
felt the wind burn with its passing.

Transcendent satisfaction in every moment of
it.

The job was done. Strenuous and fulfilling
labor complete, his senses tingling postcoitally.

His enemies were dead. He was alive. Who is
incapable of feeling joy at that?

Books by Joseph R. Garber

Whirlwind
Vertical Run (1995)
Rascal Money (1989)

JOSEPH R. GARBER

WHIRLWIND

HarperTorch
An Imprint of HarperCollinsPublishers

This is a work of fiction. Names, characters, places, and incidents are products of the author's imagination or are used fictitiously and are not to be construed as real. Any resemblance to actual events, locales, organizations, or persons, living or dead, is entirely coincidental.

HARPERTORCH
An Imprint of HarperCollins*Publishers*
10 East 53rd Street
New York, New York 10022-5299

First HarperTorch paperback printing: October 2005
First HarperCollins hardcover printing: September 2004

HarperCollins®, HarperTorch™, and ♦™ are trademarks of Harper-Collins Publishers Inc.

Printed in the United States of America

Visit HarperTorch on the World Wide Web at www.harpercollins.com

10 9 8 7 6 5 4 3 2 1

For my brother, Dr. John Garber

PART ONE

Charlie's Exile

A man who tries to carry a cat home by its tail will learn a lesson that can be learned in no other way.

—Mark Twain

I
Ah, Vengeance!

Charlie McKenzie glared over the rims of his half-moon reading glasses. Shuffling his *Washington Post* in what he hoped was, but suspected was not, an intimidating manner, he reached for his coffee. A newspaper, a cup of coffee, a dozy cat in his lap, and a peaceful morning in which to enjoy them—were they not every man's natural-born prerogatives?

Hugging two-year-old Jason to her hip, Carly brandished a portable telephone. "Dad," she said breathlessly. "It's the White House! The national security advisor!"

Apparently his daughter held the rights of men, or at least males, in low esteem. Charlie had no one to blame but himself. Up until the day she died, Mary had insisted that Carly certainly did not get *that* sort of behavior from her side of the family.

He turned in his wicker chair, looking out beyond the screened porch, past the long green expanse of a stately lawn, down to Chesapeake Bay. It was a lovely summer morning, bright but not yet hot. Perfect weather as far as the eye could see—except in the climatological zone directly above Charlie's thundercloud brow. "Tell him to go piss up a rope."

"Dad!"

"Tiss upa row," echoed Jason. To which Molly, aged six and peeking around her mother's skirts, added, "Mommy, Jason's saying dirty words."

"Your grandfather's influence. *Again!*" hissed Carly, thrusting the phone into Charlie's lap, then dragging her children away from what doubtless would be another bad example.

Charlie raised the phone to his ear. He spoke softly, gently. "Mornin', Sam."

An unctuous answer, amiability's illusion in every syllable: "Charlie! It's good to hear you, man! Thank God I caught you at home! Listen, there's a problem, a helluva problem, and the president personally asked that I call—"

Speaking in the gentlemanly tones of a sweetly reasonable soul, Charlie interrupted. "Give him my best personal regards, and tell him I said he can screw himself."

The portable phone chirped like a digital bird as Charlie fingered the Off button.

Eight seconds, he estimated as he glanced at his outrageously garish wristwatch, a solid gold Rolex President with numbers set in colored gemstones. The preposterous thing was a gift from the Philippine government. That figured. No one in that part of the world had a bit of taste.

. . . three, four, five . . .

As opposed, for example, to the Italians. It was one of their presidents—who could remember which, they never stayed out of jail long enough to make memorizing their names worth the effort—who'd given Charlie the monumentally expensive, solid silver Faema espresso maker whose ambrosia he was savoring at this very moment.

. . . six, seven, eight . . . Ring!

Perfect timing. Charlie McKenzie never missed. Clicking the On button, he smiled beatifically, a man who had been waiting two long years for Sam to call, and who planned to enjoy himself mightily now that the roly-poly little weasel needed help. "Okay, Sam, if bunny brains doesn't know how to do it, tell him first thing he needs is a dildo."

Sam's oiliness had dissipated. "Charlie, we don't have time for this."

" 'Dildo' usually is synonymous with 'national security advisor,' but not this time."

Now Sam was feigning sincerity. "This is an emergency. More than an emergency. The word 'crisis' doesn't even begin—"

"And an industrial-strength motor, the kind they use to run jackhammers."

Goodbye sincerity, hello desperation. "Okay, okay, whatever you want. Name it. It's yours." He paused, then hastily added, "Short of an apology, that is."

Charlie ran a hand down his stubbled cheek. He'd have to shave before Sam showed up on his doorstep. And that would be—he eyed his watch—in fifty-seven minutes. "Anything, Sam?"

"If it's in my power, yes."

Yup, definitely desperation. It was a step in the right direction. "Ten million dollars." Charlie heard a barely audible *Shit!* "The actuarial tables tell me I've got another thirty-five years to live. Ten million works out to about two hundred and eighty grand a year. That's not much in light of my decades of loyal and faithful service."

"Put it in T-bills, and the interest is three hundred thousand."

Charlie snorted, "Hey, Sam, if you're so good at math, how come the White House can't balance the budget?"

"Quit busting my chops." He cleared his throat before predictably wheedling, "I don't suppose I could appeal to your patriotism?"

Charlie pictured the expression on Sam's pudgy face: slit-eyed calculation. It always was. "You did that last time. This time I'll take cash."

"Damnit, man, you know there's no way I can come up with ten million—"

"The president's discretionary fund. The unaudited and un-policed account Congress dispenses once per annum. Every-one since Millard Fillmore has used it to pay for botched assassinations, fund quote-freedom fighters-unquote, and compensate that compliant abortionist on J Street who caters to careless interns."

"This is a pro-life administration, and you know it."

Rumor had it that beneath his exquisitely shellacked exte-rior, Sam concealed a dangerously explosive temper. Too bad Charlie liked playing with fireworks. "Same as every other administration, the only thing you're pro is pro-reelection."

"Jesus, what turned you into such a cynic?"

"A lifetime in government service."

There was a long silence, broken only by the nearly in-audible drum of Sam's fingers on his desk. Charlie smiled. Charlie waited. And, just as Charlie expected, Sam caved in: "Ten million. Okay. I can handle that. It won't be easy, but I think—"

"Think? You've never thought in your life, Sam. Connived, schemed, and plotted? Sure. But thinking? Uh-uh, no."

"All I'm saying is that it will take time."

"That it will. Five minutes to be precise. I'm logging on to my Swiss bank then. If my account is ten million dollars plumper than it was yesterday, I'll answer the phone when you call back. If not . . . " Charlie regretted Sam couldn't see his fine and wolfish smirk " . . . then not. Bye now, Sam."

"No! Wait! I don't have your account number!"

"Oh, spare me! My personnel file is on your desk, and my account number is right there on the first page."

"Err . . . why, so it is, but—"

The phone chirped merrily, a happy little songbird soon to be fed.

Charlie polished off his coffee, set his partially read newspaper on a wicker table, and ambled back into the house. The porch led directly to his den. His Apple Power-Book computer was already alive, alert, and scanning the Internet for such dubious data as people like Charlie always found beguiling.

He pecked out his Swiss bank's computer address, entered his password, and was just in time to watch his account grow from the token thousand dollars he kept in it to ten million, one thousand dollars and no (0) cents.

Charlie reached beneath his desk and threw a toggle switch. The computer screen flickered. His modem was no longer connected to the ultra-high-bandwidth line the Agency had kindly let him keep after dispensing with his services. Charlie was now dialing into the World Wide Web via an ordinary telephone line.

Well, not entirely ordinary.

The line in question disappeared through his floor, into the basement, and from there traveled via PVC conduit a distance of one hundred and thirty yards to his neighbor's cellar. Late one evening—or, to be accurate, extremely early one morning—Charlie had paid a hacker acquaintance to bridge the wire to the neighbor's spare telephone extension, a phone line reserved solely for emergency use by babysitters.

Any number of agencies, bureaus, and departments

monitored Charlie's high-speed data link every minute of every day. They didn't have a clue that his bootlegged hookup existed.

Charlie tapped a few keys on his computer. Ten million dollars disappeared from a Swiss bank, scampering off in multiple directions to multiple mouse holes where, in due course, various cunning software programs would tuck it into a quite select number of defiantly impregnable financial institutions.

Sam wasn't going to get his money back. He wasn't even going to be able to find where it had gone.

The phone rang.

"Hi, Sam."

"Everything satisfactory?"

"So far." Charlie emphasized the word "far."

Sam grunted a predictable obscenity. "What else do you want?"

"My daughter's child-support payments suck. That syphilitic rodent in human garb who divorced her as soon as my name started making headlines—"

"How much, Charlie? Cut to the chase, and just tell me how much."

"Another ten million."

"Why am I not surprised? I'll call you back in five."

And so he did, the government of the United States now being twenty million dollars poorer—an insignificant amount in the overall order of things, what with run-amok waste, ludicrous congressional boondoggles, the bottomless pit of pork-barrel spending, and such alike.

Or so Charlie opined.

He answered the phone with a cheery, "Well, done, Sam."

"Fuck you very much." No cheer in that voice, none at all.

"And the very same to you. Now, let me give you a word

of advice. Don't even think about trying to track down those funds."

"The NSA can find anything in the world."

"With respect, Sam, the National Security Agency is a bunch of cross-eyed computer geeks. All they're good for is collecting raw data. That's not the art of intelligence. The art of intelligence is understanding the data, winnowing through it, finding which pieces of the puzzle fit—"

"Charlie, please." Sam's patience was almost gone. Charlie wasn't happy about the "almost" part, but he'd fix that soon enough. "We have a major crisis. The worst in all my years in government. I trust, now that I've paid you, you'll spare me your sermons, and let me tell you what you have to do."

"Oh," Charlie chuckled. "*Have to do*? I think you've made a mistake there, Sam. The only thing you've bought is the privilege of speaking to me. If you want me to actually do a job, I require a down payment."

"Almost" disappeared. "Completely" took its place. Charlie held the phone away from his ear until the swearing stopped—ordinary anger, unfortunately, not the frenzied rage Charlie had been hoping for. He supposed he'd just have to try harder.

"You done, Sam?"

"Yes, I am, you treacherous Judas Iscariot sonofabitch. What the hell else do you want?"

"A small advance against any good and worthy service I might render to my nation."

"I'll give you my word—"

"I had your word the week before you hung me out to dry. Remember your testimony, Sam? 'No, Senator, the White House was totally unaware of these activities.' 'Yes, Senator, the whole sorry affair was undertaken by a rogue agent acting on his own initiative.' 'I completely agree, Senator, the man should be disciplined in the strictest manner allowable.' Remember that, you treacherous Judas Iscariot sonofabitch?"

"Twenty million ought to cover it." *Give the man credit,* Charlie thought, *he truly has no conscience.*

"Indeed it does. The debt is now settled. The invoice is now paid. All that remains is for you to buy an option on my future assistance."

"In your dreams. Be so kind as to remember that I represent the president of the United States. The most powerful man in the world. *Capice?* And if I want to mess up your day—"

"You can't do squat. Listen up, Sambo, where my services are involved, it's a seller's market. The only question is: Is you a buyer or is you not?"

After a long silence, Sam answered with audible pain, "Okay, Charlie, okay. You'll get what you want. Whatever the fuck it is."

My, my, they really *are in trouble,* Charlie thought. *Opportunity knocks.* "Get the DCI on the phone. Conference call."

"The director of Central Intelligence is not cleared for the subject at hand."

Hot damn! A President's Office Only security cover! "You don't have to tell him what he's paying for, all you have to do is tell him to pay."

Sam grunted his surrender. Seconds later, the DCI's private secretary was on the phone, seconds after that the man himself.

Sam bit the bullet and said what he had to say: "Claude, I've got Charlie McKenzie on the line with me."

Claude inhaled sharply. Charlie was feeling happier with each passing moment.

Sam pressed on. "Charlie's going to ask—no, *tell*—you to do something. I want you to do it. No questions, no delay. The president will back you every step of the way."

What are you thinking there, Claude? Charlie asked silently. *Are you thinking about how resolutely the president backed me?*

"Of course," said Claude, speaking in the tones of a man who expects he is about to be gang-raped and knows there's nothing he can do about it. "Go ahead, Charlie, tell me what I can do for you."

"My son-in-law. Ex-son-in-law, actually. The little skunk who married my daughter because he thought being a member of my family would advance his career. Then dumped her and their two children the moment he realized it would not."

Claude's voice brightened. Maybe he'd escape serial sodomy after all. "For what it's worth, Charlie, I consider Don's behavior reprehensible, and I for one wish—"

"He's history. Today. You call him into your office, and you fire him. On the spot."

Salvation! Charlie could hear the relief in Claude's tone. "With pleasure."

"Then he gets leprosy. No one will touch him. No one in government, no one in the private sector. He doesn't get to work as a consultant to any of the Agency's friends. He doesn't wind up employed by an Agency front. He's a leper, and the best job he can get is cleaning peep-show booths in a porn house."

"You're a hard man, Charlie McKenzie."

"A just one, I think."

"True. That's why I always liked you." *Liar!* Charlie shouted, although only in his mind. "You know, I rather look forward to doing what you've asked. Sam, make sure the president knows that the Agency is happy to cooperate."

Claude disconnected his side of the call. Sam, emphasizing that his problem was not the sort to be discussed on a telephone, much less committed to e-mail or fax, said he had a helicopter waiting on the White House lawn. He'd be arriving at Charlie's place in about forty-five minutes.

"Forty-three minutes," replied Charlie, who was smiling as he hadn't smiled since getting out of prison.

Irina drove.

She did not know where she was. She did not know where she was going. She knew only that she had to drive this bleak highway, bitter desert on either side, asphalt night ahead, angry death behind.

She was not there upon that road, not in any conscious sense of the word. She was—four hours earlier, although it seemed like four minutes—where Dominik had become not-Dominik, transformed into a red mist, no longer a laughing colleague sharing tedious duty but only an emptiness in the air where that which once was Dominik, who was one, became myriad, and was hurled in myriad directions.

He'd not had time to scream.

She saw the deer, too. First it had been limp and motionless, entangled in the wire. But then, the second time she'd seen it, it danced.

Dead and dancing lively, a saraband in death's embrace.

It had begun with a hollow thump like the detonation of a distant mortar shell. Pale light speared the sky beyond a ridge, flickered, then died. Dominik pulled the Jeep Cherokee off the road. He gave her the night-vision camera, taking the infrared goggles for himself.

The ridge bordered a two-lane road that Irina and Dominik cruised every week. They knew what was hidden out of sight beyond its crest: a well-patrolled electrified fence; farther still, but clearly visible to anyone who scrambled up the rocky slope, a small cluster of buildings, a helicopter pad, and no runway.

No runway, no interest. Their business was aircraft. Monitoring those other unnamed bases scattered around the American Southwest was someone else's job.

But there had been an explosion. Dominik thought they should take a look. Maybe they'd see something that would add a little spice to their otherwise drably repetitive reports:

> The attached file contains digital images taken on the nights of the 27th through 31st near New Mexico areas 57 and 12. Images 1 to 6 show modifications in the B-2 Bomber's airframe being tested for airworthiness. Images 7 and 8 . . .

Anything would be more interesting than that. Anything.

Dressed in shopping-mall denims, blue cotton turtlenecks, and good walking boots, she and Dominik picked their way up the rocky slope. The ground was still damp from an afternoon thunderstorm. The climb was dauntingly steep—a hillside rising a hundred and twenty meters over a distance of two hundred meters.

Both of them were young and fit. It was not hard.

All they planned to do was look through the fence. Maybe shoot telephoto pictures if something noteworthy could be seen. You never could tell. You could get lucky. Spies sometimes do.

They crested the ridge. The fence was just below where they stood.

That's when they saw it. The first time they saw it.

The deer. The deer and the darkness. It had electrocuted

itself trying to jump high voltage wire. Puke-sweet smoke still hung in the air. Irina's stomach turned.

Dominik pointed silently. A wire had snapped. It, and the killing electricity it carried, had tumbled into a freshly washed-out gulch. Gouged by heavy rain, the gulch cut beneath the fence. It was still ankle-deep with rainwater. The broken wire had touched it, the fence had shorted out. The resulting power surge hit the small military camp's generator like a thunderbolt.

"Flames," he whispered.

A mile away, down near the base's single paved road, a fire of no small fury burned. The generator shack? It had to be.

Dominik and Irina slid into the gully, duckwalked beneath the fence, darted low from boulder to spiky desert shrub to plump barrel cactus.

And into secret space.

A tiny outpost: a single barracks, two dozen smaller buildings that might have been civilian quarters, a motor pool, a mess hall, utility sheds, and a windowless one-story bunker that, unlike everything else, had the appearance of something built to last.

Its roof bristled with needle-thin antennae. Its walls were poured concrete shot through with glistening metallic threads. Its single door was armored metal.

She heard the distant shouts of the soldiers, not so many of them, and all of them a hundred meters away trying to extinguish the fire. Even at that distance she could see twisted sheets of thick metal glowing red. How odd to build a generator shed of such heavy material.

Dominik flashed a grin as the door swung open. Whoever had been inside hadn't locked up when they ran outside to see what had exploded.

Treading softly, they tiptoed in. *I am a mouse,* she told

herself, *a tiny mouse creeping softly, for the cat may be near.* Her senses quivered, alert for the smallest sound, the slightest movement, the least hint that someone remained in the building.

No one had. It was empty, and, if Irina read the expression on Dominik's face correctly, ripe for plundering.

But of what treasure?

They eased past a bank of cubicles covered with dove-grey sound-absorbing fabric. Nothing there except empty desks, black telephones, and gunmetal-colored in- and out-boxes.

To the left, five offices with Indian art prints on their walls. Management always had private offices. There might have been good pickings in them. But management, like the cubicle dwellers, had locked away all their paperwork before departing.

Irina thought that she and Dominik were fools. No one would have been working at this late hour. In a secure installation housing classified work, anything worth stealing would have been stored in impregnable safes long before dinnertime. No one worked until two in the morning. No one.

Yet, the door had been unlocked. Someone had been in this building. Who? What kind of masochist kept working through the wolf hours after midnight?

Dominik winked, "Computerniks. They never sleep."

She nodded. Of course, it was so obvious.

To the right, a double door opened to a laboratory and rows of workbenches—a disarray of tools, loose microchips, spools of soldering wire, and computers with their screens still glowing. The lab had a battery backup system, an uninterruptible power supply to ensure that those who worked there never lost their data.

Dominik had taken his degree in electrical engineering with a specialty in avionics. The gleam in his eye told her he knew what he was seeing on those screens: CAD drawings, circuit layouts. "Camera," he whispered. She passed it to him. He focused, played with the light meter, adjusted the aperture, pressed the shutter release.

The camera made no sound. They had been issued a Peltier-cooled ten-megapixel Hamamatsu. It could take pictures by starlight—which was, after all, the dull duty to which they were assigned.

He changed settings, taking three different exposures of the screen. Then he moved down the line to the next computer, and did it again.

Irina followed. She could make no sense of what the computers displayed. She had wanted to be an economist, but Russian economic theory had fallen on hard times. She majored in mathematics instead.

A graph caught her eye. Dominik gave it a cursory glance before walking by. She stopped, studying what she saw displayed on a bright seventeen-inch monitor: a many-lobed three-dimensional shape plotted on x, y, and z axes. What formula, she wondered, could produce a graph so intriguingly complex as this? She read terse wording above the chart: "Conductivity functions are counterintuitive."

Dominik was farther away now, prowling along the lab benches, avidly photographing computer screens. Idly, without thought, she reached out a finger and tapped the computer's page-down key. Headline: "These functions can be approximated algorithmically." This above a densely packed page of formula that, given time, she knew she could decipher.

Deciphering their purpose was another question entirely. Unless . . .

. . . unless the document on this computer was . . . ?

The title bar across the computer window top read, "ww_draft.ppt."

PPT? PowerPoint? Could it be?

She whisked a computer mouse to the menu bar. Her heart skipped a beat. What was on this particular computer was an ordinary everyday PowerPoint presentation.

She clicked to the title page. And was stunned breathless.

WHIRLWIND
—Status Report—
DefCon Enterprises
Classification: MAGMA BLACK
Unauthorized access or distribution of this document
punishable by lifetime imprisonment

Magma Black was one of the American government's highest security classifications. Whatever Whirlwind might be, one thing was absolutely certain: it numbered among the most closely guarded secrets in the United States.

Irina Kolodenkova, twenty-four years old, two months into her first FSB field assignment, had accidentally stumbled across the stuff that dreams are made of.

Another whisk of the mouse, and two clicks. The presentation's author had made a backup copy on a disk. The disk was in the computer drive. A moment later, it was in Irina's breast pocket.

"Here! Come here! Quickly!" Dominik shouted so loudly that she jumped. He was at the far end of the lab. Beyond where he stood, she saw a door—no, not a door, the entrance to a vault, all burnished steel with a wheeled ratchet in its center, two separate combination locks on either side. Opening it was out of the question. They had only minutes; cracking such a safe would take hours.

Dominik gestured at something large and brown resting atop a trestle. Color-coded gas canisters—dimethyl ether, read the label—flanked the object. Thickly clad pipes linked the canisters to a laboratory hood. *Some sort of experiment is in progress,* she thought as she trotted to his side.

His smile was broad, broader than she had ever seen it. "This," he beamed, "this means we are not turtles much longer!"

Turtles. Irina pursed her lips. Russians and Americans alike used the term. It was no compliment.

Turtles waddle slowly with their heads turned to the sky. Thus the derisive nickname given the lowest of low-level field agents, the ones who roam empty highways bordering secret bases by night, their tedious mission to take fuzzy photographs of experimental aircraft so secret that they are flown only after sunset.

It was an apprentice's job—easy training for beginners, and safe in these days of detente, old enemies become wary allies in their pursuit of terrorists. Let the turtles forage for low-level intelligence; it's cheaper than a weapons inspection treaty and requires no tendentious ratification by senate or parliament . . .

What, she asked herself, *could Dominik have found that will elevate us from the lowly ranks of the turtles?*

He had his hand on a matte-brown box almost two meters long, a meter wide, a half meter deep. His cheeks were glowing, and his eyes sparkled with triumph. He'd found something important, she knew he had.

Should she tell him about the disk? *No. Later, I will tell him later. He is excited now, too full of himself for having accomplished an espionage coup of his own.* "What is it?"

Anxious orders tumbled out of his mouth. "No time to talk! We've got to get this out of here! Come on, help me carry it. Grab that end. Be careful, it's heavy."

Very heavy. About thirty kilos. Irina grunted as she lifted her end.

"They'll have their backup generator online soon. Let's move!"

Harsh, blinding, actinic, the lights sparked on before they reached the fence. Dominik and Irina were standing targets illuminated by the fires of frozen suns.

Dominik died then. A .50 caliber machine gun mounted on a Humvee served as the machinery of his death. Its slugs shredded his body, flensed it to shining shards hurled helter-skelter across an empty landscape.

Irina lay prone, screaming surrender. Bullets tore the air above her head, aimed not at her, but elsewhere. She forced herself to look up. Directly in front of her, not five meters away, the deer hung on a fence alive again with killing electricity. From a distance, from the machine gunner's position, the animal must have looked like a man trying to climb the wires. A river of bullets exploded into the poor dead creature's carcass.

Although dead, it danced.

Machine-gun rounds snapped another fence link. And another. A strand of wire, alive with twenty thousand volts of death, whipped in front of Irina's eyes. It coiled and crackled as it reached hungrily for her face. She had to run. She could not. The air above her shrieked with bullets. The wire wove back and forth, a cobra's sway, the true and actual incarnation of mortality.

Paralysis: unable to move, unable to breathe, she could only watch. The wire darted toward her one last time, as if conscious and consciously straining to touch her. Then—as though disappointed—it recoiled, sliding into that freshly rain-washed gully beneath the fence, and into the water it contained.

Lightning split the sky. The backup generator exploded.

Irina manhandled thirty kilos of god-knows-what under the fence, over the ridge, down to the Jeep.

Bullets shattered her rear windshield. She turned the ignition, thrusting the accelerator down as hard as she could.

And she drove.

She stopped only once—the darkened parking lot of a sun-bleached motel—to abandon the Jeep, shift her overnight bag and a heavy brown box into the rear of a tourist's Volvo station wagon, cross its ignition wires, and flee back into the night.

Irina drove.

Airborne in Marine Corps One, the president's personal whirlybird, Sam settled his ample rear end in his boss's even more ample seat. Very comfy. Under normal circumstances, he would be a contented man.

Not today.

Bad enough that the National Security Agency was dithering *umma, umma, umma* about the whereabouts of twenty million dollars. Worse, pretty soon now Sam would be discussing Whirlwind with the last man on earth who should know about it. But worst of all was a mess so colossally disastrous that only a conceited sonofabitch named McKenzie could clean it up.

Not merely the best man for the job, the evil old bastard was the *only* man for the job. Everyone else with his qualifications was off chasing turbaned terrorists through third world cesspits. The only available agents were desk jockeys and raw recruits—none of them qualified for a high-stakes operation like retrieving Whirlwind.

Which left Sam with a single pain-in-the-ass choice.

He was second-generation Agency, was Charlie, the son of one of Wild Bill Donovan's handpicked buccaneers. During his long and piratical career, Charlie's old man made only one mistake: trusting Henry Kissinger. Now, a quarter of a century after leaving Washington, that one time national security advisor traveled everywhere in the company of two muscle-boy bodyguards. Sam wondered if Henry the K was still afraid of Charlie. If he had any sense he would be.

His daddy's boy, Sam thought, *in every awful regard. Obnoxiously intelligent. Braver than lions. Righteous beyond the bounds of reason.*

Righteous? Self-righteous is more like it. Charlie was the last of that galling generation who actually believed in something, the sort of loose cannon you never wanted to see in Washington—a fucking patriot.

Shit!

Sam looked out the window. The capitol dome was barely visible, haze-shrouded and disappearing in the distance. He was over the greenbelt now. Up ahead, Chesapeake Bay sparkled in the sun. Under other circumstances, he might have thought the view from five thousand feet to be pretty, maybe even beautiful. However he couldn't enjoy it—not knowing that his worst enemy was waiting for him, and, no question about it, licking his chops.

Pretty soon now, Sam would be feathering down at Charlie's lair, and the very idea of it made him ball his fists. McKenzie had twenty-five acres, a great old rambling estate he'd inherited from his father. But that's all he had. Fired without a pension, he could barely pay his property tax. If everything had turned out the way Sam hoped, Charlie would have been forced to sell the house and retire to Florida.

Or maybe Arizona. Arizona would be better. It was farther away.

Only now Charlie had what he'd never bothered to acquire during his career: a nest egg. Unless the NSA got lucky (smart was not an issue; smart wasn't even in the running when Charlie was involved), that nest egg would support him for the rest of his miserable life.

And Charlie, the man who already knew too much, would be within driving distance of the Washington press corps for the rest of his days.

Sam pursed his lips like a man who had tasted something sour.

The deal shouldn't have gone down like this. When Charlie got caught with his pants down, he should have been covered with a blanket, put in a box, and freighted far, far away.

Farther than Arizona, actually.

Trouble was, you couldn't do that with Charlie. He had too many Friends In High Places, and, yes, the capital letters were appropriate. Reagan—to pick the most egregious example—simply loved him. "I like," Dutch had mused, "having someone in this town who has the guts to disagree with me." To which he'd quickly added, "Although one is enough."

Powerful friends—they stood by Charlie to the end. They weren't able to keep him out of prison, but they did see to it that he got as sweet a deal as possible under the circumstances—circumstances that were, let's face it, pretty fucking dire.

It had gone like clockwork. Charlie should have gotten away scot-free.

Oh, sure, there was the usual journalistic whining. The *New York Times* was aghast, The *Washington Post* was horrified, and the foreign press vilified America as the Wild West complete with vigilante justice, lynch law, and all that bullshit. So what else is new?

What else turned out to be a digital camera, fresh out of the box, sitting next to one Nathaniel Whinston, the driver of a car who chanced to be in the right place at the right time. Mr. Whinston, an actuary with an entrepreneurial streak, put his snapshots up for auction. NBC submitted the high bid, but Whinston sold the photos to Fox News. Fox promised him he'd personally get forty-five seconds on-screen as part of the package.

What American could resist?

Whinston's pictures were garbage, taken at night, and from too far away. Moreover, Charlie had been mostly backlit. No one could be certain it was him.

Which didn't stop a talking-head media whore from pontificating, just outside the bounds of actionable libel, "The suspect appears to bear a slight resemblance to controversial Central Intelligence deputy operations director Charles McKenzie. Perhaps the police would be well advised to look for a man of Mr. McKenzie's stature and build. . . . "

The president freaked.

And Charlie, in the time-honored tradition of Washington, was well and truly a lamb for the slaughter.

Almost.

Somewhere along the line it was discovered that he was under heavy medication for an impacted wisdom tooth, and the special prosecutor couldn't get the dentist to budge from his story. Then too, according to Charlie's credit card records, he'd been drinking heavily that night, even though no one at McCann's Bar on Lexington Avenue had any recollection of seeing him. Add to this the right kind of lawyerly spin, and behold: a miracle! Charlie McKenzie is alchemically transformed from a run-amok CIA agent to a pitiable victim deranged by pain, confused by drugs, befuddled by alcohol, and inflamed with a righteous passion for justice.

The Senate investigating committee bought it. So did the judge—upon whom, no doubt, Charlie's heavyweight friends leaned heavily.

So when Charlie copped a plea, his honor wrist-slapped him with eighteen months at a minimum-security Club Fed.

Charlie thought he wouldn't have to pull the time. Charlie thought he'd been promised presidential immunity. Charlie thought wrong.

He served out his entire sentence quietly, and didn't say a single word, not even when his wife died. That's when Sam started to squirm. Charlie's silence was—no other word for it—ominous.

Now on his way to his first meeting with the man in two years, Sam ground his teeth. *He's known it,* he thought, *known all along that sometime, somewhere, something would go wrong—not the kind of something that you solve with an ordinary black work guy, because those punks are a dime a dozen. Rather the kind of something that nobody but evil goddamned Charlie can handle because nobody but evil goddamned Charlie can burrow into an enemy's mind the way he does.*

The spooky sonofabitch. Mental telepathy is what it is. And mental telepathy is why he's known that all he had to do was lie in the weeds and wait for the shit to hit the fan.

Goddamn the man!

Sam was mere months away from more power than he had ever dreamt of. The president planned the announcement for September. It was so close he could taste it. But he wouldn't. Unless the Whirlwind fiasco was cleaned up pronto, he wouldn't even get a sniff. Instead he'd be hurled into the outer darkness, a footnote to history and infrequent guest on Sunday morning talk shows.

If he was going to survive, he needed the best cleanup man there was. In other words, he needed Charlie. But the problem was the nosy bastard couldn't be trusted to go fetch Whirlwind like a good dog. Charlie wouldn't stop there. He wouldn't stop until he knew the what and why of the thing. And once he knew that, Sam might as well kill himself.

Well, shit, he thought, *this is an easy choice.*

The trick was to stay cool, keep his dangerous temper under control, not let Charlie provoke him during what would be, beyond any question, a difficult bargaining session. Sam would win the negotiation. Winning negotiations was what he did, and no one did it better.

Then, later, after Charlie had handled Whirlwind, well . . . Sam would arrange for someone to handle Charlie. Handle him as he should have been in the first place.

He already had a candidate in mind, an independent contractor named Schmidt. Added bonus points: Schmidt and Charlie had some history, went back a long way, and what the hell, Schmidt probably would look at the job as a labor of love . . .

The rumble of the helicopter's engines turned throatier as it began to descend. Sam peered out the window.

There was Charlie's spread in all its emerald beauty, greener than Ireland in the spring.

And there was Charlie, too. Tall, craggy handsome with snow-white hair, he was striding out his back porch door and onto the lawn. As the chopper began to touch down, Sam lifted his hand in a wave of greeting.

Charlie turned, dropped his trousers, and bent at the waist. Full moon.

Tuesday, July 21.
0900 Hours Eastern Time,
0800 Hours Central Time

"Let me make sure I understand this," Charlie growled. "A couple of munchkin turtles sashay into a top secret lab because a generator explodes. Then, having filched something outrageously valuable, one of them manages to scamper away with the swag because, for an encore, the backup generator blows up."

"In a nutshell, yes," replied Sam, who sat uneasily in one of Charlie's easy chairs.

"Said generators, and their crappy circuit breakers, doubtless having been purchased from your boss's biggest campaign contributor."

Sam's cheeks reddened. "That's a lie!" he snapped. "It was the Chairman of the Armed Services Commit . . . errr . . . "

Charlie leered.

By any measure, the conversation had not been cordial. Sam, impeccably attired by the finest haberdashers in London's Jermyn Street, began by insisting that Charlie allow a pair of NSA technicians to sweep his house for bugs. Insult to injury, the two had even trampled through Mary's beloved gardens waving their ever-so-sensitive detectors in every direction.

Six months earlier, Charlie had winced at the extra price a computer outlaw who called himself the Sledgehammer charged for shielding his underground Internet connection with the fine mesh net of a Faraday cage. Now he was happy he'd made the investment. The NSA nerds didn't find a thing.

Sam, upon hearing his minions give Charlie's premises a clean bill of health—no covert recording devices, sir; no transmitters, sir; no surreptitious electronic equipment at all, sir—at last entered Charlie's den, a high-ceilinged room whose floor was scattered with tribal carpets from a dozen countries, and whose walls were lined with old oak bookshelves. Those shelves overflowed, jumbled proof of Charlie's omnivorous reading habits, books and magazines alike. And displayed among well-thumbed volumes of history, philosophy, and science were innumerable souvenirs of a former spy's career.

Near the bottom on the left: a jewel-studded fan of hammered gold, a gift from a doe-eyed Persian lass who spent ten years in Charlie's employ, and who, not so coincidentally, had been the Ayatollah Khomeini's favorite mistress.

Top shelf, left bookcase: a Soviet tank commander's dress uniform dagger. The colonel had been out of uniform when Charlie took it, and out of uniform he stayed until someone untied him the next morning. By then he was fearsomely frostbitten.

Right bookcase, third shelf: a Cohiba cigar box bearing a scribbled message, *Hope to catch you on your next visit* —a double entendre to which Fidel Castro had appended his spiky signature.

Here and there among the books, visitors could find

signed photos of Charlie with every president since Richard Nixon, some few of whom were smiling sincerely.

Pride of place went to a treasured Exacta IIb camera Charlie had used his entire career; technologically obsolete by the 1970s, it nonetheless produced the best close-up photographs of Iraq's antiaircraft targeting systems, circa 1990, that anyone had ever seen. Right next to the antique single lens reflex sat another outdated camera—a vintage 1994 analog Sony camcorder that Charlie had used to obtain footage that made even so worldly a man as the director of Central Intelligence blush.

Sam barely gave Charlie's bric-a-brac a glance as he lowered himself into the shabby horsehair armchair to which his host pointed him.

Charlie sat facing him. "Can I ask a favor, Sam?"

"Certainly." Sam was covertly trying to kick Esmeralda, one of Charlie's countless cats, away from his leg.

"Let me click on the TV. Now that I have some investments, for which I thankee kindly, I want to keep my eye on the stock ticker."

Sam's eyes narrowed with suspicion; Charlie could almost hear him think: *What's he up to now?* "Go ahead, needle me all you want. Whatever makes you happy."

"You know," Charlie smiled, "those eighteen months I spent in the pen weren't a total waste of time." He picked up a remote control and twiddled with its buttons. Sam glanced over his shoulder at the television: CNBC, with stock prices crawling across the bottom of the screen. "I met lots of CEOs, learned how to play the market like a pro. I suppose I should thank you for that. But then again, probably not."

Sam pulled out a handkerchief and blew his nose. Charlie smirked. Sam was hellishly allergic to the feline kind.

Shooting a healthy dose of decongestant into both nos-

trils, Sam began to tell his story. At no time did he observe
that Charlie's remote control was one of those ever-so-
handy "universal remotes," a clever and useful device that
could activate not only a television set but also a VCR, an
audio system, a DVD player, and, if you happened to have
one, an outdated low-tech Sony camcorder conveniently
pointed at the chair in which you'd just seated your guest.

Charlie was still feeling smug when Carly came into the
room and ruined his good spirits. After offering Sam a cup
of coffee, she shooed Esmeralda from the room. The poor
cat hadn't managed to reach a single one of the tuna-
flavored treats Charlie had sprinkled beneath Sam's seat.

Three cups later, Sam had finished telling an embarrassing
tale. Charlie, however, was not satisfied with mere embarrassment.

A videotape of the watery-eyed national security advisor
confessing to a series of security blunders was fine as far as
it went. However, it did not go far enough. Charlie would
need juicier material when—as was inevitable—Sam tried
to double-cross him.

An admission that the chairman of the Armed Services
Committee muscled the military into buying shoddy goods
from his political bankrollers was more along the lines of
what Charlie was looking for. However, in Washington such
kickbacks were barely considered criminal; most politicians
thought of them as a patriotic tradition, rather like Columbus
Day and the Fourth of July, really.

Charlie eyed Sam; Sam studied his manicure. *What the
hell,* Charlie thought, *I've still got an hour and thirteen minutes of videotape left. The little worm is bound to make another mistake.*

Bait on the hook, Charlie cast his line. "So you call this thing Whirlwind, eh?"

"That's the project designation. But don't ask what it is, or who's sponsoring it, or—"

"Air Force code name."

Sam's jaw tightened.

"Sam, Sam, don't look at me like that. The flyboys have been using Whirlwind as a code name off and on for fifty years. First time around it was for their original realtime computer. It's been back three or four times since. Don't deny it, this is Air Force stuff, and we both know it."

"You're only guessing."

"Sure," Charlie answered with a predator's grin. "But how many times have you known me to guess wrong?"

Sam started to reply, then stopped himself.

"Okay," Charlie continued, "tell me again about how this Kolodenkova girl managed to get away."

"You should call her a woman, not a girl."

"I don't work for the government anymore. I can be as politically incorrect as I damn well please. Now let's have the story."

"I told you once. Why should I tell you twice?"

"Because I need a laugh."

Charlie's cat strolled back in. Looking daggers at it, Sam sneezed. "Okay, okay. You're wearing out my patience, but I suppose that's what you want."

Got it in one, Sambo, Charlie thought.

"When the second generator went out, things became confused. There were two foot patrols and a crew in a Hummer near the fence. Somebody tripped and discharged his weapon. The GIs in the other patrol thought they were being shot at. They returned fire. Damnit, Charlie, quit laughing. I know it sounds like the Keystone Kops, but it was—it is—

serious business. Anyway, by the time everyone worked out who was shooting at whom, the Kolodenkova *woman* had reached her car. Our boys managed to put a few rounds into it, but not enough. She hightailed it out of there. So . . . " Sam sighed. " . . . You see, it's a small base, Charlie, sixty enlisted men, five noncoms, two officers, and a few dozen civilian scientists. The only transportation they have are deuce-and-a-half trucks and Humvees—no good for high-speed pursuit. The base commander had to radio for help. Problem is the second explosion damaged the radio shack. It took a while to get communications back online."

Had to radio for help? Hmm . . . that should tell me something. "How long were they offline?" he asked.

Closing his eyes, pressing the balls of his fingers against his sinuses, Sam whispered, "Four fucking hours."

"Even if Kolodenkova kept under the speed limit, she'd have been at least two hundred miles away before—"

"You think I don't know that? You think that little fact has escaped my attention?"

Charlie always trusted his intuition. At the moment it was telling him he was pushing too hard. "Just thinking out loud, Sam. No criticism implied. Now I think you'd better let me see the dossiers on these two—the late Dominik whatever-his-name-was, and the Kolodenkova *girl.*"

Sam snapped open his briefcase. "They're right here," he said, passing Charlie two manila folders.

"How did you ID them so fast?"

Sam sniffed. "Give us some credit, Charlie, we *do* know who plays for the other team."

Nodding, Charlie opened the first folder. Dominik Grisin. Age twenty-nine. His photos portrayed a handsome lad with a high forehead, thick black hair, and a strong jaw. Born in Belgorod. That explained his good looks—Ukrainian blood.

Master's degree in electrical engineering at the University of Kiev, a fine school; its mascot, Charlie remembered, was a wise-cracking duckling. After college Grisin pulled six years of duty with the Russian embassy in Washington—one of the SigInt specialists who babysat the radio interception gear in the embassy's basement. Charlie wondered how many indiscreet cell phone calls the late Dominik had tapped. And what prices the power brokers who made them later paid.

Two months on turtle duty. Hmm . . . why was that? Was Grisin being punished? Not likely. If his dossier could be believed, Dominik had been a rising star. So then . . . he probably had been assigned short-term, a job to give him a little applied fieldcraft before he moved up the ladder.

Charlie raced through the file. No use studying the record of a player whose piece was no longer on the board. The real issue was the other player, the one who was still in the game, although where in the game was the question, wasn't it?

He flipped the folder open. His first thought: *pretty girl. No, make that a gorgeous girl. And add an exclamation point!* Quite obviously, the Agency's photographers agreed. They'd taken countless pictures of her. Here she was in a slightly dowdy gown at an embassy function, there she was in flattering light but unflattering dress leaning against a bar talking to someone with his back to the camera. . . .

Close-ups that were nearly portraits. Medium shots. Full-length photos. *Yup, boys will be boys, and boys do love taking pictures of pretty . . . hmpf! . . . women.*

Blonde hair over her shoulders most of the time, but occasionally up in a tight French twist. *Big blue eyes, and you know the kind I mean. Wide forehead, elegant eyebrows arched like a seagull's wings. A lower lip so full and ripe that even a man of my advanced and decrepit years wonders how it would taste. Perfect cheekbones, not the switchblade Slavic sharpness of your typical Russian lass, but high and smooth and wholly bewitching. Yeah, I could look at Irina Kolodenkova for a real long time, and not think I'd looked long enough.*

"A major babe," Sam opined.

"Understatement. Beauties like this . . . and more credit to her for turning down the job . . . are the kind of gals they try to pressure into becoming swallows."

"Becoming what?"

Charlie glowered. A careerist and nothing but, Sam cared so little about the art of intelligence that he didn't even bother to learn the lingo. "Swallows. Agents who use sex to gather intelligence."

Sam laughed coarsely. "She could swallow me any time."

Charlie frowned him into silence. Shuffling the photographs to the side, he turned his attention to the dossier's paperwork.

Okay, what do we have here? Third child of a naval officer, a light cruiser commander, and at his age that's as far as his career will go. Two older brothers, and both of them commissioned in the Russian navy, just like dad. A military family, through and through. But Irina doesn't join the regular forces, instead she signs up for intelligence work. Makes sense. The Russian navy is not an equal opportunity employer. Women run desks, not ships, and their career progression correlates directly with the number of senior officers they sleep with. Which this girl—who most definitely did not become a swallow—was bound to know.

Sam, although he did not know it, was in an empty room. Charlie wasn't there anymore. He'd floated off to a space outside of space. Alone and unreachable, his mind roamed free, toying with scanty, scattered puzzle pieces. *Extrapo-*

*late, extrapolate. Pieces of a puzzle—their shape and texture
and color have a message and a meaning. I can't see the entire picture, because there aren't enough pieces. But I can
imagine. I can hypothesize. I can infer.*

And nine times out of ten he'd be right because he was
one smart cookie, although when he was wrong good men
died, and he wished he'd never been born.

He almost stopped. Stopped right there. Was ready to quit
on the spot. Give Sam back his files, and to hell with it, because as good as he was, he made mistakes, and he wasn't
sure he could live with himself if he made another.

Instead he thoughtlessly flipped a page in Irina Kolodenkova's dossier. And his eyes lit up.

*Oh, lookee, lookee. She made the Russian Olympic fenc-
ing team. She even brought home the gold! We've got a talented girl here. But more than that, a smart one. Fencing is
the most intellectual of sports, three-dimensional chess and
you play it in real time. In any other game, a great athlete
beats a good one every time. Not in fencing. Physical fitness
is only half the fight. The rest is brainpower. And young Irina
appears to have a surfeit of that.*

She'd be a challenge. He couldn't resist a challenge.

He closed his eyes. The puzzle is truth. Each piece is a
fragment of truth. But truth is irreducible. It cannot be broken into parts. And therefore, if you have even the smallest
scrap of truth, you have the entire thing. The trick is being
able to examine those few shards that come your way, and
see in them what they always were and always will be. The
puzzle is not the pieces; the real and genuine puzzle is the
one and only way in which they can be assembled.

Smiling, he looked again at the dossier. *Ha! Just like
every new agent, they gave her a month in D.C. and a month
at the UN before her first real assignment—the San Fran-*

cisco legation, nice duty for any spy. Of course, same as with every virgin that comes to town, the Agency dispatched various boyos to feel her up. They're supposed to accidentally bump into her at a bar or a restaurant or a bookstore or wherever, and open a dialog. Worst case, they find out what kind of a critter they're dealing with; best case they lay the groundwork for a little counterespionage. But not this time. Oh, God, no! She made utter jackasses out of everyone they put next to her. Hellfire and damnation, reading these poor guys' reports makes even me cringe!

There's an art. Students of the craft call it cold reading. Every self-styled psychic in the world uses it. Cheapjack gypsy fortune-tellers at the county fair and high-priced flim-flams who charge movie stars and presidents' wives two thousand dollars an hour for horoscopes—they're all cold readers, each and every one. Cold reading came easily to Charlie. He didn't even think about it. It was just something he did, a talent, a gift, a knack for seeing the obvious.

Take a look at a man's shoes. Are they well kept, but oft-resoled? If so, you know something about that man's self-image and his economic status. His accent will tell you where he comes from. His vocabulary will tell you his education and his job. His clothing shouts his income. His ring finger proclaims his marital status. His place in society's hierarchy is evidenced by the authority in his voice. Get him talking and he will, without knowing it, tell you the little things from which large things are easily deduced. Then you own him. You can feed your knowledge back to him and he will gasp: *How did you know that?* If you want to earn your living as a psychic, you've just hooked another sucker. Alternatively, if you want to be a spy . . .

Mathematician. Top grades. Applied to night school at Georgetown to earn credits toward her doctorate. Wants to start this fall when she figured she'd be back from turtle duty. This is one motivated lady, a real overachiever. No, wait a minute, this is someone who is more than that. She's driven, absolutely driven. "Failure" is not in her lexicon. She's got the talent and she's got the energy, but most of all, she's got the need. Oh, yeah, Irina Kolodenkova is someone who has to succeed. Officer's daughter, champion fencer, top-ranked student—she doesn't know the meaning of the word "lose"; hell, she probably doesn't know how to spell it.

Fascinating woman. Damned fascinating.

Charlie had tried to explain to the Agency how his talent worked. They didn't get it. Even though every trainee was put through an exhaustive curriculum in cold reading—The Extraction of Information from Physical Appearance was the course's official name—they couldn't understand Charlie's hat trick. They thought it was magic. Some people thought it was more than that.

Back in the days when the boneheads piddled away more than a billion dollars researching "psychic warfare," some especially witless bastard went so far as to order him tested for telepathic powers. Charlie was not known for following orders. However, he was known for taking the scalps of witless bastards. The matter ended swiftly, although not amicably. And afterward, up until the day he left the Agency in disgrace, all that anyone could—or would—acknowledge was that Charlie McKenzie had gifts that no one else had been given.

Her father is the key. Don't ask me how I know, but be damned certain that I do. He wanted a third son to follow him into the Navy. Instead he got a useless daughter. And she got raised by a father who wanted her to be something she wasn't. That's why she has to prove herself. That's what's behind the academic excellence, the fencing, the Olympic gold. That's why she turned spy. The FSB is the only Russian military arm in which a woman can succeed on her own merits. Yeah, merits. She's got 'em in spades. Plus the mind and motivation. Smart and tough, she'll win or she'll die. Irina Kolodenkova isn't the kind of gal to settle for anything in between.

What else did he now know about her? There was something. It was . . . it was . . . just beyond his grasp. He'd read it or he'd seen it or he'd deduced it, he could nearly touch it, but it was slipping away, and damnit it was important, everything was important, but this particular thing was more important than almost anything else, and unless he locked his radar in on it right this very moment . . .

Oh, yeah. Of course. Obvious. He shuffled through the photographs, his eye glinting like arctic ice, and sure enough there it was. *Gorgeous girl. Crappy clothing. In every damned photo she's dressed like a frump. More than that: no makeup, no jewelry, God Almighty, her ears aren't pierced! Okay, beautiful, now I know you, yes, I do, I know it all, especially the things you don't want me to know, and so, my lovely lass, I own you body and soul. Irina Kolodenkova, you are mine!*

Charlie returned from a faraway place. He drummed his fingers across the top of Irina's dossier. "Sam," he said. Then he said nothing.

"What?"

Charlie drummed his fingers more.

"Speak to me, Charlie."

Charlie opened his mouth then closed it. Sam threw up his hands in frustration. Charlie finally found the words, but couldn't speak them. Laughter rendered him speechless.

Finally, taking considerable satisfaction at the mottled purple of Sam's face, he managed to sputter, "Sammy, oh,

Sammy boy, this time you've got yourself a *real* problem on your hands!"

The sun was in her eyes.

East, she was driving east. Had been for hours.

Some miles back, there'd been road signs welcoming her to the great state of Texas, drive safely, speed limits strictly enforced. Now she was seeing more signs. Big billboards advertising factory outlets, auto dealers, restaurants, and private clubs that guaranteed "the most beautiful women in the whole southwest. Friendliest too."

She was on a six-lane highway, the kind Americans called an interstate.

Not good.

Such roads were heavily patrolled. Soon, if not already, a sleepy tourist family would step out of their motel room, staring with bewilderment at an empty parking space.

The authorities would be summoned. A police officer would take note of a nearby Jeep with bullet holes in its back. Shortly thereafter, a description of both the Volvo and the Jeep would be broadcast. Then the kennels of hell would open, the hounds beginning their hunt.

The clock on the dashboard panel read 7:37 A.M. That would be Mountain time. Now she was in the Central zone, an hour ahead, 8:37 in the morning.

She was running out of time.

The outskirts of the city flew past. Every off ramp pointed to: Gas, Food, Lodging. Up ahead, at the next exit, she saw a sign she recognized. It sat atop a tall white pole, rotating slowly in the bleak morning sun: SAFEWAY, a grocery chain. One of the biggest. Irina steered up the ramp, through an intersection, into a parking lot.

A small breeze whipped dust devils across the empty lot. Ashen tumbleweed ricocheted against a light pole. Harsh, barren, hostile—it was a place where coyotes would congregate by night, and they would sing.

Asphalt may replace sand, but pavement alters no desert.

At this early hour, only a few cars clustered around the supermarket's entrance. Although she was fiercely hungry, Irina had no time for food—nor for the sleep her weary body demanded.

An anonymously blue minivan, a Ford Aerostar, glided by. Irina tapped her brake. The van nosed into a parking space near the store's glass front. A moment later, a woman stepped out. Trim in shorts and halter, she wore her hair tucked up in a baseball cap.

Irina knew she should get a similar hat when she had a chance, if she had a chance.

Sliding the Ford's side panel open, the woman lifted two toddlers from the backseat. They were of an age to walk, but not to walk quickly. Not bothering to lock her car, she shepherded their clumsy steps toward the grocery store, chattering to them as a good mother will, and never looking behind.

Irina gently edged forward, sliding her Volvo into the slot next to the Aerostar. The woman was herding her children to the store's automatic doors. Both were girls, both carried baggy, floppy, cloth dolls. Once Irina's mother had bought her such a doll. Father ordered it returned to the G U M department store. Her birthday present that year was a soccer ball.

Two steps, three. One girl started to dart back. Her mother seized her shoulder and pointed her in the opposite direction. The doors whooshed open, hissed closed. Irina brushed her eye.

The woman was inside shopping with her youngsters in tow. How long before she was done? A half hour, easily.

Ample time. Irina had all the time in the world.

Stepping warily out of the Volvo, she stood rolling her shoulders, tilting her head left and right, stretching the stiffness out while surreptitiously scanning the parking lot, studying every car to be certain that, no, grandpa was not sitting there patiently waiting for grandma to buy her morning prunes.

No one in sight.

It was too hot. They were all inside pushing their shopping carts down blessedly air-conditioned aisles.

Irina walked slowly to the Volvo's back hatch. After taking one last look to be sure that no one was watching, she moved like lightning.

The Volvo's hatch flew up. The Aerostar's extra-wide side door slid open. A weighty brown object appeared from inside the Volvo, disappeared into the Aerostar. An overnight bag followed it.

Shoulder bag between her knees, Irina was in the front seat, crouched low, tickling the wires out of the steering column. Penknife in hand, she scraped insulation off two wires, crossed them, and tapped the Ford's gas pedal.

She was back on the interstate in less than two minutes.

This time, she drove west.

The motel from which she'd stolen the Volvo was east of the place where Dominik had died. A bullet-pocked Jeep would tell the authorities who the car thief was. In a half hour or so, a good mother gone shopping would report her minivan had been taken from the parking lot of a grocery store farther east. The missing Volvo was right next to where the Aerostar should have been.

Three points on a map: a secret base, a bourgeois motel, a supermarket. Connect the dots. The line pointed east.

Someone would shout with excitement: we know where she's been! We know the direction she's headed!

They'd deploy their resources to the east. Roadblocks on every highway, every graveled lane. Helicopters on patrol. Surveillance planes stuttering along only a little faster than their stall speed. Local law enforcement officers, national security agents, soldiers in uniform—they'd all be there, scouring a bleak and baking landscape for a boring blue Ford Aerostar speeding east.

Her best hope was to backtrack west. Although alone and by itself, it was a slender hope. She had her hands on a Magma Black secret. The Americans would stop at nothing to get it back.

Of course, they'd assume she knew what the heavy brown box was; just as they'd assume she'd had time to examine the computer file in her breast pocket. Given those assumptions, given the implications of a foreign spy knowing a Magma Black secret, what must follow was simply logical: if they caught her, she would never see Russia again.

Escaping so thorough a search would take more than doubling back. Irina thought she knew what that "more" might be. It would be riskier than hijacking a suburbanite's minivan from a parking lot. Risky enough that she should be armed when she did it.

Her pistol was in her shoulder bag. Driving one-handed, she fingered open the bag's brass snaps, wrapping her hand around the familiar checkered grips of a sixty-year-old Tokarev 7.62 mm automatic.

As she touched it, the blood drained from her cheeks. And she remembered, and she remembered . . .

She is fresh from graduation, fresh in a newly commissioned officer's crisp uniform. Lieutenant's pips glow on her collar, her cap is squared on her head, and her well-rehearsed words are ready for the speaking.

A shock: when she enters the apartment, he too is in uniform. The sight makes her falter. As she grew up, you see . . . she was only a little girl . . . in her earliest memories, he was always in navy blue, always in a jacket fastened by bright buttons emblazoned with the hammer and sickle.

There is no more hammer and sickle. It disappeared years ago, the embarrassing emblem of a fallen empire. But that insignia, embossed on polished brass, is always with her. It is his badge, and every time she sees him without it, she is, in some sense of the word, shaken. The two always went hand in hand. He and the hammer and sickle were twin incarnations of all that oppressed her.

The state. Her father. No difference between them, none at all.

Seeing him in uniform, yet without his hated insignia, renders her momentarily mute.

As does his seldom-seen smile. Now he is beaming, mouthing preposterous false endearments. He pulls her close, wraps his arms around her, hugs her tight, and kisses her on both cheeks. He will not stop babbling of the honor she has done him.

No honor to him, she did it solely for herself.

Her mouth will not form words rehearsed from the moment she first heard of his treachery, of his contempt, of the humiliation he thought befitted her. But he, filling glasses brimful of vodka, rattles on; and she cannot speak her rage, but only watch disgusted as he hands one glass to each of her brothers, one to a submissive mother standing, as ever, mute in the background.

One for her, and one for him.

A toast! A toast to a warrior's child who has proven the steel of which she is forged!

She drinks. There is nothing else she can do.

He rambles on: a military family, through and through. First there were the opolchenie *serfs pressed into uniform by the czars; then there were the sergeants, promoted on the field of battle; next the revolution that elevated a sergeant to an officer's estate. Every member of the bloodline has served the motherland with valor and with honor!*

Vodka flows. There is no end to it, nor to the obligatory cocktail pickles accompanying every glass. She wants to vomit. She will not give her tormentor the satisfaction.

He is lecturing now, lecturing her as always: There's a tradition, you know, in this family there is a tradition. Every father gives every son his first sidearm. Here, this is for you. Your grandfather carried it in the Great Patriotic War. Many fascists met death when they faced this pistol; at Stalingrad alone it reduced their ranks by no fewer than seven. Take it, Irina, take it—a proud father's gift to his third brave boy.

He knew what he had done. Just as he knew she knew, and took pleasure in the knowledge.

Irina felt a tear burn down her cheek. She swiped it away. The other tears, the ones of fury and chagrin, had been less easily dealt with. She was thankful that she had been drunk, more thankful that she could get drunker because in that way only could she escape, ever so briefly, that maliciously calculated disgrace laid upon her by her father. . . .

Something caught her eye.

Her head snapped right. She whispered a curse. She was at, and was passing, the exit she wanted. She swerved hard. More than a single horn blared. She bounced over rocky soil, felt the Aerostar's rear wheels claw dirt as it bumped onto the ramp.

She pulled to an intersection a few miles west of the supermarket from which she'd stolen her minivan. She'd marked out this place earlier while driving east. Now she was back, and it was exactly what she wanted.

The SunLand Mall. Two upscale department stores: Nordstrom and Macy's. All the national chains: Eddie Bauer, The Body Shop, Ralph Lauren . . . and restaurants—six of them according to the directory at the entrance. Something for everyone: organic vegetarian to pricey faux French.

Only the coffee shops were open now, but the other stores would be opening soon. Then the acres of parking surrounding the mall would fill. A blue SUV would be only one of many, and would go unnoticed—she hoped—until the stores closed for the night, and the parking lot emptied.

That was twelve hours away. In twelve hours, she would be very, very far from here.

She cruised to the end of the lot. A thirsty row of live oaks lined the mall perimeter, prime parking, the only spaces with shade. Those spaces were not what she was looking for. Her objective, marked by a small sign pointing left, was the area designated: Employee Parking Only.

The workers will be the last to leave, she thought, *the last to notice that a car has been stolen.*

She followed the sign. The Ford crept between two buildings and into a courtyard lined with Dumpsters and heaped with empty shipping crates. More than three dozen cars were already there. There were parking spaces for at least another hundred.

After circling the lot twice, Irina chose a space nearest to the most promising vehicle: a dusty black Dodge pickup truck. She inventoried its qualities and found them pleasing:

a little old, a little battered, but still sound. Four-wheel drive; off-road tires; tinted glass. No bumper stickers. That was important. Bumper stickers were second only to vanity license plates in making a vehicle easily identifiable.

All in all, the Dodge was ideal. Here, in the American Southwest, there would be hundreds—thousands—of similar trucks on the road. For all intents and purposes, she would be invisible.

Irina tucked her pistol behind her back, leaving her blue jumper loose so that no telltale bulge could be seen. Easing watchfully out of the Ford, she began to walk slowly down the row of parked cars.

Past the truck, eyeing it from the rear.

Around to the front of the parking lane, examining her target from another angle.

She edged by it on the passenger side, glancing through its windows. The doors were locked, but that was no more than a thirty-second problem.

Another car rolled into the parking lot. Irina kept walking, entering an alley that led out into the center of the mall. She stopped just where the passageway debouched into public space. Flipping open her purse, she began to rummage through its contents—a punctual shopgirl looking for her lipstick, getting ready for her day's duties.

A middle-aged woman with unfortunate hips bustled out of the alley, barely giving her a passing glance.

Irina dropped back into the shadows, turned, and sprinted. Mall workers would be coming into the parking lot in increasing numbers. What time did most of the stores open? Nine thirty, probably. Certainly no later than ten. She had to act now, before the crowd arrived.

Moments earlier, she, who wore no makeup, hadn't been searching for lipstick. She'd been looking for the plastic shim she kept in her shoulder bag. As she slipped it into the pickup truck's door, just as she felt it engage the lock catch, she heard her luck run out.

"Hey, lady, just whut the hell you think you're doin' with my truck?"

Sam was hiding something, and Charlie knew it. Frustrated, he silently reflected on what tone of voice might shake the truth loose. *Outrage,* he decided, *icy outrage:* "One last time: What the hell has this girl stolen? Whatever that big brown thing is, and whatever is on that computer disk—that's what's driving her." He shot an accusing finger at the national security advisor. "If I don't know what it is, I'm just wasting my time."

Same as the last four times Charlie asked the question, Sam shook his head. "No can do. As I've explained, this is no ordinary secret. The Joint Chiefs, the secretaries of state and defense, and five of us on the White House staff are the only ones authorized—just us and the scientists assigned to the project. That's the way it is, and that's the way I intend to keep it. I will not, repeat will not, risk another security breach."

Another security breach? Something about those words struck a false note. Charlie silently played back the national security advisor's words, listening to them with an inner ear. *He could mean what Kolodenkova did. But I don't think so. He's talking about something else. Something he doesn't want me to know.*

"Sam, you've paid me twenty million bucks to—"

"What twenty million? There's no record of any payment to you."

Slippery sonofabitch. Even though he doesn't know he's on Candid Camera, the damned snake's fundamentally rep-

tilian instinct for self-preservation keeps him from saying a word I can use against him.

Charlie changed tactics, attacking from another flank. "Whatever. You want a girl—a woman—eliminated, and you want me to do it."

"Now, Charlie, I didn't say that."

Precisely the problem. Sam had said little explicitly, although much had been implied "Spare me your pieties. We both know what you've been talking about."

"I hope you haven't misinterpreted me, Charlie. Nobody is talking about killing Ms. Kolodenkova. Although the president and I understand it's a possible outcome, we would deeply regret it."

Charlie felt like grinding his teeth. But for one irrelevant slip, Sam had said nothing incriminating. Bad news. Win, lose, or draw, Sam would sell him out. Selling people out was his job, and he went to work every morning with a smile. If Charlie couldn't get his hands on something utterly damning, Sam would double-cross him. Again!

Another change of tactics. *Make yourself vulnerable,* he told himself. *Sad and world-weary, and a little weak.* He dropped his voice, turning his eyes away from Sam's serpent stare. "How many people do you think I've sanctioned?"

Sam shook his head. "How would I know? Fifty or so, I'd guess."

"Eleven."

Sam's surprise showed. "That few? From the stories they tell, I'd have thought—"

Ah! On the hook at last. "Eleven. Not counting self-defense and collaterals—bodyguards and such, which I regret. The number you mentioned, well, that's about the number I've been asked to go after. And turned down flat. You see, Sam, the thing is . . . the very painful thing is that I despise it, and it makes me puke. Oh sure, I know it comes easy to some. And I damned sure know that it's easy enough for people like you to order. But doing it . . . no, Sam, there's nothing to be said in favor of that. There's only what can be said against."

"But still, you've—"

"I have, and it's on my soul. When the time comes, the only alibi I'll be able to offer the recording angel is that my targets were personifications of the greatest evil you can find this side of hell."

Sam seemed genuinely astonished. "Uh . . . What can I say? I suppose I should say that I can respect that."

"I suppose you should."

To Charlie's ears, Sam's sigh of surrender sounded unfeigned. "Charlie, be reasonable. Do you think I'd be in this room if the nation wasn't in jeopardy?"

"Maybe, maybe not. I don't have enough information to decide."

Leaning back in his chair, Sam massaged his forehead to relieve what were, Charlie devoutly hoped, painfully throbbing sinuses. "Hmm . . . yes, I can empathize with that. Very well, let me try to give you a perspective. You know what happens when you build a better weapon? Of course you do. Your enemy builds a better defense. Or if you invent a better defense, then they invent better weapons."

"You're saying this is about weapons technology," Charlie spat. "That figures."

"Defensive weapons."

Charlie couldn't stop himself. "Aren't they all?"

"Your cynicism does you no service. Now, do you want to hear this or not? Fine. Then please don't interrupt. So teeter-totter back and forth—that's the way it's been since the end of World War Two. Atomic bombs through cruise missiles through Stealth aircraft—sometimes we have a little advantage, sometimes they have a little advantage. But little advantages aren't worth much. Only fools pick fights without a winner's edge. So we've got the arms race, and it never stops."

"Tell me something I don't know."

"What you don't know—and what I will deny to my dying day—is that we *can* stop it, stop it dead in the water. Listen, Charlie, suppose, just suppose, we came up with something so advanced that it puts us years ahead. Suppose we were developing a leapfrog technology, a breakthrough that wasn't just a new ball game, but was a whole new sport."

"I wouldn't believe it."

Sam drove a fist into his palm. "Believe it! It's still got four or five years of work to go. Then we deploy. Hell, we don't have to deploy. All we have to do is announce!"

"They'll still catch up."

As sanctimonious as a radio preacher, Sam grinned back: "That's the beauty of it. They'll ask their scientists, and the answer they'll get is: Why bother? We'll be at least a decade ahead, and picking up speed. They'll know they can't overtake us. It won't even be worth trying. *If* . . . and it's a big if, Charlie . . . if we can finish our research and productize the results before they find out what we're up to."

"You're saying the Irina girl—"

"You wanted to know what she stole. Now, I've told you. At least I've told you as much as I can."

"This is all true? You're not lying?"

"It is all true. I am not lying."

Charlie knew it was so. He'd been watching Sam closely, baiting him to falsehood, then teasing him back into honesty. If he read his man right, Sam was telling the truth—although not the whole truth and nothing but the truth, so help me God. His dissimulation was clear to anyone who knew the signs: eyes a little hooded, smile a little false, voice a little off pitch. Yeah, Sam was holding something back—something more important than whatever gizmo a rookie FSB girl had in her hot little hands.

Charlie ran a quick mental audit of Sam's repulsive rise. A Yalie and a Bonesman, he'd begun as a White House intern, just another newly hatched snake in a den of vipers. Then upward: a congressional aide, the Finance Committee, of course, because Sam liked to be near the piggy bank. Back then the gossip mongers whispered that Sam's career was almost derailed by his viciously uncontrollable temper. However, Sam managed to rein it in, not by the traditional Washingtonian expedient of prescription pharmaceuticals, but rather through sheer force of will. Accordingly, just before his party got booted out of power, Sam was awarded a sinecure with one of the so-called independent agencies. Once his boys were back in control, Sam reemerged as undersecretary of something or another in the Commerce Department. He devoted his tour of duty to making sure he was in the room whenever deals were cut and campaign pledges were vowed, those two activities being more or less synonymous. Thus did Sam become what the insiders call an "honest broker," getting the "broker" part right, if nothing else. Pacts, contracts, agreements, and negotiations—the exchange of services for good and worthy remuneration, some small portion of which was fairly due and owing to the middleman who arranged the trade.

But money wasn't quite enough for Sam, he wanted power too. The week after the World Trade Center went down, Sam popped up, now in the State Department. Ah, Foggy Bottom! One and a half percent of the federal workforce. Half a percent of the federal budget. All the power in the world.

Sam's definition of heaven.

Becoming a ranking official in the department that controlled, among many useful assets, the Central Intelligence Agency, sated Sam's hunger. For a while. Just long enough for him to maneuver his predecessor as national security advisor into making an appalling blunder, good-bye, farewell, so nice to know you, why, yes, Mr. President, I would consider it an honor.

Now Sam was one of the most powerful people in Washington, face-to-face with the president every day of the week. That was the good news. The bad news was that he had to spend every minute of the day looking over his shoulder, scanning the ranks of his underlings, ever watchful for ambitious young upstarts who might do unto him as he had done unto others.

Great power, like great wealth, is harder to keep than it is to get.

One slipup, one misstep, one botched job, and he was history. Welcome to Washington. Enjoy your stay, however short it may be.

Charlie warmed at the thought.

Sam, old son, you're running a cover-up. I don't know what you're hiding, but anything that would make you risk bringing me back into the game has to be major-league trouble. So then, you insect, let me tell you: if blowing the lid off Whirlwind is what it takes to clear my name, then may God have mercy on your sooty soul, for surely I shall have none.

Looking candidly at Sam, his face a mask of disingenuousness, he said, "All right, I think I have to buy what you're saying."

"Charlie, I am a man of my word," Sam lied.

"I know you are," Charlie lied back. "That's why I'm willing to take on this mission . . . " *pause, count to three, then drop the hammer,* "if you meet my price."

Sam's eyes turned to slits. "Price?" he growled. "What do you mean price? I've already given you twenty million dollars *plus* the head of your asshole son-in-law."

Gotchya! You are now recorded on videotape for all posterity. "The twenty mil was for the privilege of speaking to me. Sending Carly's ex-husband to hell was—and I believe I used the words explicitly—a 'down payment,' an 'option.' If you want to exercise that option, it's going to cost you."

"In your dreams."

"Nice seeing you again, Sam. Well, not really." Charlie stood. "I'll walk you to the door." *Go ahead,* he thought, *call my bluff.*

"Sit down," Sam whispered, soft and lethal. "Have you forgotten who you're dealing with?"

"Not for a second." *Read that one any way you want.*

"Then stop playing games and finish this negotiation. If you don't, I'll—"

"You'll what?" Cold, hollow, a wind from a burnt-out star, Charlie's voice was void of anger, void of any recognizable emotion. "What can you do to me, Sam? What can you do that you haven't already done?" He whispered sharp as the Reaper's sickle harvesting souls, "Dupe me into killing an innocent man? Turn me into a jailbird? Disgrace my good name? Fire me after more than thirty years of loyal service? Take away my pension? Keep me from my wife's deathbed? Come on, you slug, tell me what you can do that's any worse than what you've already done."

Honest hate is diamond, crystal clear and incandescent.

Charlie spilled his hoarded gems before Sam's scheming eyes, and in this he was, at last, fulfilled.

Sam had three choices: lie, stonewall, or tell the truth. Pick one of the above.

He'd been in politics long enough to know lying was a risky business. If the special prosecutor smelled an inconsistency, he'd be on you like a Doberman. As a rule, stonewalling was better. Assert national security, executive privilege or, worse comes to worst, the Fifth Amendment, and he might get steamed, but he wouldn't get an indictment. Sam stonewalled a lot. Hey, it worked.

But not this time. This time he had to tell it straight. Charlie was a thunderstorm, lightning in his heart, you could hear the electricity crackle. Back in the old days he'd hurt people, important people, there were stories about broken bones, and the fire in the dangerous bastard's eyes chilled Sam's blood.

Nonetheless, he couldn't help taking a certain satisfaction in the fact that Charlie had showed his true sentiments—the hallmark of an amateur negotiator.

I know my weaknesses, Charlie, do you? Yes, Sam was grimly aware that he had them—worst of all a dangerously combustible temper. When he lost it, his judgement suffered. Then, invariably, he made mistakes—big ones, bad ones, the kind that would spell the end of any politician's career. *That's where I'm vulnerable, Charlie. Now let's talk about you. What's your weakness, buddy?* Easy answer: self-confidence. Charlie was the most cocksure sonofabitch Sam had ever met. It wasn't arrogance or pride that made him so. It was . . . the word left a bad taste in his mouth . . . it was bravery—bravery and its galling handmaiden, honor.

If there was a chink in Charlie's armor, it was that he thought the angels were on his side, and behaved like he was under heaven's protection.

But he wasn't. A year and a half in prison proved that point. To say nothing of those other episodes in Charlie's past, bodies buried deep in unmarked graves, no tombstone engraved: here lies yet another victim of Charles McKenzie's gallant, albeit mule-headed, courage.

He's right most of the time. No problem. He thinks he's right all of the time. Big problem. So what's the best way to bargain with a grandstander like that?

Obvious answer: make him believe you think he's in the right. But don't make it easy. Make it like pulling teeth. Turn it into Charlie's personal victory. The only way to win was to make the self-righteous prick think Sam had lost.

Now, Sam smiled to himself, *let the bargaining begin.*

Dropping his shoulders submissively, he looked down as though unable to meet Charlie's stare. "I suppose it wouldn't do any good if I said I was sorry."

A carnivore's growl: "Not one damned bit."

A moment's shamefaced silence seemed called for. Charlie would be expecting it, and Sam was eager to please. He chewed his lips before murmuring, with apparent reluctance, "I believe I see the issue. You want a presidential pardon; that's what this is about, correct?"

"For openers," Charlie snapped, chin jutting and fists balled. "After that, I want an apology."

Sam sighed all the sadness in the world. "Presidents don't apologize. It fucks up their approval ratings." To which, he wistfully added, "Always excepting Bill Clinton."

"It doesn't have to be public, Sam. Just a private word from the White House to make me feel—"

Behold! Sam crowed silently, *a negotiating position!*

"Oh, Charlie," he shook his head with artful sorrow, "everyone knows the official story. Drugs and drink. The voters like the story, the voters believe the story, so that *is* the story. Take my advice: let it lie, just put it behind you, and let it lie."

Charlie seemed distracted. He squinted at his watch, then flicked his eye toward his bookcase. Sam asked himself, *He's worried about the time; why the hell is that?*

"You know me well enough to know I'll never let it lie."

"I'm afraid I do." He tilted his double chin at the ceiling, his face a mask of premeditated hesitation. "So then," he whispered, "you won't settle for anything else?"

God's voice on judgement day, "No, I will not."

Relishing the moment, Sam played his high card. "You want a pardon, very well then, you'll receive a pardon. Guaranteed." Charlie blinked in confusion. Sam was delighted. He'd found the soft spot in his opponent's defenses, and he could drive a big fat wedge straight through it. "But there are terms. There are conditions. You're going to have to compromise."

"I am not a compromising man."

Ain't it the truth. "Sorry, Charlie, but this is not a negotiation." *Of course it is.* "My first offer and my last offer are the same offer. No wheeling and dealing, take it or leave it. Understand?"

"Speak your piece. I'll listen. That's the only promise I'll make."

Puffing out his cheeks and blowing as though resigned to an inevitable and unwelcome fate, Sam did what he did only when there was no alternative: sucker-punched his opponent with the truth. "The president won't pardon you because he thinks you're guilty as sin. He thinks the whole Kahlid Hassan mess was exactly what the spin doctors said it was—a rogue agent gone berserk." Sam waited for the light to dawn. It only took seconds. "Hell, Charlie, what can I say? The orders I gave you—the president didn't know about them. When he found out, he went ballistic. So . . . Jesus, I'm sorry . . . when I said the White House would back you every step of the way . . . " Sam let his voice trail off into silence.

"You lied?" Ancient war drums in those two words, an armored legion on the march.

"Uh, no." All his years of practiced dissimulation went into his phrasing. No actor upon the stage could sound more sincerely ashamed. "Not exactly. It's more like I goofed. You see . . . Christ, I hate this . . . the boss said something, and I took it the wrong way."

" 'Who will rid me of this turbulent priest?' Is it one of those deals, Sam?"

Charlie was buying the story. Sam heaved an inner sigh of relief. "Don't I wish. The thing is I had a few drinks under my belt . . . " Three stiff ones, although there was no need to mention that. " . . . and simply got it wrong. I blew it, and I admit it. I hope you can accept that—maybe not forgive me, but at least understand. Nobody's perfect, and—"

Between clenched teeth, and savagely slow: "I went to jail because you misinterpreted the president?"

Tell the truth. The truth is the only thing that will convince him he's in the right. "You went to jail to cover my butt. If you want to kill me for that, go ahead." Sonofabitch! The homicidal prick was taking him seriously! He raised his voice, speaking more rapidly. "But the pardon, Charlie, I can promise it to you free and clear. Hell, I'll even get your pension reinstated."

"I thought you said the president won't—"

"Correct. But I will." Charlie gave him a narrow, cagey

look. Sam hated it when he did that. "The thing is . . . Charlie, understand this is one hundred and ten percent off the record . . . the thing is, the veep's ticker's worn out. He barely survived the reelection campaign. The docs give him a year unless he slows down. So . . . " *Deep breath, make him think it's really hard to confess.* "This fall, after congress's summer recess, he's resigning. The president plans to appoint me as his replacement."

Charlie was dead quiet. Sam had expected him to say something. At a minimum he should have insulted him. "So, ah, Charlie, what do you think about that?"

"Mostly that vice presidents don't get to sign pardons."

"But presidents do. Three years from now the boss's term is up. Then, who's the party's logical nominee? The vice president, that's who. In other words: me. And as soon as I'm elected, you get a pardon. I swear on my mother's—"

"Hogwash," Charlie shot back. "The public doesn't know you. You've never held elected office. You've got no organization. You've got no campaign chest. You're too damned fat!"

Sam smiled a perfect smile. "Three years as vice president. A lot can change in three years."

"Not enough. There are a dozen hungry senators waiting for the primary, and there's not a one of them who isn't better funded than you. It takes what—sixty or seventy million bucks to win the primaries. And to get elected, hell, then you're talking about *real* money. Correct me if I'm wrong, but I believe your boss spent something in excess of three hundred million to buy his chair in the Oval Office."

"I can spend more." *Ha! Just look at the expression on your face.* "I've got friends, friends you don't know about. We're talking major muscle and major money, enough to steamroll the other candidates. Make no mistake, I am going to be the next president." Sam showed his teeth. "Anyone who gets in my way is roadkill!" He started to rise from his chair.

"Sit down!" Charlie snapped.

Somewhere in Sam's mind a faint alarm bell rang.

"Sam, either we finish this conversation now or we don't finish it at all."

What was the fossilized old dinosaur up to? He sure as hell couldn't have bugged the room. Sam's NSA team carried equipment tuned to detect the most advanced high-tech recording gear. *It's just an act,* he told himself, *Charlie being Charlie, thumping his chest like a goddamned alpha-male gorilla.*

Choosing to obey the order of a man who was losing (although he did not know it) this particular bargaining session, Sam slumped back into his seat. Then spreading his palms in a well-rehearsed gesture of candor, he spoke intimately, a hushed secret shared between two friends. "Look, the president is behind me. Even back before the reelection campaign, he knew the veep was sick. Two years ago, he picked three of us—me, a congressman from Southern California, and the secretary of state. He explained what's what with the vice president, and then he gave each of us a couple of balls to run with. I was assigned Whirlwind and diplomatic relations with China—"

"The most treacherous sonsofbitches I know. Present company excepted."

"They're eating out of the palm of my hand. Things have never been more cordial." He stopped himself short. Boasting about the Chinese was a mistake. Charlie was the last person Sam wanted to know about his little diplomatic coup.

"Just give me the bottom line, Sam. I don't have much time here." Charlie's eyes darted toward his bookcases again.

Why the hell was he looking at it? Nothing there but dog-eared books, a couple of cameras, and some crap souvenirs.

"China and Whirlwind were my babies. If I managed them right, then I'd get the nod when the vice president retired. Which I did. Come this fall, I'll be vice president of the United States."

"Except that Whirlwind has gone lost, stolen, or strayed."

"Which you will handle for me. Otherwise, I'm toast." Honesty, honesty—who says it doesn't pay? Every now and then. "If I'm toast, I don't get to be president. If I don't get to be president—"

"I don't get pardoned."

"But you will." Sam felt good. Sam felt fine. Sam felt like he always did when he'd brokered a winning trade. "Find that Russian bitch, find Whirlwind, and your name gets cleared."

"The only thing that will clear my name is you admitting that Kahlid Hassan was your fault."

"Not in a million years." *The negotiation is over, Charlie. Give it up.*

"But it was, right?"

"Of course it was. I already said that, didn't I?" Charlie smiled the smile of a profoundly satisfied man. Sam wondered why.

"Sam, under normal circumstances I wouldn't trust you as far as I could throw you. However, these are not normal circumstances. I'm going to accept your offer."

Charlie held out his hand. Sam stood and shook it.

Done deal, sucker.

Disappointed that he hadn't succeeded in detonating Sam's volcanic temper, Charlie shepherded the security advisor out of his house. As they walked down the porch steps, Sam said, "Once I'm airborne, I'll order the equipment you asked for. There'll be a chopper on your lawn in two hours. Agency Falcon at—"

"I'd prefer a Gulfstream. A GV actually."

"Your wish is my command. It will be waiting for you at Bolling. Fully equipped with onboard secure radio, secure cellular, secure network access from anywhere, all that technology crap."

"Which you will bug."

"Correct. Also you get temporary credentials with your old rank back and a renewed security clearance. Full-time Agency librarian. Four squeaky-clean credit cards, one in each flavor. Twenty grand in walking-around money."

Charlie glanced over his shoulder. Jason and Molly had their faces pressed to the window. Carly, hands on her hips, stood at the screen door. "All in twenties and fifties. I presume it will be marked."

"Of course. If you cut and run, I want a way to track you down."

"Don't you wish."

Sam shrugged, continuing to read from Charlie's neatly printed shopping list. "A Steyr sniper rifle with a Trijicon scope . . . whatever that may be . . . and two FBI-accurized .40 calibers. That's everything you asked for. Anything else you want?"

Sam's Marine Corps pilot had fired up the helicopter's engine. Its blades were high above both men's heads. Neither Sam nor Charlie could keep himself from instinctively ducking.

"The father."

"Excuse me? What father?"

"The girl's. The Russian navy guy. I want his full dossier. Digitize it, and send it to me once I'm in my Gulfstream."

"It's been looked at. There's nothing useful in it."

"Send it to me anyway."

"It's your ballgame, Charlie. Ask, and you shall receive." Sam lumbered toward the helicopter's boarding steps. He did not, Charlie observed, offer to shake hands again.

"One other thing, Sam. I want your promise that you won't be bringing anyone else into this business."

"Of course I won't, Charlie."

"No hired guns at all."

"You have my word on that."

It was in his eyes, pure deceit, Charlie read it like a book. *Samuel, you are a vile lying yellow dog.* Stepping back, he gave a friendly wave as the helicopter lifted off his lawn. The gesture cost him nothing and was bound to make Sam feel good.

But not as good as Charlie felt now that he had—compliments of an outdated video camera so low-tech that the NSA's high-tech whizkids ignored it—Sam's full confession on videotape.

3
Introducing Mr. Schmidt

Irina read him. Within seconds she cold-read who and what he was.

They'd taught her well at the Institute, spicing the course with old American movies. Hollywood knew better than any intelligence agency how garb and gesture subliminally communicate persona to an audience. Posture, intonation, and expression transform the servile butler from *The Remains of the Day* into Hannibal Lecter, cannibal epicure. A red-robed cancan dolly in *Moulin Rouge!* applies putty to her nose, and dressed in stark austerity incarnates neurotic Bloomsbury's most neurotic novelist.

All the world's a stage, and all the men and women merely players. . . . Who then, she asked herself, was the actor who'd found her breaking into his truck?

A cowboy sidekick. Never the leading man, but always a good one. He would be Slim Pickens, Ward Bond, Ben Johnson. Sitting in a darkened classroom she had seen him in a dozen films.

Walking with an ill-disguised limp, he was compact and

muscular, although with an unbecoming bulge around his waist. The corners of his eyes were engraved with squint lines—sure sign that he worked outdoors. Yet his complexion was sallow; he had not been beneath the sun for months.

His dress told a simple story—inexpensive clothing recently bought off the rack at a discount clothier. New chinos purchased for a newly ballooned stomach. A white shirt bearing the creases of a garment fresh from a store, freshly put on. However, his elaborately stitched cowboy boots were expensive, and probably custom-made. One other costly thing: a heavy silver belt buckle decorated with turquoise and lapis. Words she could not make out were embossed around its rim. Was it some sort of prize—an award for athletic prowess?

No wedding ring, he eyed her with the gaze of a proud man used to women's admiration.

An athlete—he could be nothing else. *He broke his leg in an accident, and was invalided for months. Whatever his sport — rodeo, I think—he was injured so badly that he can play no more. His recuperation was long and expensive. Now he has little money and no work. He wears new slacks and shirt because his old clothes no longer fit, because they are as flamboyant as his boots, because this morning he wishes to make a good impression. He is a man who is—who has been—interviewing for a store clerk's job.*

The phrase "target of opportunity" came to mind.

"Lady, listen up. I'm talkin' to you."

Irina's English was too perfect. Its unaccented precision proclaimed her a foreigner, although none who heard her could guess her nationality. Slurring her words drunkenly would disguise that. "'S not your truck. 'S my truck. You think I dunno my truck when I shee it."

"Ma'am, I'm tellin' you that one ain't yours." The hardness in his bearing loosened, and his voice edged toward courtliness—an almost imperceptible change in tone revealing a vulnerability, telling her how to exploit it.

She tossed her head, let her hair fall over her face, giving him a peek-a-boo look. "'S too. I got my keys right here . . . oops-a-daisy." Her purse tumbled to the pavement, its contents scattering. The man glanced down. Irina slid her shim into her hip pocket. "Aw, now look what you've gone and made me do." She fell to her knees. He, chivalry in his warm brown eyes, squatted on his hams, helping her pick up wallet, coin purse, nail clippers, hair brush, and (with some embarrassment) a paper-wrapped Tampax.

"Shee. Shee right here. My keys. My truck. Jus' like I said."

"Ma'am, with respect, them ain't Dodge keys. That there is a Ford logo." Politely spoken—a cowboy gentleman who was always courteous to the ladies.

She held the keys up, closed one eye, focused the other a little beyond where it should have been. "Awww, you're right." She stood, as did he. "Usin' my sister's car today. Awww, I'm sorryyy." With that she fell forward, her arms around his neck. "Forgive me?" She let herself slump, her breasts rubbing against his chest. "I jus' got a little confused. We had us a party las' night. All us waitresses. Boss man's gonna be sore when he opens the wine cellar. Whoops! I bet I gotta go on unemployment again."

His smile said he was on her side. "Must a-been some fine party."

"Didn't end 'til the wine was *allll* gone. Now everyone's gone. All gone home. An' I gotta find my car an' go home too." She forced herself to burp. "'Scuse me."

He reacted to her intentionally foolish proposal as she'd hoped. "Ma'am, I'd say you ain't in any condition to drive. 'Sides which the local law takes DUI pretty serious."

"Aw, that's nothin' to worry about. I just give 'em my phone number an' they tear up the ticket. I got nothin' against datin' big guys, y'know guys with muscles jus' like you."

Drunkenly seductive, she smiled sweetly. He seemed at a loss for words, although clearly his thoughts were turning in the direction she wanted. "My car, sister's car actshully, oooo . . . now where could it be? Big blue whatchymacallit Ford thingy. I'll just get in an' drive out to the innerstate an' ever'thing'll be just fine."

"I'd reckon that to be really one seriously poor idea."

Irina smiled inwardly. His face told her that the seed was well planted. "You gotta better one? What? You wanna drive me home instead? Okay. Thass an okay idea." She leaned against him again, watching his cheeks flush. In a moment or two, he'd be hers.

He pursed his lips. "I suppose. Problem is, if I drove your car, then once I got you home I'd have to call me a taxicab to get back to my truck. That's an expense I don't need at this present time."

She gave him a look. No, she gave him *the* look. "Silly. I didn't mean my house. I meant your house."

A half hour later, he—Mitch Conroy was his name, and yes he was a disabled rodeo rider—pulled his truck into a cluttered carport. Covered with an old tarpaulin, a stolen secret, brown and oblong, sat in the pickup's back (" 'S a surprise," she'd said as he moved it from the Aerostar. "No peekin' 'cause the surprise is gonna be for you.").

The neighborhood was run down—stucco houses, dying lawns, thirsty dogs sleeping in the shade. You moved here when life dealt you a losing hand; you stayed here after you bet all your chips on the wrong cards. Last stop, the bus line ends here.

Mitch unlocked a side door, holding it open. "Hope you'll pardon the mess. I ain't the best housekeeper in the world. And like I said, things ain't been all that easy for me since I had to give up my old place."

" 'S not a problem." Although it was. Unwashed dishes were piled in a rust-stained sink. Crumpled fast-food cartons and pizza boxes decorated the kitchen table. The small living room looked like it hadn't been vacuumed since—a month earlier, Mitch had said—the previous renters had vacated the property. Except for a dozen rodeo trophies, his few personal possessions still lay in cardboard boxes lining the wall.

"Bedroom's right through here. If you . . . uh . . . want to freshen up any, the bathroom's that door over yonder."

She nodded so hard that her hair tumbled over her face again. Before they'd left the shopping mall, she'd told him she needed to stop at a drugstore. "Girl stuff, y'know. For when we get home." Wearing the expression of a man who knew little about girl stuff, and who did not wish to learn more, he'd stopped in front of a Rite Aid. She dashed in, then dashed back out with the brown paper bag she still held tightly in her hand.

The bathroom was what she expected—little more than a closet with an enameled shower stall, a toilet that had seen better days, and a sink that needed scouring. Mitch's shaving tackle, hair cream, toothpaste, and toothbrush sat on a small glass shelf above it.

Irina emptied her bladder, wiped herself, and took a deep breath. She wished what had to come next would be as easy as what had come before.

Mitch was a nice—indeed decent—man. He'd been

sweetly polite to her. She liked his wry sense of humor and roundabout way of talking. And he'd earned her sympathy; the tough times he'd endured since breaking his leg saw to that. Under other circumstances . . .

But there were no other circumstances. The only condition was the present condition. Irina regretted pain she could not avoid inflicting, and wished she had another choice.

There was none. She'd made a vow. Only by bringing the computer disk and the heavy brown object home could she keep the pledge she'd silently sworn a year ago, both hands clasping her mother's secret Bible: *On my honor and before God, I will outrank him, I will, and I shall make him salute me, he shall stand at attention before me and raise his hand and he shall salute me!*

She would keep that promise. No power on earth could stop her.

Setting her jaw, she studied herself in the mirror. It was not Irina Kolodenkova who stared back. Then whose remorseless face was it? Were those loveless eyes, that stony look, familiar? Could it be a despotic Navy captain . . . ?

She splashed water on her cheeks, washing away nothing.

Then, still clothed in denim and a blue pullover, she stepped into the bedroom exclaiming, "Ta-TA!" and striking a model's pose, one arm stretched high over her head, hip thrust left.

Spartan, male, not the least feminine touch, the bedroom made her pause, a caesura in time, a frozen moment during which she was transported from a ramshackle Texas cottage to the joyless room in which she had grown up. She closed her eyes, swallowing hard.

Mitch sat on the bed. He'd removed his boots, but nothing else. "My, my. You sure are a pretty thing."

Shivering, she took a step forward, a reluctant actor in an unwanted spotlight. "Awww . . . " She flopped down on the bed and steeled herself for a role she did not wish to play. "You're sweet. Bet your kisses are pretty sweet too." She knew she sounded forced and stilted.

Apparently Mitch did not notice the insincerity in her every word. "Well now, there's only one way you can find out about that."

She feigned a cat purr sound, fumbling at her belt as she did. "Lemme . . . lemme get into nothin' comfy before we start. Gee, Mitch, you know it sure is hot. You got AC 'round here somewhere?"

"That I do. It ain't worth much, though."

"Be a doll and turn it on. Then you get to turn me on." He'd want to hear a giggle now. She did her best.

Mitch walked to the window, flicking a switch on an antiquated air conditioner. Irina unbuckled her belt and unfastened the button on her Levi's. As Mitch ambled smiling to the bed, she slurred, "Aw, damn! Zipper's stuck." Then in the teasing tones of a little girl, "You know how to get a zipper unstuck, Mitch? Do you, huh?"

"I believe I can handle that." His smile widened. Reaching the edge of the bed, he began to bend at the waist. He was where she wanted him, and in the posture she desired. She lashed out her foot, a soccer kick aimed at his groin.

Badly mended leg. Pudgy belly. It made no difference. Mitch remained what he'd been all his life, an athlete. A bad fall from a bad horse had cost him his career, but not his reflexes. He pirouetted to the right, dancing backward. Irina's kick cut empty air.

"Well, hell," he sighed, giving her a look that, surprisingly, was not angry. "I sorta been expectin' sumthin' like that, but, you know, I was genuinely hopin' I was wrong."

Irina again played peek-a-boo with her hair. "Aw, I was only funnin'."

"Nah. You can drop the drunk act now. I didn't much believe it in the first place."

"Not drunk. Jus' a little tipsy." She opened her eyes wide, showed all the blue she had. It produced no effect.

Mitch put his hands on his hips, watching her with genuine sadness. "Soon as I smelled your breath back in the parking lot, I got a mite suspicious. Didn't seem like you'd been drinkin' all night long."

"Gargle. I gotta gargle every time I give a blow job. Had to gargle six times lass night."

He gave her a melancholy little smile. "That's a right good line, ma'am, but it ain't gonna work with a man like me."

Irina said nothing, although she thought much. Force was out of the question. She was strong, but he was stronger. And as swift as she was, he, quite obviously, was swifter. The only advantage she had was tucked beneath her pullover, snuggled in the small of her back. She wasn't sure she could pull the trigger if it came to that.

Mitch did not glower and did not frown. He merely looked sorrowful. "You wanna tell me what this is all about. I mean before I call the law or somethin'. If you got yourself a story, and if it's true, now'd be the time to tell me."

"I am a Russian spy," she said flatly. "The FSB—the Federal Security Bureau—that is what the KGB calls itself now."

"Right." Disgust and disappointment in his voice.

"My real name is Irina Kolodenkova, and I'm—"

The phone was on top of a lopsided dresser. Mitch stepped backward, his hand behind him reaching for it. Irina snapped the Tokarev up, both hands around the grip. "No!"

Mitch stopped dead in his tracks. "Lady, whatever your name is, I ain't got nothin' worth stealin'. Which makes me wonder just why in the hell you picked me for your sucker in the first place."

"Take off your pants."

"Ain't a-gonna do that."

Irina squeezed the trigger. The telephone turned to shrapnel.

Mitch said the only thing he could say. He said, "Yes, ma'am."

Well, sweetheart, that's about all I have to say today except that I love you and I miss you. Charlie always used the same words—more or less—to end his daily letters to the only woman in his life. I wish I had an address to mail this to, honey, I wish I knew a post office that would deliver it. But since I don't, I'll just do what I always do, and throw some kisses your way into the bargain. Love, Charlie and Carly and Jason and Molly.

He dispatched a letter to his dead wife in the only way he knew how: he hit the Delete key.

As he powered down his computer, the in-flight phone in his armrest trilled. He picked it up. "Yeah, Sam?" Pressing the handset to his ear, he glanced out the Gulfstream's window. The twin-engine jet was over West Texas, dreary hill country beloved by the natives but by no one else. He figured the pilot would be beginning his descent soon.

"How did you know it was me?"

Charlie eyed his digital recorder wistfully. No way could he press it against the earpiece to tape Sam's voice. This was an executive branch VIP jet, bug detectors built into the phones; they'd pick up the proximity of any electronic device closer than six inches and—*oogah! oogah!*— Sam would hear an alarm in his ear.

"Who the hell else is going to call me aboard a government plane on a top secret mission?"

"Good point." Sam sounded irritated. Charlie was the happier for it.

"Okay, Sambo, what do you want?" Thirteen luxurious blue leather seats in the Gulfstream, twelve of them unoccupied—Charlie swiveled, stretching long legs into the plushly carpeted aisle.

"I thought you should know that I decided to brief Claude on Whirlwind after all." Sam spoke hesitantly, a man unwillingly admitting that he'd done something he'd said he wouldn't.

Charlie lifted a glass of lemonade from his walnut burl tray table. It was tart and it was fresh, nothing but the best for passengers on a White House aircraft. "Excellent decision. The Agency isn't what it used to be, but there still are a few competent people left. Even though he's a treacherous toad, Claude will put the right resources on the job." Charlie asked an unspoken question: *A couple of hours ago, you deceitful son of a whore, you swore Whirlwind was so sensitive that the director of Central Intelligence had to be kept in the dark. Now you're having second thoughts. So tell me, Sam, how much trouble are you* really *in?*

"Glad you approve. But the thing is, uh, the thing is Claude wants to rescind your orders."

Charlie's eyes narrowed. *Now what the hell do I do? Same as usual, I suppose, run a bluff.* "Fine by me. I'll tell the pilot to turn around."

"No!" Sam barked. "That's not what I meant. I meant, well, Claude wants you to take the Kolodenkova woman alive."

I was wondering how long it would take you dimwits to figure that out. "He's right. She's been on the loose long enough that she might have made contact with her people. You won't know whether she's spilled the beans on your Whirlwind gizmo unless you interrogate her."

"That's exactly what Claude said. So what we . . . what I want is for you to, well, not to . . . "

"I'll bring her back alive. That was my plan from the get-go."

"Oh?" *Do I detect a little dismay in your voice, Sam? Has it only just now struck you that I might not carry out your orders to the letter?*

Sam dropped his voice, "Claude says we should wait until midday Friday. If you can't bring her back by then, odds are Whirlwind will be out of her hands and in somebody else's. So Friday noon. After that . . . well, you know."

"A price on her head, open contract, shoot to kill."

"Whatever. All I'm saying is that come Friday noon you won't have an exclusive."

"If I can't catch a rookie FSB girl in four days, it's time to put me out of my misery and send my carcass to the glue factory."

"I have every confidence in that." *Ouch,* Charlie thought, *I left myself wide open for that one!* Sam continued, "Now I'll let you get back to your—"

"Not so fast." He altered his tone, a throaty rumble of command. "While I've got you on the line, there are a couple of questions I want answered."

Charlie relished the wariness in Sam's hesitant answer: "Of course. Go ahead."

"Let me preface this by saying that I genuinely dislike being lied to. From now on, I want nothing but the truth. If I don't get it, there will be consequences." *Consequences. Nice word. Ambiguous. Scary.*

No surprise, Sam reverted to oleaginous type: "Charlie, I'm insulted. Would I lie to you?" *Every chance you get.* "It's true that I've kept a few facts back." *You have a talent for understatement.* "But those are strictly in the national interest." *Strictly in your interest is my bet.* "There's no reason for you to know what's not germane to the mission." *Every intelligence snafu in American history—including goddamned Kahlid Hassan—has resulted from some REMF desk jockey not giving front-line guys the information they need.* "I'm happy to tell you what I can, but please understand that—"

"Hogwash! Damnit, Sam, your people faxed me the plans of the Whirlwind base. All it took me was a protractor and a stopwatch to work out that Kolodenkova and Grisin didn't have time to paw through your secrets. The fence line is about a fifteen-minute hike from the laboratory. Given the time difference between when the first generator exploded and the second went ka-blooey, they couldn't have had more than ten minutes—and probably only five—in that lab. Are you following me, Sam? Do you see the implication?"

"That doesn't change the fact that—"

Charlie turned up the heat. "It sure as hell does! The way you told the story, this girl knows something so dangerous that she has to be silenced. But the truth, Sam, the truth is that those two kids weren't in your skunkworks long enough for anything but a little smash and grab. The girl may have her mitts on something secret, but the odds are a hundred to one that she actually *knows* what it is."

"I can't live with those odds."

"You can't kill people for those odds." *Am I mad, Sam? You bet your ass I am.*

"I'll make that decision."

When pigs fly. "You lied, Sam. More than once. Lie number two is the crap you fed me about the base commander having to radio for help."

"That was completely true. I don't see what you're—"

"The plans, Sam, the plans of that base. They show the position of every building, every road, every sewer, and every plumbing line. What they don't show, you liar, is any telephone lines. Not aboveground on poles. Not underground in conduit."

"An omission."

"Baloney. The reason why there aren't any phone lines on those plans is that there aren't any phone lines on that base."

"Your implication would be . . . ?"

Jesus, I hate these stupid games. You know what I've deduced. I know that you know. You know that I know that you know. But still, you've got to play it out, don't you? "EM weapons, that would be my implication. Zap your enemy's aircraft with high-energy electromagnetic radiation, and it toasts their electronics: the controls, the targeting systems, the onboard computers, and even the pilots' ejection buttons. All that's left is a flying brick."

"That's science fiction."

"Yeah? Then why did the Pentagon boast in *Forbes* magazine that our EM-equipped tanks can disable incoming rockets moving at three hundred meters a second? Come on, Sam, it's the generals' wet dream—Buck Rogers ray guns and Star Trek phasers, only for real. EM may be dangerous as hell and dumb as hell, but science fiction it is not."

"Just what makes you think Whirlwind has anything to do with energy weapons?"

Charlie sighed. "You told me that the soldiers guarding the lab couldn't get help for four hours because their radios were down. Anyone with half a brain would have asked: Hey, why didn't they use the phone? Answer: because electromagnetic radiation fries line loading coils, amplifiers, and repeaters. So don't accuse me of swiping state secrets, Sam. You're the one who spilled the beans."

Sam whispered his favorite obscenity.

Charlie took another swallow of lemonade, emptying the

glass. A uniformed steward trotted forward with a pitcher in his hand, offering him a refill. "EM weapons sound slick in theory. In practice they suck. Once you start beaming radiation into the sky it goes everywhere and hits everything. Including friendly aircraft. I believe the navy demonstrated that unhappy fact to everyone's satisfaction when some hairball started testing microwave death rays on Long Island Sound. And knocked down four passenger jets flying out of JFK in the process."

"No one can prove that."

"Wanna bet?" Charlie put his all into those words, every ounce of cunning he possessed. Gratifyingly, it worked. Sam muttered: "Shit happens. Besides, we stopped after the first two jumbos crashed. The others weren't our fault."

Charlie glanced at his digital recorder's time counter, nearly hidden by the stethoscope he'd hastily hooked to the telephone. Plenty of recording room left—just in case Sam chanced to make another criminal admission into a low-tech/no-tech gizmo that kept a recording machine sufficiently far from Uncle Sam's bug detectors that they never knew it was there.

"Listen up, Charlie." Gratifyingly, Sam almost sounded angry. "Forget about EM. Forget about everything except the fact I've paid you big bucks to do one simple job: get Kolodenkova and get Whirlwind."

"That's two jobs." *That ought to piss him off.*

Sam murmured, "You know exactly what I mean."

Charlie grimaced. Sooner or later he'd make the fat-boy bureaucrat lose his ever-so-tightly controlled temper. He'd just have to put his shoulder to the job. "I'm not sure I do. After all, I thought I knew what you meant when you said you wouldn't hire any freelancers. But then I sent a few e-mails from this very fine aircraft you've lent me, and guess what?

I hear from my sources that certain unnamed mercenary organizations—"

"They're on standby, Charlie. Ready reserves, backups. As I said, you've got until Friday noon. Of course, if you don't bring home the bacon by then . . . Well, now you know my fallback position."

Charlie didn't believe a word of it. "Who? Which outfit are you using this time?"

"That's irrelevant to your mission."

"I'd say not."

"Only if you don't do your job."

"Listen to me, Sam—"

"No, you listen to me." His voice was shriller. Charlie wondered how close to the edge he was. He wondered if he could push him closer. "There's only one . . . only two things I want out of you. That damned Russian and what she stole. No, let's make that three things. The third is I don't want you giving me any more lip."

If Sam had seen the glint in Charlie's eyes, he would have flinched. "Sorry, Sam, there's a little more lip you're going to have to take."

"Oh, do I?"

"Are you sitting down, Sammy boy?"

"What's that crack supposed to mean?"

"I wouldn't want you falling over and hurting yourself. Well, actually I would, but let that pass." *God, this is fun.*

"Cut to the chase, buddy. Say what you have to say and let me get on with my life."

"You won't like it."

"Will you just stop screwing around?"

"Okay. Brace yourself."

No more shrillness, Sam was positively snarling, "Quit

playing games! I've got better things to do with my time than—"

"I videotaped everything you said in my study this morning, every single word."

A long silence. Then hushed disbelief. "Impossible. I had my NSA technicians sweep—"

"The NSA couldn't find a nipple on a nudist. Believe me, Sam, I've got you live and in living color. Action News. Footage at five. The president's national security advisor confessing to his role in the Kahlid Hassan affair."

Silence. Then a single whispered word: "Blackmail!"

"Absolutely not," Charlie chortled. "It's just my insurance policy. Before I left home I digitized that tape and put it out on the Internet. It's safe and secure in a place you'll never find, an encrypted data vault that no one can crack. So, it gives me great pleasure to inform you that if you even think about double-crossing me, then that video gets sent to every media company in the world. Television, radio, newspapers, magazines, you name it, they get it. And if they do, what do you think will happen to your presidential aspirations? Hmmm?"

Sam knew the answer. Losing his appointment to the vice presidency would be only the first of many, many bad things. Accordingly, he said what Charlie expected he'd say. "I'll kill you first."

"Bad idea, Sam. Plenty bad. I've got a deadman's brake."

"What the fuck is that supposed to mean?"

"Ask Claude. Even someone so embarrassingly devoid of operational experience as the director of Central Intelligence should know what a deadman's brake is." *Click.* Smiling widely, Charlie disconnected the call and switched off a tape recorder now chockablock full of Sam saying very naughty things. Navy involvement in the crash of two civilian jetliners, the use of mercenaries on American soil, and, best of all, a death threat against that righteous paragon of godly behavior, Charles McKenzie, Esquire. *Blackmail? Sam, you clown, you don't know the half of it!*

He coiled up his stethoscope and dropped it back into the war bag between his legs. Then, heaving a happy sigh, he leaned back in his seat and shut his eyes. Beating Sam to a bloody pulp would be gratifying. Putting him in jail for the rest of his life would be better. But public humiliation . . .

"Excuse me, sir. Is there anything wrong." The steward was hovering at Charlie's shoulder.

"No," Charlie said. "No. What makes you think there's something wrong?"

"Well, sir, you were . . . uh . . . you sort of were . . . those sounds you were making . . . "

"Just laughter, son. I was only laughing."

Irina chewed her lip. Mitch's kitchen was a wasteland. The refrigerator contained only a carton of stale milk. As for the cupboards, they were bare but for an almost empty box of Frosted Flakes. A few spoonfuls of cereal lay in its bottom, small insects rustling among the grains. Hungry, but not that hungry, Irina dropped the box in disgust.

Apparently Mitch subsisted on fast food. And that was a problem. She could risk leaving his house for a few minutes, risk driving to the cluster of take-out chains she'd noticed not far from here. But she could not risk someone noticing the black Dodge truck she'd be driving. The woman at the Taco Bell drive-thru window, the clerk behind the counter at Pizza Hut, might recognize it. "Why, howdy, miss. Y'all a friend of ol' Mitch's? I see he's lent you his pickup, and that boy don't do that 'cept for his very best buddies."

Make no mistake, they'd know Mitch, and they'd know his truck. The detritus scattered across the kitchen table told her he was a valued customer.

An inquisitive clerk, a question she couldn't answer—some friend of Mitch's might worry enough to stop by the house; he might worry more than that, and call the police.

Getting food was too risky. She'd have to endure her hunger until nightfall, and she was back on the road. There were plenty of restaurants on the interstate. No one would pay attention to her; no one would guess she was driving a stolen truck.

Frustrated and famished, Irina pushed Mitch's collection of empty burger cartons onto the floor. A small green package caught her eye. She picked it up. Chewing gum. And, wouldn't you know, there was only one stick left.

She decided to save it for later—something to fool an empty stomach after she'd slept.

Sleep was more important than food anyway. Awake for more than twenty-four hours, her body ached from muscles that had been tense too long. Just a few more minutes, and she'd lie down and sleep and sleep and sleep.

She patted her hair. Almost dry. It had taken longer than she expected.

After changing its color with the dye she'd snatched up at that drugstore, she'd had no choice but to towel her hair hard and wait for Texas's arid air to do the rest. A man like Mitch didn't own a hairdryer. Of course not.

Leaving the kitchen, she walked across the living room and into the bedroom. She glanced at the closet. Mitch was inside, immobilized—nearly mummified—by the duct tape she'd found in his carport. He'd quieted down at last, stopped his yelling. For that she was thankful. She didn't want to tape his mouth. He'd already thrown up twice—the predictable aftermath of a punch in the solar plexus—and she knew a man with his mouth taped closed could choke to death on his own vomit.

Now in the bathroom, she studied herself in the mirror. Her hair had turned out better than she'd expected. No longer gold, but rather glossy brown, almost chestnut, the new color made her look . . . *more American, I think. More ordinary. Part of the crowd.*

Later, when she woke up, she'd see to her eyebrows. She'd thicken them with the makeup she'd bought, flattening their distinctive arch. She'd do something about her lips too. Pale lipstick waited on the sink, ready to mask a red that men found too attractive. Then there was the question of her nails. She'd bought a bottle of scarlet polish. She wasn't sure she could bring herself to put it on. She'd never painted her nails, in truth had never used makeup at all. Father forbade it.

She ran a brush through her hair one last time. Surely it was dry enough. Even if it wasn't, she could keep her eyes open no longer.

She stretched out on Mitch's bed, nestling her head into his pillow. The air conditioner hummed in the background. Such a comforting sound. White noise. More relaxing than silence, really. . . .

If she dreamed, she did not know it. Wrapped in sleep and forgetfulness, she knew nothing at all.

"Hey, Mitch! I know you're in there. Your truck's in the garage."

What?

"Open up the door, boy. I've got something for you." A man's voice.

Drowsy and confused, she looked at the alarm clock on Mitch's nightstand. A little before four-thirty in the afternoon.

"Quit fooling around and get out here." Not urgent, but resolute.

Still fully dressed, Irina leapt out of bed. She jerked open the top drawer of Mitch's dresser. A half dozen sets of underwear lay inside. Shedding her blue pullover, she snatched up a yellowed T-shirt.

"Mitch, I'm not leaving until I see your ugly face." A friend joking at a friend.

Off with her bra, and on with the T-shirt. Fingers through her hair, mussing it. Pistol snatched from the nightstand, slipped behind her back. Quick to the closet. A groggy man tried to speak. Once, twice, three times—duct tape crisscrossed his mouth. There still was no hatred in his eyes, and that was hard to deal with.

"Come on, Mitch. What are you doing in there?"

One last thing. The chewing gum. She popped it into her mouth, grinding it with her rear teeth.

She narrowed her eyes to slits, forced her mouth into a frown, tried to look as angrily sluttish as possible.

Her voice, her perfect pronunciation, was a problem. She knew she couldn't credibly imitate the saw-toothed tones of a Texas bad girl. But maybe, just maybe, she could fake the next most dangerous thing: a recently relocated New Yorker.

Flinging the door open, she rasped, "Yeah, so whatchya want?"

A lightning-quick reading. A tall and dignified man. Older but not too old; "mature" was the proper word. Expensive grey whipcord trousers and a pricey desert-tan bushman's shirt. An alpha male, no disguising that. But deferent and not threatening—a man who glanced only briefly at distracting breasts barely concealed by a thin T-shirt.

He carried himself . . . he stood like . . . he seemed to be . . . A businessman? A lawyer? A doctor? Surely some sort of professional. And his smile? Why was he smiling with such . . . more than friendliness . . . with such affection?

He lifted his left hand. An inexpensive wedding band on his fourth finger told her he'd started poor, but a costly gold watch on his wrist proclaimed he had risen to a higher station. What was he? And . . . *I do not believe this* . . . what was he holding in that hand?

A white paper bag. A McDonald's logo. Food! "This is for you. I figured you'd be getting pretty hungry. By the way, my name's Charlie."

Sam slammed down the telephone. Charlie, goddamn Charlie, was off the radar! The cunning sonofabitch hadn't been on the ground two hours before he dumped his thoroughly bugged car, eluded a supposedly skilled FBI surveillance team, and merrily scampered off to who knew where.

Insult to injury, he now was in possession of a bag full of untraceable cash. A courier had met him at the airport, delivering a great big leather satchel to Charlie boy. At the time, the watchers didn't know what was in it. Now they did, and there was little hope that Charlie would use the twenty thousand dollars in sequentially marked bills that Sam had given him. The evil old bastard would leave no trail at all.

"I'd kill him if I could." Sam didn't realize he'd spoken aloud until he saw Claude cock a patrician eyebrow and slowly shake his head.

Sam still wasn't sure he'd done the right thing by letting the DCI in on Whirlwind's secrets—not that he had any intention of letting the spymaster learn the most important secret of all. "I know, I know. His insurance policy, that goddamned Internet data vault." Sam kneaded the bridge of his nose, trying to rub the agony out of his sinuses. Charlie McKenzie. As welcome as a penis canker. Harder to get rid of. "Come on, Claude, surely your people could—"

"Under ordinary circumstances, we'd turnip-ize him. You know, put him in a coma, leave him on life support for thirty years. We don't dare try that now. Not if he's hooked up a deadman's brake."

"What the devil is a deadman's brake, anyway?"

The director of Central Intelligence steepled his fingers. "You ever ride the New York subway, Sam?"

"Please!"

Claude flicked an invisible speck of dust off his pin-striped lapel. "I thought not. You don't exactly keep in touch with the common man, do you? No criticism implied. Anyway, when a subway train is in motion, the engineer squeezes two levers together. As long as he does, the train keeps rolling. If he loosens his grip—falls over with a coronary or something—the brake circuit closes and the train stops safely. Dead man's brake. Charlie's using a similar gimmick. He'll have arranged some sort of signal—maybe he's supposed to send an e-mail every Friday to the same address, or maybe visit a certain Web site once a month. I doubt if we'll ever know. All we know is that if the signal doesn't get sent, whatever is in his vault will be broadcast automatically to every journalist in the world."

"There's nothing you can do?"

"A waste of time. Charlie's on a first-name basis with half the hackers on the watch list. They'll have set up an un-crackable system for him."

"Get your people to work anyway!" Sam slapped his palm on his desk. "Getting rid of that bastard is an alternative I want open to us if . . . " A smile formed on his lips. He had a fresh idea. "What about his kids? If we had them, we'd have leverage."

"I already thought of that." Claude sighed. "His youngest son is an anthropologist. He's somewhere in Borneo, but who knows where? It'd take months to locate him. The other one—his name is Scott—is a surgeon with the Indian Health Service in Arizona—"

Sam snapped, "Right. Free health care for the redskins. I'd like to see that expense lined out of the budget. Have the FBI bust the little twerp. Put him in custody as a material witness or something."

"Too late. Young Dr. Scott McKenzie has a private pilot's license. He disappeared out of the Three Turkeys clinic this afternoon, flew off somewhere in his Cessna. We're running a search, but it's a big country out there. Little dirt airstrips all over the place. He could be anywhere."

Sam's eyes narrowed. "Charlie got word to him? How did that happen? I thought we were tapping every phone he touches."

"Maybe his daughter made the call. She's been in the Israeli embassy since—"

"What!?!" He was on his feet. "She's where?" A floral paperweight shattered against the wall. "Why the fuck, just why the fuck" — his trash can spilled its paper guts across a carpet of presidential blue — "hasn't anyone told me this wonderful fucking piece of news?" Was he reaching for Claude's shirt? Why, yes, he was. And his hand was no longer a hand, it was a fist. "That motherfucking cocksucking sonofabitch, I'll—"

What will you do? he asked himself. *Punch out the director of Central Intelligence? Go postal in the Executive Office Building?*

Charlie fucking McKenzie. Insubordinate pricks like Charlie *always* drove him into . . .

. . . pure . . .

. . . crimson . . .

. . . frenzied . . .

Swallow it, he ordered himself. *Clench your teeth and swallow as hard as you can.*

It wasn't easy. He did it anyway. He didn't like the way it tasted, liked even less the expression on Claude's face. Inhaling deeply, he lifted a carafe of ice water. Claude flinched. Sam wanted to smash the pitcher in his face. Instead he poured a glass, drank, and poured another. "I, uh, shit! Sorry, Claude. My allergies. It's my meds. I have a reaction to them. Gotta get the prescription changed."

Claude gave him a long slow look. Sam recognized it for what it was: wary reappraisal. "You all right now?"

Sam slumped back in his seat. "Yes," he murmured weakly, "yes, I am. I apologize for that. Really. Christ, Claude, I take a tablet and something comes over me. Who's our point man at the FDA? I should talk to him about this stuff. It's a public menace." He reached into his pocket, removed a small brown bottle of harmless allergy pills, and with a flourish emptied them into an ashtray.

Claude seemed to buy the act. "Can I get you something? Should I call someone?"

"No, thank you. The last thing I need is more chemicals in my bloodstream. I'll be fine." Sure he would. As long as he kept it controlled, and as long as there weren't any more nasty surprises, and as long as that cunt McKenzie . . .

Don't go there, Sam. Keep the reins held tight.

He puffed up his cheeks and blew a long sigh. "Look, just forget about it, okay? Let's get back to the problem." Eyes firmly locked on Claude's, Sam seemed a soft-spoken model of rationality. "McKenzie's daughter, her name's Carly, right? How come I haven't been briefed that she's hiding out with our Hebrew brethren?"

Claude still looked like a nervous man who didn't want to

provoke another explosion. "We've been e-mailing you status reports every hour."

Sam bit his tongue. "I didn't see it. Tell me what it said."

Sam knew little about computers, distrusted the things, considered them beneath his dignity. His secretary, Josephine, was supposed to print out e-mails so he could dictate his replies. Today, she'd left early.

Claude, faintly amused at a superior's weakness, answered, "Ms. McKenzie, accompanied by her two children—names Molly and Jason—and six pieces of luggage, entered the Israeli embassy at approximately noon today. I expect she will remain there until . . . well, I suppose until all this is over. We can't touch her, Sam."

The Mossad, Sam thought. *A.k.a. the Institute for Intelligence and Special Tasks.* Charlie was asshole buddies with them. They'd give the daughter and the grandchildren sanctuary as long as Charlie wanted.

"Do you think she's helping him?"

"Unlikely. Charlie always made a big deal about keeping his family life and professional life separate. If anybody in the Agency tried to . . . well . . . there was this chap named Cole who asked Charlie's wife to do a courier job. Charlie found out. Now Cole signs his name with his left hand. The right one doesn't work very well."

Sam drummed his fingers on his desk. "If his daughter isn't involved, how did he get all that cash?"

"Someone—the Israelis, I presume—ran a wire transfer through an offshore bank. Then a courier flew up from Belize. He gave Charlie the goods as soon as he deplaned."

Sam's sinuses throbbed. His eyes watered with the pain. "You're saying I have to worry about the Mossad too?"

"No, I think not. They won't directly involve themselves.

Moving money is one thing. Mounting operations inside U.S. borders is another."

Pressing his fingers hard against his eyebrows, Sam muttered, "Great. Charlie's talking to Israeli intelligence, and we can't hear what he's saying. They've already sent him a bucket of laundered cash—probably with clean credit cards and fake ID. Next time, they'll send him . . . what? That's the question that worries me."

Claude nodded. "The other worrisome question—if you don't mind me asking—is how is the president taking this?"

"Better than expected." Sam left it at that. No need to tell the DCI that, immediately following his morning security briefing, the man in the Oval Office had politely—politeness being a hallmark of that fundamentally decent, fundamentally dim soul—described the fate that awaited Sam if a certain recently stolen object was not recovered "toot sweet, Sam, very toot sweet."

Immediately following that remarkably unpleasant conversation, Sam—pale and shaking—returned to his office and started working the phone.

First call: the secretaries of state and defense. Second call: the director of the Federal Bureau of Investigation. Then calls to everyone else—every federal law enforcement agency down to and including the park rangers. After that, the spook shops. There were twenty-eight, count 'em, twenty-eight intelligence-gathering organizations tucked away in various federal agencies. Sam alerted them all, even the yahoos at the Department of Agriculture.

Next-to-last call: Max Henkes, chairman and CEO of DefCon Enterprises, the prime contractor for the Whirlwind project.

Max hadn't been a happy camper. In fact, he was so furious he less spoke than stuttered, yada-yada, what do you expect? Sam was happy to let him get it out of his system until Maxie boy stepped over the line. " . . . more than tuh . . . tuh . . . ten billion dollars worth of research in the hands of the goddamned Ru-Ru-Russians!" Max howled. "And you're re . . . re . . . responsible, you goddamned in-in-incompetent!"

Well, that was enough of that. The man had to be put in his place—and that place was many, many ladder rungs below the national security advisor. "Incompetent? Good word, Max. The way I see it, if some airhead had bothered to lock the lab door, this never would have happened. So who's incompetent? I'll tell you who. DefCon Enterprises is incompetent. And you, Max, *are* DefCon. The buck stops on your desk. If you want to look for incompetence, I suggest you look in the mirror."

"You . . . you try to blame me! When your own so . . . so . . . soldiers—"

"Drop it, Max. One more word out of you and I will indict your corporate ass for criminal negligence, and you will be in a world of pain."

Max went silent. When he spoke again, the stuttering had disappeared—although not the anger. "I don't deny we have to shoulder our share of the blame, but you have to understand that it was one of the junior staff. She was up late, polishing a progress report for presentation the next morning. I, for one, think it commendable that one of our employees was putting in extra hours to—"

"Write a computer file that's on its way to Moscow. Is that what you want to commend?"

"No, of course not. All I'm saying is that the woman was tired. Here it is, two o'clock in the morning, and she's been working her tail off. She hears something explode. She runs outside to see what's going on. Then she sees a fire. So she pitches in to help douse it. In my estimation that's praiseworthy."

"We'll give her a medal after she gets out of jail." Sam smiled. Doling out torture was preferable to being, as he had been most of the day, on the receiving end.

"Sam, listen—"

"No, you listen. This is the second time you people have caused me grief. First, there was that Wing boy—"

"Dr. Wing's your man, hired at your recommendation. You sure as hell can't blame DefCon for his son's mistakes."

"I can, and I do. Jesus! It's not like the stupid kid kept his plans secret. Your company travel agent booked the tickets. Wasn't anyone in your shop paying attention? Hey, our chief scientist's brat is planning on visiting mainland China, the son of a man running a Magma Black project wants to rub shoulders with the commies, is this a good thing or a bad thing? Tell me, Max, how fucking dumb can you get?"

"Do we have to go over this again? Don't we have more urgent things to talk about?"

Sam nodded appreciatively. Henkes had just fed him his straight line. "Yes. Yes, we do. But the point, Max, the very clear and very obvious point is this: we've got a bad problem on our hands. What Wing's kid did makes it about a thousand times worse. You understand me?"

Henkes's voice was still angry, but it was a frightened anger. "I'm afraid I do."

"Good. Then understand what comes next. I'm putting a lot of uniforms in the field. But it's not enough. I need a different sort of talent. The kind you get with the Navy SEALs or Delta Force. Unfortunately I can't use 'em. They're all committed overseas. Besides, those lads . . . well, their operations tend to be a little less understated than the present situation requires. I can't afford that. Not in America. If we were chasing jungle bunnies in some third-world shithouse, it'd be a different story. Dead colored boys aren't prime time news. Dead white boys are."

"Don't tell me the media are involved!" No anger now, only fear.

"We've got them locked down for now. But if the body count starts to mount . . . "

"So what are you going to do? How can I help?" He was on the edge of panic, exactly where Sam wanted him.

"Subcontractors. Somebody effective but discreet. There's an outfit I've used in the past. They can get the job done. Problem is, I can't pay them direct. There's no way I can let a money trail lead from people like that back to the White House."

"You want them on my payroll?"

"Got it in one."

"No sweat. We're on a cost-plus contract. We'll just pass the expense through. My company is happy to do any-thing—let me emphasize that—*anything* to get Whirlwind back."

Done deal, another fine negotiation brought to a satisfactory conclusion.

Sam had told Max to expect a quote-consulting contract-unquote to arrive on his fax machine within the hour. The letterhead would read "The Specialist Consulting Group, Inc.," and the contract would be signed by that organization's president. All Max had to do was countersign it and fax it back. He didn't even have to read it. In fact, he'd be better off if he didn't.

Max understood. Max agreed.

Only then did Sam make his last call. As he dialed, his skin crawled.

Now, two hours later, he was keeping his eye on the clock.

Quite soon, only a minute to go, Sam's oversized plasma TV would switch on automatically. Then he and Claude would watch a closed-circuit broadcast—dangerous men being briefed by the even more dangerous man to whom Sam had made his final phone call of the day.

Sam knew him, had met him more than once, had more than once shaken his astonishingly cold hand. He tried to picture his face. Oddly, he couldn't. Whenever he tried to recollect his features, all he could think of was a pale tiger with hunger in its heart and no mercy in its soul.

He could remember the voice, though. It was not a voice you forgot easily—low and guttural, an Afrikaans accent, throaty as a hunting cat's growl.

The television blinked on. The Specialist Consulting Group's red eagle logo appeared on the screen. An announcer spoke: "Please stand by for a briefing from our chief executive officer, Mr. Johan Schmidt."

Good afternoon, gentlemen.

I should like everyone to know . . .

Excuse me, would someone kindly cue the music. Thank you. Ah, an excellent choice. The cavatina from *La Forza del Destino,* not inappropriate, I do believe.

Well then, to recommence. I want all of you here in the auditorium, and all of you watching from the field, to know how much I appreciate your deferring your other duties to participate in an uncommonly important mission.

As you are aware, our organization has gone through trying times. A few years ago, one of our consulting teams failed to perform to standards. As a result, a significant client dispensed with our services. Bonuses have been scant, and perquisites have been few. We have had to run lean and mean.

However, I have been working hard to reestablish credibility with that client, doing all in my power to win back his trust. I am pleased to report that I have been successful. We have been given a second chance.

Accordingly, to quote a famous maxim, failure is not an option.

First slide, please.

This is the heart of our mission. I do not know what it is, and our client has requested we not attempt to find out. Suffice it to say that it is oblong, sixty-two inches in length, thirty-five inches wide, eighteen deep. Weight: seventy-six and a half pounds—twenty-eight and a half kilos. It is essential that this article be secured. No price is too high to pay to achieve this objective.

Next slide.

A seemingly ordinary backup disk. It is our second objective, and quite as important as the first. A crucial fact, gentlemen: this disk is not to be put in any computer. Security codes are secreted throughout it. As soon as it is inserted in a drive, the disk determines if it is connected to a classified file server—and a very high level of classification it is. If no secure server is found, then, in nanoseconds, the disk destroys itself.

Another crucial fact: as those of you with a technical bent know, such protection schemes can be breached. A man with the right skills can subvert any security system protecting any disk. For this reason, our client is keenly interested in whether or not the disk has been compromised. If any of you tamper with it . . . well, our client would find that disappointing.

As would I.

Next slide.

Ah, I see I have your attention now. Yes, despite her graceless dress, she is rather comely, isn't she? You at the projector, show the boys the next five slides. Whistle and applaud as much as you want, gentlemen, because this beauty is our third objective. Irina Kolodenkova is her name, and she plays for the Russian team. You will find a full dossier on her in the information package that will be distributed after I conclude my remarks.

The computer disk and the rather large brown object are in Ms. Kolodenkova's possession. Secure one, and you will have secured them all.

Yes, question in the back.

Ha! Of course! Most certainly you can strip search her when you catch her!

There will also be a full body cavity search. You see, the rather tasty-looking Ms. Kolodenkova was in a place she shouldn't have been. She may have had a digital camera in her possession at the time. Such cameras can record photographs on small magnetic strips. Sad to say, such strips can be swallowed. It should be self-evident that if the strips exist, our client wants them retrieved. Accordingly, a comprehensive autopsy is planned.

However, and I cannot emphasize this enough, it is absolutely critical that the woman be taken alive. The possibility exists that she has spoken to another agent, transmitted a message, or simply dropped photographic strips into the mail. For this reason, she will need to be questioned. I myself will administer the interrogation. It will go quickly, I think. She's a pretty woman. A pretty woman is a vain woman. The closer a straight razor comes to her pretty face, the more voluble she becomes.

But we all know that, don't we?

To repeat and reemphasize: my cardinal point is that Ms. Kolodenkova is to remain alive and in reasonable health until questioned by me, questioned personally. This is not to say that you cannot amuse yourself with her. It is the right of warriors to use the enemy's women as they wish. So enjoy. After all, no one will be filing charges.

Let me add one salient point. There is a time element in this mission, and the clock is ticking. In the unlikely event we do not apprehend Ms. Kolodenkova before noontime Friday, she becomes an open contract. Were a competing party to take her, we would forfeit our performance bonus. Gentlemen, that would be unacceptable. Completely unacceptable. Am I understood? Good. Now, should this woman remain in play after Friday noon, the rules change. When you see her—when, not if—you are to kill her where she stands. That will earn us our head price, although I'm sure we all would be happier to provide full satisfaction to our client by delivering her before the deadline.

I have every expectation we will.

Final slide.

Here we have the fly in our ointment. The gentleman's name is Charles McKenzie. Some of you may remember him from the newspapers two years ago. Older hands will recollect our firm's previous, distasteful experiences with him.

Be advised: Mr. McKenzie is a good news/bad news proposition. The good news is our honorable profession has never known a better manhunter. Much to everyone's advantage, he is in pursuit of Ms. Kolodenkova. I should be quite surprised if he does not find her. Therefore, if we follow McKenzie, he surely will lead us to her doorstep.

Following him will not be as easy as it might sound. He already has eluded those charged with watching him—

Yes? Ah, I am afraid so. The FBI. Gentlemen, please hold down the laughter. Our time is short, and I have a great deal more information to share with you. Good, thank you. Well then, McKenzie is out of sight for the moment. However, he will resurface. He has no choice. Once he does, we will be alerted. Then we, rather than the lackluster lads from Quantico, will be in charge of keeping an eye on him.

That brings me to the bad news. The bad news is that there's more to McKenzie than his tracking skills. Succinctly stated, he is a highly competent professional, a master of the arts in which we all have so diligently trained. Approach him cautiously. Expect the unexpected. He is dangerous—and that is an egregious understatement.

More bad news, our client believes McKenzie may have an agenda of his own. Having secured Ms. Kolodenkova and the objects in her possession, he is quite capable of behaving in a manner inconsistent with our client's best interests.

Question? Yes, on the aisle.

There are more scenarios than I care to enumerate. I'm told he might try to use Kolodenkova as a bargaining chip. Alternatively, the materials she has stolen involve a secret that McKenzie could use against our client. Blackmail, apparently, is not out of the question. Why this is so is none of our affair. Our sole job is to deliver the results expected of us.

What? No, absolutely not. Under no circumstances is McKenzie to be terminated. Our instructions in that regard are regrettably specific. I say regrettable because I personally would welcome some quality time with him. Unfortunately, the privilege is denied me. At most, we are allowed to incapacitate him—although not in earnest. A bullet through the ankle is acceptable, I suppose, but little more than that.

Gentlemen, I do recognize that such unwelcome limitations to our flexibility raise the possibility of casualties in our ranks. The only consolation I can offer is that our company's survivors' benefits package remains the best in the business.

Yes?

Excellent question. Thank you for asking. There does indeed exist some possibility—however remote—that Ms. Kolodenkova will be captured by another agency. Both local police and federal officers are searching for her. Should one of them get luckier than he deserves, you are to relieve him of his prisoner. If he resists, you are authorized to employ appropriate force. The word "appropriate" is defined as whatever it takes to do the job.

Now, let me move on to procedural matters.

First: civilian wear. You must look and act like ordinary citizens. No battle dress, and, unhappily, no Kevlar or M5. The deer and the antelope play in the great American Southwest. Likewise the tourists. Protective coloration is the order of the day.

Next, light weapons only. You'll be issued nothing more powerful than varmint rifles—.17 and .22 caliber rimfires. Again, I apologize for the inconvenience. Our mission requires that Ms. Kolodenkova be interrogated, and therefore we cannot risk somebody inadvertently rendering her unavailable for questioning. For sidearms, no one is to carry anything heavier than a .25. Don't use them unless you must. If you do use them, shoot to wound.

Yes? Right you are. Stun grenades will be issued. Likewise tear gas, shock batons, and such other non-lethal arms as the company armorer can provide. And I should mention that we will deploy five airborne teams armed with automatic weapons. In accordance with the restrictions placed on us, they will be using rubber bullets.

For vehicles, it's civvies again—except for my command car. That means no Hummers, and more's the pity because our prey will most likely be found in desert country. However, I have arranged a fleet of high-performance four-wheelers. You can take comfort in their anonymity, and in the fact that—in that part of America—well-stocked gun racks are common on every highway.

Another point. I will be assuming personal command of this mission. As soon as we're finished here, I'm boarding the company jet. I expect to be on the ground in West Texas at approximately twenty-one hundred hours local time. The usual chain of command will be in force, but with one exception. That exception is: if any of you come across anything that even hints as to McKenzie's or Kolodenkova's whereabouts, do not go through channels. Report to me immediately.

As per usual, we'll be using field names. Given the likelihood that most of this mission will play itself out in the desert, those names will be taken from the herpetology handbook. I am King Cobra. Directly reporting to me will be three zone commanders, Messrs. Nishikawa and Ortiz, and Ms. Jäger—a.k.a. Adder, Fer-de-Lance, and Cottonmouth. Their orders are my orders. Their will is my will. Never think otherwise.

Finally, and not to belabor a point known to all, our fine firm is not the largest competitor in its field. However, it is my hope that one day it will be so. This mission—this absolutely crucial mission—will move us closer to that objective. Accordingly, we *will* reestablish our bona fides with our client. We *will* deliver the results expected of us. We *will* succeed.

You—all five hundred of you—are the elite, battle-proven warriors with top performance ratings, handpicked from the ranks of more than four thousand men-at-arms worldwide. You are our company's A Team. I have every confidence in you. You should have every confidence in yourselves. Be proud, gentlemen. Be proud that you are among the chosen. Be proud and you cannot fail.

Now to summarize, you are to think of this operation as a minimally intrusive surgical procedure, leaving no scars behind. Our first step must be to find and follow Charles McKenzie. However, that is only a first step. We will not have earned our fees until we secure Kolodenkova and the materials in her possession—and until I obtain her full and enthusiastic answers to an intensive interrogation.

Does anyone have any questions?

No? Very well, gentlemen, I've nothing more to say. Let's saddle up and ride.

4
Liar's Poker

"I like your hair. The color becomes you," said Charlie, who had never trusted a blonde in his life.

Irina, her mouth full of Big Mac, gestured irritably with her Tokarev.

Handcuffs rattling against the sink pipe, Charlie leaned against the bathroom wall. As planned, she'd taken him prisoner. As expected, she used his own cuffs to immobilize him. Right on schedule, she was grilling him. "Just trying to be polite," he smiled. "Well, anyway, to answer your question, finding you wasn't all that hard. Everybody—the FBI, the state police, all of 'em—are convinced you're headed east. The going theory is that you're running for the Gulf, that you'll try to steal a boat and sail to Cuba. Damfool theory, but then we're dealing with damfool people."

He'd chosen his tone of voice carefully—the inflection of an irascible old fart. "The nincompoops are breathing their own exhaust, believing their own publicity. You know, it was my dad who cooked up the Cuba strategy—demonizing Castro, painting him as the incarnation of all that is ignoble, base, and vile. The idea was to convince you Russkies we thought he was a real threat—which the dummies in the Kremlin swallowed hook, line, and sinker. Whereupon they started hurling money at the clown. Heh! Just what we wanted! So then after the Soviet Union went Chapter 11, Fidel saw the writing on the wall. He may not be the sharpest needle in the haystack, but he's got some brains. Two years after Yeltsin took power, he was ready to roll over."

A harmless, rambling antiquity with too many memories—he hoped she was buying the act, although he couldn't tell for certain. *You just can't read a face that's wolfing down an overstuffed hamburger.* "My source—the number-two guy at your embassy as a matter of fact—told me that Fidel had his pen out, ready to sign just about anything we sent him. The poor schmuck probably would have applied for statehood if we asked. But by then Congress had come to believe all that mud slinging. Add to that the fact that the sugar lobby is one hell of a big political contributor which most definitely does not want Cuban competition. Plus Bill Clinton was too spineless a wimp to stand up to them—"

Irina waved her gun again. Charlie smiled inwardly. He'd made most of the points he'd wanted to. The rest could wait awhile. "Sorry. I was just explaining why I knew you wouldn't be hightailing it for Cuba. Let me start over. The cops found that blue Ford buggy you swiped. By the time I got to the shopping mall, they'd made every clerk behind every cash register check whether his or her car had been heisted. Of course, nobody's had. So they start going around the stores again, this time asking the managers if all their employees showed up for work this morning. Sure enough, a couple hadn't. Well, lemme tell you, the sirens howled as those boys zoomed off to see if those employees were home with a tummy ache, or home with a gun to their head."

He gave her a cunning grin. *I'm just your foxy old grandpa, sweetheart, and you can trust every word I say.* "I knew better. Hostage-taking isn't your style. So, I went looking for a store with a Help Wanted sign in its window. Found one. Sporting goods and such. I talked up the manager. Sure enough, early morning—just about the time you stole the Aerostar—he'd interviewed a hard-luck cowboy named Mitch Conroy." Charlie raised his voice in a sneer of prissy insolence, " 'While having a professional athlete in our store is highly desirable, a rodeo rider simply would not be consistent with the outdoor adventure image we wish to project.' The pompous ass still had Conroy's application form and address on his desk—which I swiped and burned. After that, all I had to do was get rid of my car—it was bugged forty ways from Sunday—and dump the people who were tailing me. And now, you lucky girl, here I am."

He gave her his best boyish smile, confident he was convincing her that he was a garrulous fool, so indiscreet as to identify a double agent in the Havana embassy. She was a spy. She couldn't help wanting to hear more.

"Excuse me? I didn't quite understand that, what with your mouth being full. . . . Oh, my car? Well, that was easy. They gave me an Explorer registered under my own name. I cruised around until I found a row of auto dealerships. Then I sashayed into a BMW showroom and told the salesman I had a low-mileage four-wheeler I wanted to trade in. He asked how low. Twenty-eight miles, says I, and he allows that, yessir, that's pretty low mileage. So I offered him thirty-eight thousand bucks plus the Explorer for a new X5. Then I started counting the money—cash greenbacks—out on his desk. Well, he started playing silly car salesman games—jabbering about having to check with the manager, and how he'd have to get the mechanic's opinion on my Explorer, and all that stuff."

Skilled actors use their entire bodies to create a character. Charlie, hampered by a handcuffed left wrist, did his best to become someone an FSB-trained agent would badly misread. He jutted his jaw and wagged a remonstrative finger. "I said, look, son, you're earning twice your best-ever commission on this deal; now here's the thirty-eight grand; I'm walking up the street to buy a couple of burgers to eat in my new luxury sports-ute; when I get back, either you're going to have that X5 waiting outside with the engine running, or I'm going over to the Mercedes showroom and buy an M-Class. Well, he was unhappy, wasn't he? Here he was making more money off a single sale than he'd ever seen, and I was taking all the fun out of it. Ruined his day. Howsomever, the X5 was waiting when I got back. I signed the forms, climbed in, and floored it. While I was picking up your lunch, I'd timed the stoplights. I knew exactly when to peel out of that dealer's lot. One of the FBI boys following me tried to run the light, but, you know, he didn't make it. I was miles away—switching license plates, actually—before the rest of the feds managed to get around the wreckage."

Irina licked her fingers, wolfed down a handful of French fries, and chug-a-lugged a swallow from her giant-sized Coke. Charlie still couldn't quite read her reaction, although her words were encouraging. "And you claim you were not followed? You claim you are alone?"

"Like I said earlier, there's no SWAT teams hiding in the bushes. I'm all by my lonesome. No one here but you and me."

She started unwrapping her second hamburger. "You are lying. Saying that you are not here to arrest me—this also is a lie."

"I could sort of tell I was having credibility problems when you chained me to this pipe." *Damn*, Charlie thought, *it's fun telling the truth to someone who doesn't believe you.*

"Why should I trust you?"

"Well, for one thing, I'm unarmed. For another, if I'd wanted to take you down, that hamburger you just finished eating would have been spiced with enough thorazine to knock out an elephant."

Irina goggled. She dropped her hamburger and flung up the toilet seat. "I will put my fingers down my throat!"

"Oh, give me a break! We both know that if I'd sprinkled that stuff on your lunch, you'd already be asleep on the floor. Calm down and eat the rest of your food. It's good for you."

She gave him a disbelieving look. "A Big Mac?"

Charlie snorted. *Good,* he thought, *she made a joke. We're making progress.* "Look, just like I said when you stuck that shooting iron in my face, I'm not who you think I am, and I'm not doing what you think I'm doing."

Lowering the toilet lid, Irina sat down again. She leaned forward and thrust the Tokarev's muzzle under Charlie's chin. *Oops, maybe we're* not *making progress.* "So then tell me what you really are, Mr. McKenzie. In your wallet there is a Central Intelligence Agency identification card with your photograph on it, and I do not believe it is a forgery."

I'll be damned. She didn't buy a single word of my act. Nuts. No choice now but to be myself. "It isn't. I tried to explain things earlier, but you weren't in the mood to listen. This time," he snapped, "try to pay attention. One: I spent my whole life with the Agency. Two: they screwed me. Three: I'm going to get even. Four: you're the way I get even. Five: P.S. I get to clear my good name into the bargain."

She gave him a narrow look. "Why has a disgraced agent been assigned to my case?"

Charlie let his voice turn into a growl. "Because I am very,

very good at what I do." Her nostrils flared. He'd struck the right note. "And because they are very, *very* worried about what you've got. Too damned worried. If they're desperate enough to hire me, they're worried about more than whatever you filched." He showed his teeth. It wasn't a smile. "Now that little fact piques my interest. I think they're covering something up. If I can find out what that something is, if you help me—"

She was taken aback. "Why should I help a secret policeman who wants to arrest me?"

Now he'd make her a little scared. "Because they'll kill you if you don't."

"Nonsense!" Irina tossed her head. "America does not execute intelligence agents. Show trials are a valuable source of propaganda."

"Do you want to know how I know they plan to kill you?"

Almost sneering, she replied, "Convince me if you can."

"Because I'm the one they sent to pull the trigger." A bald-faced lie, of course, since Sam had called off that part of the job—not that Charlie planned to sanction the girl anyway. Regardless—be it truth or be it lie—his words produced the desired effect. Irina Kolodenkova was stunned into silence. *Well, I believe I've scored a point at last.*

Her pistol was still aimed at Charlie's head, but—no question in Charlie's mind—there was considerable uncertainty in the way she held it. She gasped a half dozen short breaths before managing to speak. "I should shoot you now. Yes, this is the right thing to do."

Charlie grinned. *Good line,* he thought, *crappy delivery. You weren't cut out to be an actress, my girl.* "Killing me would be the dumbest thing you could do."

The pistol wavered. Not defeated, but surely indecisive, she murmured, "Why?"

" 'Cause I'm the only one who can get you out of this mess."

"Oh? Is that what you think?" Her eyes sparked. The color returned to her cheeks, and there was anger aplenty in her glare. *Uh-oh,* Charlie thought, *I just said the wrong thing.* "You think I am a weak little girl who cannot succeed on her own. If that is what you think, Mr. McKenzie, your thinking is in error."

He had no choice but to bull his way through it. "Maybe. Maybe not. You're good, Irina. You wouldn't have gotten this far if you hadn't been smart, nimble, and fast—a damned fine tactician. But tactics is all it is. There's no strategy, no plan. You're just thinking on your feet, and grabbing opportunities. That's no criticism. Hell, if I was your boss . . . " *Or your father, but I'll leave that unstated.* " . . . I'd be proud of you. All I'm saying is that you are new to the job, and simply do *not* know what the other team will throw at you. You need somebody experienced enough to tell you how to get past them. You need a strategist. You need me."

"I can do very well on my own, Mr. McKenzie."

"I don't doubt it for a moment." *Reinforce her, build her up.* "My point is that 'very well' isn't good enough. They want you bad, and they'll send the best they have to bring you down." *She's thinking. Good. Now let's knock her a little off balance.* "There's another reason why you need my help. You don't have a clue as to what you've stolen—Project Whirlwind and that computer disk."

"The DefCon Enterprises presentation?"

Charlie could barely control his glee. *DefCon, eh? Now I've got a name, and that is one hell of a lot more than Sam gave me.* "Exactly. You know if you try to read the disk, it'll blow up?"

"Of course. I am no fool." She raised the pistol. "And you are mistaken. I know precisely what I have my hands on."

Nice bluff, lady. "You know as much as I know—zero, zip, zilch, nada. Both of us are in the dark. All we can be certain of is that you've got your hands on a secret worth killing for."

"You are mistaken about what I do or do not know."

"Baloney. They faxed me a topological map of the base you burglarized, and a floorplan of the lab. I measured the distances, and I checked the times—when the generator failed, when the backup came online. Under the best of circumstances, if you and your partner had been standing at the fence line when the lights went out, you had ten minutes in that lab. Probably less. You stole the disk because the presentation on it looked interesting. You stole Whirlwind because . . . why? . . . my guess is because your partner, a trained engineer, knew what it was."

"He did. And he told me."

"No, he did not." Charlie could see it now, see how it unfolded. Given the time and distances involved, there was no other way it could have happened. "You didn't have a chance to chitter-chatter. With armed guards all around, the most you two did was whisper a few words to one another. You sure as blazes kept silent once you were out of the lab and running for the fence. Dominik Grisin may have known what he was stealing—or at least made a good guess. But he didn't tell you. Don't lie to me, Irina, you're everything a spy should be, but you simply aren't seasoned enough to fool an old fox like me."

Resignation in her eyes, she nodded. "You said you were good at what you do. This is true, I think."

Okay, now we're getting somewhere. "Thank you. Now are you going to do the right thing?"

"What is the right thing?"

"Whatever you think is right." Her eyebrows shot up. *Oh,*

yeah, score one for Charlie! She was expecting some fatherly quote-advice-unquote, same as I bet her dad gave her every minute of her waking life. Nope, my sweet, I'm not falling into that trap. "Look, I've been in this racket a long time. I know what I'd do if I were in your situation. I also know that when I was your age the last thing I'd do would be to trust an enemy who claimed he had a grudge against his own people. So, like I said, you do whatever you think you should. If it works out for you, great. If it doesn't, I'll be around to give you a hand."

She smiled. *Pretty smile!* "I think not. You will be handcuffed to a sink for quite some time. I will be far away."

"Sure you will. But I'll be coming after you."

"You don't know where I'm going."

"Wanna bet?"

She drove one-handed on an empty highway, night surrounding her, darkness shrouding her soul.

To be born Russian is to be born in bitterness, centuries of oppression your only heritage. You are a child of a nation that has bowed beneath the indistinguishable tyrannies of czars, of Party apparatchiks, of elected kleptocrats and their Mafya henchmen. No matter how many joys life may bring, foreboding and suspicion weigh upon your every thought. Distrustful of life, resigned to death, you look upon the outer world as an impoverished child looks through the window of a toy store, angrily envious of delights that can never be yours.

Hope is denied. Despair is certain.

But now, just at this time, she had a chance to rise above a fate foretold. An accomplishment beyond the grasp of ordinary men lay within her reach. All she need do was seize it. Then would be a victory that none could question, none belittle.

Good grades are not enough. I expect no less of my blood than perfection. Sit with me, girl, I will show the proper way to approach these problems. . . .

Being a member of a winning team is an achievement of little individual merit. You will come with me tomorrow. A Navy trainer will make you a true athlete . . .

The state honors you for your Olympic medal. In four years, they will honor another. You will be forgotten. . . .

They would honor her again, honor her for a triumph that none could deny, none could denigrate. Irina set her jaw. *You will salute me, father! You will stand at attention and salute your superior!*

She'd made a mistake. She was running. The enemy expected that. Doing what they expected was the wrong thing to do.

What, she asked herself, would they not anticipate? No police can search every hiding place. She had to find a place where they would not think to look.

If that McKenzie man had been telling the truth, and he probably was, the Americans had concentrated their security forces to the east—although, no doubt, hunters prowled every point of the compass. North, south, east, or west, they expected her to run somewhere. And therefore unexpected was . . .

She flipped on the Dodge's turn signal, eased into the right lane, and took the next exit. She turned left, then left again—back onto the interstate, back to the city whose borders she'd left an hour earlier.

They know I was there. They will be sure I have moved on. What is the most unexpected thing a fugitive can do? Answer: not flee.

She wouldn't run. She would stay put. It was the only feint they might not foresee.

Besides—she cursed herself—only a fool would drive this barren countryside at night. In the empty hours, out in the vastness of New Mexico and Arizona, hers would be the only vehicle on the road. Easily seen, easily stopped, she might as well have painted a bull's-eye target on her truck.

Lay low. Find a motel. Get out of sight.

What kind of a motel? Her choices were limitless. She could afford anything.

The very peculiar Mr. McKenzie had shouted at her as she left Mitch's house: "My car doors are open. There's a present for you on the backseat."

An understatement. She found a large brown shoebox on which, in an elegant script, he'd written, "For Irina Kolodenkova." It contained fifty thousand dollars in one-hundred dollar bills, a Texas driver's license bearing her photo but another woman's name, and both a Visa and a MasterCard. He'd attached a small note to the driver's license: "Irina, the credit cards are issued by an Israeli bank. They're *prozrachnyj,* what my side calls glassies, totally safe and untraceable. The cash has been laundered. The driver's license comes from the Mossad's finest forgers. Good luck, Charlie."

She'd gaped. McKenzie never expected her to cooperate. He'd walked unarmed into Mitch's house *knowing* that she would take him prisoner, and *knowing* that she would flee.

What is his game? Does he truly seek revenge against his own?

She shook her head. The questions were not answerable. Clearly he had his own agenda—an agenda that must be as dangerous as the man himself. The best she could hope for was to elude him the same as she planned to elude all the others who sought to keep her from her victory.

An hour later she saw the sign: Airport, Next Exit.

Perfect. There will be motels nearby. Everyone will be a transient, and I just another traveler passing through.

She swung off the expressway onto a four-lane artery. Three stoplights later, she passed a T intersection—the airport access road to her left, to her right a row of motels with familiar signs: Ramada, Day's Inn, Motel Six, Marriott Courtyard, and—*the largest, a convention hotel with trade show facilities. I will be lost in the crowd*—the Airport Hilton.

Pulling into the parking lot, she glanced at her overnight bag. She'd kept it with her all day, transferring it from Jeep to Volvo to Aerostar to Dodge pickup truck. It was not large, but she thought it large enough to look like an air traveler's luggage. The desk clerk might not notice.

The desk clerk did not notice. She was an older woman, olive-skinned, perhaps of Mexican blood. She asked only if Irina had a reservation ("No. My flight was canceled. I drove straight here from the airport."), whether she preferred a smoking or non-smoking room ("Non-smoking, please."), and what credit card Irina planned to use ("Visa," said Irina, handing her a card bearing the name Caroline Sonderstrom).

Five clocks were fixed above the reception desk—one showing local time, the others marked Tokyo, London, Los Angeles, and New York. *How pretentious,* Irina thought. Although, perhaps, Americans did not grasp the subtleties of time zones as readily as other nationalities.

"Thank you, Miss Sonderstrom. You're in room four-oh-four. Checkout's at eleven. Complimentary continental breakfast is in the lobby lounge between seven and ten. The elevator's just past the restaurant on your left. You have a nice stay, hear?"

Irina nodded politely, picked up her bag, and started toward the elevator.

Behind her she heard the lobby's automatic doors hiss open, then a Germanic voice so resonantly basso that it made her turn: "Sleep comfortable tonight, gentlemen. It could be a long time between soft mattresses." The speaker was slender, pale, aglow with power. Even though it was nighttime, he wore tinted glasses. She could not see his eyes. For reasons she couldn't explain, she was certain they were as cold and grey as the North Sea.

Other men crowded behind him—two Africans, a single Arab, and a half dozen crop-haired whites. None looked like the man with the dark glasses, but, in some sense they all looked like one another: well exercised beyond civilized norms, primitively muscular, insolently self-confident. They swaggered with a braggart's arrogance, spoke with a bully's contempt: "Long way between women, too. I wish we had that Russki blonde babe to play with tonight."

"Patience, gentlemen. All good things come to him who waits. Even tasty young spies."

Whispering among themselves, they snickered of their appetites, and how they'd sate them.

Charlie almost missed the party. Thank Kolodenkova for that. No sooner had he pulled his spare handcuff key out of his socks than he noticed something a wee bit wrong with the lock. The damned girl had stuffed chewing gum in the keyhole.

Sneaky, devious, and tricky. I admire that in a woman.

What he didn't admire was the sweaty work it took to pry a rusty drainpipe out of the wall, or the time wasted running hot water over the cuffs to loosen the gum. Add to that more distractions: first, freeing an angry cowboy hog-tied in a closet; second, calming down the aforementioned wrangler; third, swindling the lad into doing something imprudently dangerous; fourth, jury-rigging the wires of a shattered, 1960s-vintage telephone to his PowerBook computer so that, fifth, he could send urgent e-mails to an Israeli friend and to a hacker who called himself Sledgehammer.

Add it all up and it was just about nine in the evening when he belly-crawled to the top of a low bunker some distance from the airport terminal. He'd expected to spot a few suspicious planes parked near the general aviation hangar. That he arrived in time to watch—through the clear bright lenses of 10x42 power Leica binoculars—a private jet taxiing toward the debarking area was a lucky bonus.

Less lucky was the familiar logo on the jet's tail: a stylized red eagle falling for the kill.

The plane rolled to a stop. As its engines wound down, a rear door swung open, stairs deploying automatically. Sniffing the night air, tasting it and drinking it down, a man in darkened glasses stepped out: bad news personified, the big kahuna himself, Johan Schmidt.

Charlie gasped liked he'd been gut-punched. *Jesus,* he silently cursed, *Sam's put that thing of darkness on the payroll! Nobody hires him unless they're scared witless. Goddamnit, what kind of unholy hell is this Whirlwind thing?*

Ash blonde and cat-graceful in tailored tropical garb, Schmidt was followed from the plane by nine plug-ugly henchmen. They strutted toward five different vehicles, four of them ordinary-looking pickup trucks (although Charlie was willing to bet their engines had been tinkered with). The fifth vehicle, the one that Schmidt seemed to have reserved for himself, was neither ordinary nor anonymous—a military model Mercedes Gelandewagen 500.

Used, the brute would set you back twice the price of its civilian cousin. God only knew what it cost new. Mean, muscular, and totally bad assed, G-Wagens *ate* Humvees. The thing could clock over a hundred and twenty miles an hour, hit sixty in about seven seconds, and climb slopes that would intimidate a mountain goat. Bulletproof, rugged enough to take a triple roll and keep on truckin', and strong enough to tow an elephant, oh, yeah, Schmidt's little toy gave new meaning to the phrase "mean machine."

Refocusing his binoculars, Charlie scanned the rest of the airport. The Gulfstream GV that had brought him here was still parked near the hangar. Next to it sat two Falcon 50s—Agency aircraft from their identification numbers—and an old Learjet. FBI? Probably. A couple of clearly marked Bureau choppers were out on the tarmac—and, more troubling, five olive drab helicopter gunships. *No military markings. Not the property of the Air National Guard, I think.*

He pointed the binoculars back at Schmidt and his minions, now clustered around their trucks. *Damn you, Sam. I figured I'd find a mercenary plane or two here. But Schmidt and his thugs? Hell, if I had any sense, I'd bail out of this assignment right this second.*

Charlie swiveled to the right, scanning the length of the terminal, then letting his binoculars roam the full length of the runway. Idly wondering where Schmidt was planning to sleep that night, he aimed the Leicas up the airport access road, picking out the row of hotels across from the T intersection where that road ended. *Hmm, I wonder if brother Johan has booked a room at the same hotel as me. Now that would present a fine opportunity for bloodshed on an epic scale . . . what? . . . aw, no, say it ain't so. . . .*

Streetlights illuminated a black Dodge pickup truck waiting at the intersection for the light to change. A tarpaulin-covered box rested in its bed; a chestnut-haired woman sat in the driver's seat.

I do not need this. I do not, do not, do not!

The light changed, and wouldn't you know it, she pulled into the Hilton parking lot.

God damn *this!*

Schmidt was in his G-Wagen, his gorillas were in their trucks. Their convoy rolled toward the exit.

What are the odds they're headed for the Hilton? Five hotels. One in five? No, worse. He's on Sam's expense account, and that means he won't stay in a Motel 6. Son. Of. A. Bitch!

Charlie leapt to his feet. He'd left his BMW sports-ute on a dirt-surfaced maintenance road near the end of the runway—a road that could only be reached from the airport. Not enough time to circle back to the terminal; his only hope of intercepting Schmidt was to drive cross-country and pray that he could cut the man off before he reached the motel strip.

Let's see what this Beamer is made of.

Four-wheel drive, and precisely the kind of suspension you'd expect German engineers to put on an off-roader. The X5 handled well. Besides, the ground was hardpack. He didn't have to worry about sinking up to his hubcaps in sand. On the other hand, he did have to worry about hummocks and washes and boulders and—

Ouch! Where the blazes did that come from?

Twenty miles an hour was the best he could manage. Anything faster jolted the steering wheel out of his hands.

Too slow, too slow.

The lights of five trucks in convoy sped away from the airport. Charlie was still a hundred yards from the road when they passed in front of him.

He gunned his accelerator. The X5 leapt forward. Luck was on his side. The ground was level, obstacles few, he could move faster here and . . .

Oh, hell!

His headlights picked out a drainage ditch separating open desert from asphalt. He slammed on his brakes. The BMW fishtailed. A cloud of gravel fountained into the air, rattling against the side panels. His front bumper tilted down. Charlie locked his fingers to the steering wheel, his stomach falling as he plunged down a thirty-degree slope.

Jerking his foot from the brake, he seized the gear lever and downshifted to first. The Beamer was sliding sideways, ready to roll. Charlie wrenched the wheel, steering into the slide, wrestling to regain control. A concrete sluice lined the ditch's bottom. The BMW's bumper hit it hard. A rooster tail of sparks sprayed by the driver's side window. Charlie gritted his teeth as the truck skidded left.

The X5 tipped sickeningly onto two wheels. Gripping the steering wheel with one hand, Charlie unsnapped his safety belt, hurling his weight right. The BMW tottered. Charlie's shoulder was on the passenger seat. He twitched the wheel left, then pulled straight again. The Beamer weaved, shifted balance, and thudded back onto four wheels.

Flooring the gas pedal, he pulled himself erect into the driver's seat. The BMW's ventilation system sucked the smoke of burning rubber into his face. *Traction!*

Grinning fiercely, he accelerated up the sluice. Thirty miles an hour. Thirty-five. Forty. High beams bright, he kept his eyes left looking for the right, for the perfect . . .

No rocks. Not an easy angle, but better than anywhere

else. He aimed for it. The BMW's front wheels clawed dry earth. Charlie held steady, and held tight. The speedometer read a bit more than fifty miles an hour. Air bags or no, if anything went wrong, he was in trouble.

He fumbled for his seatbelt.

The world tilted sideways. The Beamer exploded up the slope. Its undercarriage shrieked across a rock as it reached the crest, bounced four wheels into the air, and thudded down hard.

He was on the road, and safe.

Which was more than could be said for the Kolodenkova girl. Schmidt's convoy had already passed through the intersection. Charlie, cursing furiously, watched them turn, one by one, into the Hilton parking lot. She'd only be minutes ahead of them.

Murphy's law being what it is, the traffic light at the intersection turned red just before he reached it. Murphy strikes again, a darkened police car sat directly across the street. Inside a patrolman unlimbered his radar gun, preparing to trap unwary speeders.

There'd be no running this particular red light. Charlie cursed louder.

The light winked from red to green. Keeping within the speed limit, Charlie turned left, cautiously signaling like a good citizen, and pulled into the Hilton's driveway. Mitch Conroy's stolen black Dodge pickup was the first thing he saw.

The second was Schmidt and his punks waltzing through the hotel's front entrance.

No time to park, Charlie braked to a halt in the loading zone. Leaving his keys in the ignition, he ran for the entrance.

There they were. *Aw, God,* there they *all* were. Ten wolves loped laughing toward the reception desk. Not three yards away, Irina Kolodenkova stood frozen like a deer in the headlights. All Schmidt had to do was glance up to see her. He'd recognize her as soon as he spotted her. Dyed hair and inept makeup wouldn't fool a pro like Schmidt, not for a second.

No choice, no plan, no time—the only thing Charlie could do was improvise. "Hey, Schmidt! Yeah, you, you dumb Dutchman!"

Ten men turned. Nine of them were reaching gun hands beneath their jackets. Schmidt merely frowned. "Charles McKenzie," he purred. "How unexpected." He flicked his hand, signaling his followers to leave their weapons out of sight.

The receptionist's eyes went wide. She started to lift the phone. A bear-like paw—one of Schmidt's aides—snatched it off the counter. "Cool it, lady." She backed out of sight.

"Charles, I am astonished." That creepy Boer voice, utterly devoid of emotion; Charlie wondered if he practiced it every night. "I heard you'd gone walkabout. Now I find you, Daniel in the lion's den, greeting me at my own hotel. Tell me, Charles, how did you find me so swiftly? I can't have been in this wretched city more than fifteen minutes."

Charlie kept a large supply of smirks in inventory. He put on the most irritating one. It fit just fine.

Her face drained bloodless, Irina blinked.

Schmidt's voice, hollow as the grave, was in and of itself a death threat. "Best tell me what you've been up to, Charles. Best tell me how you managed to track my spoor."

Schmidt's lips tightened as Charlie winked at him. "Trade secret. However, I will tell you I'm staying just up the road. At the Marriott. I like the breakfast at the Marriott. The Marriott knows how hungry a traveler can be in the morning." He'd said it three times: *Marriott, Marriott, Marriott.* Had she understood? Charlie couldn't tell. "You ought to try it, Johan. Hell, they'll probably even have bananas for your pet monkeys." Charlie flipped a disparaging hand at Schmidt's followers. Good news: they glowered. Better they should look daggers at him rather than glance around the lobby. "Peel 'em with their toes, I bet." Faces changed color. "By the way, Johan, be sure to call Sam. I bet he's been sweating bullets since I dumped his bloodhounds. If you tell him I'm in the Marriott, he might sleep a little better, although I hope not."

Irina had gotten his message. She took a halting step backward. Baggy jeans, oversized shirt, hasty hair—her garb didn't draw eyes in her direction. That was a good thing, Charlie thought. Despite her motivation for dressing drably, at this present moment her clothing choices were a very good thing indeed.

"Samuel will want to know what you've been up to, and why you cut and ran."

"None of his business. Yours either."

"But it is, Charles, it is." Schmidt began to turn. "Come over here, let's sit in the lounge and chat." In a moment he'd be facing her head-on. "My colleagues can see to checking me in."

Charlie stopped him cold, body three-quarters toward Irina, pale face paler with anger. "Your colleagues can see to whatever they want because they don't wear dumb damn sunglasses all the time. I've always wondered what's behind those shades. I bet you've got little pink rabbit eyes, my lad—you know, darting left and right, worrying where the big bad wolf is." Charlie broadened his smirk as if to add: *and I am that wolf.*

Schmidt's lips twitched. "I conceal my eyes because men find my gaze . . . unsettling."

Charlie chortled. He made the sound as exasperating as possible. "Look, Johan, my car's out front with the engine running." Nodding her understanding, Irina edged backward. "Besides, it's getting late and I need my beauty sleep. I trust I'll see you in the morning. In my rearview mirror, no doubt."

Schmidt's voice was wind off a glacier. "You won't even see that. I'm going to kill you one of these days. I presume you know that."

Down to the end of the corridor and almost out of sight. Nobody noticed her. Now, if she had any sense, and Charlie knew she did, she'd hightail it out the back door, then wait for him near his BMW.

"Yeah, yeah, yeah. I heard you the last time you made that particular promise."

"*This* is the last time."

"Fine. Give it your best shot." Charlie stretched his arms out, offering his chest. "Come on, Johan, now's your chance." Schmidt set his jaw. "Oh, sorry. I forgot. You can't do it face-to-face, can you?" He spun on his feet. "Is this better? Come on, buddy boy, I'm trying to make things easy for you."

Feeling gun-sight eyes on the back of his neck, Charlie began counting slowly to sixty. By the time he reached thirty, he was nauseous. At fifty, he wanted to dive for cover. But sixty was his target, and sixty it would be, and he would not shake or shiver, but instead would hold himself rock steady until he ticked off the last terrifying second of one full minute. Fifty-seven, fifty-eight, fifty-nine, thank you, God, sixty. "No sale, eh? Well, I always said you were pussy."

Laughing, Charlie hobbled to the door, feigning a limp that he was sure Schmidt's men would remember the next morning.

Only when he was outside did he wipe the sickening sweat from his forehead.

Let's not try that trick again.

Schmidt wouldn't be off balance for long. Give him a few minutes to collect his thoughts and he'd order a pack of watchdogs to stake out the Marriott. Charlie had a little prank to play before they left the lobby and ran for their trucks.

He lifted the X5's back hatch, snapping open his war bag as he tugged it out. Pen in hand, he neatly printed "For road expenses <u>ONLY</u>," on four ordinary envelopes. Into each he tucked five thousand dollars' worth of the marked bills Sam had given him earlier in the day.

Shimming the locks of the four trucks flanking Schmidt's bad-boy G-Wagen, he slid four envelopes under four passenger seats, making sure each seat was too far forward for comfort. In the morning, Schmidt's no-brow apes would roll the seat backs, and, surprise, surprise. . . .

Charlie almost laughed out loud.

As he was closing the door on the last truck, a shadow darted from beneath a tree. A frightened woman's voice whispered, "How did you find me? How did they find me? In the lobby, they were laughing about me, they were saying they would—"

"No questions," Charlie barked. "They'll be out here in seconds. Just get in my car. No, don't worry about your Dodge or Whirlwind. They're safe here. I'm the one they'll be watching."

"No. I cannot—"

No time and no patience. "Just get the hell in my car, okay? If you don't, I'll clock you, and we won't be able to argue about things until you wake up."

Sam slumped behind his spacious desk. His tuxedo jacket was crumpled on the floor, his bow tie flopped limp beneath the collar of an unbuttoned shirt. At this late hour, he was one of the few people at work in the Executive Office Building. Nobody else was around except the security guards, the communications people, and a handful of eager young Iagos, each of them as treacherously ambitious as he'd been at their age.

He hadn't wanted to go to the party that night, but he'd had no choice. Above all else, Washington was a social town. Those who did not pay obeisance at ten-thousand-dollar-a-plate fund-raisers were vulnerable. More than one cabinet secretary had been exiled into the outer darkness because he'd failed to trade bon mots with the right people while sipping a glass of overpriced California wine.

Nine to five is when you shuffle paper. The real work begins at cocktail time.

Or, in Sam's case, a little before midnight. The Whirlwind mess—to say nothing of Charlie *goddamn the man* McKenzie—had put him behind schedule. He had to get caught up. The president was making a major address the next day, and the speechwriters had turned in two thousand words of crap. Shoving aside a stack of phone messages . . . shit, three of them were from Dr. Sangin Wing, and *he* could stew until the morning . . . Sam began to read: "As Middle East negotiations evolve—"

Evolve? Christ! You can't use that word. The votes of twenty million fundamentalists depended on never, ever implying that anything evolves.

Grimacing, Sam laboriously pecked out the word "unfold" on his loathsome computer. He hated the thing, never learned how to type, looked with contempt on upstart yuppie white trash with their laptops and their Palm Pilots and their Web-browsing cellulars and . . .

The phone rang. Not the regular office phone, and not the president's hot line. The other phone. *That phone.*

He snatched it up and heard the sound of music playing faintly in the background, something classical, a familiar tune: *The Anvil Chorus* from some wop opera. He gritted his teeth. There was only one man he knew who listened to nothing but opera. . . .

"Good evening, Samuel. Johan Schmidt here."

Even when he was politely saying hello, Schmidt managed to be menacing. "Johan. Thanks for calling. Any progress to report?"

Schmidt was so emotionless that you knew there was only murder in his heart. Presuming he had one. "Some. I have located Charles. He has taken a room in the Airport Marriott here. Two teams are on duty outside the hotel. You need not worry about him eluding observation again."

Sam sighed with relief. "Any idea what he's been up to?"

"He declined to say. However, whatever it was, it injured his leg. He's walking with a pronounced limp."

"Glad to hear it. You know him personally, don't you?"

"He and I have a certain history."

Sam could detect not the least hint of a change in Schmidt's voice. Nonetheless, the words made the hair on the back of his neck rise. "Be careful. He's dangerous."

"We have that in common."

Sam's sinuses throbbed. "Any word on Kolodenkova?"

"Not yet, but it's still early days."

"We don't have days."

"I am aware of that, Samuel. It was only a manner of speaking."

"Understood. Look, Johan, I have bad news. McKenzie's daughter is in the Israeli embassy. She's under Mossad protection and—"

"The Mossad? How uncommon. The *Memuneh* rarely

consents to granting another nation's agent 'jumbo.' That's the term they use—"

"Claude told me what it means. And he told me Charlie's got it."

"Does Charles's privileged status extend to field support?"

"They'll never go that far."

"A pity. One of my firm's clients, a gentleman in Dubai, pays a handsome bounty for Mossad genitals."

Something bubbled in Sam's throat.

"But that is neither here nor there. Why is McKenzie's daughter an issue?"

"She's not. But the Mossad is. They're in communication with him."

"Then I would advise you to silence them. The more isolated Charles is, the better are my odds of success. The more he has no one to rely upon but himself, the easier my job will be."

The pain was getting stronger, creeping up the bridge of Sam's nose and burrowing into the bones above his eyes. "What do you want me to do, blow up their embassy?"

"If you prefer. Although I should think, as you have done in the past, declaring certain embassy workers persona non grata would suffice. Expel a few and they'll leave Charles to his own resources."

"Not likely. Back when the Israelis were planning the Jericho casino, he went over to negotiate intelligence access. While he was there, a bigwig Mossad officer walked into a trap up in Syria and was bundled off to the Tadmor prison. You know what the Syrians are like, electric needles through your dick, saw-toothed whip handles up your—"

"The old ways are best."

Sam did his best to ignore the implication. "So Charlie

disappears—totally unauthorized, by the way. Two days later he shows up with a smirk on his face and the bigwig in the back of a stolen Syrian Jeep. Ever since, the Israelis would walk through fire for him."

"Regrettable. Well, at least try to find out what information they're feeding him. It would be helpful if I knew."

"Never happen. Charlie's got too many hacker friends. They've given him codes that even the NSA can't break. Plus the sonofabitch has got a secret vault out on the Internet that he's using to . . . uh . . . that . . . well, forget about that. Forget I even mentioned it."

Schmidt inhaled sharply. After a moment's silence, the South African spoke—and, unless Sam misread his distant voice, there was a certain hunger in his tone. "Do I sense a problem here, Samuel, a little something you've neglected to tell me?"

Sam narrowed his eyes. Should he confess the truth about Charlie's hidden data repository? Could Schmidt neutralize it? *Neutralize Charlie too, if that's the proper word.*

"Samuel, Samuel, you know you can trust me."

If there was any power on earth who could take Charlie down, Schmidt was it. And if the mercenary could crack Charlie's data vault into the bargain . . .

"We've known each other a long time, Samuel. There should be no secrets between us."

True. Schmidt really was the only man in the world whom Sam could trust. Which was, when you thought about it, a fairly damning self-indictment.

"Come, Samuel, anything you tell me about Charles is to our mutual advantage. Moreover, if you have some—shall we say—secondary issue with him, perhaps I can offer my assistance. You know I would be pleased to be of service where he is involved. Why, good gracious, old friend, I might even waive my standard fee."

"I doubt that."

"As well you should. However, a discount is not out of the question. Now, Samuel, please do tell me what's troubling you."

And Sam did.

Acid in Irina's every word: "So now you have a pretty Russian girl in your hotel room. I suppose you think this means you can screw her."

Ignoring her, McKenzie raised the television's volume. She understood his ploy: the human voice makes glass vibrate; a microwave signal bounced off a window can eavesdrop on those vibrations; however, a television's blare—he'd tuned it to MTV—neutralizes the technique.

"This is surely what is on your mind. I am in your power. Your wife is far away—"

"My wife is dead," he said, not rebuking, merely explaining. "Leukemia. It lasted a year and a half. Three remissions to give us hope, four declines to teach us despair. She weighed seventy pounds at the end. It was a death I'd wish on no one."

Irina wrapped her arms around her waist. She knew what he was doing—trying to win her sympathy. Sympathy is the first signpost on the road to surrender.

His eyes seemed duller than they had been, a little life siphoned from his lively glance. "At the end, just near the end, I made a vow. I didn't make it to God. He and I weren't on speaking terms at the time. I made it to my wife. I'd been faithful to her every day of our marriage; I swore I'd stay faithful after she'd gone. Mary didn't hear me speak the words. She was in the hospital. I was . . . somewhere else. That wasn't important. Only the promise was important."

Bad liars do not prosper in the espionage trade. Only the gifted survive. McKenzie surely was a brilliant liar. Why then did she believe him?

She looked away, taking a moment to compose herself. The death of a wife, deeply loved or not, was irrelevant. The vital point, the only point, was that she'd been captured by a man whom she'd underestimated—worse, by a man old enough, arrogant enough, to be her father. Now she must discover his weaknesses, turn them against him, use them to escape. "How did you find me?"

Turning his back, McKenzie sluffed off his sweat-soaked shirt. Had he been perspiring in fear when he confronted those men? If so, she could not fault him.

Next, he peeled off his equally wet undershirt. Bone-white scars rippled across his shoulders, brutally ugly, jagged lightning bolts, and there were many. She wished she could avert her eyes, although she could not.

He muttered, "This is what happens to cocksure pigheads. The lucky ones, I mean. They should have taught you that at the Institute."

Speechless, aghast, she did not want to think about how much pain this man must have endured.

"The long ones running left to right, that's what you get in a Burmese jail. They have a martial arts master on the payroll. He soaks his rattan canes in brine before he flogs you. My sentence was twenty-five strokes. I thought I'd die. But the truth is, I got off easy. I was using a Canadian passport, they didn't know I was American, they didn't think I was a spy."

Less flesh than leather, the hide of an ancient animal who'd survived a lifetime of battles for survival.

He pulled fresh clothing from an overnight bag. "Down there on the left, you can see what a combat knife will do to you. Guy was trying for my kidneys, and if he'd been better at his job, you and I wouldn't be having this conversation. As it was, the blade skittered off my ribs. Took a lot of meat with it. Medic had to stitch Kevlar webbing under there to keep my innards from falling out."

She swallowed hard. He was doing this—must be doing this—to gain her pity. Pity an enemy? Never!

He shook open a T-shirt and began pulling it over his head. "See that gouge on the right. Tonight you met the man who gave it to me. Yeah, Johan Schmidt. He doesn't know about it, though. He was shooting blind in the dark, and there was no way in hell I was going to let him know he hit me. Instead I forced myself to laugh, then cracked a dirty joke about his mother. That makes a real tough hombre, right? Sure it does."

The expression on his face as he turned toward her had nothing to do with toughness. It was only sorrow, sorrow and self-mockery.

"Honorable wounds, Irina. That's what they call 'em. But I've got news for you. There's no such thing. The only kind of wound there is, bleeds and hurts and screams that you're not Superman and bullets don't bounce off your chest; you're only an ordinary Joe, and you've been overconfident again. And conceited, self-righteous idiot that you are, you've made another damn dumb mistake, and one of these days you'll make another, and it will be your last. Or worse, somebody else's. Welcome to my world, Irina Kolodenkova, if you had any sense, you'd move to a different planet."

His intent was transparent. She would not be beguiled by so flimsy and feeble a ploy. This man wished to win her over. Let him wish in vain. Narrowing her eyes, she demanded, "You did not answer my question. How did you find me?"

She knew the smile he returned was meant to irk her. "I told you I was good. Now you know how good."

"You put a tracer on my truck."

"Nonsense. You're smart enough to check for bugs."

True. And there'd been no tracking equipment on the dashboard of his ridiculously luxurious SUV. Which meant . . . "You have an assistant. He followed me."

McKenzie jacked his Macintosh PowerBook into the hotel phone. "Nope." He grinned. "If I'd had backup, you would have seen him when I was needling Schmidt and his punks. I wouldn't have faced down those hyenas by myself unless I had no alternative." The PowerBook chimed. McKenzie was connected to the Internet.

"Then it was luck. You found me because you were lucky."

"Oh, I wouldn't believe that if I were you." His fingers raced across the keyboard. He cocked an eyebrow at the screen, nodding satisfaction at the results.

His smugness abraded. Worn and exhausted, she grunted, "What are you doing with that computer?"

"Take a look."

She stepped behind him. Meaningless rows of numbers scrolled down the screen. He was downloading an encrypted file. "Pardon me," he said, "for doing this now, but Schmidt's people will slap a tap on every phone in this hotel. I wanted to get this stuff before they have a chance."

"You are a fool. They will check the hotel's phone records." She regretted the jibe. He'd have an answer—his kind always did.

"Sure. And eventually they'll pinpoint the Web site I visited. Not that it will do them any good. You see . . . " The download ended. McKenzie clicked his cursor and the screen changed, " . . . this is a public bulletin board—one of the ones where encryption freaks hang out. Everybody posts coded messages, and everybody tries to crack each other's code. It's all a game for them. For me too, I suppose. My daughter and I play code games. It's fun. We've been trading messages here for, oh, nearly twenty years now. Nobody has cracked our cipher yet. Although, God knows they've tried."

Irina's voice turned brittle. "Your daughter has followed you into the CIA?"

"Nah." Disconnecting from the Internet, McKenzie leaned back and knitted his fingers behind his head. "She's got a master's in music. None of my children have anything to do with the government. For which I am duly thankful."

"Your children? How many?"

"Two sons and a daughter."

Cold crept up her spine. Two boys. One girl. A domineering father. She knew the life such families led.

McKenzie leaned back, a mellow smile on his face. "When I was young, I wanted to be a journalist. Took my degree at Columbia. I still hang out with reporters. They're good people. All they want to do is learn the truth. Everybody lies to them when they try. I can relate to that."

He would have been a tyrant to his children, molding them like putty, turning into mirror images of himself. No man of his temperament would do otherwise.

"But my dad twisted my arm until I joined the Agency. I liked it well enough—or at least I did for a while. By the time I stopped liking it, I'd become what I'd become, and there's never any changing that. Howsomever, somewhere along the line I made myself a promise: my kids could be whatever they wanted to be—follow their own star, not mine. Now my oldest boy, Scott—he's named for my father-in-law—is a doctor. He's spent the past six years helping some pretty needy folks. The youngest, Mike, is an anthropologist. He's started making a name for himself. Not that fame matters to him; he loves his work, and that's all that counts. I'm proud of 'em. I suppose I shouldn't be because I didn't have anything to do with their choices. But you know, when you're a father, it's hard not to take pride in your kids."

No! She would not believe it. He was lying smiling lies, trying to put a good light on what was—what had to be—a story of subtle brutality and secret intimidation.

He pulled out his wallet, displaying a photo in a plasticine window—two handsome men, one the very spit and image of his father, side by side with a woman whose delicate features were spoiled by a frown. "That's Scott and Mike on the right. My daughter Carly's on the left. She's the only one of the three who's messed up. The last thing Mary and I wanted was for her to become another damned Washington wife. But wouldn't you know it, no sooner than she finished her master's degree than she fell in love with the wrong man, married the skunk, and walked straight into cocktail party hell." He sighed. "Well, it's over now. She's got two great kids . . . here, wait a second, let me pull this other picture out . . . Jason and Molly, cute little devils, aren't they? I'd say they're a pretty good consolation prize for a rotten marriage and an even worse divorce." He slipped the photo back in its holder and slid the wallet into his pants. "Anyway, now I'm hoping the rest of Carly's life will be better than the past two years have been. If she needs it, I'll give her all the help I can. But Carly's as ornery as me. She'll never ask."

Liar! You are a liar and you are trying to dupe me into believing you are a loving father, a doting grandfather. It is mere acting, a cheap masquerade. I will not believe this sham! "She sends you coded messages. You taught her spycraft as a child." This in frigid tones of anger.

"Nope. What happened was—oh, she was about nine years old at the time—she was trying to read a quote-secret message-unquote in one of those kids' magazines. I offered her a hand. One thing led to another, and pretty soon we cooked up a private code—you know, just for us, our secret. Because I used to be out of the country a lot, I'd send her postcards with coded messages. That drove the Agency nuts because they couldn't read what I'd written. Ha! They still can't."

False. False again. She was certain of it. "Impossible. There is no unbreakable code."

"Disposable onetime pad. Invented in 1919, and no one's broken the original inventor's secret message yet. Carly and I use a computerized variation on the theme. Nobody can bust it." He smiled, damn him, he smiled gently. "Look, if you don't believe me, I'll give you the URL for my little cryptographer's playground. You can log on and try to crack my code. I'll post a message to you on that Web site. My screen name is Gryphon. We'll make you Red Queen—"

She shouted, "I am not a Party member." *But my father is. A steadfast believer in scientific socialism who will hail the day when the red flag flies again from his vessel's stern.*

"Whoops, sorry. I'll call you White Queen instead." He laughed.

"We are wasting time!" Although she knew she shouldn't, she still was shouting. *"You* are wasting time! Letters from your daughter! Are there not more important—"

The swiftness with which his voice changed caught her off guard. Suddenly he was all iron, face and intonation alike. "Nothing is more important to any father. But that's not what I downloaded. Some . . . shall we say 'friends' have sent me DefCon Enterprises' full public record. The Dun and Bradstreet reports, the S&P file, articles of incorporation, biographies of the management, and all the newspaper stories they found on the Web."

He studied the screen, eyes narrow while he cursored through pages of now decoded information. "California company. Incorporated back in the Clinton years. Privately held. Venture-capital funding. Three hundred and twenty employees—mostly an R&D shop. Chief exec, Maximilian Henkes, age fifty-two. MIT grad, MBA from the Sloan School. Worked for Lockheed before starting DefCon. The chief financial officer is a Lockheed alumnus too. Vice president of operations comes from Martin Marietta, and the controller from General Dynamics. They all have defense contractor backgrounds. Everybody does except the chief scientist—Sangin Wing, a Chinese defector with a doctorate in materials science. Says here he wrote his Ph.D. thesis on superconductors. Now that's interesting. . . . "

He leaned back again, this time shutting his eyes. His lips moved soundlessly. Suddenly he showed his teeth, a hungry fox. His eyes popped open—bright, electric, frighteningly intelligent. What, she asked herself, did he see in these minuscule fragments of information? How could any man make sense of so few irrelevant facts?

McKenzie abruptly flipped the PowerBook's screen down, shutting the computer off. "There's a ton of material here. We can look at it tomorrow."

"We?" She was on fury's edge. His self-composure, his nonchalant friendliness—she knew they were meant to both charm and seduce her. That he thought she could be so easily bewitched was maddening.

"I hope so. On the other hand, if you want to make a run for it again, that's your privilege. I won't stop you."

She could kill him. He hadn't taken her pistol. He was so

gallingly self-assured that he did not bother to disarm her. She'd never killed a man, but this man . . .

"In fact, I'll even give you your gun back."

What?

"Once your temper has cooled off, I mean."

She patted her waistband frantically. The Tokarev was no longer there.

Her shoulders slumped. No, she was not defeated. She'd never be defeated. But she was on the defensive—a painfully unfamiliar position.

The problem . . . the problem was that she was drained of her last reserve. This day had exhausted her like no other. She'd seen death, and known fear. It had left her vulnerable and bereft of the strength she needed for the parry and thrust of conversation with this infuriatingly cunning opponent.

"Look, Irina, I am not your enemy."

"No?" she spat. "Then what are you?"

"Just a guy who wants to protect you."

She wiped spittle from her lips. "I need no . . . no . . . guardian angel!"

"Like it or not, you've got one. Call me Saint Charles." There was that dullness in his eyes again. She still could not interpret it. "Nah, on second thought don't call me Saint Charles." His face softened and his voice came from far away. "Plain old Charlie is better."

Was a weakness hinted at, some vulnerability she could turn to her advantage? She pressed him. "Why not Saint Charles?"

He smiled faintly, distracted, a man mulling over a pleasant memory. "It's the name of a place, a little town, a village really. Not Saint Charles, but the Spanish for it: San Carlos—San Carlos do Cabo. Saint Charles of the Cape. Down on the California coast, south of Big Sur. Mary and I . . . my wife and I . . . we had happy times there, some of our happiest. You know, we were going to retire there, that's how much in love with it we were. . . . " His voice sank, and the light faded from his eyes.

I have him if I want him, she thought. *A lonely widower mourning his wife—at just this moment I can harvest him as a well-trained swallow would, harvest him body and soul.*

It was the right thing to do. It was what they would want her to do. And when she had done it, she would be no better than her father's dockside whores.

McKenzie shook himself like a wet dog. "I need a drink." He pushed himself away from the desk and fumbled open the minibar. "Do you want something?"

The opportunity had passed. She knew she should feel guilty for letting it slip by, but instead she shivered with relief. "No. Yes. A soda. No, a fruit drink." *"Rattled" is the word an American would use. I have lost my self-composure and must recover it.*

He brandished a cold can of orange juice, mixed himself a gin and tonic. "You want ice with this?"

"No." After pouring it into a glass, he passed it to her with a napkin. The spark was back in his eyes, and the wry smile on his lips. She'd lost him.

Sipping his drink, then sighing in satisfaction, he said, "Anyway, like I was saying, I'm on your side. At least for the here and now. The guy you have to watch out for is the one whose tail I was twisting at the Hilton, Johan Schmidt. He's bad medicine, the worst I can name. He's a merc, a pro, and he'll have five hundred men or more behind him. You've got the most dangerous mercenary organization I can name on your case. As if that weren't bad enough, you also have to worry about the civilian police, the FBI, and a whole bunch of alphabet-soup agencies. A lot of people want to take you down; I'm pretty much the only one who doesn't."

"I will escape them." She would. And it was important that this McKenzie man know it.

"The government guys? Sure. There's no doubt in my mind you can get past them. But Schmidt is a horse of a different color. Look, we don't have anything like your country's Spetsnaz in America. Heavily armed, highly trained special forces who do the dirty work *both* abroad and at home just aren't the American way. So, the laws of supply and demand being what they are, private enterprise—"

Her temper ignited. She found herself sneering as her father would sneer. "This is your much vaunted free-market economy at work."

McKenzie chuckled. "I guess. It all comes down to the same pig-stupid libertarian philosophy. Yeah, sure Johan Schmidt's the personification of the free-market economy. He and his people are only in it for the money. Patriotism, duty, ordinary human decency—they're irrelevant to that crowd. All they care about is cash on the barrelhead. The profit motive, my girl, is the most powerful motive there is. Once you understand that, you'll understand how much danger you're *really* in."

True, Schmidt was to be feared. The very sight of him had frightened her. But his men were mere hooligans. They would be no challenge.

"Don't make the mistake of believing that Schmidt's gang are all brawn and no brains. His soldiers—the monkeys you saw with him an hour ago—aren't particularly bright, although they are exceptionally well-schooled. His officers are a different story. One officer for every ten foot soldiers, they're the best money can buy—smart, seasoned, and not easy to fool. I'm damned good, but as good as I am, I'd rather keep out of those guys' way."

He is back in control of this conversation. How did that happen?

McKenzie continued. "Which should be your objective if you decide to run. Look, I'm leaving here early tomorrow morning. They'll be following me—or at least they'll think they are. If you wait until after I'm gone, you should be able to get out of town unseen. After that . . . well, I don't know what your best route is. Southwest, probably. More traffic that way, you'd be lost in the crowd. Yeah, the route over to Southern Arizona is your best bet. Phoenix, Tucson—big cities are always a good place to hide. Although the truth is you'd be safer if you stayed here until I get back."

She glared at him, unable to decide what to say but knowing that she would never, *never* accept his advice.

"If you do run for it, get some decent clothes to replace that junk you insist on wearing." Irina winced. "Stop at some upscale shop, and look for the St. John Sport label. Mary always was a knockout in their stuff, and it would look great on you. Schmidt's people aren't searching for a well-dressed posh kind of woman. If you're wearing fancy clothes, you might slip by them. I doubt if you'll find the right kind of store in this town. Maybe in Tucson or Phoenix or Sedona—one of the resort towns, anyway."

Why is he helping me? He is up to something. There is a trick here.

"Okay, it's getting late. We should go to bed—*chastely* to bed. Wearing our britches by the way, because Schmidt is quite capable of kicking down the door at three in the morning. But before we do, there's something I want to ask you. Be patient. This will only take a few minutes."

All she wanted was sleep. If she could put this day—the most hideous in her life—behind her, she could deal with this man and with whatever sly gambit he was about to attempt. *Or has attempted, and I am too tired to notice.* She shook her head, trying to clear her mind of its fatigue, and of all the chemistries of fear and flight that had bewildered it.

He withdrew a handful of photographs from his satchel. Some were black and white. Others were color. He spread them on top of the motel desk. Her cheeks flamed. Such was her outrage and such was her shock that she could feel the heat. *How dare he? How dare he show me this?*

"These snapshots were taken mostly up at Beloye More and over at Lake Ladozhskoye. This is your father, right? That's you. Those are your brothers and your mother."

She teetered on the brink. The precipice was high. The pit bottomless. The photos were too much, too much to be borne. This day—horrible, horrible—Dominik dying in a fog of blood, cars stolen where any man might see her, the expression on sad, sweet Mitch Conroy's face, McKenzie finding her not once but twice, and the gloating obscenity of Schmidt's henchmen. . . .

She did not know how much more she could endure. Surely she could not endure the sight of these . . . of these . . . damnable photographs!

"So here you all are on holiday, and every holiday your father takes the family sailing. You must have been six or seven when this first one was taken. And in this last one, out in the Gulf of Finland I think, you look to be about seventeen."

"Eighteen." She could barely get the word out. Her throat was constricted. Choking memory rendered speech impossible. She felt her hands shake, knew that she burned with terrors best left unspoken, and wanted nothing—*nothing!*—more than to open her mouth and shriek.

"Same as every other spook shop in the world, the Agency just loves collecting snapshots of foreign military guys. So we've got this full photographic record of you growing up.

Dozens of shots of you and your family on vacation. Usually you're all out on the water. But the thing is . . . see here in every picture . . . the thing is that while everybody shares the boating chores, there's one chore we never photographed you doing. I'm curious about that, Irina. I mean, I was just wondering—"

An explosion. A house condemned to demolition. Its walls crumble. Nothing is left but dust and rubble.

"Never!" she shouted, "never!" She would not cry. This man—no man —could make her do that. "Never once! Only my brothers! Not me! I was *never* allowed! He would *never* give me the chance to prove myself, and . . . " She swallowed hard, gulping back the pain.

"He never let you take the tiller, never let you steer."

"I was a girl. I was not good enough."

"That's what he said."

"Always. About everything. I was never good enough!"

"So you never really knew?"

"Knew what?"

"Whether he was right. Whether you're good enough. You don't know that."

"I do know."

"You only think you do."

"No!"

"The truth is . . . " He stretched out his hand to comfort her; she pushed it away. " . . . you never can be certain how good you are."

She hated him. The power of the emotion staggered her. She began to speak—to shout, really, but stopped herself short.

She stopped because she could see it. It was in his eyes, a hint, not a flagrancy, the flickering ghost of unspoken knowledge.

He knew more, knew that secret thing, knew what her father had done, knew her humiliation, the shame she denied because if she admitted it she would scream and scream and scream.

It was written in his eyes. And it was written that he would never speak of what he knew, but keep it hidden inside of him, locked as deeply as it was locked within her.

For this she hated him most of all.

She slapped him. She slapped him as hard as she was able.

He merely looked at her sadly, as though she had somehow disappointed him.

PART TWO

Charlie's Love

De l'audace—encore de l'audace—toujours de l'audace.

—Danton

5
Roadwork

Charlie pitched his voice loud to penetrate the closet in which Irina hid. "Good morning, Mitch!" he boomed as he flung open the hotel room door.

With two shopping bags and a greasy box of Krispy Kremes clutched to his chest, Mitch Conroy hobbled in. "Mornin', Mr. McKenzie. Am I on time?"

"Five forty-five to the minute. Punctuality is the virtue of princes." In grey slacks, white shirt, and a Sears sports coat, Mitch looked like a small-time businessman—a car dealer, an insurance broker, a shoe store manager. Charlie was confident Schmidt's watchers hadn't given the rodeo rider—walking slowly to conceal his limp—a second glance. "Is that breakfast I see? Why, bless you. And quit calling me 'mister.' My friends call me Charlie."

"Yessir, I'll try to remember to do that, Mr. McKenzie." Wearing a puppy-dog grin, Mitch put his shopping bags on the floor, then perched on the edge of the bed.

Laughing at the cowboy's sly wit, Charlie sat beside him. This was a good man, he told himself, one miscast in the risky role he'd volunteered to accept. More to assuage his conscience than anything else, he asked, "Look, son, are you sure you want this job?"

Mitch opened the donut box, revealing four cups of hot coffee and a dozen gloppy confections. He peeled a plastic lid off one of the coffees, then picked a sticky bun with hot pink icing. "Only work I seen in a long time."

Charlie took a coffee for himself. He eyed the pastries, choosing the one that seemed least likely to trigger coronary thrombosis. "You're going up against some pretty bad people, Mitch. They might rough you up some."

"I been ridin' rodeo since I was sixteen. I reckon anybody as whups up on me can't do more than some horse already done twice." He licked his fingers with relish and took another donut.

"Just so long as you know what you're getting into." Charlie passed a manila envelope to Mitch. "I've signed the BMW's title over to you. The registration and all the paperwork are in here. Plus the twenty-five thousand cash I promised. When you get to Las Vegas, don't blow it at the tables."

"I ain't no gambler. Most I'll do is catch me a show and have a good steak dinner."

"Smart man. Okay, now let's go over the plan one last time."

Mitch nodded. "Well, sir, like you told me, I bought me some khaki clothes same as yours. Also got built-up shoes to make me look taller. And I found a store out near the state college that sells makeup and wigs and such, so I got that stuff too. In a minute or so, I'm walkin' into your bathroom, and when I come out I'm gonna look a mite like you—leastways at a distance. Then I'm headin' downstairs with a satchel similar to yours, goin' out the back door—"

"The BMW's parked beneath a tree right by the fire exit. They're watching it."

"I'll be limpin' fast and keepin' my head down. Then I'll climb in that fancy vehicle of yours. Always did want me one of them German cars." He smiled boyishly. "As the crow flies, we got 'bout six hundred miles between here and Vegas. If I take the long way around, I won't get there 'til dark. Whereupon I drive up to the Mandalay Bay, throw my keys to the valet, and as soon as I go through the door, the wig and all goes into my satchel. Then I check in under my own name, and I stay there 'til I hear from you—or for three days, whichever comes first."

"If you get pulled over—and it won't be by the police— what do you do?"

"Tell the truth. Tell 'em everythin'. Even 'bout that pretty girl."

Charlie looked warily at the donuts. Still hungry, he selected something slathered in chocolate and oozing whipped cream from the center. "Especially about that pretty girl. And make sure they know that I'm the one who paid you to drive a high-visibility BMW from here to Vegas. You're not part of this, Mitch, you're just a hired hand. If they understand that, they'll probably let you off easy."

Mitch drained his coffee. "Will do. And now . . . " He pulled a folded envelope from his slacks pocket. " . . . here's the papers for the car I got you. Ain't much of a car. Beat up old riceburner, actually. Most folks in this part of the world would sooner walk than be seen in a Jap car, so I got a right good price on it."

"It's not going any farther than the airport. By the way, I presume you had no problems chartering a private jet for me."

"Nothin' that wavin' a big ol' wad a hundred-dollar bills didn't solve. They's a-flyin' in from Dallas. Be waitin' for you at seven o'clock sharp." He began to reach into his rear pocket. "Which reminds me, I got plenty of money left over from what you gave me yesterday."

"Keep it."

"Can't do that. It's close to two thousand dollars."

"Put your damned wallet back in your damned pants. The money's for you."

Nodding, Mitch hefted the shopping bag containing his disguise and walked to the bathroom. Five minutes later, he was gone. Five minutes after that, Charlie followed.

When he returned to the room, Irina was sitting at the desk. She'd wolfed down three donuts and was working on her fourth. Charlie blackly observed that she'd polished off both remaining cups of coffee. He'd wanted a second cup for himself.

"No trouble?" she asked.

He pulled up a chair at the desk, peeked into the donut box, and decided that no power on earth could persuade him to eat another one of the things. "None. The night clerk is still on duty. He checked me out and went back to his nap."

"Will Mitch . . . " Charlie noted the hesitancy in her voice. " . . . will he be all right?"

"Sure. Oh, they'll be mad as hell, but that won't change the fact that I skunked them into following the wrong man. If they stop him, I figure Mitch will walk away with no more than a bloody nose. No one's got any reason to hurt him."

"I hope you are correct, Charlie. He has a good heart."

She'd stopped calling him Mr. McKenzie. Charlie rather liked that. *Of course it's only appropriate to be on a first-name basis after spending the night with me, and damn but I had trouble falling asleep. . . .*

"Charlie?"

Hell, is it showing? "What?"

"I feel badly about what I did to him. Do you feel badly about what you did to me?" Caught off guard, Charlie returned a poker-faced stare. "Showing me those photographs, taking advantage of a weakness, playing mind games—this is not so different from what I did to Mitch, I think."

After a moment's reflection, Charlie pursed his lips, "That's good, Irina, in fact, it's first-rate. If you make me feel guilty, then you'll have the upper hand. Congratulations, you've scored a point."

"You have not answered my question."

"Two points. Now get ready to lose one. The answer is if you feel guilty, you're in the wrong line of work. In this business, the only thing you're entitled to is pride when you win and bitterness when you lose."

"You still have not answered."

Charlie chortled, although not happily. "Game, set, and match. Yeah, I do feel guilty. You were vulnerable. I took advantage of it. Even though it's all part of the game, I feel like a louse. Now, are you satisfied?"

"Not really. I too feel guilty. Guilty in my heart." She gave him a flat, emotionless look.

I loathe this job. I truly, truly do. He drew a deep breath, "If it's any consolation to you, that confession makes you a better person than ninety-nine percent of the other guys."

She refused to meet his eyes. "Now what? You will arrest me, and return your precious Whirlwind to its owners, I suppose?"

"Dead wrong. Make no mistake, Irina, if Whirlwind is critical to the national defense—and I suspect it is—I'm not letting you get it out of the country." A small fire sparked in her eye. *Good,* Charlie thought, *let's see some spunk, girl.*

"On the other hand, I have no intention of bringing either it or you in until I know what it is. I've said this before, I'll say it again: there's more going on than meets the eye. They wouldn't have brought me back from exile—and they sure as hell wouldn't have hired Johan Schmidt—unless there's a secret behind the secret. That second secret is the important one. If I can crack it, then I might just get what I want. If I do, if you help me, then maybe we can work something out between us."

"I will make no deals with you, Charlie."

No hesitation, nothing but resolution in her voice. Charlie would have been disappointed if there hadn't been. The night before he'd mounted a full scale assault against the weakest place in her defenses. She'd fought back like a champ. The most he'd been able to accomplish was to plant a seed of self-doubt. That seed wouldn't bloom until she started questioning her motives. *And then, my dear, you belong to me.* "Fair enough. Leave the deal-doing to me." He glanced at his jeweled watch. "Look, I'm going to have to leave in a few minutes. I'd like to ask you some questions before I go."

Astonished, she blurted, "You are leaving me here? I may do what I wish?"

Gotchya! "Yup. Right now, Schmidt and company are burning rubber trying to catch up with Mitch. They'll be on his tail all day because they think he's me, and they think he'll lead them straight to you." He smiled a smug cat smile at his own cleverness. "Okay, so right now according to the Marriott's computer system this room is vacant. The cleaning crew won't show up until nine. If you want to make a run for it, your best bet is to wait here for a few hours, then scoot over to the Hilton, check out, and hit the road. I'd be happier if you stayed holed up. That's the safest thing to do. But I won't stop you if you want to hightail it. Leave here at nine, and you can make it to Phoenix by late afternoon, get as far as San Diego or LA by ten tonight."

She blinked in confusion. He could almost hear her mental gears grinding as she tried to puzzle her way through his motives. She opened her mouth twice, but said nothing.

"Okay, Irina, will you answer a few questions for me?"

She responded warily, "Only if you answer my questions too. Why have you chartered a plane? Where are you going?"

"California. That's where DefCon Enterprises is. A chartered jet will get me there and back in jig time." She nodded, although not trustingly. "My turn for a question. Tell me everything you saw when you stole Whirlwind—every detail. I need to know it all."

Irina began to speak. Charlie slouched back in his chair. As on the night before, his fingers were knitted behind his head. He closed his eyes. There, but not there, he emptied his mind, making it a blank slate upon which Irina would write. If he concentrated at all, he concentrated on not concentrating. Outside his own reality, he was inside hers.

An invisible ghost, he hovered over the desert night. Below he saw two figures flit like hunting owls through the darkness. Shadows danced in blood-orange firelight. An impenetrable building was penetrated.

Two curious cats intrigued by an open cupboard pawpadded their way to innocent predation. The mouse was plump and slow. They pounced.

Black flared white. Searchlights speared the sky. Angry bullets flocked in a killing hailstorm. Frightened rabbits fled the hunter's horn, and fresh-spilled blood puddled on a sandy slope.

Irina fell silent. Charlie shook himself out of the world where he'd been and into the world where other men live.

Her skin was sallow. Charlie regretted that. Reliving those moments of terror could not have come easily. But she, a good soldier, had given him what she knew he wanted. He admired her for that. *Which,* he reflected, *could become a problem.*

Hands on her hips, she demanded, "Now I shall ask you a question, and you must answer truthfully."

Damn she made a fast recovery. "Fire away."

"What did you do with the disk you stole from me?"

Charlie froze. For a moment he could neither move nor react nor think. Then he exploded into laughter. Snorting and wiping his eyes, he barely managed to get the words out. "You know, I've never met my match before. But you . . . dear God!" He reached into his war bag, ran a fingernail along an invisible seam, and teased open a false bottom. "Here," he said, handing her a disk. "Anyone as smart as you deserves it."

Irina leaned across the table, took the disk, and flipped it over her shoulder. "I would like the real one now."

"You are good, lady, so very, very good." Abashed, Charlie opened a shirt button, fished a hand beneath his khaki, and pulled a disk from a secret pocket. "Is this what you're looking for?"

She answered with a single crisp nod as she dropped it in her breast pocket.

It took no small effort to keep a straight face. The disk he'd given her had come from beneath the left side of his shirt. The disk she wanted was secreted on the right. "Okay, we're square now. And I've got to hit the road. Just let me get two things straight. First: are you sure those generators were shielded?"

"I did not say they were shielded, only that the shed was made of thick metal. The fragments I saw from the explosion were very heavy. This is not so significant, I think."

"I'll be the judge of that. Second: you said there were gas canisters hooked to a lab hood. Do you remember what was in 'em?"

She pressed a fingernail to her lip. *Such a pretty gesture,* Charlie thought. "No, the light was poor and . . . wait, I do remember . . . something . . . an anesthetic, I think."

"Ether?"

"Dimethyl ether, yes. Why is this important?"

"Not an anesthetic, not in that lab."

Her eyes sparked. "A coolant? It is quite cold, I think."

"Liquefies at minus twenty-five degrees," said Charlie, who hadn't missed an issue of *Scientific American* since age fourteen. "Freezes somewhere under a hundred, a hundred and forty maybe."

"Why would they need something that cold?"

"Think about it. You're a smart cookie, you'll work it out."

She snapped her fingers. "Ha! They have developed a new superconductor!"

Damned smart. Girl, I'm going to have to keep my eye on you. "Got it in one. A material that conducts electricity with no resistance. Electrons zip through and they don't even know it's there."

"But there are no practical applications for superconductors, not even the so-called high-temperature ones. It is merely an interesting phenomenon, a toy for experimenters."

"It's more than a toy. If they were using that ether to cool down that box you stole—"

"I am not so sure it is a box, Charlie. I have carried it three times. There's no lid or lock. It is solid, I think."

Charlie shut his eyes again. "An ingot. Not metal, not plastic, right? A ceramic composite. Yeah, it would be a composite." He was close, so tantalizingly close. They were there, all the puzzle pieces. All he had to do was shuffle them around, looking for their connecting points while he worked out the real, the undeniable, the absolute truth—

No time! His head snapped up. "Irina, I've got to leave now. Before I go, tell me you'll hide out at the Hilton. Tell me you'll be waiting when I get back."

She shook her head.

"Are you sure? I'll be back from California no later than four or five this afternoon. You'll be a lot safer if you join forces with me. I think we'd make a pretty good team."

Another shaken "no."

"Have it your way. But for God's sake, be careful. If they get their hands on you, you're going to get hurt."

"They will not catch me."

Charlie stood, picking up his war bag with his left hand. It struck him that he'd like to plant an unbecoming good-bye kiss on her cheek. But that would never do.

Glancing over his shoulder, he walked to the door and turned the knob. "Okay then, I'll see you this evening. To-morrow morning at the latest."

Her eyes flashed and her jaw jutted. "You will never see me again!"

Charlie chuckled as he left the room. Of course he'd see her again. He knew where she was going. Hell, he even knew when she'd get there.

A furnace on wheels, the black Dodge pickup sponged up the sun. Irina drove with the air conditioner on high, the vents aimed at her face. Mitch, she imagined, did the same.

She smiled at the recollection of that gentle cowboy— calm brown eyes, and an aura of comfort that fit him as well as his Stetson. *He does not doubt himself. Like Charlie, he is wholly self-confident. But Charlie wears his confidence like a badge. Mitch has no such need. It is inside him, and is part of his honor.*

Both were men of virtue: Charlie the proud knight who flaunts his valor; Mitch a man without pretense; both so different, but neither so conceited as to believe himself . . .

. . . never wrong. No matter what the facts, he could never admit that he had made a mistake. If he so much as misadded a column of numbers, the fault lay not in him but in the illegibility of another person's handwriting, a broken gear in an adding machine, the distraction caused by a little girl at play.

Error was easily explained. Its name was Irina.

She would be happier, she thought, if she could be so cheerfully self-assured as Mitch or Charlie. If she did not always have to prove her mettle, if she could lose gracefully, she would be the better for it. But she was her father's child. Like him, she could not blame herself. Like him, she must always blame another. Like him, she blamed . . .

. . . I blame my father for faults that are only my own.

Bad thoughts, and a bad time to be having them. Doubting herself was a luxury she could not afford.

Shaking herself from her reverie—hypnotic introspection triggered by a highway too straight, a countryside too featureless—she wondered what the outdoor temperature was.

One hundred degrees? More? She did not know, knew only that this desert was deadly, and without mercy.

The land bordering the interstate was lifeless pepper and salt. Only distant cliffs relieved its barren hostility; they, sharply lined in crystalline air, were paint pots of ochre, cinnamon, and arsenic green. As for the rest—dusty sage, saguaro cactus in fractal cruciforms, strands of ropy vine with tiny dead leaves—it was a reptile nation, enemy to all that was human.

Her truck shuddered as a sixteen-wheeler roared by her.

She was driving at a steady seventy-five miles an hour; the trucker was rolling at more than ninety. On this, the fastest route west, speed limits were ignored by drivers whose instincts warned them not to linger in a land that did not welcome the presence of man.

The dashboard clock read ten minutes after noon—11:10 in the Mountain time zone. Remaining on this highway any longer was foolish. She'd encountered three roadblocks in as many hours—lean state troopers in peaked hats and gabardine uniforms. One had waved her past. Two had stopped her. May I see your driver's license, ma'am? Certainly. Says here your hair is blonde. It was, but I tired of it and let it grow back natural. You don't sound like you're from these parts. Utah; I am going home. Well, you drive safe, ma'am, you hear? Yes, officer; thank you, officer.

Now a hundred and fifty miles into New Mexico, she should leave the interstate. Back roads would be less closely patrolled, and should danger present itself, finding a hiding place would be easier.

Glancing at the map spread out on the seat beside her, she decided to take the next secondary road, a meandering route north, hill country with towns few and far between.

North. Yes, that made sense. Although she could not say why, her intuition told her that the northern part of the state would be safer than the south. *I shall turn west again once I am past Gallup. After I cross the Arizona border, there is nothing but Navajo villages and empty roads. I will be safer there.*

Her fuel gauge's needle pointed to one-eighth. She'd need to fill the tank before driving into the deserted uplands.

A green sign marked an approaching intersection, State Highway 24, the road she planned to take. A gas pump icon was directly beneath the sign.

She slowed, flicked her turn signal, and exited. A small town clustered at the crossroads, nothing remarkable, wood-fronted and adobe buildings, a handful of shops, a fire station, a small church.

Whenever father was at sea, mother took her to church. Together they would kneel in cathedrals thick with incense. Illuminated by constellations of candles, they prayed beneath gilded icons, chanted ancient hymns, accepted sacraments from priests robed swan-white, gold-threaded patterns woven in their sleeves.

She'd been eleven when he found out. That was the only time she'd ever known him to strike her mother, a light slap really, more rebuke than punishment. Punishment was reserved for Irina.

She averted her eyes, and drove on.

The service station was directly to her right—Arco: AM/PM Market.

She knew the chain—small tidy stores stocked with comfort food, prewrapped sandwiches, and cold drinks. She and Dominik had often bought provisions for their night watch at such places. Dominik . . . she'd always laughed as he gravely compared AM/PM fare to 7-Eleven to Subway, as though he were a critic for *Gourmet* magazine, and she would never smile at his solemn joking again.

Stopping the Dodge beside one of the pumps, she spoke aloud, although no one could hear her. "When my father salutes me, Dominik, it will be your victory too."

Mitch had left a duck-billed hunting cap tucked behind the driver's seat. She pulled it over her head, tucking her long hair out of sight. Entering the blissfully cool store, she handed the clerk one of Charlie's hundred-dollar bills. "A hundred on number five," she said, using America's cryptic commercial shorthand.

The clerk, a bored teenager in a checkered shirt, whisked the bill through a counterfeit detector. "Pump number five" is all he said, and he said it like he'd spoken the words a million times before.

Outdoors again, she topped off her tank with ninety-two octane premium. It seemed only right to pamper Mitch's truck. She thought he would approve.

The pump chimed full.

Back in the store, she idled down an aisle looking at cans of Pringles, bags of Lay's, packages of Oreos. A cooler filled the store's entire back wall—rows of overstuffed sandwiches and bottled beverages barely visible through glass wet with condensation.

"Forty on pump six."

Irina froze at a voice she'd heard before.

"You handle the gas. I'll get us some rations."

"Miller's fine just as long as it ain't lite."

Her every nerve ending screamed.

"No beer during duty hours. Cobra would have our balls."

Two of them, muscles rippling beneath white T-shirts, necks like oxen, steroidal stupidity in their eyes. The first to speak . . . he was the one . . . the one in the Hilton lobby who smirked, *I say we make the bitch take it every way she can, and all at once. Three on one is always fun.* "Here's another twenty," he grunted to the clerk, pulling a crisp bill from a white envelope. "Ring it up to cover the chow."

The clerk slid the bill into the counterfeit reader. "Sixty on number six." His boredom was beyond imagining.

As his partner walked out the door, the second man started down the aisle, rolling his hips with cock-of-the-walk insolence. She faced him straight on. There was no alternative. Seen from the front, her heavily made-up face might conceal her identity. But in profile . . . ?

In profile, the makeup would not matter. He'd recognize the line of her forehead, the curve of her jaw, the tilt of her nose—they'd have photos from every angle, and he'd know her in an instant.

The stolen Marriott towels she'd wrapped around her stomach to alter her waistline would not fool him. Nothing would fool him. If she turned sideways, he'd have her.

Snapping up a bag of tortilla chips and a package of chewing gum, she walked toward the exit. He bully-boyed forward, a man who would not step aside, no not at all, he'd make her push past him, rub against him, shrink but not escape his touch.

Her breasts brushed his upper arm. She caught the flicker of his smirk. As she slid by, his hand went down, caressing her buttocks. She fought the urge to lash out. It was better to let him have his sordid pleasure than to provoke a man like this.

Past him now, she hurried to the checkout stand. "Pump five," she said, shoving her chips and gum across the counter. The boy didn't seem to hear her. His face was tense, and his eyes blinked nervously at his counterfeit detector. "Pump five. Could I have my change now?" He jerked, muttered something she couldn't hear, and rang up her sale.

He gave her ten dollars too much in change. Irina thrust the money into her shoulder bag and fled.

A white GMC Sierra was parked directly behind her truck. Its mud flaps displayed the silvered silhouette of a nude woman. Pulling her cap as if adjusting it, Irina walked toward Mitch's truck. The man pumping gas did not look up.

Even though the air conditioning had been off for fewer than five minutes, the Dodge's interior was scorching. She flinched as she gripped the wheel. Turning the ignition, she drove—neither fast nor slow—away from the station.

She should have realized that a skilled mercenary like Schmidt would never concentrate his forces. Some, but far from all, of his minions followed Charlie's BMW on a wild-goose chase to Las Vegas. Others would disperse all across the countryside.

How many men were under Schmidt's command? Charlie had said more than five hundred. If they traveled in teams of two, at least two hundred and fifty patrols were searching for her. *Two hundred and fifty!*

Fear is not cowardliness. Encountering those two killers in the store had frightened her. But she could not—would not—fall into panic's eager grasp. Victory favors only those who master fear.

She assessed her position with ruthless objectivity. Outnumbered and on her own, she would never survive a confrontation. If she could not outfight her opponents, then she must outwit them.

What would *they* do? What was *their* best strategy for capturing her in this wasteland of too few roads?

Short patrols, she thought. *Each team will be assigned a thin stretch of highway, perhaps no more than fifty miles. They will cruise abbreviated circuits, weaving a web of watchfulness, no team more than a hundred miles from the other, on average all teams closer than that.*

With two hundred and fifty cars, they'd cover every road between here and California. She'd never pass unseen.

A chilling thought: she must have been seen already—probably more than once. Her dyed hair and thick makeup had been sufficient to fool a driver glancing out his window at an oncoming pickup truck. Blind luck: no one had time to study her features.

Would her good fortune last? Perhaps for a few more hours. Certainly not for the two days it would take her to reach the one place where safety was certain: San Francisco and the West Coast *Rezidentura.* Eighteen hours of driving, every minute of it a peril, and she would need to stop and rest and . . .

Something white.

In her rearview mirror, a white vehicle closing fast.

A GMC Sierra.

Wary of highway patrolmen and their radar guns, she'd kept within the speed limit—sixty miles per hour on this two-lane blacktop. The Sierra was doing eighty.

A straight and empty highway lay ahead. No side roads, no places of concealment, naked desert all around.

A trickle of sweat burned into the corner of her eye.

She couldn't outrun them. Schmidt's trucks might look ordinary, but no mercenary's vehicle would carry an ordinary engine beneath its hood.

The Sierra grew larger in her mirror, its driver and passenger shadows without face or feature. She imagined their wet smiles. She weighed her alternatives.

She'd scored well in her vehicular combat course. But they would be as well trained as she. If she tried to force them off the road, they would know how to counter her attack. It would be an equal match, and therefore a risky one. *Engaging an opponent who is your equal is the last resort. Never engage without an advantage.*

Now clearly seen, mere meters from her bumper, one wore sunglasses, the other did not.

Irina snapped open her handbag. The Tokarev—old and black and ugly—was comforting in her grip.

The mercenaries accelerated into the oncoming traffic lane. There was no oncoming traffic. On this road, only the hunter and the hunted drove.

Right-handed she was a superb marksman. Ninety-three

out of one hundred shots in the center ring. Left-handed was another story. She'd never mastered ambidextrous shooting.

Tense but confident, she shifted the pistol to her left hand. A fusillade, the trigger snapped fifteen times to empty a fifteen-round magazine, precision was irrelevant, fill the air with enough bullets and her target would be hit. At this speed a disabling shot was as good as a killing one, and a wounded enemy would die in flames.

She glanced left. The Sierra was almost by her side. Keeping a finger loosely on the trigger, she rested her thumb against the Dodge's window control. She inhaled, a shooter's breath to be expelled halfway before firing.

She depressed the window button. Hot wind flooded the Dodge's cabin.

Any moment now, in just a second, the Sierra's driver would swerve, aiming his bumper at her fender. That time would be her time. As he began his run-up to ramming her, he'd be at his most vulnerable as she emptied her pistol, raking fifteen rounds into the face of a . . .

The Sierra raced by, swinging back into the right lane, and gaining speed.

The distance between the two trucks grew. They hadn't recognized her. They didn't know. She was safe.

Her hands shook as she returned the pistol to her bag. She'd been wound tight as a spring, ready for the moment and perhaps even looking forward to it. That nothing happened was a relief, but also—the admission worried her—a disappointment. Was she so hard a person that escaping a killing fight . . . ?

A quarter of a mile ahead the Sierra fishtailed onto the shoulder. The driver spun a loop back onto the road, accelerating toward her.

No time to retrieve the Tokarev, Irina held the wheel with

both hands, fingers so tight that veins rose on the back of her hand.

The Sierra whipped past. The driver—she saw him clearly—peered at her intently.

Brakes shrieked. She glanced over her shoulder. The white Sierra slid sideways in a moonshiner's turn.

They'd seen her in profile. They knew who she was.

She locked her leg, standing on the gas pedal. The speedometer needle ticked up. Seventy. Eighty. Ninety . . .

The Sierra was faster. She'd not outrun it.

. . . one hundred and ten. One hundred and twenty. Her tachometer crossed the red line. The Dodge's engine howled. One hundred and twenty-five miles per hour, but no faster than that.

The steering felt loose as though her front wheels were lofting off the road. Mitch's truck was not meant for this sort of speed. Neither was the Sierra, although modifications surely had been made.

It was close, so close. She could see both men's faces, their teeth shining white between pulled-back lips.

They wouldn't try to ram her fender. At high speed, a tap on her rear bumper was all they needed. They—custom engine and custom suspension—would not lose control. She would.

There was nothing she could do. The Dodge would go no faster. Pulling on to the graveled shoulder was suicide. Braking would slam them into her rear, and send her spinning out of control.

Her only chance: decelerate slowly, be ready with the Tokarev when they came.

Two guns against one. Not a contest of equals. She steeled herself. Equals or not, she was as deadly as they, and would not sell herself cheap.

"Pull over!" A voice through a loudspeaker. The piercing whoop of a siren. "Slow down and pull over!" Whiteness behind a white Sierra, white striped green, a row of colored lights across the roof.

"Both of you dragsters. This is your last warning. Pull your vehicles off the road."

The men in the Sierra were so near that she shrank at their fury. The driver's eyes bulged, a moment of indecision. Then a clenching of the jaw, a bunching of shoulder muscles. He'd made his choice. No hick cop was going to stop him now. He had her, and he was going to take her, and fuck you, Deputy Dawg.

He swerved into the left lane. Irina caught a glimpse of the highway patrol car, a single officer, his features grimly resolute.

The Sierra exploded forward. He planned to ram her after all. She glanced left, seeing the driver's meaty arms ripple as he readied himself to turn the wheel.

Wait for it! Wait!

His right hand edged up the steering wheel. His grip tightened. He said something to the man in the passenger seat.

Now!

Irina slammed on her brakes. The Sierra sliced in front of her, missing her bumper by inches, juttering off the road, over the shoulder, into the sandy desert. The highway patrol car screamed into a slide. Irina jerked her foot from the brake pedal, kicking the gas pedal hard. The Sierra spewed dirt into the air. She wove blindly through an alkaline fog, pumping the brake, slowing the Dodge. She heard the slap of pistol fire behind her, nails hammered into concrete, hard and flat, five shots fired, then six.

The Dodge jolted to a stop. Snatching up her Tokarev,

Irina sprang from the truck. She bent low, running into the gritty dust cloud, two hands gripping her weapon, ready to fire at the first target that presented itself.

Wind whisked dirty plumes across the highway, impenetrable haze becoming translucent smoke.

Both of the Sierra's doors were open. One man sprawled limp on dry earth, his head twisted in a sickening angle. A second, still alive, slumped in the driver's seat. Blood pulsed from his chest, poured to the ground, hissed as it puddled onto hot sand.

A highway patrolman with a pistol in his hand staggered drunkenly up the road. He stumbled, and fell. His legs drummed on asphalt as he died.

The Sierra's driver, the man vomiting blood from an open wound, held something in his hand, fumbled with a console on the dashboard.

Irina ran.

He twisted a knob, depressed a switch, lifted the radio to his mouth. Red spittle bubbled from his lips as he tried to speak.

Well beyond conventional range, he was a difficult target. Irina stood like a statue, quarter turn right, knees flexed, elbows locked, left hand cupping the right, finger gentle on the trigger, deep breath in, then exhale half the air, and squeeze gently, ever so softly . . .

She killed her first man cleanly, and with a single shot. She took no comfort in the fact that he was already dying, and was sickened at the pride she took in her marksmanship.

Glowering, Sam strode toward his office. Junior staffers scuttled from his path.

Allergies raging, he felt as if his world was tilted two martinis into the evening, and the itch that needed scratching most was the one behind his eyes. Charlie's damned cats had left his sinuses vulnerable to every virus in Washington.

Jesus. What could be worse?

Easy answer: the Chinese. They'd caught wind of trouble with Whirlwind. Now they were on the warpath, and who needs this grief? Calming them down had been tough. Keeping them that way would be tougher.

He slammed his office door, strode to his desk, and dry-swallowed a Claritin.

Sitting down, he glanced at the stack of messages waiting for him. He really wasn't in the mood to deal with them. All he wanted to do was curl up in bed and sleep. Reluctantly, he flipped through the green slips. The senator from Oklahoma. Dr. Sangin Wing. The secretary of the treasury. Dr. Sangin Wing. The chairman of the Senate Intelligence Committee. Mr. Cobra. Dr. Sangin Wing . . .

Oh hell!

Mr. Cobra. 12:05.
Asks you to call his service on the secure line.
Says you know the number.

Sam reluctantly picked up his phone, hesitantly tapping in both Schmidt's number and the eight digit password that gave him access to the South African's messages, said messages always being accompanied by some opera singer's emotional counterpoint to a serenely unemotional voice.

Good afternoon, Samuel.

This voice mail system is secure. I intend to leave you progress reports every three hours. Do try to review them in a timely manner. If you need to speak to me in person, you have my cell-phone number.

Regarding our status, at the moment I am nearing the Arizona border, following Charles's ostentatious vehicle. His planned destination is unclear. Tucson, perhaps. Possibly Phoenix. No doubt he has a specific objective in mind. I expect that as we move closer to that objective, he will attempt to elude me. You may have every confidence that he will not.

We do not yet have a sighting of Miss Kolodenkova. I remain certain that she is headed west, not, as the always obtuse FBI imagines, east. Accordingly, I have every road and highway between here and California under surveillance. She'll not slip through my net.

Now, with regret, I have disturbing news. When I accepted this mission, you advised me that you'd given Charles a tidy sum in marked, sequentially numbered bills. I assume either you or the FBI broadcast an alert regarding them to the local law enforcement lads.

Where an ordinary adversary is involved, I would deem this to be a clever ploy.

However, Charles seems to have turned the tables on you. Or rather on me. He has played an irksome prank with your bills. Somehow he managed to get them into the hands of my team. The consequence? Six of my men used that money to pay for food or fuel. Four of them are, at this present time, under lock and key. Two are dead.

Naturally enough, a policeman is as well. When uniformed law enforcement officers intrude in matters beyond their competence, the outcome is predictable.

However, in the instant case, because my subordinates are armed—at your direct command—with small-caliber weapons, two good warriors died. A risk of the trade, to be sure, but nevertheless vexatious.

Please understand the gravity of the situation. A policeman was killed by two men, since deceased, who passed marked currency to a momentarily attentive gas station clerk. Four other men carrying the same currency have been taken into custody. These four were arrested in trucks modified in ways similar to that driven by the late deceased, and bearing similar equipment. Well, you can imagine the furor. County sheriffs, town constables, highway patrolmen, and others of that amateurish ilk are behaving in a counterproductive fashion. Indeed, their intervention threatens to disrupt my mission.

Sort this out for me, Samuel. It is a distraction I do not need.

Finally, I wish you to reconsider your orders that Charles not be harmed. At the moment, both I and my people are in a punitive frame of mind. Once Kolodenkova is located, I genuinely believe it would be in everyone's best interest if we are permitted to neutralize him in a manner that insures he plays no more of his insufferable practical jokes.

Do give this matter some thought, and call me at your earliest convenience.

Swallowing another Claritin tablet, Sam laid a yellow legal pad on his desk. He always found it easier to reach a difficult decision if he prepared a ledger listing the pluses and minuses of a given course of action.

Uncapping his Mont Blanc pen, he started to write. Five minutes later, he leaned back in his chair and studied the surprising outcome of his analysis. The number of minuses were fewer than he'd expected.

Only one really mattered.

That fucking Internet data vault.

If someone could find it and crack it, Charlie was Schmidt's meat.

6

Air Charlie

Wednesday, July 22.
0915 Hours Pacific Time

San Francisco! Charlie loved the place.

Alarmingly pierced Goth girls, hollow-chested Lawrence Ferlinghetti wannabes, graceful street jugglers, in-your-face gay activists, tie-dyed sixty-year-old hippies who remembered the summer of love as if it were only yesterday (and, the by-product of too many drugs, probably thought it was), and the cooks—*yeah!*—the cooks, caring for each dish and every serving as if it were a newborn child. Hey, you! Food is fun. If you aren't here to enjoy it, the chef politely recommends you go back to New Yawk.

Mary came here for the opera. Not for her the ponderous gaudy of New York's Metropolitan. Every winter, she'd be in San Francisco. Charlie, no matter what he was doing, managed to join her. Two seats on the aisle and four hours time-travel to a more innocent era when heroes were gallant, villains wore capes, and heroines were e'er willing to Die For Love.

These are good things to believe in, Mary said. Believing in Romance with a capital R makes us human.

Except at the last—she in the hospital, he in prison—they'd visited San Francisco every year of their married life. But that city was only their starting point. They roamed all up and down the state, overnighting in B&Bs, four-star resorts, and anonymous little back-road motels that provoked Mary to more than ordinary lasciviousness. All in all, they'd behaved liked two overgrown kids, playing hooky, no adults to deny their whims.

Toward the end—those final years before whispering death wooed her for his bride—they found themselves returning to one place, a single spot that had become their personal Shangri-la. Love at first sight, they instantly knew it for their destiny. Turn off the main highway; drive down a prosaic two-lane road; pass quiet farmlands and lush coastal groves. Then the sudden glory of a Pacific sunset, the sky liquid gold, infinite beauty, and it struck them to their hearts.

San Carlos do Cabo, a tiny seaside village at the tip of a broad cape. A few hundred delightfully quirky citizens. Victorian houses of lively color. Fields of infinite flowers. A wind off the ocean bearing air that no man had breathed before.

"This," Brigham Young had said, "is the place." Mary said the same. Charlie added, "Damned right."

Land was cheap, at least by California standards; building a good—a perfect—retirement home was affordable; they'd have two fireplaces against the summer fogs, a big broad porch for sunny winter days, an enormous backyard garden for Mary to putter among the flowers she adored, and Charlie would breed fine pedigreed cats, and the world could go to hell because both of them had found what few are given, and would be together always, always smiling, until the end.

A tear beaded at the corner of his eye. Embarrassed, he brushed it away. Life, which is never to be trusted, had different plans for Charlie and Mary McKenzie, and he'd never see San Carlos again.

Pushing aside old memories—the happy ones and the sad—he steered a course through San Francisco's backstreets, circumventing yet another protest march, the city's favorite outdoor sport. Dropping down from Presidio Heights, he wheeled his Hertz Rent-a-Weenie onto the Golden Gate Bridge's feeder road. Traffic was light. He was ahead of schedule.

His plane had arrived at SFO twenty minutes earlier than the flight plan called for; the pilot was a hundred dollars richer for every minute of it.

Charlie trotted across the tarmac. Sledge, well groomed for a change, was waiting for him in the general aviation terminal.

If Sledge had a real name, Charlie didn't know it. No one did. In the subterranean world of computer hackers, you only needed to know that Sledge, short for Sledgehammer, was the man who could crack anything.

He hung out at U.C. Berkeley. Not a student, most definitely not faculty, he was one of those ageless eccentrics found in every university's computer sciences department—a lone gunslinger without title, position, or stipend who nonetheless had his own cubicle, his own hot-rod workstation, and plenty of money for late-night pizza.

"Whadya got, Charlie?" Sledge reserved polite greetings for his equals. As near as Charlie could tell, Sledge acknowledged no equals.

Handing the hacker the floppy he'd filched from Irina,

Charlie answered, "Mission Impossible. This disk will self-destruct in—"

Sledge peered down his nose. "Been there. Done that. Got the T-shirt. When do you want it back?"

"Three hours. Here at the airport."

Aloof and abrupt, the hacker asked, "Ten grand sound about right?"

"Cheap."

"Fine, it'll be fifteen."

Charlie peeled the bills off a roll. "I need the original disk back in pristine condition."

"You think you're playing with kids? Insult me again and it'll cost you twenty." So saying, the hacker dropped both cash and diskette into the pocket of his expensive-looking Norfolk jacket. With only a sneer for a farewell, he spun on the heels of tasseled Bally loafers, and loped away.

Most people didn't like Sledge's style. Charlie could name more personable frogs.

Now across the Golden Gate, through the Waldo Tunnel, and rolling north up Route 101, Charlie recalculated his timetable. Earlier he'd thought he'd need several hours to pry Whirlwind's secrets out of DefCon. However, as he'd settled into the luxuriously appointed cabin of a chartered eleven-passenger Cessna Citation on its way to San Francisco, fragments of an incomplete puzzle fell into place.

A laboratory building with wires woven into its walls? That was the same principle as the Faraday cage Sledge used to safeguard Charlie's illicit Internet connection. Shielded generator shacks? Obviously to protect them from stray electromagnetic weapons' rays. No telephone lines and a radio that couldn't be restored to service for four hours? Yeah, well—set phasers to stun—EM pulses will fry communications gear every time. Dimethyl ether coolant? A Ph.D. materials scientist who wrote his thesis on superconductors?

Ha! It's too easy! Superconductors are the holy grail of computing and telecommunications—the perfect transmitter of electricity. If you want the fastest supercomputer or an information highway of infinite bandwidth, then you need a material through which electrons pass instantaneously with no resistance at all.

But—beam me up, Scotty—all this Star Trek technology has a little problem. Superconductors don't work unless you cool them down to preposterously low temperatures—usually below the temperature of liquid nitrogen, but, theoretically at least, maybe the temperature of liquid ether, same as Irina saw in that lab.

Charlie slumped in his seat, sipping his morning orange juice. At the front of his spacious cabin, a red LED panel displayed flight information.

> **ALTITUDE:** 34500 FEET
> **GROUND SPEED:** 523 KNOTS
> **HEADWINDS:** 15 KNOTS
> **OUTSIDE TEMPERATURE:** -34°C

Bingo!

Puzzle pieces danced together in a waltz of elegant simplicity, each dovetailing with the other, all swirling together in the one way, the only way, in which they could fit. It was pure poetry, and as full of ineluctable joy.

An epiphany, in fact.

There is a pattern that dictates the contour and texture of all things animate and inanimate. To be sure, much is random, and the goddess Eris (latterly known as Lady Luck) rolls her dice. But where chance is, necessity follows, for they are two sides of a single coin. Study necessity's obligations, follow them to their logical conclusion, and there you will find, as Charlie found, that one inevitable pattern that explains so much.

He knew what Whirlwind was. He knew because it could be nothing else.

But there was another mystery, and it was more than a big block of a super-secret superconducting ceramic filched from a no-name New Mexico skunkworks. Browsing through the computer files he'd downloaded the night before, Charlie scented a deeper, darker riddle—perhaps the *true* reason why Sam had been desperate enough to bring him back from disgrace.

The clue? Newspaper stories off the Web. Two dozen of them. They all said the same thing: CHINESE ARREST AMERICAN STUDENT AS SPY.

Ten column inches, sometimes twelve, you've read it all before. It's one of the games the Chinese play. An American citizen of Chinese derivation visits his ancestral homeland; maybe he's an academic on a research trip; maybe he's a businessman overseeing the construction of a factory; maybe he's a journalist or just an ordinary tourist. It doesn't matter. No one takes the trumped-up espionage charges seriously, least of all the Chinese government. It's just their way of sending a message to every expatriate: if you're of Chinese blood, we own you, boy.

Twenty-three-year-old Michael Wing had been in diapers when his father and mother, both students at Cornell, renounced their Chinese citizenship. More than two decades later, he returned to China on a student exchange program. A week later, he was behind bars.

As Charlie studied the digitized newspaper clippings, the hairs on the back of his neck lifted. Something was wrong. Something was missing.

Where the hell was the president's traditional statement of shock, outrage, and dismay? *I personally lament the unwarranted charges laid against a wholly innocent individual, and wish to remind the Chinese government that the United States takes a sovereign interest in the well-being of its citizens, blah, blah, blah*, and it was all on the Executive Office's word-processing system, and they printed it out at least once a year.

But not this time.

Young Michael Wing got busted on February the sixth. In Washington, nobody said a word.

Ditto on February the seventh.

On February the eighth, another two dozen newspaper stories appeared. The Wing kid got sprung. The photos showed him in Hong Kong, smiling for the cameras with his father's arm around him.

Dr. Sangin Wing, who had been speaking at a scientific conference in Tokyo, met his son in Hong Kong, and you bet your ass they caught the next flight home.

What is wrong with this picture?

Never, under no circumstances whatsoever, do defense scientists like Sangin Wing set foot on Chinese soil, that's what's wrong. If they even think about it, large gentlemen in dark suits show up on their doorstep to admonish them.

And another fishy fact: a high muckety-muck, one of the People's Republic's most exalted statesmen, expressed his government's regret for the arrest of Michael Wing.

Regret? Regret!!! The Chinese government never regrets, never apologizes, and never, never, never admits it has done something wrong.

The Beijing spokesman went on to explain that the incident had resulted from a miscommunication among Chinese law enforcement officials, several of whom, he added, would be disciplined for "excessive zeal."

NFW, thought Charlie. *And I don't mean North Fort Worth.*

There should have been an exchange of strongly worded diplomatic messages. There should have been a barrage of presidential press releases. There should have been smug Chinese replies. And there most definitely should have been a show trial. Then, and only then, would the Chinese make that unctuous gesture of benevolent goodwill they'd planned all along, and release their falsely accused, falsely convicted victim.

That was how the game was played. The moves never changed.

Only this time they had. Instead of spending three months in a Chinese dungeon, Michael Wing spent three days.

Somebody bought a get-out-of-jail-free card for the son of Whirlwind's chief scientist.

Charlie wondered what the card cost, and who paid for it. Once he knew that, he'd have a get-out-of-jail-free card of his own.

Twenty-five minutes north of the Golden Gate Bridge, Charlie pulled into DefCon Enterprises' parking lot.

The defense contractor occupied an anonymous, single-story building in San Rafael's low-rent district. Cheap brick and miser's windows, it could have housed an industrial tool maker, a software start-up, a real estate broker. There were a million buildings like it in America, and no one knew what went on inside.

As he pushed open the front door, he checked his watch.

If everything worked the way he hoped, he'd be back on the road in an hour and fifteen minutes.

Being a California company, DefCon did not belittle the chin-tucked redhead, pretty in a desperate way, manning its front desk by assigning her so politically incorrect a job title as "receptionist." Her nameplate informed visitors that Ms. S. M. Jacobson was "Coordinator of Visitor Access."

"I'm here to see your CEO, Max Henkes," Charlie flashed his CIA identification card.

"Do you have an appointment?"

"I'm here to see him *now*." He knew how you did it: leaning forward, squaring your shoulders, narrowing your eyes, whispering in a soft Clint Eastwood voice, are you feeling lucky today, punk?

The coordinator of visitor access was very far from being equipped to deal with Dirty Harry McKenzie. "I'll buzz him and—"

"Tell him the man standing in front of him has even less patience than he has time." Charlie marched six quick steps through the reception room, flung open a door, and strode into DefCon's inner offices.

The usual cube farm. Fluorescent light. Wear-resistant beige carpet. Pastel abstract art spaced at twelve-foot intervals on every wall. Industrial psychologists had concocted the color scheme. Any environment that soothed rats was sure to do the same for office workers.

Charlie followed his nose. Nine times out of ten the head honcho had a corner office—the one with the best view and the least exposure to the sun.

Northeast corner. A small brown sign on a large oak door: Maximilian Henkes. Charlie didn't knock.

Henkes was the big boss, and he looked the part. His skin was evenly tanned, his blonde hair expensively styled, and his waist was as trim as five miles of daily jogging could make it. He wore a robin's egg blue shirt with his initials monogrammed on its French cuffs. Charlie reckoned the tie was from Brioni, and guessed it cost as much as dinner for four at the best restaurant in town.

"He just came in," Henkes said, setting down the phone. "Yes? I'm Max Henkes. What can I do for you, Mr. . . . err—"

"McKenzie," snapped Charlie, flipping his ID card on Henkes's quite empty desk. "Central Intelligence."

"Directorate of Operations," Henkes read with a worried frown. "Deputy director, I see." He pursed his lips, then did his level best to look at ease. Charlie's temporarily restored rank seemed to render him a most pliable man. "Yes. Well, yes. Welcome to DefCon. Can I offer you something to drink? Tea? Mineral water?"

"No, thanks, my time is short." Charlie gave Henkes's office the eye. DefCon's CEO favored stark white—the walls, the carpet, the leather furniture—a poor choice in Charlie's opinion. Poorer still, Henkes's taste in art: monochrome stipple-work portraits of war pilots posed before their aircraft. "Have you been swept recently?"

"Every Friday evening and every Monday morning."

Charlie nodded official, albeit feigned, approval. Same as every other defense contractor, two out of three DefCon employees frittered away their days filling out the mindless bureaucratic reports the government demanded of its suppliers. The only people employed at corporate headquarters were pencil-pushers. No spy worth his salt would bother to burgle or bug a place like this. The secrets were elsewhere.

"Glad to hear it. All right, let's get down to business."

"This is about Whirlwind, I presume?"

"At this point *everything* is about Whirlwind." Charlie let his words hang in the air, waiting for Henkes's reaction.

Henkes's blinked. "I . . . you're here to give me a status report, aren't you?"

A spy's life is a poker game. You don't win by studying your cards; you win by studying your opponent's face. Solemn and slow, Charlie shook his head. "I'm here to ask questions. You're here to answer."

"Uh . . . I, ah, I had a conversation last night with . . . well . . . and he assured me—"

"The national security advisor." The light in Henkes's eyes changed. It was enough to tell Charlie that, yes, Sam had spoken to Henkes. That information was all Charlie needed to begin running his bluff. "Sam told me all about it."

Henkes's head bobbed nervously. Charlie slipped his hand into his pants pocket and flipped a switch. If Max Henkes was a security nut, he'd have sensors in his office capable of detecting the minuscule magnetic field generated by a battery-powered tape recorder. However, Charlie doubted he had, or could even afford, the kind of technology needed to sniff out a solid-state recorder—twelve milliamps of power that tucked digitized sound into high-density CMOS memory.

"Did Sam tell you I signed that contract? As soon as it showed up, I signed it and faxed it straight back to that German—"

"South African?" Charlie appended a faint question mark. If he'd guessed wrong, his inquiring tone gave him an out.

"Whatever. Chap named Schmidt. The Specialist Consulting Group."

Cold reading is easily transformed into hot reading. First you tease the scantiest handful of facts from your victim. Then, you play them back to him. Not recognizing that he himself is the source of everything you know, the sucker will believe you know more than he does.

Charlie cast his hook. "Expensive, aren't they?"

Henkes took the bait. "Five million dollars a day, yes, I'd say that's expensive."

"You get what you pay for." Another intentionally bland remark.

"You mean what *you* pay for. This is going to show up on my next invoice."

Charlie milked Henkes's indiscretion for all it was worth. "Plus the usual markup, I presume."

"Twelve percent on a cost-plus contract. By the way, is there any way you people can speed up processing our bills?"

"Not my department," said Charlie, delighted to have just recorded the sort of statement that inspired Senate investigating committees to bay at the moon. "And not germane to the reason why I'm here."

Henkes leaned forward. "And that would be what, Mr. McKenzie?"

"Dr. Sangin Wing."

Henkes clenched his fists. "Da . . . da . . . damnit, I thought that incident was behind us."

Paydirt! "It's not the sort of thing that's ever behind you. Not really." Charlie was trolling, dragging a line through cloudy water, and not knowing where the fish were.

"I don't see what this has to do with Whir . . . Whirlwind."

The ignorant confuse stuttering with stupidity. Charlie knew better. Stutterers are often smarter than the glibly eloquent. "Maybe nothing, Mr. Henkes. Maybe a great deal."

"Sam sa . . . sa . . . said it was the Russians."

"What Sam didn't say is that the Russians desperately need hard currency. They'll subcontract to anyone willing to pay the price."

Henkes's face showed naked fear. "You mean the Chin . . . Chin . . . Chinese?"

Thank you, Mr. Henkes. I do appreciate knowing you're worried about the Chinese. "Their own agents don't exactly blend into the crowd, do they? Sure, sometimes they can insert a legend—an operative under especially deep cover—into a defense project. But conventional fieldwork? They need a Westerner for that, don't they?"

"But Sam told me, they had prom . . . promised to leave Whirlwind alone."

A promise? From the Chinese? What the blazes is that supposed to mean?

Charlie still knew next to nothing. He framed his next sentence carefully, choosing words that Henkes could misconstrue. "Not everyone keeps their word. People break their promises."

Henkes reddened. "Your pe . . . pe . . . people didn't hold up their end of the bargain? Is that what you're say . . . say . . . saying? That the Chinese hired some Russians to steal Whirlwind because you broke the deal?"

A reciprocal agreement. The White House gave the Chinese something, and the Chinese gave the White House something. Charlie turned both of his palms up, the universal gesture of open candor. "Now I didn't say that, Mr. Henkes."

"But you're imp . . . imp . . . implying it."

"Not at all. I might be implying that Dr. Wing cut a side deal—"

"Bullshit!" No stutter in his voice, Henkes suddenly was furious. "He's your damned man, personally vouched for by the national security advisor!"

Sam? What the hell? Christ, I'm out of my depth here!

"Not that I objected. Dr. Wing is a brilliant scientist. Whirlwind wouldn't have succeeded without him. But more to the point, he hates the Reds, hates them with every bone in his body. Yes, he made a mistake by going to the mainland to recover his son. But, no, he made no deals, promised no promises. I know that, and you know that. How the hell many lie detector tests did you give him anyway?"

For a moment Charlie thought about explaining what an utter crock polygraphs were—a hocus-pocus technology in the same league as perpetual motion machines. Instead, baffled by Sam's personal involvement with Sangin Wing and needing—badly needing—more information, he tried to calm Henkes down. "I apologize. I trust you understand why I had to raise the issue."

Henkes was in no mood for apologies. "If the Chinese are behind this, then the only question you should ask is what promise the White House has broken. I don't know what agreement Sam negotiated. Quite frankly, I didn't want to know and I still don't want to know. The one thing on my mind was getting a vitally important employee out of a dangerous situation."

Nuts! This guy is out of the loop. Whatever is going on, it's between Sam and the goddamned Chinese. "Understood. Consider the matter closed. Now, if you don't mind, I have a few other questions for you."

The world contains few sights as glorious as San Francisco seen from north of the Golden Gate Bridge. Coming out of the Waldo Tunnel, Charlie drove into light like liquid honey, the bridge luminous, a hue such as Tintoretto might have used. Beyond its breathtaking towers lay that white city whose gossip-laureate had immortally nicknamed "Baghdad by the Bay."

Four hours south, Charlie thought. *Not that far a drive. You go down a coast that's God's grandest sculpture, turn onto a little back road, and there you are. There we were. Me and Mary. We'd start out here, and we'd wind up there, and maybe that's what I should do after all. I can afford to move there now. It'll be a fresh start for me, for Carly, and most of all for Jason and Molly. I don't want my grandkids growing up to be Washington brats. By God, once this mess is over, I'm going to buy that seaside ranch Mary and I always talked about.*

Once this mess is over . . .

Well, hell, that was the problem, wasn't it?

Now that he was certain what Whirlwind was—Henkes had unknowingly confirmed Charlie's theory—he knew that Irina Kolodenkova was in a great deal more peril than he'd imagined. In and of itself Whirlwind was worth killing for. Worse yet, he still didn't have a clue as to what else Sam was covering up. All he could say for certain was that whatever it was, it had to be even more dangerous than Whirlwind. *Jesus wept,* he asked himself silently, *what have I gotten myself into?*

Charlie braked to a stop at the toll plaza, passing the booth attendant five dollars. As he pulled away, he flipped open one of Sam's scrambled cell phones. No doubt every law enforcement agency in the country was on the alert for its roamer signal. Charlie didn't want to disappoint them.

Thumbing the On switch, he keyed in Sam's private line.

One ring, then, "Yes."

"Hi-ya, Sam." Charlie eased into the right lane, taking Nineteenth Avenue—a shortcut to the airport.

"Charlie!" No joy in his exclamation. "I've been wondering how you're doing. Have you made any progress? Where are you, anyway?"

"To answer your first question, yes. To answer your second, in San Francisco."

"What!?!" Utter disbelief. Charlie had been hoping for

foaming rage. Oh, well, sooner or later he'd ignite Sam's powder-keg temper. And that's when the useless ape would start making mistakes.

"Pretty close to Golden Gate Park actually."

Confused, Sam muttered, "Schmidt said you were in Arizona."

Charlie felt a happy smile creep across his face. "Hey, Sam, if you send a boy to do a man's job, don't be surprised at the results."

"Why are you in California anyway?" Sam's voice was pitched higher. Ditto Charlie's spirits.

"Interviewing your buddy Max Henkes at DefCon Enterprises."

A low groan, a wounded animal: "How did you find out about DefCon? Just how—"

Come on, Sam, you know you want to go ballistic. Be a good boy and blow your stack. Here, I'll give you a little incentive.
"Irina told me. You know Irina. Nice girl. I like her a lot."

"Kolodenkova? You've got her? Thank God! Good news at last!"

"Good for me at least. We spent the night together." It was a petty thing to say, and thus doubly pleasurable. "At the Airport Marriott. Just up the road from the Hilton Schmidt stayed at. You know, Sam, he really is a bonehead."

"Forget him. Just fucking forget him. Bring me Kolodenkova and—"

"No can do, Sam. I let her go."

Gratifyingly, Sam was propelled past the point of shouting. He could barely whisper. "You're lying."

"No lie. I kid you not." Charlie gunned his rent-a-car through a yellow light, cut across traffic, and wheeled onto Route 280 south. If he pushed it, he could hit the airport in fifteen minutes. He planned to push it. Likewise Sam.

"If you had your hands on that bitch and you cut her loose . . . Fuck! Do you know what I'll do to you? Do you have any idea?"

"Twice, Sam. I had her twice. So to speak. Turned her free both times. But not to worry—there'll be a third time. Although maybe I'll let her go then, too. Maybe not. That's up to you. No, Sam, do not swear at me, do not insult me, and least of all do not make me angry. Making me angry could put me in a vindictive frame of mind. You don't want me in a vindictive frame of mind, Sam. Uh-uh, no. Trust me on this, if you piss me off, to use your very own favorite word, you're fucked."

"You want more money, right? Of course you do. Well, I'm certain we can work something out."

Charlie laughed. He was on a roll, having a grand time. "Hell no! I've got all the money I need!"

Sam spat, "Then what? Tell me. Name your fucking price." He was on the edge, right on the brink, and Charlie could explode him like a toy balloon.

Tempting, mighty tempting.

However, a pleasure postponed is a pleasure doubled. Besides, the only way Charlie could be sure of getting *everything* he wanted was to do it face-to-face. "I will. But not now. Meet me at the Albuquerque airport in . . . oh, adjusting for the differences in time zones . . . meet me at three forty-five local time. If you tell your pilot to put the pedal to the metal, you can make it. But don't be late, Sam. If you're not on the tarmac parked next to Air Charlie—which is a blue and white Citation—at exactly three forty-five P.M., I'm outta there. And you, Sambo, will be left twisting slowly, slowly in the breeze."

So saying, Charlie hit the disconnect button and tossed the cell phone out the window.

Well now, he grinned, *that has well and truly set the cat amongst the pigeons.*

Glancing at his speedometer, Charlie tapped the accelerator. Eighty miles an hour. Safe enough on this particular road, the scenic route to Silicon Valley. The highway patrol didn't even blink unless you were clocking ninety.

Timing was everything now. He had to get airborne fast, had to be on the ground in New Mexico a few minutes before Sam. If he wasn't, his plan wouldn't work.

It was a good plan, or at least he hoped it was. It had only one flaw—Mitch Conroy. Letting Sam know that he, Charlie, was in California was as good as telling Schmidt that the black BMW X5 he was following was a red herring. As soon as Sam's plane was in the air, he'd be on the radio giving the mercenary the reaming of his life. Schmidt would be livid. If he was mad enough, he might take it out on Mitch.

Nah, Schmidt's not that dumb. By now, Johan would be at least three hundred miles from Albuquerque; once Sam called him, his top priority would be getting there ASAP. Yeah, he'd grab Mitch for a quick Q&A session, and yeah, being the sadist he was, he'd probably leave a few bruises. But Schmidt was a pro. He'd understand that Mitch was hired help, an innocent bystander, and he wouldn't waste his time doing serious damage to someone who didn't deserve it.

Charlie turned his thoughts elsewhere. What he wanted now was quiet time—a couple of airborne hours to relax, empty his mind, and sift through the miserably few pieces of information he had about a defense scientist named Sangin Wing. Something wasn't right, more than a single something. The story told by the newspaper downloads didn't cohere; Sam's role was twice the mystery it had been; the whole damned puzzle had blown to smithereens and nothing seemed to fit.

He was missing the heart of the matter. Infuriating, it was

like . . . it was . . . *suppose you've mislaid something important. Suppose you know there are only four or five places you could have put it. Suppose you look in every single one of those places but you can't find it. Nonetheless, you know it's there. It's in the drawer or on the shelf or under the counter, and damnit, it's probably even in plain sight. But you look and you look, and you can't see it for the life of you. Some inexplicable mental blind spot is keeping you from finding what you know is there; and try as hard as you can you just can't remember and the only thing to do is . . .*

Forget about it for a while, then come back afresh.

That's what he'd do on the flight to Albuquerque. He'd reread his downloaded files, then he'd shut his eyes and meditate. Sooner or later he'd see it, because he always did, and that was the one thing he did best of all.

* * *

SAN FRANCISCO INTERNATIONAL AIRPORT
MAIN TERMINAL LEFT LANE
CARGO AND GENERAL AVIATION RIGHT LANE

Sledgehammer was waiting at the private plane boarding area. Charlie didn't like the frog's smirk on the hacker's face. He figured he was about to hear some distasteful news.

"No refunds," Sledge said, handing Charlie a computer disk.

"You damaged it?"

"Don't be ridiculous," Sledge sneered.

"Then what's the problem?"

"Nothing on it, man. It's virgin. You paid me fifteen grand to crack a blank disk."

Charlie blinked, shaking his head with disbelief. "You sure?"

Sledge drew himself straight, mastery addressing amateurishness. "What do you mean am I sure?"

"Sorry. Of course you're sure. Which means . . ." Charlie's mouth broadened. " . . . which means . . ." A smile spread from cheek to cheek.

And he laughed.

He roared and rollicked and guffawed, and could not control himself as he doubled over whooping like a loon, immobilized with hilarity, gasping breathlessly at Irina Kolodenkova's outrageous, monumental, positively epic brazenness.

"You all right, man? Like, are you having an attack or something?"

"No!" It was so diabolically funny he could barely stand. "I mean yes!" She'd flummoxed him like a raw recruit, switching disks, and he'd never noticed. It was beautiful. It was perfect. And he was . . . he was . . .

"Then what are you laughing about? I mean, fifteen grand to scope out a blank disk is not so funny to me. So tell me the joke, man, what am I missing here?"

"What you're missing, Sledge . . ." Another gale of laughter erupted. "What you're missing, my friend," Charlie gasped, "is that I think I'm in love!"

"In my personal estimation," reflected Mr. Schmidt, "A. G. Russell is the finest knife maker in America."

Mitch Conroy watched the mercenary through a single swollen eye. The other was crusted closed with blood. "I've heard that said," he mumbled, his lips bruised and numb.

Not far from Mitch, a portable CD player rested on a rock. Act I of *La Boheme* echoed through the arroyo, Mirella Freni's voice soaring as she sang that she was only a humble seamstress, an ordinary girl nicknamed "Mimi."

"This particular knife," Schmidt continued, "is one of two hundred and fifty, a genuine rarity. Titanium case, one-handed operation, and a damascened blade sharper than a surgeon's scalpel. I've taken a man's hand off with it. Flesh, sinew, and bone—a single stroke. The fingers were still wiggling when it hit the ground."

"I can believe that." Mitch forced himself to nod. It was the best he could manage with his wrists lashed behind a stunted juniper tree, his legs wound tight with towrope.

"The important thing, Mr. Conroy, the very important thing for you to know is that you won't feel it. Not at first. That's how sharp the edge is. It cleaves clean and fast. You don't notice until quite a few seconds later. Then your nerve endings sense something's missing. Neurons fire signals to receptor cells that are no longer there. When they receive no answer, they fire harder. I am told the pain mounts to astonishing levels. Any man who's lost a limb will assure you the agony is quite beyond comprehension."

"There ain't no need for this, Mr. Cobra. I done told you everythin'. Heck, I told you the whole story before you and your boys started whuppin' on me."

(Now Rodolfo sang, the incomparable Domingo as the struggling playwright.) Mercenaries stood at some distance, unmoved by the music, more interested in their cigarettes than anything else.

"So you say, so you say." Cat-like, Schmidt stalked back and forth across loose cobbles. The sun was behind him. Mitch squinted painfully as he watched him prowl. "I suspect you have told the truth. Indeed, I'd assign a high probability to it—ninety-nine percent, shall we say. Alas, that leaves me one percentage point's uncertainty. Under normal circumstances, I'd let so trivial a figure pass. However, these are not normal circumstances. First, you have annoyed me mightily—"

"Ain't nothin' compared to what you've done to me."

Schmidt's voice was level, neutral, carefully modulated to communicate no emotion whatsoever. "You have annoyed me by playing a wicked little prank. You have annoyed me by wasting a considerable amount of my valuable time. You have annoyed me by making sarcastic remarks—"

"That's just my way of speakin'. It don't mean nothin', and there's no insult intended."

"And you have annoyed me by interrupting me. Please do so no longer." Schmidt put his hands on his hips, examining Mitch from behind smoky eyeglasses.

Mitch swallowed hard. "Yes, sir. But can I say something, Mr. Cobra?"

"Certainly." Schmidt waved his hand in a gesture worthy of a king granting a petition to a commoner.

"T'wasn't a prank or a joke or nothin'. Weren't no malice in it at all. Like I said, that McKenzie fellah, he paid me good money to drive his truck. It was just a job that come my way when I needed one bad."

(The seamstress and the playwright stand in a chilly garret, dumbstruck by love at first sight. Their impassioned voices soar as they are drawn into one another's arms.)

"And rewarding employment it was. Twenty-five thousand in cash. A brand-new BMW—I am sorry that it's no longer in pristine condition, but I trust you have insurance—yes? Well, Charles is a generous soul. Suspiciously so. That is my second concern—second to the annoyance you have caused me. My third concern is a wholly understandable apprehension that you have omitted something from your tale, some small and seemingly irrelevant fact that could shed light on the whereabouts of Irina Kolodenkova."

"Sir, I honest-to-god don't know. Last time I saw her was in my house. You say she was in that Marriott with Mr.

McKenzie. Well, I guess I gotta believe you, but I sure didn't know it. I didn't see her, I didn't hear her, I figured she was long gone by then. Everythin' I know about her, I've told you. Told you three or four times now. I just can't think of anythin' else to say."

"Perhaps if I prod your memory something fresh will come to mind, eh? A little something to jolt your system might open up fresh channels of thought, and, behold!, you will recollect some few other facts."

"Mr. Cobra—"

"Ah, listen." Schmidt cupped his hand to his ear. "That sound you hear is an approaching helicopter. It will dust down above this gully in just a few short moments. The pilot's bringing someone quite singular with him, one of those exceptionally few specialists whose skills exceed my own. My most sincere counsel to you, Mr. Conroy, is to tell me everything now. You really and truly do not want this gentleman interrogating you."

"If I could think of one other thing to tell you, I surely would. Let me start over at the beginnin'—"

Pressing a finger to his chin, Schmidt tilted his head. "No, no. That won't do. I shall ask a question or two instead. Minor matters. Small sources of perplexity. Question the first, what kind of a vehicle is Ms. Kolodenkova driving?"

"Can't rightly say. She was tryin' to steal one of them suburban utility buggies when I bumped into her. After she left my house . . . well, hell, I just don't know. I suppose she stole one of the neighbor's cars."

"And your pickup truck? We've checked the DMV computer. You own a black Dodge. Where might that Dodge be at the present time?"

"Probably out at the airport. Like I told you, that Mr. McKenzie and I traded cars. He said he was headin' for the airport, and I'm pretty sure he was 'cause I'm the one who chartered a jet for him."

Behind Mitch, out of his limited field of vision, a helicopter thundered in descent. A gale of dust whipped down the slope of the arroyo. The engine revved then fell silent. Mitch heard the sound of boots sliding down a dry river bank.

And a lilting Irish voice, thickly accented. "Cobra. Good to see ya. And this wee shite all wrapped up beneath the tree, this would be my party favor?"

The voice's owner sidled into view. He was short and paunchy with dark, greased-back hair. Despite the desert heat, he wore a black leather jacket, and his bandy legs were ill disguised by loose blue jeans.

Schmidt glanced from one man to the other. "Mr. Conroy, let me introduce Mr. Keough. He hails from Belfast, and his former employer was the Irish Republican Army."

"Sinn Féin, actually," said the Irishman, bending at the waist and placing a tool chest on the ground.

"A trifling distinction at best. Now understand, Mr. Conroy, that men enlist in the IRA either because they wish an excuse to steal, or because they enjoy hurting people. There are no other reasons. The brotherhood's kitchen serves only those two flavors of soup. I'm sure you can guess which flavor Mr. Keough represents."

(Their duet complete, the orchestra falls to a hush, sweet notes of love, gently played. Mimi and Rodolfo have found their destiny: each was meant only for the other.)

"Ain't gonna serve no purpose to hurt me more."

"Ah, but it will. It will serve to make me happy—although Mr. Keough will be happier still. Unless, of course, you can convince me that you've told me everything you know. Do that, Mr. Conroy, and you are free to go, and will be none the wiser about Mr. Keough's arts."

"I don't reckon. You and all your boys been callin' each other by snake names. Only this fellah you call by his real name. I figure that means once he's through with me, I ain't goin' nowhere."

Schmidt pressed his lips together. It might have been a smile, if he were capable of that. "How unfortunately observant you are." He walked to the left, out of Mitch's sight. "It appears I need to administer a small object lesson in being less attentive to my subordinates, and more attentive to my questions."

Schmidt's hand appeared in front of Mitch's face. It held something. Mitch blinked. Sweat dripped off his forehead and into his one good eye. His vision was blurred and he couldn't quite see . . . but could begin to feel . . . growing, mounting, rising . . . pain that defied belief . . . and the horrifying agony of it jolted up his arm like an electric shock.

Johan Schmidt put Mitch's little finger between the cowboy's lips. "Bite down hard. I'm told it helps with the pain."

Mitch screamed.

"Zippo," said Schmidt, lifting a hand. One of his men tossed him a lighter. He snapped its cover open, spun its wheel, and held the open flame to Mitch's severed joint. "This will cauterize the wound. We can't have you bleeding to death, can we?"

Head turned to the sky, Mitch howled a cry he had not known he had in him.

"You may think the removal of your finger painful. In this you err. You do not know what genuine pain is. The severing of a single digit is not even—metaphorically—an overture. It is merely the orchestra tuning up. The real symphony, Mr. Conroy, begins when Mr. Keough steps to the podium."

(Outside the garret, Rodolfo's friends summon him to the

Cafe Momus. It is Christmas Eve, and he has promised to join them in celebration. With Mimi hugged to his side, he calls out that they should go, that he will catch up later.)

Keough squatted by his toolbox, the lid open. He removed a car battery, a power cord, and an electric drill. Smiling like a child, he said, "Back when I was a young 'un, the provos shot Protestant bastards in the kneecaps. Primitive, would you not say? Bang, and it's over and done, and where's the fun in it? Now we use Black and Decker, and the advantages are numerous, numerous. No wasting valuable ammunition. A man can take his time. And the boyo at the receiving end of the business always finds he has more information in him than he thought he did."

Mitch whimpered.

"A quarter-inch bit, I think. Now where's me Allen spanner, I've got to open up this chuck a bit."

"Sir!" Another voice, a man who called himself Boa. He stood at the top of the arroyo, calling down to Schmidt.

"Not now. I'm busy." Schmidt's tongue whisked across his lips.

"Sir, it's important. I have Cottonmouth on the radio. She says she's found her, found Kolodenkova!"

Schmidt spun. "Where?"

"About ninety miles northeast, sir. The chopper can get you there in thirty minutes."

Leaning forward into Mitch's face, Schmidt showed his teeth. "Well, well, well. It appears that fate has intervened on your behalf, Mr. Conroy. I see no need to squander any more of my time talking to you." He turned toward Keough. "Sorry, old friend, you'll have to put your toys away. But don't feel badly. I'm sure that in roughly half an hour's time you'll be able to put them to good use."

(Singing "Amor, amor," two young lovers leave the stage,

their fading voices hanging in the air as they depart for dinner on a Christmas Eve.)

Schmidt stepped behind the juniper tree to which his prisoner was tied. A single slice of a damascened blade severed the jugular. Mitch watched his blood fountain out from beneath his chin, a wide red geyser that splashed maroon on desert sand. He felt nothing, and was dead before he understood what the caress of Schmidt's knife had done.

Someone asked, "What about the body, sir?"

"Leave it for the coyotes." Schmidt climbed toward the helicopter. "But I'll want the finger for a souvenir."

(Upon one final *"Amor,"* the curtain falls.)

* * *

I'M NOT IN YOUR HURRY

read the bumper sticker on a wheezing Winnebago camper. Agonizingly slow, it sluggishly climbed a twisting back road. Immediately behind, a spa-toned couple in a Porsche Boxster fretted and fumed, the driver darting into the left lane to see if there was room to pass, darting back because there never was.

Irina inched along behind the Boxster.

A cream-colored Silverado pickup truck followed her.

Schmidt's people, she was sure of it. A husky, broad-shouldered man sat at the Silverado's wheel. Irina could see the bulge of his biceps in her rearview mirror. His passenger was a woman, sharp-faced with straight blonde hair. When she moved, her pale green jacket revealed shadowed metal holstered beneath her armpit.

When the Silverado had first pulled behind her, Irina's heart almost stopped. Still shaken by the deaths she'd left behind two hours earlier, she nearly pulled off the road.

If she had, they would have known instantly.

Controlling her fear hadn't been easy. Doing the right thing—the thing she'd rehearsed over and over—was harder still.

Crawling uphill at twenty miles an hour, she'd let her dashboard clock tick off three minutes. Then she'd turned her head slowly so that the two mercenaries could see her profile. She'd smiled at the Silverado's driver and had given him a hopeless shrug, as if to say: these old fogies in the Winnebago are slowing me down too, but what can I do about it?

The driver nodded at her. She'd gotten away with it.

The trick wouldn't have worked in open sunshine. Shadowed inside Mitch's Dodge, she was eight meters from the hunters. If they'd been closer, they would have seen the shape of her nose had been clumsily disguised by a wad of chewing gum across its bridge. However, from a distance and observed through tinted glass, she bore the beaky profile of an English aristocrat.

Now the mercenaries had been behind her for a half hour. The Winnebago had painfully breasted a mountain pass. The road had straightened enough on the downhill run for three cars to pass the lumbering yellow elephant. Out on the flats, another three had managed to speed by.

Then another climb, an endless climb, and there were only four vehicles left in the slow-moving convoy: a Winnebago, a Boxster, Irina's black Dodge pickup truck, and a Silverado the color of vanilla ice cream.

Again the Boxster shot out to pass. The next blind curve was too close. It pulled back in front of Irina.

She kept her eye on the rearview mirror. The Silverado's driver and his passenger exchanged a few words. A water bottle passed hands. The woman stretched. The man rolled his shoulders. And every fifteen minutes, the woman lifted a microphone from its cradle.

Status reports—she was calling in at quarter-hour intervals. The web Schmidt wove was fine indeed.

The road ahead seemed endless. Hairpin curves, less than thirty meters of straightaway, then another switchback. To her right, a narrow shoulder bordered empty air. A hundred vertiginous meters below lay a valley pocked with boulders and tawny hummocks of wild grass. To her left: the chiseled rust orange of a mountain whose slope had been dynamited and jackhammered to make room for a preposterously narrow two-lane blacktop.

No exit. Nothing but curve after endless curve.

Hazy streamers of sand spit across the road. The wind was stiffening, evidence that they were nearing the top.

How far was the summit? A mile at most. Then the road would go downhill. The Boxster would rocket around the Winnebago, and she finally would be able to pass the ponderous camper. If she timed it right, she might be able to leave the Silverado stranded behind, be trapped at twenty miles an hour, while she sped away.

She'd pick the place carefully. She was sure she could do it.

More wind. Her truck rocked in a gust bursting over the ridge.

Something flickered in her rearview mirror. Green. Cloth. The tarpaulin.

The wind lofted its corner. She heard it snap, saw an unfastened rope whip into the air.

The woman in the Silverado turned to the driver, spoke a few terse words, then snatched the microphone from its cradle, pressing it close to her mouth.

It wasn't time for her check-in report. Only minutes had passed since she'd made her last call.

Irina sweated. The sweat was ice.

They'd seen Whirlwind. When the wind lifted its tarpaulin cover, they'd seen it clear as day. A matte-brown ingot a meter wide, a half meter deep. They knew what it looked like. They knew they'd found it.

She twisted her steering wheel left, accelerating into the passing lane. No hope. The next curve was too near. The Boxster's driver—moussed hair, aviator glasses, tailored shirt—looked angrily over his shoulder. She slipped back behind him.

The man in the Silverado fumbled one hand over his head. He was reaching for something . . . for what?

A rifle. He took it from its rack, and laid it across the dashboard.

Turning to him, the woman said something. The man's sole answer was a hard-eyed nod.

Irina asked herself what words had been spoken. The logical . . . the probable . . . scenario was that the woman had radioed her superior—perhaps radioed Schmidt himself. He would have given her an order: don't try to take Irina Kolodenkova on your own; she's trapped in slow traffic on a road from which she cannot exit; stay on her bumper, but do nothing else; a full backup team is on the way.

It made sense. Once Schmidt knew where his prey was, he'd order every available soldier to the scene. He'd make sure that she could not escape, that she could not even hope to escape.

Of course, she thought, *of course that's what Schmidt has done. I know because I reasoned it out, and Charlie would have reasoned it in precisely the same way.* Inexplicably, the memory of Charlie gave her comfort. She held it tight, a shield against her fear.

What else would he say? He would say he is a strategist and long-range thinker, but I am only a tactician who seizes opportunities and makes the most of them. So be it. What tactical opportunities do I have?

The two behind her did not know she'd guessed who they were. There was an advantage in that. Another advantage: the high mountain pass was nearer with each weary minute. Once across it, she might be able to outrun the Silverado.

But running would be futile. Schmidt's army was surely on its way. By now all of them knew the make, model, color, and license of the vehicle she drove. No matter how fast she ran, she'd be dead before dusk.

Irina steered into another hairpin curve, no hope of passing the Winnebago.

The Boxster's driver thought otherwise. He gunned left, flooring his gas pedal. The Porsche's engine was not as spunky as its styling. On a seven percent grade its puniness showed.

It edged past the Winnebago's left. The Winnebago's driver did not slow down, probably could not slow down without stalling. The Boxster's front bumper drew level with the Winnebago's, and it was all happening painfully slowly, and the road curved out of sight, so near, so dangerously near. . . .

A dark blue Chevrolet truck slewed around the curve, straight into the Boxster's path. It pulled a trailer bearing two Arctic Cat all-terrain vehicles, both looking like ugly four-wheeled motorcycles. The Boxster could not pull right without ramming the Winnebago. Instead, its driver whipped left onto the shoulder, his wheel skimming the mountainside. The Chevy slammed on its brakes, blue smoke streaming from its tires. Its trailer whiplashed into the Winnebago's path, out of control.

Tactics. Seize the opportunity. Irina threw her gearshift into neutral.

The Boxster made it by inches, its badly frightened driver weaving as the Chevy slid across the road in a cloud of oily smoke, its trailer clipping the Winnebago's front fender and flipping, sparks everywhere, two Arctic Cats tumbling and rolling, gasoline spilling from their ruptured tanks.

Irina threw open her door.

Metal crumpled. Someone shouted.

She leapt backward from the still-moving truck, landing in a parachutist's crouch, twisting slightly to the left, taking the fall on her shoulder, rolling head over heels like a circus acrobat.

The Chevrolet teetered on the edge of the precipice, its trailer dragging it down.

Pistol in hand, Irina was up and running. Schmidt's gunmen rammed Mitch's truck, hitting it hard enough to trigger their air-bags.

A bullet whined by Irina's ear, a shot from behind. She whirled. The Chevy's driver was leaning out his window, a revolver clenched in a two-handed combat grip.

They too were part of Schmidt's team. They too would die.

She raised her Tokarev, finger to the trigger. The Chevrolet's front end tilted up. The driver screamed a curse. A last, meaningless, slug passed high over Irina's head, and then the shooter, the truck, the ruined trailer were gone, only a shattered railing to mark where they had skidded backward over the cliff.

Irina spun and ran. The Silverado's air-bags deflated. The driver slapped at shiny aluminized fabric. She reached the Silverado's side-panels, and she drew a bead on his head.

Bad shooting conditions. His window was rolled up. Its heavy, laminated glass would deflect the bullet. A ricochet was more likely than a killing shot.

The driver's expression changed to animal stupidity, death's final insult. His face painted a red brushstroke against the glass as he slid down to where the dead men go.

The woman—the passenger—had recovered faster than her partner. She'd tried to shoot over his shoulder. She'd missed.

Irina hurled herself to the ground, rolling under the Silverado as a fusillade of shots shattered its windows. She pulled herself up on the passenger's side, flung open the door, and—muzzle aimed at the woman's throat—whispered, "Drop it."

The woman, still wearing her seatbelt, lashed out with her foot. Irina slammed the door on her ankle. Bone cracked, and the woman shrieked. Opening the door again, Irina seized her enemy's pistol, hurling it over her shoulder.

Sobbing, the woman cradled her broken leg. Her features were contorted with pain, her unfeigned tears sea blue in prismatic sunlight. She wore the sort of long skirt favored by women who are ashamed of their legs; sometimes Irina wore the same, although for different reasons. Still crying, she slid her hands the length of her leg, stretching toward her ankle. Irina whipped her pistol barrel against the woman's temple, then snatched down to her enemy's ankle holster, jerking out a short-barreled automatic.

The pistols—both of them—were small caliber, .25s. Irina was surprised. She'd expected Schmidt's employees to carry nine millimeters or .40s. The rifle that lay across the dead man's lap was equally surprising. It was—and Irina was insulted by the discovery—a short-action Sauer model 202, a small-game gun. *Why?* she asked herself. *Why so light a weapon? An armalite automatic would make sense. Or a Weatherby Magnum. But these? Both the pistols and the rifle are not what a professional would carry. You would have to be very close to kill someone with them—very close, or very good.*

The woman groaned. At first glance she looked to be in

her early thirties. Irina knew better. The telltale signs of skin too diligently cared for told her true age, as did the bitter experience in her eyes.

"I can kill you," Irina said. "Or I can give you a chance. Which shall it be?" Was that true? Could she really kill in cold blood? Irina did not know.

"What chance?"

"Reach over, reach slowly, and put the gearshift in reverse."

The Silverado's engine still rumbled. The woman shifted gears. The truck lurched away from Mitch's Dodge.

"Now what?"

"Pray that your seatbelt holds."

The woman's eyes goggled. She shouted, "No!" as the Silverado's rear wheels jolted over the edge of the road. Irina stepped away. The truck rolled backward, down a drop the length of a soccer field. It bounced, somersaulted, slid sideways upside down. Irina tasted her own blood, a lip bitten too hard.

"My God." He was small, white-haired, and freckled with age. "My God, what's going on here?" He inched forward nervously, tiny steps in orthopedic shoes, a toy poodle of a man.

His wife, blue-tinted hair and a termagant's face, stood by the Winnebago's rear. "You keep away from her, Peter. You just stand back and let her get on with her business."

"They were shooting at you. I saw it. The folks who came around the curve. The people in that truck behind you. Gunmen. Shooters. And now they're gone. Gone all the way to the bottom. My God."

Irina lowered the Dodge's back gate, wrestling the Whirlwind ingot off the truck bed. "You," she said to the woman, "what's your name?"

"None of your business."

The man said, "Patricia. She's my wife. I'm Peter. We're retired. We're touring the country. We don't want any trouble."

"Patricia, open your camper's back door."

"When hell freezes over."

"Pat, do what she says. She's got a gun."

"I do. Please do not make me use it."

Patricia wrenched the door wide, then moved angrily to the side. Irina carried her heavy brown secret to the Winnebago, shoving it firmly in the back. Once it was safely out of sight, she returned to her truck for her overnight bag, and for the roll of duct tape that had already served her well.

"Peter, I will tie you up and put you in the back. Your wife will ride up front with me. If you cooperate, you will not be hurt."

"I don't give a damn what you do to him. He's insured."

Irina shut her eyes. *Is there nothing in my life that will be easy?*

"Change of plan. Peter, you shall be up front with me, hands tied. Patricia, come over here, I will tape you so you cannot move."

"That'll be the day."

"Your mouth too."

"Young lady, you can just—"

Irina snapped off a shot, muzzle aimed three feet to the left of Patricia's feet. Patricia folded limply to the ground. Irina sighed with relief. So did Peter.

Patricia was mummified with duct tape in the Winnebago's back. Peter, who'd asked permission to urinate before she tied his hands, was in the front seat.

Ready for any contingency, the two kept a five-gallon jerrican of gasoline strapped to the back of their mobile retirement home. Irina splashed it liberally over Mitch's Dodge. Putting the truck in low gear, she turned the wheel toward the cliff edge. As she jumped, she flipped a lit match into the cabin. Flames boiled through the open door. It did not explode until it shattered at the bottom of the precipice.

No one could descend that slope without ropes. The valley beneath was too narrow for a helicopter. It would take Schmidt and his men hours to make their way down, sift through fiery rubble, and discover that neither she nor Whirlwind was in the wreckage.

Better still, the fire blazed high, thick smoke billowing in an ever-mounting cloud. Rangers would see it, and firemen and state troopers. Would they let a civilian like Schmidt interfere with their rescue efforts—and later, their investigation?

Johan Schmidt was going to be a frustrated man.

Tactician, she thought. *That's what I am. I should be proud.* Then another thought. Unbidden. Horrible. *You have done well, daughter, you have done what I would do.*

Unable to stop herself, Irina Kolodenkova, murderer of many, doubled over vomiting.

Pain chewed at Sam's sinuses. As his plane descended, air pressure drove phlegm and agony into his Eustachian tubes. He swallowed hard to clear the blocked passages. No success. His inner ears felt ready to explode.

Cursing cats, the unquestionable source of his suffering, he shut his eyes and tried to concentrate on the problem at hand: Charlie McKenzie in possession of a videotape that could—that would—spell the end of Sam's career.

Best case scenario: if the media found out about Sam's role in the Kahlid Hassan debacle, he'd become a political pariah, lucky if he could land a job as lobbyist for the North American Man-Boy Love Association.

Worst-case scenario: jail time, hard time, and plenty of it.

Which was unfair. He'd been drinking. His judgement was impaired. The worst you could say was that he'd misconstrued—that was the word, "misconstrued"—the president's wishes. It could have happened to anyone. After all, the chief wasn't the most articulate man in the world.

"This is a disgrace, Sam. I simply cannot believe the jury found that man not guilty!"

"New Yorkers. What do you expect?"

"There are plenty of countries where things like this never would have happened—where things like this never would have made it as far as a courtroom."

"Wouldn't have happened in Russia. Not in China either. And Israel? Hell, the prime minister calls the Shin Bet, and—bang!—case closed. Likewise the coffin."

"Damnit, Sam, my predecessors had a lot more leeway in these situations than I do. They used . . . oh, what's his name . . . you've brought him to my breakfast briefings. McKenna? McKinley? Something like that."

"McKenzie. His name is Charlie McKenzie."

"Right, that's who I mean."

So who could blame me for misconstruing the president's wishes? Shit, it sounded like he wanted that fucking camel jockey iced. Turns out I was wrong. I admit it. Anyone can make a mistake. Everybody understands that.

Except Charlie. Charlie wasn't a man who forgave and forgot.

Sooner or later he's going to blow the whistle on me. So this should be an easy decision, right? Choose one from column A or one from column B. Either McKenzie goes or I do. No contest, and I should have had him taken care of two years ago.

The pilot's voice came over the intercom: "We have begun our approach to the Albuquerque airport. Passengers please return your stewardesses to the upright position." Sam's eyes popped open. "That boy's fired," he growled to no one in particular.

He frowned out the window at Albuquerque's shoe-leather landscape, Sandia Mountains crouched to the east, two inadequate highways crossing in the center of town, and traffic—as usual—backed up for miles.

Wheels touched the runway. The engine reversed. Sam's jet, an Agency Falcon compliments of Claude, slowed, taxiing toward the general aviation terminal. A ground crew from Kirtland AFB was already trotting forward to service the VIP plane.

Charlie's white and blue Citation was parked off to the left. Charlie himself was standing in the hatch. As Sam's plane braked to a halt, the damned old dinosaur walked down the stairs and onto the tarmac. No surprise, he wasn't limping.

Unfastening his seatbelt, Sam waved two secret service agents out of sight, then stepped through the open door. He forced himself to smile. Being from Washington, he'd had lots of practice. "Charlie, come on up. I'll pour you a drink."

Standing a wing's length from Sam's plane, Charlie shook his head. "No, Sam, I think it would be better if you came over to my plane. Less probability of bugs. No probability of armed goons hiding in the toilet."

Sam laughed. He'd had plenty of practice at that too. "Of course I have bodyguards. They come with the territory. But I don't have any recording equipment. And I can assure you my bar is better stocked than yours. Come on, Charlie, let's try to be friends."

Charlie's eyes went into that damned mule-headed squint of his—the one that said: *do it my way or else!* "Sam, I don't have time for games. Haul your pudgy butt over to my plane."

Sam felt his blood rise. Doubtless that was what his antagonist wanted. "I don't take orders from you, Charlie. In this country, I only take orders from one man."

Graceful as Fred Astaire, smooth and fluid in every gesture, Charlie swept a Smith & Wesson .40 caliber automatic from behind his back, took aim at Sam's tires, and emptied a fifteen-round clip. Rubber shredded, air percussed, the plane sagged left. Jacking out the magazine and slapping in a new one, he frowned. "I don't want to go to your plane, Sam. Your plane is broken."

"Jesus!" Sam was frozen with shock. "You are totally fucking insane."

Charlie drew a bead on an underwing fuel tank. "In fact, your plane looks unsafe. It might catch fire any second now."

Sam cursed himself. The secret to conducting a successful negotiation was to let your opponent win the first point—a token freebie to make the other party feel good. Waving off a clutch of Air Force technicians and ordering his bodyguard to stay put, Sam hustled down the stairs. *All right, McKenzie,* he thought. *As long as you've got that tape, we'll do it your way. But once I've got my hands on it, the terms of our contract will be subject to renegotiation.*

Charlie didn't holster his pistol until Sam was safely inside the Citation, the hatch securely latched.

Taking a seat toward the front of the plane, Sam looked daggers as Charlie toyed with his notebook computer. He seemed to be tapping into a wireless Internet connection—what did they call it? Wi-Fi or something? Who knew? Who cared? He snapped, "Can I get a drink in this rent-a-wreck?" instantly regretting the exasperation in his voice.

"The bar's at the back. Fix me a gin and tonic while

you're at it." Now Charlie was tweaking some sort of green computer mouse left and right.

Grudgingly, although not showing it, Sam slouched to the drinks cabinet, poured himself an amber tumbler of Laphroaig and, for Charlie, a G&T that was more T than anything else. He returned to the front of the plane, slapping Charlie's drink in front of him. "Okay, Charlie, let's talk."

Charlie tapped a few computer keys, then took a seat across the aisle. "Okay, let's."

"You first." *Oh hell, the sonofabitch is smirking.*

"Gladly. I know everything. Whirlwind, DefCon, Dr. Sangin Wing. All of it."

"Bullshit." Charlie started to make a comeback. Shaking his head with artful sorrow, Sam cut him off. "Charlie, do you think I'm an amateur? Come on, give me some credit. I know how your little con game works. You have a pissant collection of discombobulated factoids. You dribble them out one by one. The sucker sees a few crumbs and thinks you have the cake. So he starts spilling his guts. Every indiscreet word he drops, you pick up and throw back at him. Then, by God, the poor bastard is convinced you know even more than he does. Right, Charlie? That's the scam you're trying to run on me, isn't it?"

Smiling, Charlie opened his palms wide. "Ya got me, officer! Guilty as charged." Then he laughed. "Or I would be if I didn't know that Whirlwind is a superconducting material that activates at, oh, probably around minus twenty or thirty degrees Celsius. That's the temperature aircraft encounter above thirty thousand feet. By aircraft I mean fighter bombers, of course. So tell me, Sam, is this a crumb or is it a cake?"

Sam felt his stomach sink. "Keep going."

"Big problem at the Department of Defense. A while

back—at the end of the last administration if I remember correctly—the British discovered they could use modified cellular radio signals to detect Stealth aircraft. Siemens and BAe Systems are building prototypes. Call it 'Celldar.' Of course you guys kept the story out of the press. After all, you had the Viper coming up for appropriation, and didn't want to jeopardize yet another overpriced weapons boondoggle. However, the truth of the matter is that any country with the infrastructure and the engineering smarts can spot Stealth planes. That's why you need something new, something better. You need Stealth Two, the next generation, and that's what Whirlwind is."

Sam nodded, praying silently that all Charlie knew was what he'd just said.

The Lord wasn't listening.

"Right now, a Stealth bomber works its magic mostly because of its geometry and because the plane is coated with a special polymer. That's okay, but it isn't perfect. If the enemy tunes his radar just right or uses the cell phone gimmick, he can lock an antiaircraft missile on your tailpipe. But suppose you armored your bomber with a superconductor. Ah-ha! Different story. That *would* work perfectly. The radar signal would zip in one end and out the other. Your plane would be totally transparent. From an electrical standpoint, shielding a plane with a superconductor is the very real world equivalent of a Klingon cloaking device, and thank you very much, Captain James Tiberius Kirk. Right, Sam? Am I right?"

"You're right." Sam had come to one of those extremely rare moments in his life when truth was the only option. He didn't like the experience. "We call it 'S2'—S-Squared, Super-Stealth."

"I bet you call it super for another reason—superconductors. Interesting thing about that stuff—it's not only invisible to radar, it's also immune to EM warfare, to high-energy electromagnetic weapons. I think we've already established that the Department of Defense is hot to trot with EM. Or it would be if it weren't for the ugly fact that there's no way of predicting how a death ray will propagate once you zap it into the skies. Big problem there. Fire an EM microwave cannon and you're as likely to toast your own aircraft as the enemy's." Charlie grinned a Cheshire cat's grin. "How am I doing, Sam? So far so good? This is one hundred percent cake I'm feeding you, right, no crumbs at all?"

Sam wanted to grind his teeth. "Nice try, Charlie. Don't expect me to confirm a word of this . . . this *hypothesis* of yours."

"It's no hypothesis, and you know it. Coat your warcraft with a superconductor, and you've got a squadron that is not only invisible to the enemy but that also can burn the bad guys' planes out of the skies without risking any harm to themselves."

Sam forced himself to keep his mouth closed. He didn't intend to give the bastard an inch.

"So, Sambo, am I right or am I right? These are not little factoids. This is the straight scoop on a major scientific breakthrough. Just like I said, I know it all. Hell, I'm even willing to bet that the Whirlwind material—probably a stable fluoroargenate doped with quantum dot crystals—works because you've got buckyball nanotubes woven through it to act as waveguides."

Stunned, Sam blurted, "How did you find that out? Damnit, that information is so highly restricted—" Realizing he'd been outmaneuvered, Sam snapped his mouth closed in midsentence.

Charlie leered. "I didn't find out until just this very second, for which you have my undying gratitude. Oh, don't look at me like that, Sam. I was pretty sure I'd figured it out. All you did was confirm it for me."

"You're just guessing."

"Sorry, Sam, but I *do not* guess. What I do is Dumpster-dive in the data, then extrapolate and deduce. Want to know what I extrapolated from? I'll tell you: Dr. Sangin Wing's Ph.D. thesis was on superconductors. I've got a copy on my computer. Guess what its title is? 'Low Temperature Properties of Buckminsterfullerines.'"

Sam felt a red moon rising. His temper was up, a rumbling in the beast's throat, claws scraping at the bars. Unleashing that hungry predator, letting it freely feast and glut and gorge would feel good, damned good, as good as sex, and maybe better. But he didn't dare. It was exactly what Charlie wanted: Sam ranting and raging and saying things he shouldn't. Nonetheless hard words were irresistible, a little hors d'oeuvre to feed an inner animal. "Goddamn you to hell!"

"Not likely. I'm on the side of the angels. In fact, Sam, for once in our lives we both might be. I know as well as you do that if an enemy gets his hands on your Super-Stealth material—and my bet is that the ingot Kolodenkova swiped is a trial run of a compound that's damned difficult to manufacture—then he'd be able to leapfrog a decade's worth of scientific research. He wouldn't catch up with us, but he'd be a lot closer. To catch up, he'd need Kolodenkova's computer disk." Charlie pulled a beige square out of his pocket. "This disk." Sam snatched at it. Charlie laughed and put it out of sight. "Uh-huh. I thought so. This has got all the good stuff on it—chemical formula, performance parameters, algorithms, all that and more."

"Give me the disk, Charlie! Give it to me now!"

"There's a price."

"There always is." Sam did his level best to look accommodating. "What did you have in mind?"

"Presidential immunity for Irina Kolodenkova."

Sam couldn't believe his ears. For a moment he couldn't even speak, and that was an unprecedented experience. Finally he managed to gasp, "You're joking."

"I'm dead serious."

Sam shook his head and spoke very, very softly. "Charlie, that bitch broke into a top secret installation. She stole the most important technology since the A-bomb. God only knows what she saw while she was doing it. God only knows what secrets she has locked in her head. And you want the president to let her off? You want a woman who knows what she knows going home to Russia? Are you out of your mind?"

"She won't go home. I'm working on her. She's got some psychological vulnerabilities. I'm pretty sure I can persuade her—"

"No! Abso-fucking-lutely no! You got that, Charlie boy? N. O. Spells 'no!' This is not a negotiation." Not now it wasn't. Things had gone beyond the point of being negotiable. "We are not bargaining. There is no give-and-take. A compromise will not be reached. *Capice?* I've paid you good money, big money, to do a job. I've promised you a presidential pardon. We have a deal. Now all I want is for you to deliver the goods. *Numero uno,* that disk. *Numero duo,* the Whirlwind material. *Numero* whatever comes next, Kolodenkova. After that, your job is done, and I'll handle the rest."

"The rest being," Charlie whispered, "killing her?"

You and her both, if it can be arranged. "I didn't say that. But we both know the answer."

"Suppose I decide not to let you."

If she stays on the loose, the Chinese will freak. And if they freak, I might as well kill myself. "Then I'll move up my Friday deadline—just take my cell phone here and call Johan—"

Charlie seized Sam's arm, wrenching it down painfully and sending the cell phone skittering across the aisle. A second later it was shards of plastic and silicon beneath his heel. "Don't screw with me, Sam. Just do not screw with me."

Sam tilted his head back, giving Charlie a long, appraising stare. *Goddamn you, McKenzie. I need you inside the tent pissing out, not outside pissing in. At least until Schmidt burnbags your fucking video. After that, I don't need you at all.* "Okay, Charlie, calm down. Look, we both know what this is really about." He put on his best schmoozer's smile. "It's your pardon, right? That's what it all boils down to. Kolodenkova is just a bargaining chip. Okay, Charlie, okay, I understand. Honest to God, I do."

"You don't understand a thing."

Sam didn't like the undertone in Charlie's voice. He spoke faster. "I believe we can work something out. Maybe get you a more equitable arrangement than the one we agreed to. After I returned to the White House yesterday, I began thinking about your situation. No question, you have a legitimate grievance. The truth of the matter is that justice was not done. You have every right to be upset. So what I did, Charlie, what I did was I went and had a long heart-to-heart with the boss. I did it for you. Me personally, on my own initiative. And guess what? The president wasn't totally negative. While we were talking, a thought crossed his mind—"

"Short trip."

"I'll ignore that. The thought was this: if you retrieve

Whirlwind, you will have done the nation a service that should be rewarded sooner than three years from now. That's what he said. And as God is my witness, he means it. If you do the job, find Whirlwind and Kolodenkova by Friday, you'll receive your pardon. And I mean immediately. This is good news, correct? You don't have to wait for me to take office. The president will sign it for you the minute Kolodenkova is in a body bag. And this is an unconditional offer. No terms and no strings. All the president asks is that you make a public apology for the Kahlid Hassan affair, and—"

You could almost hear Charlie's temper explode. All at once he was towering, dark as a thunderhead, God's wrath incarnate, lightning crackling in every word. "Get off my airplane!" A volcano in eruption, fire from the skies. "Do it now! If you don't, they'll need a dustpan to scoop you up!"

The irony was not lost on Sam. Two hotheads, one trying to infuriate the other, but guess who it was who'd lost his cool? He couldn't resist making it worse. "Oh, calm down. I'm offering you a reasonable, no, downright generous—"

Charlie's fists were balled tight, punches ready to be thrown. "An apology! You want an apology! I have nothing to apologize for! The only thing I did was follow—against my better judgement—some lard-assed White House bureaucrat's orders because I thought . . . I *thought,* they came straight from the president . . . because I *thought* I had presidential immunity . . . because I *thought* I'd been told the truth . . . because I *thought* I was doing something honorable for my country! Do you think I should apologize for that? Do you, you damned buffoon?"

He grabbed Sam's arm, yanked him from his seat, and frog-marched him to the plane's door. "I'm owed a pardon, Sam, and I'm owed more than that. It is not my intention to apologize to get what's due me."

It was happening too fast. Charlie was a human hurricane. Sam couldn't collect his thoughts, couldn't think of a way to pacify him, and there was no resisting the almost supernatural force of his rage. He tried to say something, anything to salvage the situation. The words wouldn't come. He wasn't sure he wanted them to anyway. He stumbled as Charlie stormed him down the stairs and onto the tarmac. And then, finally, he found his voice, and found himself saying what he'd been wanting to say all along. Even as he spoke, he knew that his self-control was slipping, slipping, slipping away. "Fuck you, buddy! Just remember we have a deal!"

"To hell with your deal, and to hell with you!"

Two secret service agents burst through the door of Sam's plane. Both gripped their pistols with practiced skill; both drew beads on Charlie; both slowly began to squeeze.

Sam shouted an order: "Stand down those guns."

Charlie kicked him sprawling onto the runway. A Smith & Wesson appeared in his hand for a second time. For a second time he emptied its clip. And, for a second time, federal property exploded into ribbons. Its recently replaced wheel shot to shreds, Sam's plane tilted sickeningly.

Sam looked up from where he lay. Charlie, blood in his eyes, towered over him. A thin wisp of blue smoke swirled from his gun barrel. "You computer-illiterate chowderhead. Remember that little green ball I plugged into my Macintosh while you were fixing the drinks? It's a digital camera. It uploaded our entire conversation to the Internet. If any harm comes to Irina, any at all, I'll release it to the press. Every damned word. Stealth, Super-Stealth, EM weapons, and the national security advisor engineering the murder of a twenty-four-year-old girl."

You're dead, McKenzie, Sam answered, although he did not say it aloud. *As of this moment, you are a fucking corpse.*

Johan Schmidt is your undertaker, and I'm the one who's pissing on your grave.

Charlie spun on his heel, stalking back toward his plane. One of the secret service agents called out, asking for instructions. "Let him go," Sam spat as he pulled himself to his feet. He choked back his fury, smothering words he did not dare speak, *Deadline! Friday noon! Either you deliver Kolodenkova or it's open season, big bucks for whoever brings the cunt in, shoot to kill, hang her up by her heels and gut her and skin her like a deer in season, I'll have her fucking head on my office wall, no more games, McKenzie, it ends, fuck you, it ends! Deadline! Read my lips! Dead! Line!*

"Deal!" he couldn't stop himself from roaring. "We have a deal. And you damn well better honor it!"

Charlie was in the Citation's hatch. He glanced over his shoulder, extending the middle finger of his right hand. Within minutes his plane was airborne, turning lazily northwest and disappearing from sight.

He was gone, long gone when the helicopter—a stylized eagle logo on its fuselage—feathered down on the runway beside Sam's Falcon.

And Johan Schmidt—summoned from a canyon of corpses and carnage—nodded briskly at his new orders.

Betrayals

Wednesday, July 22.
1930 Hours Mountain Time

Arizona, early evening on a lonely road. Sam heard the two men's voices long before he saw them. Hell, you probably could hear them in the next county: "This is a federal matter, Captain! Order your troopers out of that canyon!"

The speaker was a tenor, shrill with frustration; the answerer, big and basso with a beefeater's tones: "Get that tin badge out of my face, junior! This is a state investigation!"

With Johan Schmidt by his side, Sam picked up his pace, jogging around a blue-striped, white Chevy Blazer to confront two lawmen on the verge of a fist fight. One of them was a rangy Marlboro man wearing a beige Stetson and a crisp poplin uniform. The other was a charcoal-suited FBI lad straight from central casting—Ethan Hawke, Ben Affleck, Jude Law, take your pick because who can tell the difference?

They stood at cliff's edge above a valley turned wheat-gold by approaching dusk. To Sam's eyes it looked like the cop was about to make the FBI munchkin part of the scenery. He glanced at Schmidt. "You'd better handle this."

Shaking his head, Schmidt faded back into the shadows.

His whisper hung in the air like forgotten perfume. "I do not show my face to law enforcement officers. Never, and under no circumstances. This is your problem, Samuel. Solve it."

Squaring his shoulders, Sam stepped forward. "Gentlemen," he said, donning his most diplomatic smile.

"And just who the hell are you?" His nameplate identified him as Captain Thornton of the Highway Patrol, and Captain Thornton was not a happy man. "This is a crime site. No civilians allowed."

You ignorant country hick, Sam thought. "Who am I?" he replied sharply. "I am the president's national security advisor, that's who I am."

"And I, jackoff, am the merry queen of the May." Thornton laid his hand on his pistol butt. "Now, mister Security Advisor, you'd do yourself a service by getting out of my face. Better yet, get out of my state."

Not trusting himself to speak, Sam flipped his wallet open, displaying an identification card in a plasticine window.

Thornton eyed a professionally lit photograph, a presidential seal stamped in Williamsburg blue, a legend across the top proclaiming Office of the President, United States of America. He became mighty quiet mighty fast.

Humiliation and anger, Sam reflected, *are a dangerous combination. Best not to make a proud man lose face.* "Captain," he said with forced cordiality, "I empathize with your situation, I genuinely do. Under normal circumstances no federal agency would intrude in an accident investigation—"

"SOC team down there says it's no accident."

With practiced piety Sam whispered, "The matter is more grave than I anticipated."

"Three dead men, one woman pretty damned close. Yessir, I'd call that grave."

Sam felt a jolt of pleasure at the word "woman." If Kolodenkova was at the valley's bottom, so was Whirlwind. "All the more reason to sort out who has jurisdiction in a matter involving stakes higher than you know. Were those stakes lower, I would order Agent . . . Agent . . . what's your name, son?"

An awed FBI man replied, "Special Agent Küpper, sir."

"Captain, I assure you I would like nothing more than to order Agent Küpper and his team to defer to your Scene of the Crime team and allow local lawmen do what local lawmen do best. However, I trust my presence—the presence of someone directly under the president's command—will persuade you that what lies at the bottom of this cliff is a matter of national security." Sam lowered his voice, speaking intimately. "As you know, ever since nine-eleven certain matters are better left in the hands of federal experts."

Now seriously worried, the captain rubbed the side of his cheek. "You saying those are terrorists down there?"

Sam played his fish. "I'm afraid I can't answer that question. I suspect you can guess why." He forced himself to count to five, before adding in a whisper, "Captain, I urge you to evacuate your people . . . " *pause, look him straight in the eye, and add an exclamation point to the sentence . . .* "quickly!"

"Bioterrorism?" His leathery complexion pale, the lawman jerked a bullhorn to his lips. He strode to the cliff's rim, shouting orders downhill. Troopers and pathologists looked up, and, shaking their heads, began to pack their kits.

The nice thing about amateur negotiators, Sam thought, *is that if you wait long enough, they'll always feed you your straight lines.*

Within twenty minutes Thornton's team had swarmed up three hundred feet of rope ladder, climbed grumbling into their vehicles, and driven into the dusk.

Sam stood at Agent Küpper's shoulder until the last state officer was out of sight.

"Sir," Küpper said, "I want to thank you very much. Having a bunch of hillbilly cops tramp around a crime scene—"

"What's at the bottom of that canyon is X-rated, junior—adults only. Get your fanny out of here. You and all your yuppie buddies. Hit the bricks, boy, and do it now."

Nightfall, or near enough. To the east, a discomforting darkness, stars so bright they did not twinkle. In the west, a dying sun splashed bloody spears among the clouds. Sam, far from city lights, shivered with an inner cold.

He sat on a rock at cliff's edge. No power on earth could have forced him down a hundred precipitous yards to sift through mangled bodies and wrecked vehicles. That was what you paid people like Schmidt for.

Schmidt . . . Sam closed his eyes and shook his head. It was a little late to be having second thoughts about hiring the mercenary. But still . . .

He remembered—when was it? a decade ago—the first time he'd used The Specialist Consulting Group's services. The results were impressive, more than he'd asked for, "exceeding expectations," as the jargon goes.

Later, after the bills were paid and the bodies bagged and tagged, he'd decided he should get to know Schmidt better. The future is uncertain, and you wanted to have someone with his particular talents available, just in case.

They'd met in a bar down in Fredericksburg, far enough south of Washington that there'd be no one around to recognize Sam. Or, for that matter, Schmidt—presuming that anyone who knew him by sight lived to tell the tale.

Somewhere along the line—Sam was on his third Cutty Sark, Schmidt three-quarters of the way through a single Campari and soda—Sam's curiosity got the better of him.

He'd asked Schmidt how he'd gotten into his, well, unusual line of business.

Schmidt's lips twitched. He slowly stirred his drink with a swizzle stick. After slightly too long a silence, he replied: "When I was seventeen, a platoon of ANC guerrillas attacked my church during Sunday services. I was altar boy that day. My father, my mother, two sisters, and a brother were in the pews. The blackies burst through the rear door carrying cheap Chinese AK-47s, and extra magazines— drum magazines, forty rounds per drum. They sprayed bullets, reloaded, and sprayed again. Ten men. Ten guns. I am told they fired more than twelve hundred rounds that day. My family died. Almost everyone died. Only I and six others survived. I chanced to be standing behind the minister at the pulpit. Three slugs to the chest, he fell on me, protected me. Rather biblical, don't you think? What is it the good book says? 'The God of my rock; in him will I trust: he is my shield, and the horn of my salvation, my high tower, and my refuge, my savior; thou savest me from violence.'

"Just so. He is my shield. Never forget that, Samuel. He is my shield.

"In any event, that Sunday, the *schwartzers* were not to be satisfied with mere rifle work. They set off explosions, too. Grenades. One rolled directly across the altar. The sight of it is my last memory of the day. I came out of a coma a week later. My first waking thought, the very first, was that spending the rest of my life killing coloreds would make for a tolerable career. Later, having developed a certain aptitude at the business, I realized that the pay was better if I broadened my horizons, did not discriminate, embraced the brotherhood of all mankind. And so you find me, one of this disposable world's rarest individuals, a man who treats everyone alike—equitable and impartial in every regard. Can you say the same of yourself?"

Sam didn't bother to answer. He paid the bar bill and drove into the night promising himself that he'd never speak to Johan Schmidt again.

But he did.

And never regretted it. Not even now, nightfall and the stink of charred corpses faint in the air, he never regretted it. If you had regrets, you had a conscience. Ambition didn't allow that luxury.

A serpent coiling out of darkness, Schmidt silently materialized at the cliff's rim. He neither sweated nor breathed heavily. That was no surprise. Sam would only have been surprised if he did.

"Kolodenkova?" Sam asked hopefully.

Dusting his hands, Schmidt looked outward toward falling night. Sam watched him in profile. *That's odd,* he thought, *I never noticed the thickness of his glasses before. The frames are designed to disguise the lenses' dimensions. I always thought those shades were an affectation, dark eyeglasses for a dark soul. But they're prescription, they have to be, those glasses are a quarter inch thick. The man must be half blind without them.*

Silence endured until Sam asked again, "Is she down there?"

Schmidt grunted, "No. The dogs have sniffed a half mile in every direction. The only dead are my dead."

"I'm sorry." It seemed the thing to say.

"Sorrow is inappropriate. They did what they were trained to do. That's what counts."

"Any idea as to what happened?"

Schmidt nodded, a last glimmer of light sparking his prescription lenses. "Cottonmouth survived long enough to out-

line the story. I had to spike her heart with fifty ccs of epinephrine to wake her up, and another fifty to keep her talking."
He stared into the night, then back at Sam. He said nothing.

"And?"

The mercenary inhaled deeply, let the breath out slowly. "After sending two of my teams over the cliff, Kolodenkova set her own truck on fire, then pushed it off the edge. The Whirlwind material isn't in the wreckage. Our opponent moved it to another vehicle—presumably the one she's in now. According to Cottonmouth, it's a vintage Winnebago, faded butter-yellow with brown stripes."

Sam whispered, "Shit, it's the height of the tourist season. How many campers are on the road? Thousands? Tens of thousands? We'll never find her."

"Not so. She won't be moving fast, not in an oversized RV. She hasn't had time to get far. We have a manageable search radius. It's merely a matter of time."

"I devoutly hope so." As an afterthought, he added, "Give my thanks to ... did you say Cottonmouth was his name?"

"Her. A woman. Cottonmouth was a woman. Now she's just another KIA."

Killed in Action. "Oh," Sam grunted.

"An old hand, a fine soldier. With me from the early days. Not a friend, you understand. Commanders can't afford friends. But she was someone I talked to. I'll miss her."

"Sorry."

Schmidt jutted so close that Sam could feel his dry breath. "I believe I have already indicated that your sorrow is neither befitting nor welcome."

Suddenly frightened—*enormously* frightened—Sam stumbled back. "Certainly. Of course. My mistake."

"Good. I am pleased we understand one another."

Was that an emotion? From Schmidt? Sam was unable to

answer his own question. He knew only that Schmidt, always a terrifying man, suddenly had become more so. Sam wished he was elsewhere. Anyplace would do so long as it was far, far away.

"I need to get back to Washington, Johan."

"You're with me for the duration."

A needle through the sinuses, Sam's allergies were back, more painful than ever. For a moment he thought about objecting to Schmidt's order. Then he thought some more. "Whatever you say."

"Precisely. Whatever I say."

Schmidt left his words hanging in the air. Sam shuddered.

"I have a piece of good news, Johan."

"I would welcome that."

"Claude called while you were down there with your people. He has a lead on McKenzie's data vault."

"A credible one?"

"Sounds that way. Ever since the World Trade Center attack, we've been watching airport Internet links like a hawk. While Charlie was . . . uh . . . while he and I were in Albuquerque, somebody used the airport's wireless system, used it in a big way." *Did the user send enough data for a half hour's worth of video?* Sam had asked. *Why, yes,* replied the director of Central Intelligence, *how did you know?* Whereupon Sam had cursed and hurled a borrowed cell phone into the darkness. "They traced the transmission to a fly-by-night Internet operator—the kind Charlie would use."

"Were they able to read his message?"

"Of course not. Charlie's using encryption techniques the NSA has never seen before."

"But they do know the ISP, the Internet company? They do know where it's physically housed?"

"Northern California. It's run by a bunch of hackers—

most of whom are on the watch list. They call it 'the Underground Empire, dot.com.' "

"Single site—all the servers and disk drives in one place?" Schmidt's voice was, as ever, flat and neutral. With eyes masked by tinted glasses and a voice that was almost a monotone, he was impenetrable. In anyone else Sam would have found such icy remoteness infuriating. But with Schmidt . . . well, maybe he was better off not knowing what was on the man's mind.

"Can't say. I don't know much about computers."

"Nor do I. However, I do know Charles. There are but a few people who can compromise the kind of computer security he'd use."

"Who? Give me a for instance."

"That's of no interest to you, Samuel. All that need interest you is whether or not I have access to any of them."

"Which you do?"

"Of course."

Sam thought back to his earlier conversations with Schmidt—one over the telephone the night before, the other only hours ago at the Albuquerque airport. "Put him on the payroll."

"There will be an additional fee."

"Add it to Max Henkes's bill."

"And am I to presume that if we do eliminate Charles's data vault, I have your authorization to—"

"Add that to the bill, too."

She should have been so famished that she'd eat even this sad salad of wilted lettuce, three alleged cherry tomatoes as juicy as Ping-Pong balls, spitball-soggy croutons, an ancient anchovy deceased across the top.

Caesar salad? No, Brutus was the chef.

For the main course: a steak of her childhood, Soviet gristle served with corn too yellow to be natural—the hue of a hazardous waste warning, and as appetizing.

Not that it mattered. Though famished, she could not bring herself to eat, although she knew she must.

Hunger, they'd taught her, blunts the senses, and slows the reflexes. *If your enemy has you on the run, his first objective is not to capture you, but rather to exhaust you.* Who said that? One of her instructors. Captain Petryshyn, a rare teacher who cared for his students. *The thirsty are found near water; the starving are taken near food; the agent who stumbles with weariness stumbles into the arms of his pursuers. Stamina is survival. Eat well and live!*

A different voice, prideful and domineering: *Eat well! At home and at sea, that is my law. My crew honors me less for my rank than because aboard my ship they do not dine, they feast! The loyalty of inferiors is bought with red beef, fresh greens, fat cakes full of rum and brown sugar. If you would lead men, forget their minds, for they have none. Forget their hearts. Those belong to street sluts. Remember only their stomachs! Feed them, and they are yours forever! But never cook, girl, never! That is woman's work. . . .*

"Hi. Mind if I join you?"

It was Charlie. Of course it was Charlie. Who else could it be? Too exhausted to look up, she merely shrugged.

He sat down. "Happy to see me?"

A weary nod.

"Surprised I'm here?"

A resigned shake.

"What's good on this menu?"

A blank look of hopelessness.

He studied the menu disapprovingly. "The farther you get

from the oceans, the worse the food is. Right now, we're just about on the Continental Divide, so . . . Oh, excuse me, miss, could I have a BLT, coleslaw on the side. No, I don't think I'll try one of those salads, and a real Coke, you know, Classic Coke with sugar and caffeine and all that politically incorrect stuff. Bring the same for my friend, only put extra mayonnaise on her sandwich, and give her a chocolate milkshake instead of Coke. We'd like some corn bread and butter, if you have it. Yes, please take away her . . . uh . . . steak, I suppose. Thank you. Irina, you just look like hell."

After checking into the motel—garishly decorated with a potpourri of Navajo, Zuni, and Hopi motifs—Irina had caught an unwanted glimpse of herself in the bathroom mirror. Her eyes were bruised, her skin sallow, her lips raw and chapped. It pained her that Charlie was seeing her in this condition; it pained her more that she was embarrassed in front of an enemy.

He spoke again, genuine concern in his voice, "I'd say you've had a rough day." Pity kindled in his eyes. "Very damned rough."

"You could say that." Less spoken than croaked.

"Tell me."

"Then I would have to think about it." She felt like crying. *No, that is not possible. I will never cry again.*

Charlie nodded knowingly. "You're all right now, aren't you?"

The truth was necessary because Charlie, inexplicably, had become a man to whom one could only tell the truth: "No, Charlie, I am not. I am not so sure I will ever be again."

"How many did you kill?"

He understood. She should hate him for that. "Enough. Too many."

"Give me a number."

What right had he to ask that? "Seven, I suppose. It is a matter of how you look at it."

"It's a matter of what your conscience tells you." He gently took her hand. She didn't pull away, although she could not say why. "Irina, thirty-some years ago, I had to deal with it for the first time. It sucked, but I got over it. So will you. Give it time, and you'll get over it."

Bitter, she was so bitter. "Is that supposed to console me?"

"Nope."

"Will I be a better person once the memory fades?"

"Doubtful. But you won't be a worse one either. We live our lives, and if we do our best, we've got nothing to feel guilty about."

"Seven people are dead. The guilt is mine." *I am questioning my suitability for this life—I, who never question myself.*

"My presumption is that if they weren't dead, you would be. In my book that means the guilt is theirs."

"They were seven. I am one."

"Tell me true, Irina, were any of them in the right?"

"No. Yes. One. A policeman." His legs had drummed a tattoo on the asphalt. He was so young.

Charlie's eyes glinted diamond bright. "You killed a cop?"

"No, they did, those men from the hotel. But they did it because of me. It is my fault."

He threw up his hands. The gesture was blatantly theatrical. He was such an actor. "Baloney! That's like telling the money it's responsible for the bank robbers!"

He was right. The knowledge was no solace. Beyond any doubt her superiors would applaud victories she found more wounding than defeat. What should have left her triumphant, disgusted her. *If . . . when . . . I return to Moscow, give me no medals, pay me no praise. And if you promote me, promote me to a desk job.*

"Tell me about it," he murmured. "Everything. Minute by minute. Get it out of your system."

She answered, flatly recounting the terrors of her day. All the while, he stroked her hand, although only softly. Then, story told, she fell silent, studying him. Nothing could disguise the decency in his eyes. She opened her mouth, ready to say who knows what in response to the kindness of his touch. A plate clattered in front of her. She jumped.

"Two BLTs, one slaw, one Coke, one shake, basket of corn bread." The waitress truculently ticked each item off. "Anything else?"

"Butter," said Charlie.

"In the bread basket." Disdainful, she walked away, a woman who earned few tips, and was not disposed to make the effort necessary to do so.

"Eat," Charlie ordered.

"I am not hungry." A small anger pricked her. Who was he to tell her what to do?

"Eat anyway." He took two healthy bites from his own sandwich, washing them down with a swallow of Coke.

She bridled at his command, thought to make a sharp retort, but could not find the spirit. Instead, she sampled her food. It was tasteless, difficult to swallow, and sat heavily on her stomach. "Charlie?"

"Yes."

"Tell me one thing."

"Whatever you want."

"How did you find me?" *Curiosity is the only emotion I can feel. Will I ever feel another?*

The corner of his mouth drifted up—half a smile. "You won't like the answer."

"All the more reason to hear it. Maybe I will learn how to escape you next time."

He laughed a deep, rolling belly laugh. She liked its sound but could not bring herself to smile in response.

"Okay. But don't say I didn't warn you." He took another sip of Coke. "It was a con job. A flimflam. A cheap trick, same as you played on me by switching disks—"

"You noticed?" She was chagrined. That was wrong. She'd outmaneuvered her opponent. She had nothing to be ashamed of.

"Not when you did it. I found out later. At considerable expense, I might add. Anyway, let me explain the scam I ran on you. Same as a card shark suckers his mark into drawing the card he wants, I suckered you into driving toward northern Arizona. Last night and this morning, I dropped all sorts of little hints that I expected you to take the southern route toward Tucson and Phoenix. Oh, I didn't say anything overt; it was all subtle subliminal message stuff to plant an idea in your head. I wanted you thinking: wicked old Charlie is certain I'm going to go south, therefore I must go north. Which you did, just like I wanted. Another thing: I figured you'd stick to the back roads. There are only three you could have taken, and all of them are pretty slow. Nine or ten hours of driving time would wear you out. You'd only get so far. About this far."

He wasn't telling her everything. It could *not* have been that easy. Her voice rose. "You are lying. You walk into my motel, into this restaurant at eight thirty and—"

"Cool down. My son's with the Indian Health Service. He's stationed at the Three Turkeys clinic, about two hours from here. My wife and I used to visit him every summer. I've driven every mile of paved road and dirt track in northern Arizona. I know this part of the country like the back of my hand. Which means I know where the very few motels hereabouts are located. All I had to do was phone. 'Has Ms.

Caroline Sonderstrom checked in yet?'—that being the name on the clean credit cards I gave you. I would have checked every damned fleapit between here and Las Vegas if I had to. However, because I am a good and God-fearing man beloved of the angels, I struck paydirt on the third call." He pitched his voice higher, " 'Sorry, sir, there's no answer from that room. Would you like me to take a message?' "

Irina almost laughed. Charlie made it sound so simple that any fool could do it.

However (of this she was certain), not every fool could. The shrewdness with which he'd nudged her north, his almost supernatural certainty that she'd stop when she did, his confidence that she'd use a credit card rather than cash—how had he known those things? She herself had not known until she'd made the decisions. She could have just as easily continued north, turned east or west, or . . .

"Of course, finding you wasn't the hard part." Charlie beamed. "Swiping Whirlwind from that ridiculous new sports-ute parked outside your motel room wasn't hard either. The tough part—the part I really was *not* looking forward to—was coming into this restaurant, sitting down with someone I genuinely respect, and having to tell her that as of this moment, she's busted. Irina Kolodenkova, I'm placing you under arrest. Stay put for a minute . . . now where did I put my Miranda card? . . . oh, here it is. You have the right to remain silent. You have the right—"

She lashed out a slap. Charlie snapped a handcuff on her wrist.

"Who are you to say you will save me!?!"

Charlie had handcuffed her to a motel bedframe—something she'd angrily denounced as demeaning until he'd reminded her that cuffing him to a bathroom sink might, in theory that is, be considered even more mortifying.

That shut her up. Although not for long. "I am perfectly capable of taking care of myself!" This in the tones that Charlie found reminiscent of a cat being shampooed. "I am trained and I am competent!"

Yup, good analogy—she definitely was as mad as a wet cat. Prettier though. Pretty as a picture all flushed and furious. Of course he'd never tell her that. "Irina, you haven't got a prayer of getting away from Schmidt and his goons on your own."

A fine feline hiss: "What gives you the right to *force* your unwanted help on me?"

He didn't even stop to think about his answer. "Like I said last night, maybe I'm your guardian angel sent down from on high."

"Pah!" she positively spat. "I do not believe in God."

It had been a long time since Charlie had a good rip-snorting argument with a woman. He'd forgotten how much fun it was. "If you did, maybe he would have assigned you a higher class guardian. Me, I'm just a beat-up, worn-out old avenging angel recycled and repurposed to custodial duties."

Damn, but she could arch her eyebrows. He'd never seen it done better. Always excepting Mary, that is. "Saint Charlie?" she sneered.

"Yeah, sure." He laughed, and the laughter felt fine, "They even named cities after me. Seven of 'em in the U. S. of A. Five 'Saint Charles,' and two 'San Carlos.' "

Tight-lipped, still frowning. "You told me that last night."

"Did I?" *Hmm*, he thought, *so I did. Why the blazes did I do that?*

"You said you want to retire there."

"That's the plan. Want to join me?" *And, for that matter, why did I just say that?*

She glared at him. "I have been there. It is an ugly little freeway town." Her eyes weren't quite as bright as they had been. She brushed her unshackled hand across drooping eyelids. Charlie figured sleep was settling. And about time too.

"That's the one in Silicon Valley. The other one, San Carlos do Cabo, is down the coast on a cape that juts way out into the ocean. Sometimes, mostly in the summer, it's so foggy you can't see your hand in front of your face. But when the sun comes out, it's God's glory returned to earth, all green, the prettiest green you've ever seen. Every house has gables and chimneys and big front porches, and the farms are so beautiful that you just want to walk through the fields until the world ends. Mary and I . . . I mean . . . I've fancied moving there for the longest time. Raise cats and cows, but mostly cats. Buy a nice Catalina sailboat, park it at the marina, and on quiet days I'll go out and do some serious fishing—which basically means doing nothing at all. The rest of the time I'll just lounge on the porch or lie in the hammock, drink lemonade, and read all the things I've meant to read twice but never quite got around to. And I'll live the rest of my life out in peace. After all these years, I think I'm entitled to a little peace."

"Peace." She was slipping away now, her lips barely moving.

"That hammock is particularly on my mind. I mean to string it between two old walnut trees. I can see myself lying there in the afternoon shade with a couple of cats on my belly. I'll be napping, of course, because there's nothing more conducive to napping than having a dozy cat or two around. Cats have the skill of the thing and can teach you all you need to know about snoozing in a genuinely professional manner."

Barely perceptible, her lips moved again. Charlie thought she might be trying to say "cats," and that would be the last word she would say until morning. He'd talked her to sleep, as intended—or rather talked her into yielding to the power of the two powerful soporifics he'd slipped into her milkshake about twenty minutes earlier.

Good night, sleep tight, I really do care about you, you know.

Yeah, well, that was an unfortunately honest self-confession. He genuinely and sincerely did feel something that a man of his years should not feel. What? He was unsure, a bit confused about his emotions, in fact, downright befuddled.

Not that it was a problem. He could clear things up easily enough. Same as every other occasion when he wasn't certain about his own sentiments, he'd talk it through with his wife.

He'd made a promise to her, more than a promise, a sacred vow. He'd sworn on his honor and on his love that he would never, under any circumstances, involve their children in any of his messes.

Today he'd broken that oath. Now, pecking on his computer's keyboard, Charlie McKenzie confessed his sin. Mary was the one person to whom he never lied, not once in his entire life.

The Mossad, he typed, had forwarded a covert message to Scott asking him to do three things: first, arrange for one of his Navajo friends to chauffeur Charlie from Gallup to the reservation where he suspected Irina would go to ground. Second, procure a few unregistered fire arms. Third, arrange for a mutual friend—another doctor who, like Scott, was a bush pilot—to meet Charlie next morning at the Indian Health Service's airstrip near the village of Three Turkeys.

It was innocent stuff, Charlie wrote, and nothing that could put Scott in danger. Nonetheless, he'd broken his word, and he begged Mary's forgiveness for that.

If he'd printed his apology out, it would have filled three single-spaced pages—and another page for a renewed oath that he would never again, under any circumstances, embroil either children or grandchildren in the deadly affairs that were the daily life of Charles McKenzie, assassin and spy.

At last, having settled with his conscience, and being reasonably certain that his wife would forgive him just this one time, he went on to tell her everything that Irina had told him: the gunplay, the sickening carnage, the hijacking of a Winnebago that, later, she'd hidden behind an elementary school, and how she'd replaced it with an enormous, fire-engine-red Cadillac Escalade.

He grinned as he wrote about that. Irina's audacity reminded him of his own.

Whirlwind? That was safe and sound, he wrote. After stealing it from Irina's Escalade, he'd paid his Navajo driver to take it, hide it, and never say a word. If Charlie didn't know where Whirlwind was hidden, then nobody could make him tell.

He looked up from the computer screen, glancing at Irina. She was deep asleep, a Botticelli angel in repose. It was hard to take his eyes off her. After a while, he forced himself to return to his typing.

Once Whirlwind was safe, I sashayed into the restaurant, and there she was. Cool as a cucumber, she didn't even blink an eye. It was almost like she was expecting me.

Whereupon I arrested her. Oh, but it was a joy to behold! You've never seen anyone so mad. Wildcats aren't the half of it. Despite her eloquent criticisms of my character, morals, parentage and what not, I'm pretty sure she'll play ball with me tomorrow when I try to get her out of the soup. But just to make certain, I handcuffed her to her bed. Now she's out like a light (two Dalmane capsules administered in a sneaky fashion will have that effect), and after I finish typing this up, I'll be sleeping right next to her, this being one of life's little rewards for an old fossil in the sunset of his years, and don't give me any lip, okay?

But I have to admit, sweetheart, she's giving me conniptions. Trouble is she reminds me a lot of you. Not on the outside, although she is a looker. But what I mean—what is getting to me—is what she's like on the inside. It's her heart and her brain that are the admirable things. She's solid at the core, Mary, as solid as you.

So what is it with me and this girl, or young woman, or whatever I'm supposed to call her? You tell me. I'm buffaloed. Maybe it's that the world has a shortage of genuinely good souls, and I'm not prepared to let anyone harm an endangered species. Maybe it's that when I look at her, I see you. Maybe I'm just a damned old fool. Or maybe, just maybe, it's something to do with the way I lost you, how there was nothing I could do, how I just had to stand there helpless as a child, and I will be thrice damned to hell if I'm going to stand by impotently again, not when I can do something about it.

I don't know.

Nuts. I need a drink. Or a shrink. Or both.

He settled for the drink, a short gin and tonic from the motel's minibar. Then he typed the last few paragraphs of his daily letter to his wife: What was Sam up to? What role did Sangin Wing and his son play? What was the puzzle inside the puzzle, and the secret inside the secret? Pretty soon, he wrote, he'd know. The Mossad was turning on the vacuum cleaner; tomorrow they'd send him every speck of data they could find about the Wing family, and especially about what DefCon Enterprises' chief scientist was up to February seventh through the ninth. Wing had been attending a scientific conference in Tokyo then, chairing a panel when his son was arrested. Charlie wanted a transcript of the panel discussion, bios of the other members, news reports from the scientific journals, photos, anything and everything. He wasn't sure what he was looking for, he typed, but by God he'd know it when he saw it.

Leaning back, he rolled his shoulders, cracked his knuckles, then typed what he always typed at the end of his letters to Mary: love, loneliness, and regret.

He read his letter two times over, changing a word or two, and smiling to himself. Then, as he did with every letter he wrote his wife, he deleted it.

She'd get it anyway, of that he was certain, and the celestial e-mail system was one that not even the NSA could tap.

He stood and stretched. His fingers brushed the speckled ceiling of Irina's sad little motel room as he inventoried its squalor: a cheap writing desk; worn blue carpet; tacky Indian scenes on the wall; a thin mattress; yellowed sheets.

Nothing here worth wanting. Nothing worth having. Nothing worth keeping.

Except for a woman as innocent as her dreams.

Only a day ago, he'd thought no more of her than he would of a plastic pawn, a game piece to be moved and sacrificed as he forced Sam to checkmate. Now things had changed, changed a lot. He couldn't say why. All he knew was that he was responsible for her, a guardian angel to be sure. Whatever happened from here on was his fault and no one else's. Arrogant ass that he'd always been, he'd thought he could muscle Sam into telling the truth. Instead, cocky, pompous, and too damned certain of his own self-righteous superiority, his neat little scheme had blown up in his face. Now Sam would kill her for sure—if for no other reason than to punish him.

So, yeah, he'd done it again. Bold, brave Charlie, the guy with the foolproof plan and the lionhearted valor to pull it off. Most of the time he did. Every now and then he didn't.

Problem. Big damned problem. He was afraid that this time would be one of those other times, blood-soaked times, and it hurt less when the blood was his own than when it was someone else's. *I know you, old man,* he told himself, *and with all due respect, this time, you self-centered simpleton, you've bitten off more than you can chew.*

He studied the face and form of an enemy of whom he was too fond. He smiled. Looking at her made him smile and he just plain couldn't help it. Then he turned to the mirror and smiled again, this time at himself. The smiles were different. The first was tender, the second sardonic.

Thinking only cynical thoughts, Charlie headed for the shower. Soap and water would wash today's dirt off easily. Would that he could do the same for his soul.

Charlie didn't check his e-mail at all. His daughter Carly checked hers too late.

Message 1:
From: sledgehammer@undergroundempire.com
Wed Jul 20 23:07:55

```
Date: Wed, 22 Jul 23:19:55 +0300
From: The Sledgehammer
<sledgehammer@undergroundempire.com>
Reply-To: sledgehammer@undergroundempire.com
X-Accept-Language: en, fr
MIME-Version: 1.0
```
To: "Carly M Family" <charliesangel@potomacmail.com>
Subject: Forward to your father
References:<200195192323.QDD08478potomacmail.com>
Content-Type: text/plain; charset=x-user-defined
Content-Transfer-Encoding: 7bit
X-UIDL: 1e705e5e2111117130f9fc99bsa0acqa

```
Miz C.

Pls relay to Mr. McK in case he misses the msg I
sent him direct that I'm unavailable to help him
anymore. Also tell him I owe him zero, zip, zilch.
But since he's been a good customer, he gets one
favor. Only one. The favor is I'm telling him I
just took on a job for a dude named Schmidt.
Remind Mr. McK that when I'm paid to do a job, I
do the job I'm paid to do.


Sledge
```

==
This message may contain confidential and/or privileged information.
If you are not the addressee or authorized to receive this for the
addressee, you must not use, copy, disclose or take any action based
on this message or any information herein. If you have received this
message in error, please advise the sender immediately by reply
e-mail and delete this message. If you elect not to cooperate in this
matter, I will scrag your disk, melt your motherboard, and nuke your
CPU. So don't fuck with me, man.

==

8

Cliffhanger

Souls are shaped in childhood. Bodies age, but character does not. Eager youth is always in us.

On the occasion of his twelfth birthday, Charlie had been given two books. The giver was his godfather, later his father-in-law. The gift was Homer, the *Iliad* and the *Odyssey* in prose translation, a beautiful boxed set bound in grey canvas and illustrated with two-color linocuts.

In later life, the *Iliad* would enthrall an adult Charlie. At age twelve, the *Odyssey* bewitched him, stamping a lasting mark. Crafty Odysseus became first among his heroes, and, perhaps, his permanent, although never-acknowledged, ideal.

The *Odyssey*'s adventures were thrilling to be sure; he shivered with delight. But they came at a price: that saga of a wandering warrior gave young Charles McKenzie nightmares.

Or say rather *a* nightmare, one single recurring malignant dream that rendered him paralyzed, sweating, stiff with terror.

He dreamt it still.

At Circe's instruction, Odysseus sailed to the shores of

Hell. By the black banks of the River Styx, he dug a pit, filling it with milk, wine, honey, water, crisp barley grain, and fresh blood from the throats of sacrificial sheep.

It was the blood that did the work.

The dead came forth. From down below they cockcrowed, belly-crawling out of Hades to sip at the offering, gurgling with pleasure as they lapped life's never forgotten wine.

Dead, all dead, every death since the dawn of time, men Odysseus knew, and women too, they crouched like sooty animals at the feast. Even Achilles, of all mortals greatest, was unable to resist the scarlet scent. That most courageous soldier, or rather his hungry ghost, fell to its knees, ringing its lips with gore.

Once a hero, now a drooling beast.

Some among the dead spoke. Hearing them was worse than seeing them, for the greater portion chittered insanity. But Achilles could be understood. Oh, yes. Easily. "I'd sooner be the lowest farmer's lowest slave than king of all the dead." Thus spoke the bravest of the bravest, whom every man idolized and sought to imitate.

Then a million, million mourning ghosts pressed 'round Odysseus in their insatiable hunger, their inextinguishable despair.

Charlie dreamt the dream more often than he admitted, and when he awoke . . .

"Charlie?"

"What?"

"You are shouting in your sleep."

"It's nothing, Mary. Just that dream. You know that dream."

"No."

"I've told you. It's scared me ever since I was a kid."

"No, I am not Mary. I am Irina."

Charlie sat bolt upright. He heard Irina fumble at the lamp.

"You are crying, Charlie."

For once in his life, Charlie McKenzie had nothing to say.

"Schmidt." It was how he answered the phone. One word. It was enough.

"Fer-de-Lance here, sir. Sorry to call at this hour but—"

"Report." One word was enough for most situations.

"McKenzie's data vault has been cracked, sir."

"Excellent." Soldiers need the simplicity.

"It's a two-terrabyte partition on a file server out here in California. Mirrored on a second server at the same site."

"Contents?" Verbosity breeds complexity.

"Unknown. This computer geek . . . calls himself Sledge-hammer . . . was unable to decode a single word of it. He told me it would take a neural net processor array to break the encryption key."

"Status?" Complexity requires thought.

"Erased, sir. This, uh, Sledgehammer overwrote both partitions with ones and zeros several hundred times. Whatever data McKenzie had on them is gone forever."

"The hacker?" Thought impedes obedience.

"I was at his shoulder every second, sir. Watched him like a hawk. There's no way he made a backup for his own use. Those files are deleted permanently. Guaranteed."

Schmidt smiled faintly. McKenzie was now a man without armor, his head an easy trophy for anyone who wanted it. "Your insurance policy has been canceled, Charles," he whispered.

"Sir?"

Vulnerable at last—it was a warming thought, and Schmidt allowed himself a few seconds to relish it. Then back to business: "This Sledgehammer character, Fer-de-lance, he has a reputation. No matter how closely you supervised him, there exists a possibility that he pirated those data."

"I am aware of that, sir."

"A single keystroke is all it would take. He could have copied McKenzie's files and sent them off to some other site on the Internet. Neither you nor I nor any man would know that he had done so. There's profit in McKenzie's files, blackmail profit."

"Yes, sir."

"I need assurance that such will not occur."

"I'm seeing to it now, sir."

"Ah. I am delighted to hear you've taken the initiative. Do bear in mind that it would be best if his remains are in a condition that hinder identification."

"In progress. No fingers, no fingerprints. No teeth, no dental records—"

"DNA testing?"

"Only if the fish don't do their job. At the moment, I'm in a boat about three miles off Stinson Beach. They say there are sharks in these waters."

"They say correctly. Great whites, I believe. Well done, soldier. I'm pleased with your work."

"Would you like to speak with Mr. Sledgehammer before I put him overboard, sir? He may be difficult to understand, but he can still talk."

"No, thank you, Fer-de-Lance. But do leave the line open so I can hear . . . well, whatever is to be heard."

"My pleasure, sir."

"The pleasure is all mine."

* * *

The northern Arizona landscape was new to Irina, scenery so different from the sterile deserts of the south— distant buttes like stately ocean liners; black lava tufts, each tall as a skyscraper; salmon-pink cliffs; tabletop plateaus speckled with piney groves; cloud armadas billowing across an infinite sky. The road ran arrow straight, and on every side the vista would lift all but the most sullen heart.

Irina's heart was, although she did not think of it in these terms, most sullen.

They were on the Navajo reservation, the "rez" Charlie called it because he was an old hand out here and knew the lingo. Dead dogs lay by the road, milestones on a highway from no place to nowhere. Infrequent intersections were prostituted with garish signs importuning tourists to visit . . .

. . . the casino . . .

. . . the pottery shop . . .

. . . the historic trading post . . .

Leave your dollars, please, then leave.

Open spaces again, nothing profaning them, not even electric pylons. Rolling plains of coral-green sage, mustard-yellow rabbit bush, jimsonweed with corpse-white flowers. A huge black raven soared in surprise from the road's verge, startling Irina as much as her passing had startled it.

"Water?" Charlie asked, one hand on the Escalade's leathered steering wheel, the other offering a bottle of Calistoga.

She shook her head.

"Better take some. We're at six thousand feet here. It's dry country. You dehydrate without noticing."

Having already said to Charlie everything she had to say, she neither wished to reply, nor to see him smile his infuriating smile, nor hear him assert over and over again that it was his firm intention to protect her whether she liked it or not.

How dare he?

She had been trained by the best, been at the top of her class in every discipline, finished first in every competition, won every—

"Just because the air is cool, it doesn't mean you're not sweating. Moisture is wicking out of your skin as fast as it would in the open desert."

She refused to look at him, the arrogant man. Superior, she was superior to him in every attribute except experience. What gave him the right to be so overbearing?

"Drink some of this water, and stop your sulking."

Snatching the bottle from his hand, she hissed, "I am not sulking."

"Oh, excuse me. Would 'pouting' be a better word. How about 'grumping'? I know damned well the only accurate word for the expression on your face is 'scowl.'"

She savored the water, had needed it more than she had known. After a second swallow, then a third, she twisted the cap back on, dropping the bottle in his lap. "I am capable of looking out for myself."

"We had this argument before. You lost."

"You will not succeed. I will not be put in jail. I will return to my nation."

"Had that argument, too." He was grinning again, damn him!

"You have done more than I would have believed possible. I am . . . " she licked her lips, the word didn't come easily " . . . beaten. You have Whirlwind, whatever it may be. You have my computer disk—"

"Not yours. Belongs to my government."

She felt herself flush with fury, and liked it like that. "Arresting me serves no purpose. Only my humiliation. Is that what you want? What is that wonderful American phrase, the one you use to teach bad puppy dogs good behavior—'rub my nose in it'?"

He answered with maddening reasonableness. "At the risk of repeating myself, I'm trying to protect you from people who think you know more than you should."

"I know nothing. Only the code name of a project. Only the location of a laboratory that probably has been moved."

"Nobody knows what you saw in that lab except you. Maybe you don't know a thing. Maybe you do. And if that's the case—if you do happen to have a few of our national secrets locked away in your very sharp mind—then you're a dangerous proposition. Doesn't matter that Whirlwind's safe and sound. Doesn't matter that I've got that disk in my hip pocket. What matters is that you may have knowledge that—"

"I do not. How many times do I have to tell you? You know the truth. You worked out how much time Dominik and I spent in that laboratory. We had no chance—"

"Give it a rest, Irina. I believe you. The only information you've got is what I've given you—and that isn't worth diddly. But my opinion doesn't count. I've said this before, and I'm going to say it again, and by God, I hope this time you listen. *I am not your problem.* The people whose hands I'm trying to keep you out of—they're your problem. They honestly and sincerely think you know something of vital importance to the national defense. There is no way on God's green earth that you can persuade them otherwise. I'm the only one who can do that. If I can get you to safety, yup, I think I can do that very thing."

"You are not telling me everything." A shot in the dark. But it felt right. As she spoke the words, she knew they were true. "There is something else." She could read him now, read him like a book.

Charlie frowned at her.

"What is it? Tell me, Charlie."

He chewed the corner of his lip. His eyes focused less on the road than on some inner space she could not touch, but which, given time, she knew she could reach.

"Do you think I am weak? Do you think I cannot take it? Am I just a little child who is not to be trusted with the truth? Is that how you see me?" He winced. She'd pricked him. "I can handle it, Charlie. Whatever it is, I can deal with it. I might even be able to help. I am good, Charlie, you know I am good. Tell me, and we can work it out together."

His jaw tightened. "No," he snapped. "Not now. Maybe later."

"Unacceptable! I am the one who is in danger! You cannot—"

"Sure I can." With a wolf's grin, he tightened his grip on the steering wheel and locked his eyes on the road. "You know that flying saucer stuff?"

He was changing the subject on her. Unbearable! "No, and I do not wish to."

"It was back in 1947. The Air Force was launching radiosonde balloons from Holloman base, looking for high-atmosphere radiation in case Stalin was testing nukes. They called it Project Mogul."

"I am utterly uninterested."

He ignored her. She might as well not even be there. "So one of these balloons comes down on a ranch outside of Roswell, New Mexico. Well, of course the military runs scampering to fetch its top secret equipment. Then some local rancher tells the newspapers that he thinks an alien spaceship has crashed, and the Army's trying to hush it up—"

"You are treating me this way because I saw you cry." As soon as she spoke, she regretted it. No man wishes to be seen in his weakness, not even a man as strong as Charlie.

He did not so much as blink. For this Irina, now abashed, was thankful. "Well, my dad figured that was a God-given opportunity to mess with the Russkies' heads, so he sets up an operation to convince your people we really did have our hands on a UFO—"

As furious at Charlie as she was at herself, Irina turned her face to the window.

"Hamadryad to King Cobra. Do you copy?"

"Cobra here. I copy."

"I'm in chopper four. We've acquired the target."

Schmidt reached out a finger, ejecting *Rosenkavalier*'s silvered harmonies from his Gelandewagen's impeccable Harman stereo. "Position?" he asked.

Hamadryad shouted to be heard above the roar of his helicopter's engine. "Unmarked dirt road, sir. Runs parallel to the west side of Mitchell Canyon. Can you find that on your map?"

The G-Wagen sported a wide-screened GPS display. In the passenger seat, Coral Snake, once a Gurkha on India's northern frontier, now a master sergeant of no nation, tapped a query on the keyboard. "Found it, sir. Mitchell Canyon. Thirty-six degrees and three minutes north. One hundred nine, eighteen south." His clipped English was flawless, not the least hint of that colonial lilt that always reminded Schmidt of his homeland's conceited Hindu bourgeoisie. "Our position is almost directly south of it. No roads are shown near the west rim."

Lifting the microphone to his lips, Schmidt depressed the Send button. "Are you certain it's our target, Hamadryad?"

"Affirmative, sir. Lollipop-red Cadillac Escalade. There's no missing it."

Schmidt touched his tongue to the corner of his lips. How many luridly colored Escalades could there be on northern Arizona's back roads?

Only one, Kolodenkova's.

A bit after seven in the morning, a janitor found a vintage Winnebago parked behind a school building, muffled cries coming from within. He'd called the local law. Soon thereafter, an aspiring Wyatt Earp, sidearm drawn and hammer cocked, had cautiously opened the suspicious vehicle. Two red-faced retirees were tied up in the back. One of them had wet his pants.

Miss Kolodenkova's work, no doubt about it.

The girl's MO was to steal another car as soon as she abandoned whatever she was driving. However, there'd been no auto thefts in the town, not a single one. Schmidt only had to think about that fact for a moment before ordering his men to roust every automobile dealer in the area out of bed.

It didn't take long to find the right one.

A more than merely nervous used car salesman burbled that yesterday, just before closing time, a woman calling herself Caroline Sonderstrom paid cash for a distinctive used Escalade. Yes, sir, the official Cadillac designation for that Escalade's exterior is poppy red, but it's more of a fire-engine red, you know, or maybe cherry, 'cause it's the brightest red you've ever seen. Stands out like a hard-on in a nudist colony, if you know what I mean. Aw, sure, she fits your description to a T, only her hair is brown, but the thing is, when I took down her driver's license number, I noticed her photo showed her blonde. No, sir, I didn't even think about it for a second, because you know the ladies—they change their hair more often than most boys around here change their jockey shorts.

Gratifying.

It was about time Charles slipped up. He'd used old photos for the girl's false ID. Unfortunately she dyed her hair to disguise herself. Had Charles been a bit more professional, he would have been prepared for that particular contingency. Schmidt most certainly would have been.

Glancing at the GPS systems's digital map, he pressed the Send button again. "Which way is she headed?"

Hamadryad responded, "North."

"Our GPS database does not seem to portray every dirt track and cattle path in Arizona. Hamadryad, you're going to have to help me find the turnoff. I'm on Navajo road thirty-four, repeat three-four, headed west. We've already passed a number of ranch roads. There's no way we can tell from the ground which one Kolodenkova is on."

"Stand by, Cobra. I'll drop back toward the highway and see if I can spot you."

"I'm switching my emergency flashers on. We should be easy to recognize."

"Copy that."

Hide in plain sight. He gave Kolodenkova credit for her cleverness. The girl intentionally chose a high-visibility vehicle. His soldiers would be looking for an anonymous car or truck—Dodge, Chevy, Ford, all the common nameplates found on every highway in the West. What they would not scrutinize was something so ostentatiously eye-catching that no fugitive would dare use it.

Clever, uncommonly clever, she was a worthy opponent. The endgame would be sweeter for that.

"I see you, Cobra."

Schmidt craned his neck. His G-Wagen had just passed

through a pungent coniferous forest. Now on open plains, wild grass and grazing sheep, he peered into the distance. Two o'clock high, a tiny black dot hovered above a mesa layered like a cake. He flashed his high beams three times.

"You just gave me three flashes, correct, sir?"

"Correct, Hamadryad."

"And there's a white van behind you."

"That's Puff Adder and five team members. Correction, four plus a supernumerary. Our client is accompanying us, albeit not entirely willingly. Now where's the turnoff?"

"About five miles ahead of you, sir. You'll pass one, no two, ranch roads. The one you're looking for is the third. It angles back northwest almost as soon as you get on it."

"And our target?"

"Approximately thirty miles north of the intersection. I estimate her current speed at about twenty miles per hour. She's kicking up lots of dust. I'd say it's a lousy road. She's not going to make good time on it. Neither will that van behind you."

"The van has been modified for difficult terrain. Puff Adder may not enjoy the ride, but he'll keep pace. As for myself, why, Hamadryad, a Mercedes Gelandewagen is a miracle of German engineering. At fifty miles an hour, I doubt if we'll experience more than modest discomfort."

In the seat next to Schmidt, Coral Snake gritted his teeth and tightened his seatbelt.

"Hamadryad, how much firepower is your chopper carrying?"

"A .223 caliber chain gun, sir. That's all we could find on short notice."

"Then I would encourage you to put it to the use God intended. Slow Kolodenkova down, stop her if you can. We'll be there soon enough."

"We only have rubber bullets, sir. That was your order. I don't know if—"

"Ah, but neither does she. Pepper the ground in front of her and she'll think it's full metal jackets all around. Inexperienced girl that she is, she'll probably pull over and step out with her hands above her head."

"Copy that, sir. I'm on it, sir."

Schmidt watched the distant helicopter bank into a turn, disappearing as it raced north.

Usually his world was grey, was Johan Schmidt's. All that caught his eye was cover, concealment, and camouflage. But every now and then, quite rarely, his personal clouds lifted, a sun of startling purity illuminating the very palette God used when painting His creation.

So it was at just this delightful moment. He could *taste* the colors of plains, buttes, the sky. It was a feast!

At one with the world, he nestled back in his Gelandewagen's soft leather and breathed deeply of sage-spiced air.

All that was missing was the appropriate music. *Something triumphant*, he thought. He fingered through the collection of CDs in his G-Wagen's console, selecting, as always, the perfect choice. He slid the disk into the player, tapping his finger as he stepped through its tracks. Track seven. Act Three, Scene Five, *Die Meistersinger von Nürnburg* by Richard Wagner. A festive meadow outside of Nürnburg. Beneath a blessing sun, good burghers preen their gaudiest finery. All is joy as the guilds march in to celebrate this most important of feast days. The first to enter are the *Schusters,* the cobblers, singing jubilant praise of their patron saint, *Sankt Krispin lobet ihn! War gar ein heilig Mann, zeigt, was ein Schuster kann.*

Johan Schmidt savored a wide delight, anticipation of greater delights to come.

* * *

"Goddamn it to hell!" The helicopter was in Charlie's rearview mirror, closing fast.

"What?" It was the first word Irina had spoken for the last half hour. Charlie wished he had the luxury to enjoy it.

"Behind us. Bell AH-1. Vietnam-era gunship."

He slammed the accelerator down. The Escalade had a plush comfy suspension, just what you wanted if you were a well-to-do pensioner retired to a golf resort condo. However, it was not made for bomb-crater-sized potholes on a badly maintained Navajo dirt track. It wallowed all over the road like a drunken hippopotamus.

Irina appraised the surrounding terrain coolly; he expected no less of her. "There is no cover."

Charlie observed that her eyes were open wider than they should be. But resolution showed in the set of her jaw, and that was good. Growling, he wrestled for control of the lurching SUV. "Tell me something I don't know." *Grazing land. This is the worst place in the world to get caught in the open.*

"Charlie, he is swinging sideways. He has a machine gun!"

He downshifted to first gear as he threw the Escalade's transmission into low-power four-wheel drive. "That drainage ditch on the right-hand side—keep your eyes on it. I need a spot where it's shallow enough to get this pig off the road without leaving the undercarriage behind."

"Off the road? There's no place to hide. It is flat, all flat."

Fear? Yeah, there was fear in her voice, but also courage and confidence. There was no one he'd rather have at his side in a situation like this. Not that he'd ever tell her that. "Optical illusion. Mitchell Canyon is . . . damnit! . . . " The

Escalade bucked like a rodeo bull. Seatbelt notwithstanding, Charlie's head bumped the cabin roof. "The canyon's about a mile and a half to your right. Cuts straight through this plateau. Five hundred feet deep in places. You can't see it until you're on top of it."

The gunship was directly behind him. The buffet of its blades made the Escalade even harder to manhandle. "The ditch, Irina? How deep?"

She shouted over the helicopter's roar. "Too deep! Five feet! Six!"

A .50 caliber machine gun sounds like a buzzsaw chewing oak. The road exploded, sand geysers fountaining three feet above its surface. Charlie swerved. A trail of bullets cut in front of his bumper, kicking dirt so high that flecks of gravel pocked his windshield.

"Warning shots. Next time they'll blow the hell out of us. What do you see?"

"Nothing! Charlie, nothing!"

His skin prickled, he felt his muscles tense. It was always like that. The body knew what was about to happen before the brain. It readied itself, mustering resources for what was to come. Suddenly he was calm, so calm, quite thoroughly relaxed. "Well hell, looks like it's going to be one of those days."

He tapped the brake. Not hard, barely enough to flash the rear lights, signaling his enemies he was slowing down. *Here we go again,* he thought, because he'd been here before and this time would be no different. "Blue sports bag. My war bag. In the backseat. Get it."

Irina swiveled in her seat, wrestling the open satchel into her lap. "Guns," her voice was so low that Charlie almost didn't hear her. "Four pistols."

"Two old FBI-style .40 calibers. Two Browning Hi-Powers.

I'll take the Brownings. The Smith & Wessons are yours. Lock and load." It came to him that he was actually looking forward to it. There's a real pleasure in doing those things you do well, and too bad if what you do best is kill your enemies.

Irina flicked four safeties, slapped four clips into four butts, racked back four slides.

He saw how the game would play out. A chess master sees the same. The pieces are in this position. In six moves they will be in that position. There's no other way it can be. "Take two, tuck 'em behind you, beneath the belt, over your fanny. Give me the other two. Fetch a couple spare magazines for each of us." He took the pistols from her hand, arched his back, slipped them under his waistband. "Okay, I'm coming to a stop. When I do, we both climb out with our hands above our heads. We walk to the back of this pimpmobile, and stand near the edge of the ditch. How are you at ambidextrous shooting?"

"Not so good. With my right hand—"

"Good enough to hit a helicopter at twenty or thirty yards?"

"Yes."

"When I give the word, sweetheart, when I give the word."

"Cobra, do you copy?"

"I copy."

"There are two of them, sir."

"Two what?" Schmidt snapped angrily. He was, he acknowledged, irritable—an unseemly emotion under the best of circumstances, and certainly ill-suited for a man who had victory in his grasp. Nonetheless, he could not help himself.

This road—although that word was overly generous for the wretched sheep path—was worse than could be imagined. Its ruts were gouged more than a foot deep, a washboard for giants. Beach-ball-sized rocks littered the route. Every few hundred yards, the track disappeared, washed out, nothing but treacherous sand. He'd expected to be able to move at twice Kolodenkova's speed. As it was, he felt lucky to hold the speedometer needle at thirty miles an hour.

"In the Caddy, sir. It's not just the woman. Someone's with her."

Could it be? Oh, please, God, let it be!

"Description?"

"Good build, six feet-plus, white hair. Wearing khakis. We're kicking up a lot of dust, Cobra, and I can't make out his features."

McKenzie is with Kolodenkova! Perfect!

"Your position?"

"About thirty-five miles, make that thirty-eight, from the turnoff."

The Gelandewagen bounced. All four wheels left the ground. Schmidt grunted. In the seat next to him Coral Snake cursed. Schmidt, sunglassed eyes locked on the wretched route ahead, hissed, "Zip it. Not a word."

"Sir?" Hamadryad was shouting from a helicopter more than twenty miles from Schmidt's current location. How irksome. At his present rate of progress, it would take a half hour to reach them.

"Hamadryad, you've called in additional support, have you not?"

"Affirmative, sir. Rattlesnake and two other vehicles are converging on the north end of this road. They're coming up around where Mitchell Canyon dead ends. ETA is forty minutes."

Not good enough. "Other whirlybirds?"

"Problem there, sir. Number five is low on fuel; he's on his way back to base. Number three is the only other chopper in range, but he dropped down into Canyon de Chelly to check out a suspicious vehicle. Once he went below the rim we lost radio contact."

Needs must when the devil drives. "Keep airborne, Hamadryad. Do not attempt to land. Do not attempt to apprehend the fugitives. I'll be on the scene in, oh, shall we say, twenty minutes. King Cobra out."

"On this road?" Coral Snake gasped. "Are you crazy?"

"Two observations. One, never use the word 'crazy' in my presence again. Two, if you do not know the meaning of the phrase 'hairy mission,' you are about to learn it."

Charlie felt more than good. Charlie felt like God.

"Now!" he shouted, whipping two blue steel Brownings from behind his back. Eight inches and two pounds of righteous weight. Thirteen rounds in each magazine, one in each chamber. What more could a man ask for?

Arms stretched to their uttermost, elbows locked, don't aim, just point. "The pilot! Kill him!"

The machine gunner had been calling over his shoulder, his eyes not on his targets. That moment of distraction was all Charlie wanted or needed.

The pistols were finely balanced things, beautiful machines in their way, sweetly engineered to their lethal purpose. The rake of their butts nestled comfortingly in his hand, three fingers around the grip, thumb curled snugly above, and trigger finger . . . well, where else would his trigger finger be?

Black iron silhouetted against a dusky grey target, the

notches of his rear sights lining up so elegantly with the muzzle blades that he felt as if these guns were put here in his hands as a predetermined part of destiny's plan.

Two hammers clicked back with a most satisfying snap. Squeeze gently and . . .

When you're really in the heart of it, you don't hear it. The ignition of the powder, the percussion of the bullet blowing through the sound barrier, the harsh flat crack of a pistol shot . . . no, you don't hear a thing, not if you're doing it right.

However, you do feel it. The recoil hits your wrist first, then shocks along your arm, and no matter how hard you try, the jolt will send your barrel up and off target. A good marksman knows that, is ready for it, is already tensing those tendons that will bring his aim back down to the killing zone. Because if you know what you're doing and you've done it many times before, then doing it again is just doing what comes natural.

The helicopter's left window starred frosty white. Charlie fired again. He heard the roar of Irina's pistols. No need to look, he had every confidence in her. He squeezed his triggers another time, knowing that he'd done it well.

The machine gunner was back on the job. A little too late for that. Look away for a moment and your barrel drifts. Up in the air on an unstable platform, it takes time to get the sights realigned with your target, time this man did not have.

There is no such thing as bulletproof glass. There is only bullet-resistant glass. Hit it with enough jacketed rounds, eleven hundred foot-pounds of energy in each and every one, and star-shaped impact points form and crack. Hit it again the cracks widen. More bullets, please, the glass fractures. Jack fresh magazines into the butts of your weapons;

start firing again. The face behind the glass fogs into blood pudding.

And a machine gunner who has finally drawn a bead on his target is filling the sky above and the ground below with wild shots from a warship whirling out of control.

Charlie hurled himself left. He didn't have to look where Irina was standing because he knew where she was standing, knew it in his heart. His shoulder clipped her in the upper rib cage. Grunting, air expelled from her lungs by the force of the blow, she windmilled off the road, slipping then tumbling into the drainage ditch. Charlie leapt after her. She landed facedown in the sand. He threw himself on top of her, pressing her flat, covering her.

Protecting her.

Metal shrieked. A thin wailing scream, human perhaps, rose above the forges of destruction. The sky itself shattered, iron thunder, and the rain that fell was a rain of hot steel. The ground shook as a helicopter burst to shards. A fragment of its blade whipped over the ditch; Charlie felt the wind burn with its passing.

Transcendent satisfaction in every moment of it.

The job was done. Strenuous and fulfilling labor complete, his senses tingled postcoitally. His enemies were dead. He was alive. Who is incapable of feeling joy at that?

Irina squirmed beneath him. Nice, very nice indeed. . . .

Uh-oh! He rolled off her.

Gasping, she crawled on hands and knees out of the ditch. "Oh," was all she could say. Just "oh."

Charlie took a look. The carnage was most agreeable: twenty million dollars of finely tuned aerodynamics rendered into scrap.

Less agreeable was the condition of a poppy-red Cadillac Escalade. One of the helicopter's tail rotors had sheered through its front fender and was—spectacularly to Charlie's eyes—embedded in the engine block.

As for the rest . . . *Well, hell,* Charlie reflected, *a posse of twenty men with shotguns would have trouble doing that much damage.*

Irina, cheeks smudged and clothes gritty, pulled at the Escalade's door. It dropped to the ground. She fumbled inside, found the water bottle, and drank deeply before passing it to Charlie. "Now what?" she asked.

Charlie swallowed once, twice, three times. It was cold and good. A beer would have been better, maybe. But water was just fine. He stood for a moment studying the landscape, then answered, "We need to be on the other side of Mitchell Canyon. It's too far to walk around the north end. Only way to get where we've got to be is through it. Mile and a half that way . . . " he pointed east " . . . and we climb down. Three miles or so up the canyon, and we climb out. I've been there before. I know the way." He smiled fiercely. "You up to it?"

"Do I have a choice?"

That's my girl! "Nope. Those guys in the helicopter will have radioed for backup. Probably a couple of busloads of goons are headed our way from both directions on this road. Unless you feel like re-enacting Custer's last stand—he lost, you know—we go cross-country."

She reached back into the ruined Cadillac, pulling out a four-foot-long matte-black bolt-action rifle. "Who carries this?"

"Me. That's an Ed Brown Savanna gun, and I've always been envious to own one. The kid who got it for me . . . well, I was so downright delighted, I tipped him extra."

"Perhaps I am a better shot than you."

Charlie laughed. There wasn't any pride in her voice, she was just stating the facts. "If it comes to it, we'll see. Now sling a couple more bottles of water and all the ammo you can find into my war bag, grab your own kit, and let's make tracks."

Irina picked two pistols off the ground, flicked their safeties on, and muttered, "Whatever you say."

Charlie wasn't fooled. "Go ahead."

"Go ahead, what?"

"Go ahead and say what you really mean."

She smiled like a lioness. "Whatever you say. For now."

I am not frightened, Irina told herself. *I have done harder than this.* To which, unwanted, a mocking voice appended, *On a combat course. With safety nets.*

Angry, she shook her head. *I* can *do this! I can!*

Not you, girl, you're not good enough. . . .

She'd swallowed hard when she first saw it—the land sloping down gently, peach sand specked with flowering purple Rocky Mountain bells, an apricot-hued boulder beneath which a weary hiker might rest, tortured junipers nestled in shallow crevices, a terrain that would have been most pleasing to the eye had it not disappeared into hollow emptiness, nothing to be seen until, a mile away, the striated walls of a canyon side rose out of cool morning shadows.

That was the *other* side. The one that had to be climbed up once *this* side was climbed down.

"Do you need to catch your breath?" Charlie said, relaxed and looking like he was born in this place, squinted over his shoulder.

He was belittling her again. She reddened. "A ten-minute run is nothing."

"Good. I see dust kicking up back toward the road. Company's coming."

Irina peered warily over the precipice's edge. Straight down, more or less. A sheer drop but for a few craggy outcrops. To the north, the canyon was terraced, a rust-colored staircase for titans, each step ending in a hundred-foot drop. To the south, sheer ochre rock shot through with mica sparkling in the morning sun.

He expected her to be hesitant, apprehensive, uncertain. She did not intend to give him that particular satisfaction. "I hope the climb is not too strenuous for a man your age."

His answer was a snort—that and a smile so knowing that she ground her teeth.

He began trotting north, a leisurely jogger's pace, his feet picking out the easiest path among lichen-pocked stones and water-carved pits, each as smooth as her mother's kitchen bowls. She kept step close behind him, he with his eyes studying the cliff's jagged edge. He'd said he had been here before. He said he knew where he was going. She had her doubts.

"Ah!" a grunt of discovery. She followed his eyes, seeing only eroded stone so red-orange that it reminded her of tangerines. The ground was littered with sullen grey pebbles. Miniature cactus, clawed like tiny kittens, sprouted in the sand. In the sky, turning and turning, a turkey buzzard hovered. She heard no sounds but the sigh of wind. Suddenly, surprisingly, it came to her that there was an enormous beauty here, peace as well, if only one had the time to accept the gift.

Charlie stretched out his hand. "Give me my war bag and your purse. No way in hell can we carry them down."

Fetching a handful of loose karabiners from the bag's bottom, he used them to clip water bottles to his belt loops, and to hers. He stuffed a box of Hornady .30-06 cartridges into his left pocket, six nine-millimeter pistol magazines into his right pocket, and slung a pair of black Leica binoculars around his neck. She, in a man's denims, slid four spare magazines for her own guns into her pockets, then silently accepted the wickedly long Buck hunting knife he offered her.

"One pistol each. Give me your second one." She obeyed. Charlie dropped two handguns and her purse into the bag, zipped it closed, and, spinning like an Olympic hammer thrower, hurled it off the cliff. "If we find it down below, we take it. If not, we do *not* go looking for it." He had his khaki shirt off, was knotting the right sleeve around his money belt; the left dragged in the dirt. "This is the best I can do. It'll dangle maybe ten inches under my feet. If you feel yourself getting into trouble, grab it. It's a Filson; it can take your weight." To which he added, a worried look in his eye, "Whether I can is another question entirely."

He was going over! But there was nothing here! Flat, wind-polished sandstone without so much as a crack into which she could wedge her fingers. It was madness. She couldn't stop herself from shouting, "You are insane! There is no—"

"Trust me." He tightened his rifle bandoleer around his chest.

She trusted no one. Once, perhaps, she had. But that was long ago, and when her father said those words, she soon discovered that the only person she could trust was herself.

Charlie continued, his voice low and serious. She forced herself to listen. No power on earth could force her to believe. "The Anasazi, the old-time Indians, they were cliff dwellers, built their adobe fortresses all up and down these canyons. Back then, life was war to the knife—all against all. So they chose the most inaccessible spots, the places where no enemy could creep up on them from below, sneak down on them from above. There are ruins right beneath us, big ones, maybe housed a hundred and twenty people who planted their crops here on the plateaus. Came up by day to work them. Went down by night for safety. And the way they went up and down—the way they moved through *all* these canyons—was by cutting trails into the virgin rock."

Irina stared into the abyss. The cliff wall fell away, an almost imperceptible slope, terrifyingly steep. Far, far below broken scree bordered the tangled tops of dusky olive trees. "There is no trail here."

"See where the stone is gouged out there—looks like natural erosion, but it isn't. Those are handholds. You're lightest, you go over first. Hang on tight, probe with your feet. You'll find the recesses the Anasazi carved; they're spaced maybe two, two and a half feet apart. Take it easy. Test each one. Don't put your weight down until you're sure it's solid. The wind and rain have had centuries to work on them. They can crumble like burnt toast. Be careful. And like I said, if anything goes wrong, grab for the sleeve of my shirt."

"You are a crazy man. I will not do this."

And he with his unspeakably infuriating grin replied, "You're not afraid, are you?"

I am not frightened. I have done harder than this. On a combat course. With safety nets.

She shook her head. *I* can *do this! I can!*

Irina slid over the edge.

Exhilaration.

Nothing *nothing!* was better than putting yourself to the test and triumphing. Irina reveled in her mastery—flawless control of muscle, of breath, and, most important of all, of mind.

The least mistake would fling her into empty air. A hundred and fifty meters, gravity's prisoner, she'd die a wet pulp on a rocky canyon floor. For this reason, fear was irrelevant. She felt not the least hint of its touch. Her thoughts were elsewhere. The texture of sandstone. The salt sweat running down her cheeks. The whisper that preceded a gust of wind, and the tensing of her fingers as she braced herself against it. The delicate caress against her toes as she probed for another thousand-year-old handhold, sliding her foot into its shallow stirrup.

She wore size seven shoes; the ball of her foot barely fit into those ancient notches.

Press. Press ever so gently. Feel windblown sand slide beneath your feet. Has the rock rotted and crumbled? Will it bear your weight? Lower yourself a little more, test it, do not act in haste.

It held. She lowered herself another two-thirds of a meter.

Pure euphoria. Risk it all, risk it with every step. Every centimeter is a victory. Every victory brings joy.

She was centered only on this, the apex of physical achievement. Her mind and body were one, transfigured in mutual elation, a unity collaborating with exquisite grace to master the unmasterable.

Above her Charlie, he as lithe and muscular as she, called out little encouragements. His shirtsleeve, an unnecessary precaution, really, dangled not far from her face. She glanced up, not often; he was doing fine. On the whole, she ignored him. He was not what was important. All that was important was the deed and her self-imposed imperative that she execute it flawlessly.

In some sense she wished she could continue forever. In

some sense she was disappointed when her feet reached a razor-thin ledge.

Bottom of the climb. She'd descended a hundred meters of sheer rock. From here on the path was a childishly easy walk, a half-meter-wide trail hewn out of virgin sandstone. It cut down the cliff, not sloping steeply, five switchbacks before it reached the canyon floor.

Charlie was beside her. "You okay?" he asked.

"That was fun." Her skin tingled fresh and bright. She almost wanted to run the rest of the way.

"Take a deep breath, Irina. You're on an adrenaline high."

"Do not tell me that," she snapped. He was spoiling it, casting a shadow over the joy she felt.

"Right." His eyes were narrow. She loved the deep lines around them. He was an exceptionally handsome man. How had she not noticed that earlier?

He continued. "I'll lead from here."

"Catch me if you can, Charlie!" and she danced down the ledge, pacing herself to keep just beyond his reach.

The fall, when it came, was neither long, nor hard, nor painful. She lay laughing among dappled grasses beneath the adobe walls of a millennium-old ruin.

Johan Schmidt did not smile, although he was tempted. The spectacle of a plump-bottomed Washington bureaucrat vomiting in terror was, by any definition, amusing.

Samuel, that unfortunate desk jockey, had reacted predictably poorly to descending a five-hundred-foot cliff, child's play though it was with two brawny Nigerian mercenaries belaying the ropes, and a third rappelling at his side. Now he was on his hands and knees, wiping his lips with a handkerchief as white as his face. It was, Schmidt acknowledged, a deliciously droll sight. The troops were having trouble controlling themselves. He shot them a warning glance. Their grins faded to thin-lipped seriousness.

It was useful for people such as Samuel, the people who paid the bills, to see what the work was like. Not until they were up close and personal with field personnel doing what field personnel do best did they genuinely understand the value they received for their money.

"Give him water," Schmidt ordered. Samuel glugged a canteen's contents down too fast, then started puking again. Predictable. Such was the sort of behavior you expected of civilians.

He turned his attention elsewhere. Almost all of his men were now at canyon's bottom. Two remained above the scarp, working the ropes as they lowered a pair of Honda ATVs that would, quite soon now, bring this time-consuming affair to its predestined conclusion.

Charles, Charles, there's a butcher's bill to pay. Good men are dead, and the time has come for you to settle a debt due for decades.

The girl, as well. Kolodenkova. She owed him a certain price. Cottonmouth, who had died in his arms, was more than a comrade. They had consoled one another, he and she; in difficult times and in troubled circumstances, they'd gifted each other with solace and oblivion. That so fine a woman, a born warrior, had gone to her grave burned black at the bottom of a ravine . . .

Schmidt felt his anger rise. Anger was good. Anger befitted a soldier. But it was better to husband and hoard it, saving it for the moment when it served its purpose best.

He turned his thoughts elsewhere.

How far ahead were Charles and his companion? Ten minutes. Perhaps a little more. It made little difference. Be it ten or be it twenty, their lead was no advantage—not with two all-terrain vehicles on their trail.

It would have been better to overtake him up on the plateau. However, the best that could be done was to follow him at a slightly faster pace than poor aging Charles could run. In this regard, Schmidt's Gelandewagen had proved its mettle, crossing (although not easily) a deep drain ditch so that it could follow in the fugitives' tracks.

Follow slowly, given the terrain and the G-Wagen's load.

Three other trucks bearing additional troopers had arrived from the north. Those men had to be packed into Schmidt's already crowded off-roader. Happily, one of those trucks towed a trailer bearing two Honda ATVs, four-wheeled motorcycles with balloon tires that were capable of making good speed over even the most broken ground.

Eighteen people in total, sixteen skilled fighters, a bitterly complaining national security advisor, and Schmidt himself. Two men had mounted the Hondas. Another five rode on the G-Wagen's roof, two more on the sideboards, the rest crushed in the Gelandewagen's cabin . . . the rest except for Sidewinder.

Ah, Sidewinder! He was the best tracker Schmidt had ever known, better by far than any man under Schmidt's command, and indeed better than Schmidt himself. True, Britain's innocuously named Special Air Services, the SAS for short, were beyond question the best-trained commandos in the world—as was evidenced by the fact that while America's Delta Force had gotten all the media coverage in Afghanistan, it was the SAS that had done the heavy lifting.

Even for an SAS-schooled soldier, Sidewinder was uncommonly talented, preternatural in his perception of shape, shadow, silhouette, surface, and spacing—those five "s-words" encompassing the stalker's art.

Who is the deadliest soldier? Let there be no debate: it is the skillful tracker of men.

Sidewinder—blue-checked shirt and dusty chinos—had sprawled clinging to the G-Wagen's bouncing hood, eyes roving the route ahead, calling out the course in a raspy Yorkshire accent. "Crushed dung beetle o'r th' right. Gee us a sixteen-degree tarn." "Loose leaves by yon brush, downwind not up." "Tracks. Deep a' th' heel. Walking back'ard, th' cunning buggers."

Piece of cake.

Sidewinder had led them straight to a pair of faint scrape marks, unmistakable signposts as to where the likely-to-be-late Charles McKenzie had slid over the edge of a cliff.

From there it was but a few minutes of well-practiced drill—ropes fastened to the Gelandewagen's tow motor, rappelling harnesses donned, down the rock wall faster than Charles and Kolodenkova possibly could have climbed. A rather sharply worded order was needed to encourage Samuel over the edge. Weapons, ammunition, radios, and the other necessities of the hunt followed the sweating civilian.

It had moved with military precision, which was the point of the thing. Every man knew his duty as well as he knew the moves he had to make. Schmidt was honored to command them.

Now the ATVs bumped down from above, the Gelandewagen's motor regulating a swiftly unwinding spool and two high-tensile ropes. The right men and the right equipment—all was as it was supposed to be. The mission would be accomplished professionally and with pride.

He'd send two outriders to the fore. On the ATVs they'd soon overtake the prey. Once the targets were seen and marked, ordinary rifle work would pin them down. Schmidt and the rest of his force would jog toward the sound of gunfire, and then . . . why then, what hope had an old man and an inexperienced girl against sixteen skilled mercenaries under the command of none less than Johan Schmidt?

One problem, only one: no camo and no ghillie suits. All of Schmidt's men wore civvies: colored shirts, denims and khakis. That made them easy targets. Charles, being Charles, would have a long gun. Casualties were inevitable.

Regrettable.

"Sir!" Sidewinder trotted back from his recon. His Yorkie accent turned the word into "sah!" Schmidt liked that. He asked, "Found their spoor?"

Sidewinder showed brown horsey teeth. He fingered a half-smoked cigarette stub from the pocket of his blue-and-white-checked shirt. Igniting it with a match, he nodded. "Dead easy. Some bugger's leggin's took th' shine off a bush's leaves near yon brook. Creek sediment's mucked up. Bit of a bother when they take to water. But ye've got a broken spider web upstream the bank, nice top mark that, and some splashes in th' sand. They're gone for th' north."

"Map," Schmidt ordered, holding out his hand. He did not bother to look at the aide who instantly obeyed.

Schmidt studied a U.S. National Imagery and Mapping Agency topographical map, nicely detailed at a half kilometer to the inch. Mitchell Canyon was an eight-inch ribbon disappearing off the map's southern border, dead-ending to the north. *A box canyon, how convenient.* While the rutted west road he'd had to travel did not appear on the map, a Navajo highway did. It lay just beyond the canyon's northern border, no more than six miles from where Schmidt stood. A small side road intersected that highway to the east of the canyon, running a few miles south to what he guessed was an Indian farm village—doubtless one of those pathetic clusters of weather-worn trailers and sheet-metal-roofed hovels that were sprinkled all across the Navajo reservation.

Obvious, so obvious. Charles, you disappoint me.

He raised his voice so that everyone could hear him. "McKenzie and Kolodenkova are running north. They'll try to—"

Something thudded behind him. He glanced over his shoulder. The Honda ATVs had arrived. Up above, high on the rock wall, the shadows of his last two men could be seen, abseiling swiftly down to the canyon floor.

Perfect. In mere moments everyone will be in place. The hunt can begin.

He continued, "Our targets are attempting to reach the end of the canyon, approximately ten klicks north. There's a road up above the rim. I expect Charles's plan is to ascend to it and flag down a passing vehicle. He will be at his most vulnerable while climbing out of the canyon. However, it would be my preference to stop him before he makes the attempt. I do not know how well traveled that road is, but there appears . . . " he slapped his hand against the map " . . . to be a village or trading post nearby. Three Turkeys it's called, and there may be sufficient traffic in and out of it—"

"Johan?" *How irksome,* Schmidt thought. He loathed being interrupted—especially while issuing orders. Nonetheless, the man was a client, and so patience if not deference was due. "Yes, Samuel."

The bureaucrat waddled toward him. He was in shamefully poor physical condition, exhausted by what had been little more than the sort of training exercise one administers to new recruits. Moreover, he was soiled and unshaven. That was an affront to Schmidt's standards. Regardless of the circumstances, he insisted that his men look sharply professional. A soldier who takes pride in his appearance is a soldier who takes pride in his work.

More irritation: Samuel was wearing his crybaby expression again—an overgrown infant who needed his diapers changed. The man had become simply insufferable. Last night he'd gone so far as to pull Schmidt aside, complaining of the number of foreign soldiers involved in this mission. Silly civilian that he was, he did not appreciate how difficult it was to recruit qualified American warriors, the best being patriotically if not profitably employed hunting turbaned terrorists in unpleasant climes. Happily, Schmidt explained, there always could be found in the ranks of every nation's special forces troopers whose excessive zeal discomforted their commanders. If they were trained and motivated, one simply did not care that they learned their skills as Angolan mercenaries, as Bosnia ethnic cleansers, or in one of those surprisingly good training facilities operated by gentlemen of the Muslim persuasion.

"Johan, did you say Three Turkeys?"

Something would have to be done about Samuel's insistence on calling him by his first name. That simply wasn't allowed. Least of all in front of the troops. "Yes, I did. Why do you ask?"

"Charlie," Samuel wheezed, "he has a son. Well, two sons. I think . . . I'm certain Claude mentioned that one of them is with the Indian Health Service. He said . . . I know he said . . . he's stationed at the Three Turkeys medical clinic."

No commander worth his salt shows the least dismay when his subordinates are present. Schmidt merely pressed his lips together, coldly collecting his thoughts. "Well, Samuel, that is disturbing news. I'm disappointed you saw fit to keep it secret until now."

"I . . . ah . . . but . . . "

Schmidt spun on his heel, again facing his men, raising his voice to drown out Samuel. "Belay those orders. It would appear that Charles's destination is somewhat closer than we imagined." He consulted the map. "Likely he plans his ascent no more than three miles from here. Our time is shorter than I wished. Sidewinder and Copperhead —" for just a moment he reverted to his native Afrikaans — " . . . *opsaal!*"

Slinging rifles across their shoulders, the two mercenaries straddled their ATVs.

"Sidewinder, take the point, follow their tracks. Copperhead, ten yards behind. Find them. Force them to seek cover. Shoot to pin them down, not to hit. I want them taken alive. The rest of us will catch up with you. Do not put yourselves in harm's way until we're on the scene."

"Yes, sah!" Sidewinder gunned a 633 cc engine into a throaty growl.

"You. Asp," Schmidt now was facing his radio operator, "broadcast an alert to all units. I want them converging on Three Turkeys ASAP. Map coordinates are—"

"No can do, sir."

Interrupted again! Schmidt felt his temper flare. "I. Beg. Your. Pardon."

"I tried to establish contact as soon as we reached bottom, sir. This canyon . . . signals just bounce off its walls. I can't raise anyone."

Heat. In his belly. In his chest. The rage was building.

Asp added, "If we had satellite radios, sir, it wouldn't be a problem. But we couldn't requisition any. G-4 even sent a request to this gentleman here" —he pointed to Samuel— " . . . and one of his people e-mailed us back that everything's allocated to military use. So you see, sir, we're one hundred percent off-line."

Schmidt could have let his anger show. It would have been a welcome release. But no. Better to keep it bottled up, stored, reserved. Save it, hoard it, keep it boiling hot until he had his hands around Charles's throat.

The longer you wait for your supper, the better it tastes.

Charlie believed if any trace of Eden was left on earth, it was to be found in these Arizona canyons.

Parklands of airy cottonwood and dun Russian olive traced the course of a tender brook. A tamarisk grove, willowy branches graceful as ballet dancers in repose, made a green tunnel through which he and Irina raced. It opened to a narrow defile pocked with shallow caves carved by wind and rain for aeons beyond reckoning; inside their depths, carved in stone the color of maple sugar, Charlie caught glimpses of ancient petroglyphs, sun signs and dancing animals, Kokopelli the priapic flute player calling the tune.

His heart sang. Fleeing for his life, Charlie's heart sang.

With Irina by his side, he sprinted down a wash that wound beneath a jutting overhang striped with desert varnish. White alkaline leeched out of its base, rendering the water in these beautiful bottomlands unpotable for humans.

But the deer adapted. Charlie knew they did. They and the bears and the cougars and all those other creatures blessed to live in secret gardens unknown to humankind.

Men almost never visited Mitchell Canyon. It was too prone to floods to be inhabitable, too remote for tourists, too steep a climb for the neighboring Navajo shepherds.

Oh, to be sure, the Anasazi had dwelt here once. Their fallen castles still stood above the canyon floor. But the Anasazi's era was a time of more forgiving weather. Nor had the Indian tribes yet raped the high plateaus of their forest cover, tree roots to siphon heavy rains, protection against the floods that now came almost every year.

Humanity moved on, paradise forgotten.

Irina—young ears—heard the sound first. She grasped his shoulder. "Listen," she said, hesitation in her voice.

Charlie stopped, tilting his head. The rumble of engines was distant, but coming closer. "Dirt bikes," he muttered. "Or ATVs. We've got company."

He admired the lightning intensity of her glance. No more crazy lady laughing at the thrill of a suicidal climb, she was back on an even keel, studying the terrain with an outdoorsman's eye. "There," she said, pointing eighty yards ahead to an eroded cave. "The canyon is narrow. A choke point. I'll have a clean field of fire."

Well, that was to be expected. *I'll have a clean field of fire.* Not you. Me.

He'd give her a chance. Worst case, she'd miss, and he'd have to take the rifle away from her. Best case, she wouldn't, and he'd earn himself a few points with the prickly Miss Kolodenkova.

Shoulder to shoulder they broke into a run. The growl of gasoline-powered motors mounted. Charlie figured there were only two, and was thankful for that.

Irina sprang on the balls of her feet, an easy jump to the cave's rim. The words "lithe" and "beautiful" flashed through Charlie's mind. They were, he assured himself, an aesthetic and not emotional judgement.

He clambered up the rock beside her, unslinging his Brown Savanna Rifle. God, it was a beautiful thing, light and graceful, only seven pounds, a fiberglass stock that begged to nestle into his shoulder. Less a weapon than a lovingly handmade piece of craftsmanship, it was a tool he begrudged letting out of his hands.

She, clearly a woman of taste, smiled approvingly as she weighed its elegant balance. "This is . . . " she said, saying nothing more because she did not have the words.

He passed her a handful of ammunition. "A work of art."

She smiled open and true. It came to Charlie that he'd won her. Just then, at that very moment, she—probably not knowing it—had yielded to a simple gesture of trust. Who would have believed it would be so easy a thing? *I trust her, so she trusts me. Brother, you should have worked that one out long ago.*

Bending at the waist, she plucked two weathered branches off the cavern floor. Sinking into what might have been mistaken for a yoga position, she folded her legs, crossing the branches and resting the rifle into the notch they formed.

Buffalo sticks—the hunter's classic ad hoc shooting rest.

The butt rested against her shoulder. Her head tilted right, one eye shut, the other gazing down a black Leupold six-power telescopic sight.

"Shoot to wound," Charlie said.

"I know that."

Well, of course she did. When you've got a hunting pack on your trail—and Charlie was pretty sure they did—you do your level best to put their scouts on the medevac list. A wounded man slows down the rest of the enemy because every soldier worthy of the name stops to give succor to fallen comrades.

Here they came. Charlie lifted his binoculars, Leica 10x42 Trinovas, sharp and bright with an excellent field of vision. Two of Schmidt's mercenary thugs rode atop forest-green ATVs—better for this sort of terrain than dirt bikes, which was an unfortunate credit to that South African bastard's planning abilities.

The front rider wore a blue-checked shirt. Its left cuff turned scarlet as his hand exploded.

Mighty fine shot, Miss Kolodenkova. Shattered the throttle into the bargain. Sent the ATV whirligig over a boulder, up into the air, and down at an ouchy angle. That particular vehicle is not going to be salvageable, and suck on that, Johan Schmidt.

Irina dealt with the second rider before Charlie could move his binoculars. Same shot in the same place, and that man's arm flew up spitting an arc of blood where his wrist had been. His ATV slewed into the creek. Steam sizzled as its engine hit the water.

Two down. How many more to go? Well, we'll find out soon enough.

Irina clicked two rounds into the Brown's internal magazine. "Here is your rifle back, Charlie. I did well, I think."

"Ha!" he exploded with delight. Then he kissed her on the cheek, and felt perfectly comfortable that it was the right thing to do.

Especially since she gave him a little hug in return.

Now they ran again, but the running was different because they ran as one. He and she were together in this. For this moment, and for whatever came next, they were closer than twins, not two individuals alone in their minds, but an inseparable whole, each part of the other, synchronized in thought, and action, and emotion.

He might have called it "love," although that was too feeble a word.

Less running than floating, her long hair streaming, slender as the wind—who was the old Greek goddess of hunting?—Diana, she was Diana come to earth, and Charlie felt such pride in her that he could not speak, but rather ran joyfully past pinyon pine and ponderosa, every now and then a Gambel oak thicket, and water birches with their witchy branches where songbirds startled at two animals of rare and unrecognized species.

So green, so green, such trees consecrated a landscape that Charlie thought to be in some sense holy. Here he was young again, his soul alive as it had not been for longer than he cared to remember.

The gnarled remains of an ancient apple plantation were the landmark he sought. Sometime—maybe a hundred years ago because those trees were old trees—a settler had planted them near the canyon's sole sweetwater spring. Nature favored him long enough for the trees to mature, but she favored him no longer than that. All that remained of the homestead was an orchard too old to bear fruit, and the melancholy stones of a washed-out cabin's foundation.

Foundation stones . . . They stored up the sun's heat, radiating it back at night. Rattlesnakes gravitated to the warmth. And now, at just this particular hour—he glanced at his watch: quarter to nine—they'd be slithering out. Breakfast time for venomous reptiles. Ugh.

Irina understood where they were headed, he saw it in the sharpness of her eyes. She'd picked out the one and only practical route up the canyon wall.

Long ago, the canyon side had caved in, creating a steeply narrow gulch. Centuries of rain washed through the cleft. Each passing storm carved it a little deeper, tumbled a few more boulders into its twisting course—beetling rocks where a man could rest his weight; others he could wrap his fingers around; a slope that could not be walked up, not exactly, but which could be crawled up, hand over hand.

"Drink some water," he said. She had already begun unclipping a karabiner from her belt. She'd known what he was going to say before he said it. Again he felt so close to her, closer than it was possible for any human to come to another.

After drinking deep, she passed him the bottle. He emptied it. Reluctant to litter a pristine place of beauty, he gave it back to her. Understanding and agreeing, she fastened it back on her hip.

"This is a tricky climb, Irina. I'll lead. I've been this way before."

"You climbed the trail down before, too. So why—"

"Nope. No one in their right mind would try that." Her jaw dropped. He relished the moment. "But I've climbed this route. Come on, let's do it."

The first thirty yards were loose scree and fist-sized cobbles, easy enough. After that it was solid rock all the way; climbing it would be only slightly less difficult than trying to scale a building side. Charlie wedged his left foot in a cracked boulder the size of a small truck. He pushed up, hooking his fingers over its crumbling rim. Sliding up the fissure, he levered his body waist high to the top. Irina, not as tall as he, couldn't find purchase for her fingers. Charlie lowered his hand, took hers, pulled her up.

They clambered up a natural stairstep of unnatural steepness. Charlie paused, remembering the way. *You've got to sidle around here, off to the left I think. Yeah, that's right, aw, hell, this next part is bad news.*

A slab the size of a house roof tilted crazily against the canyon wall. Wind and water had etched thin ridges into its face. If you took your time and watched your step, you could use those furrows as fingerholds and toeholds. It wasn't easy, but he'd done it before.

He did it again.

More than forty feet of climb-crawling at a vertiginous angle—he couldn't go straight up; there weren't enough handholds. He had to slide across naked stone, sandy grit abrading his shirt as he clung to the slab's uneven surface. Tilting his head to look for the route was not an option. The only way to negotiate the rock was by touch. He'd learned that lesson the hard way—how long ago?—years back when young Scott, a first-year medical student, had been a summer intern out here. Mary had climbed with him that day. He smiled at the memory of her whipcrack voice. "Charlie McKenzie, I'm nearly fifty years old and I don't have to prove anything to anybody." Ah, but that had been a good— *a perfect*—day.

Just like this one.

"You okay, Irina?"

"I am right behind you."

He rolled himself onto the top of the slab, again stretching a hand out for her. The bullet whistled over his left shoulder, percussing harsh and sharp into sandstone.

"Sonofabitch!" He jerked Irina up over the edge, tumbling her down behind it and out of sight. He followed. A bullet pinged above him.

Crouching low, Irina whispered, "I did not expect them to come so quickly."

As he'd scuttled for cover, the Brown Savanna gun's bolt had dug painfully into his back. He kneaded the sore place, knowing he'd have an ugly bruise. "No need to whisper. Nobody's near enough to hear. And they haven't come for us, not yet."

A third bullet cut the air, grazing the top of the slab, whining into a patch of juniper clinging to the canyon side.

"But they are shooting at us!"

Charlie shook his head. "There is no 'they.' It's one man. If Schmidt's whole mob was down there, it would be rapid fire, and lots of lead in the air. Put enough bullets into the rocks where the enemy's hiding, and one of them is bound to ricochet into your target. The guy who's shooting at us isn't trying to hit us on the bounce; he's just trying—successfully I'd say—to make us keep our heads down." He flinched as another shot slapped into the stone above him. "He's spacing his fire—one round about every ten seconds. He wants to keep us pinned here until his buddies catch up with him."

"But who—?"

"One of the men you shot. One of the ATV riders. Not both of them, or they'd be firing more rapidly."

"I hit both." Her voice sounded defensive.

"That you did. But one of them has bandaged himself up and followed on foot."

A crack of shattered stone, and a small hail of grit. Charlie glanced up at the bullet mark. He looked back at Irina, preparing to ask her for ideas on just how the hell to get out of this mess. . . .

Wait a minute. Something's not quite right here. He looked back up at pockmarked rock. *Now what could that be? Come on, McKenzie, something's nagging your subconscious. What is wrong with this particular picture? You're supposed to be good at this sort of thing—figuring out what's what, and then using it to skunk your opponents.*

He waited, silent and patient. The next bullet hit more or less when he expected it. Grains of sandstone puffed into the air, raining gently down on his head.

I'll be damned.

He scrambled forward, scanning the ground. Soon enough he found what he was looking for.

He plucked it—still hot—between his fingers, holding it out to Irina. Her eyes widened. Charlie smirked. "Seventeen caliber long rifle," he drawled. "Look at the holes it gouged in the sandstone. You couldn't put your pinkie finger in

them. Our friend down below is shooting at us with a goddamn squirrel gun."

She was confused. She didn't see it. "Schmidt wants us
alive," he explained. "Or at least you. He wants to find out
what you know about Whirlwind."

"I have told you, I know nothing."

"And I've told you, I'm not the one you have to convince."

"But—"

"But nothing. A pro doesn't use a .17 to kill a man. It's not
enough gun. The only reason why that lad down there is using
a small-caliber rifle is to . . . " Charlie drifted into silence. A
hypothesis was tickling the back of his consciousness. *Yeah,
that's the question. That and his marksmanship. That evil little
mongrel is one of Johan's people, and Johan's people simply
do* not *miss their targets.* All at once—same as usual because
that was the way it always happened—his hypothesis crystal-
lized. He felt a grin form on his face, and knew it was the kind
of grin that showed his teeth.

*Good news: I've got a theory. Bad news: there's only one
way to put it to the test.*

Charlie stood, straight and tall, an easy target in plain view.

Irina gasped. "Get down, Charlie! Get down! He will—"

Three quick shots, one left, two right. Neither of them
close enough to make him blink. "No, he won't." He ducked
back down, hypothesis confirmed. "That man is under orders to *not* hit us. If he wasn't, right now I'd be using your
tweezers to pick the bullets out of my hide."

"I do not carry tweezers."

The very thought seemed to offend her. "Didn't think you
did. Okay, let's do a little creative thinking. When I watched
that guy you shot through my binoculars, I saw he had a long
gun slung on his back."

"They both did. I saw them through my scope."

"No magazines jutting out the bottom, though?"

She closed her eyes, visualizing what she had seen. "No. I do not think so."

"Me either. You can buy a forty-round banana clip for any small-caliber rifle, but only gun nuts do that. A man who knows what he's doing wouldn't be caught dead with one. So let's make a little guess here. Let's guess he's got a built-in bottom-loader trapdoor magazine like my . . . our . . . Savanna Gun. And let's guess that it takes . . . hmm . . . how many? . . . let's guess seven rounds." He lifted the binoculars over his head, passing them to her. "I want you to spot for me. I'm the sniper. You're the partner. You know the moves, correct?"

"I know all the moves, Charlie."

"I never doubted it for a moment." He smiled at her, pure affection. "All right, get ready. When I give the word, stand up, find that sinner, and tell me where to aim." So saying, Charlie raised his head above the rock. A bullet's whine welcomed him. He ignored it. Head and chest visible to his enemy, he scuttled left. The shooter fired again, high and to Charlie's right. Charlie kept moving. Another round exploded in front of him, this time at eye level about three feet ahead. No question about it, Schmidt's gunman was trying to send him a message.

Charlie bent over, duck-walking a few steps, then raised his head again. That produced two more shots, his enemy trying to persuade him that he was facing triangulating fire and had better lie low. Charlie knew better. He bobbed his head down, then back up. Two more bullets slapped home. *Unless I'm wrong about the seven-round magazine, now's the time.*

"Do it, Irina! Do it!"

Tall and proud and straight and fearless, she stood with

the binoculars at her eyes, weaving a zigzag search across the canyon floor. Charlie silently counted a seven-round magazine being recharged. *One bullet. Two bullets. Three bullets. Four bullets. Five—*

"Five o'clock." She was calm about it, exactly what you wanted from your sniping partner. "The ruined cabin. Left corner."

Ah, yes, there you are, you sweet thing. He was damnably well concealed, prone against heavy foundation stones. Nothing showed except the thinnest ribbon of a blue-and-white-checkered shirt, a hard target but it would have to do. Charlie caressed the trigger and felt the sweet bounce of the butt against his shoulder.

"A hit." She kept her voice low, doing her job just the way it was supposed to be done. God, he loved the way she handled herself.

Deep breath, Charlie, and level the barrel, squint through the telescopic sight, get the crosshairs on your mark again because one bullet is rarely enough.

There he was and he was arched with pain. Distant, distant, you could barely hear it, although the man no doubt was shouting at the top of his lungs, "Aw, fookin' hell!" *I creased his side. Maybe skipped my shot across his ribs. Won't even slow down a tough guy like that.*

Charlie's second shot shattered his enemy's elbow. *That boy is out of the game.*

"Charlie," Irina said, no little awe in her voice, "Charlie, that was amazing."

Yeah, well, yeah, it was. On the fly. One hundred and fifty yards. A snap shot from the shoulder. *Who's king? I am king!* "All in a day's work, darling. Now let's get our fannies out of here before the posse shows up." *Did I just call her darling?*

They scrambled away from the slab. The next few min-

utes' climbing were easy—easy being a relative term because it largely was hand over hand, using outcrops as rungs
on a crazy man's ladder. Charlie didn't like it one little bit.
They were too visible, their backs inviting targets, no cover
anywhere. The sweat on his forehead had little to do with
exertion.

*Made it. What's next? If memory serves, a short run
through that dry wash.* He was feeling pretty good about
things right now.

There were boulders everywhere, a whole nation of boulders, giant fathers and three-foot-high toddlers, this was the
place where boulders came for their holiday vacation.

Charlie scrambled around them, picking his route so that,
most of the time, he and Irina were shielded from being seen
by anyone beneath them. Once they had to shin a mottled
grey pillar like a tree trunk—a short climb, but uncomfort-
ably exposed. Charlie's back itched while they ascended,
and he detected a certain hastiness in his movements.

Next they scrabbled up a fall of gravel, this one steeper
than the scree at the bottom of the cliff. Treacherously unstable rocks rolled beneath their feet; Irina gave a little cry
as she slipped, but Charlie was fast, and he had her hand, and
they were past it.

Indeed, they were past almost all of it, agonizingly close
to the canyon rim, when a fusillade of many guns rattled the
canyon walls. Charlie looked up hungrily. Sixty or seventy
feet—little more than the height of an ordinary telephone
pole. It was infuriating; another minute and they would have
been up and safe and screw you, Johan Schmidt.

He angrily threw the Brown to his shoulder. Cold, wholly
indifferent to the clap of bullets all around him, he picked
out his man, drew a line down his torso, leveled the
crosshairs on his groin, and sent him screaming to the

ground. There was another one racing forward, a chunky brute; he looked like a football tackle charging the quarterback. Charlie castrated him and took satisfaction in a scream easily heard, even at this distance. *One more, oh, God, give me just one more.*

"Charlie," she was spotting for him again, bless her, "are you doing that on purpose?"

"Get down!" He dropped as he spoke, reaching a hand for her belt. She didn't need the help. As the rocks around them exploded, she flung herself to the ground. "Yeah. We're up against seasoned fighters, blooded men. They're used to seeing their buddies take a bullet. It goes with the territory, and they really don't give a damn. Kill a few, and the rest just shrug it off. But if you hit a couple of them in the privates— well, that makes any man reconsider his career alternatives."

She grinned like a wicked child. Her blood was up, no different from his, a killing glint in both their eyes. He and she were two peas in a pod; mortal danger had the same intoxicating effect on them both; and it was hard, damned hard, not to roar like a hunting lion and make as many corpses as you could.

None of that. I'll have none of it. Neither will she. Charlie held himself rigid until it passed, and until cool sanity returned.

He emptied a box of cartridges, filling his shirt pocket and feeding three fresh rounds into the Brown. At times like this you preferred a detachable magazine. Empty it, eject it, jack another in, and keep up continuous fire. *No use wishing for what you don't have,* he told himself.

The reports of enemy gunfire echoed through the canyon. Charlie hated that. It desecrated a place dear to his heart. Another reason to paint a few more of the bastards red.

He knew his best chance of nailing them was while they

were still scurrying for cover. Besides, they were aiming to keep him pinned down. Right now, right at this very moment, the punks were just tin ducks in a shooting gallery.

He started to rise.

"Charlie, no."

"No choice. Schmidt's people have radios. They'll be calling for help. Cars and trucks and helicopters. We have to get out of here now." He rolled left, pulling himself erect, rifle at the ready, telescopic sights searching for a target, searching for . . . *I'll be damned. Dark glasses. Lean and loping like a tiger. It's the big boss himself, pleased to see you, you hyena, and I think a head shot is in order.* . . . "Jesus!" A thunderbolt burst up his leg. The pain of it, raw and electric, was unimaginably shocking.

Charlie's world went white.

When he opened his eyes—it could only have been a minute or two later—Irina was bent over him, fumbling a water bottle to his lips.

Aiming to keep us pinned down? So much for that theory. He accepted the water gratefully. "How bad's the damage?" he asked.

"It is your upper thigh, Charlie. There's an entrance wound but no exit wound. To stop the bleeding, I packed it with tissue paper, Kleenex. I had some with me in case—"

She blushed. Talking about having to go to the bathroom made her blush. If he wasn't hurting so badly, he might have smiled. "Twenty-two caliber, I bet. Feels like it's drilled into the bone."

"It must hurt."

"Nah," he lied, "not much." *Screwed up again. Cocksure again. Goddamn me, I'll never learn.*

"Stay there. I will take the rifle—"

"Like hell." She suddenly had that expression on her face.

Yeah, *that* one. Charlie appreciated the emotion behind it, but it simply wouldn't do. "Look at that slope," he growled. "Do you think I can get up it with a slug in my thighbone?" *You're not paying for my mistakes, sweetheart. I'm never letting anyone else pay, never again, you least of all.*

Irina studied the short ascent, straight up between layered red walls. She saw the same thing Charlie saw: a route that would have to be climbed like a chimney, no handholds but for precarious-looking juniper shrubs clinging to the rock. Turning to him, iron in resolve, she replied, "I will not leave you."

Oh, hell, Charlie thought, *now I'm in a Hemingway novel. Me and Robert Jordan.* He spoke rapidly, his words tumbling over one another. If he slowed down, she'd hear his pain. "You have to. Schmidt's gorillas are going to be arriving topside on the double. If you stay here, both our gooses are cooked. If you get away, then best case Johan'll leave me where I lie. I'm not the one he cares about." *Lie, you old bastard, lie like you never have before.*

"What is the worst case, Charlie?"

She would ask that. "It'll involve some humiliation, but not much else. He can't lay a hand on me. If he so much as tries, I'll dump a garbage truck full of muck on his boss's head. I've got insurance, Irina. The guy who hired Schmidt is dismally certain that if anything happens to me, his dirty linen gets shipped to every newspaper in the world."

"Charlie—" Her voice was soft and soothing. Listening to her, letting her talk, just plain basking in the way she spoke was damned tempting. He gritted his teeth. *Who played Robert Jordan? Cooper. Yeah, Gary Cooper.*

"No way. You're out of here. When you get up that notch you'll be right at the end of an airstrip. There's a plane waiting. Pilot's a bush doctor named David Howard. Once you're in the air, he can radio his clinic. They'll get a couple of medics out here to help me—that is, if he has a radio in that beat-up antiquity he flies, which he may not."

Now you are going well and fast and far. . . .

Charlie closed his eyes, a wave of pain almost tumbling him into safe unconsciousness. He could see . . . could see . . . the Three Turkeys airstrip . . . a pasture with scrawny cows . . . a stained white tank for aviation fuel . . . a faded orange windsock fluttering in the wind . . . that silly adobe building someone built as a tiny passenger terminal, hummingbird feeders dangling in front of every nicotine-stained window. . . .

"I cannot leave you like this."

Next thing, I'll be calling her my little rabbit. He shook himself awake. "Insurance. You need insurance, too. Something to bargain with, a gun you can hold to their heads." He chewed his lip, making his decision. "I'll give you the disk, the Whirlwind disk. Hide it somewhere. As long as it's out of their hands, they don't dare—"

"I have the disk, Charlie." Soft words, shy and slightly embarrassed. "I picked your pocket while we were in the car."

"The disk in my pocket was a decoy." He unzipped his fly, gingerly fingering a pouch sewn into the crotch of his slacks. "If you'd tried to filch the real one, I'm pretty sure I would have felt it."

Her expression transformed from chagrin to a blushing smile. "I would have made sure you felt it."

As he handed her the disk, Charlie forced a faint laugh.

Her last words to him were, "I will come find you. Wherever you are, I will come to you."

It was a lie, probably, one of those things you say to make someone who feels bad feel better. Charlie doubted he'd really brought her around to his side. The more he thought about it, the more certain he was that he'd been fooling himself—just another old man fooling himself about a pretty young woman, and we've all seen that before, haven't we?

She didn't give a damn about him.

Which wouldn't stop him from protecting her, no sir, it wouldn't stop him at all.

By the time she'd backed out of sight, Charlie had crawled forty feet or so left of where he had been. Every inch was agony. He didn't know how he'd kept from blacking out. *I guess I'm not awfully good at pain.*

Tumbled boulders formed a shadowed firing niche. The canyon lay nearly five hundred feet below; such beauty; a willow-lined creek, a dappled apple orchard, sand the hue of old gold. Men—a dozen of them, or thereabouts—dodged from tree to rock to bush, the classic tactics of a platoon advancing on a fortified redoubt. No one was in the open for more than seconds. Everyone moved fast and low.

Advantage: Charlie. He could see them; they couldn't see him.

He waited patiently for his first target, a soldier in a sweatshirt and phat pants concealed behind an oak. Patience paid off. The man broke his cover, scurrying for a sand bunker. Charlie shot and missed and cursed.

That first shot had been the signal to Irina. She sprinted toward the cleft. Its deep walls provided shadow and concealment. Schmidt's mercenaries wouldn't see her easily. They'd have to search for her through their scopes and binoculars. Charlie didn't plan to let them do that.

He snapped off another round, this one aimed at a declivity where a mercenary might—or might not—have been crouching.

The point wasn't to hit any of them—although that would

be a welcome bonus. Charlie's goal was to keep them down, cowering in fright—fear being an appropriate emotion when confronted by a marksman who aimed for the testicles.

He fired again.

Not that he was a marksman. Not any longer. His hands shook, sweat drenched his shirt, and his wounded leg was a nauseating pillar of agony. His nerve endings were on fire; if screaming would have helped, he would have screamed.

Instead he forced himself to look for a target, look close, look hard, concentrate then pull his trigger. *Nuts, missed again.*

The Savanna gun's magazine clicked dry. He flipped the rifle over, one hand feeding fresh rounds to the trapdoor magazine, the other extended through his firing niche holding a Browning automatic aimed blindly as he worked the trigger. At this distance he hadn't a hope in hell of hitting anything with a pistol. He fired only to keep his pursuers—Irina's pursuers—lying low, and not, most definitely not, searching the shaded crevasse where a nearly invisible young woman climbed.

He rolled back, rifle ready, and started seeking targets again. By now someone had worked out his approximate location. That someone's bullets whined in the air above him. Charlie couldn't find the shooter. Bright yellow spots danced in front of his eyes. Hard to spot an enemy with clown balloons cluttering up your vision.

Empty again.

The pistol again.

Back again.

His mind had shut down, mostly. He was on autopilot, a fleshy robot programmed to do a very few, very simple things. That was all that was necessary. Anything else would have been superfluous—and, in any event, beyond his nearly depleted powers.

Somewhere along the line he heard the buzzing rasp of an airplane engine. That surprised him because he didn't think he'd been shooting long enough for Irina to get to the top and make her way to safety. But then again, both boxes of .30-'06 ammo seemed to be empty, so he supposed he'd been doing this for longer than he thought.

How many rounds left? Five in the palm of his hand.

He looked at the ground: two empty water bottles at his feet; he didn't remember drinking them. He'd given Irina, he supposed, all the time she needed.

Charlie's world no longer contained colors; it wasn't even monochrome. Satisfied that he'd done his job, he faced the waiting darkness, sighing as he sank into its welcome embrace.

Sam was late to the party. It had taken two of Schmidt's big boys to hoist him out of that canyon, and neither of them had been polite about it.

Now filthy and exhausted he limped toward where the survivors of this expedition—this *failed* expedition—clustered at the ass end of Dogpatch International Airport.

He couldn't hear what was going on because Schmidt seemed to have a ghetto blaster with him. One of his underlings must have hauled the thing all the way down the cliff, through the canyon, and back up again. Creepy—no less creepy than Schmidt himself.

The boom box was playing that classical garbage Schmidt loved, volume deafeningly loud, a bass trio booming in who-knew-what-language, *"Ad nos, ad salutarem undam . . . "*

Not until he shoved his way through the circled soldiers did he see Schmidt or hear his unemotional, "This should turn your urine the color of cherry soda," as he drove a fist into his prisoner's kidneys.

Charlie's face was Christ crucified on an antique icon. A pair of Schmidt's henchmen held him up. He'd passed the point of having the strength to stand. To Sam's eyes it looked like Schmidt had mostly left the face alone. A rivulet of blood trickled out of Charlie's mouth, and his left cheek was swollen with an incipient bruise. His torso was another matter. Or so Sam supposed. He didn't want to know. The sort of marks Schmidt was putting on Charlie's body were something you were better off not thinking about.

Then too there was his leg . . . Sam looked elsewhere . . . it was a sick wet red where Schmidt, quite obviously, had repeatedly battered a bullet wound.

Schmidt rolled his left shoulder back, throwing the entire force of his weight into his next punch. "Charles, Charles, you do have the strongest ribs. I haven't heard a hint of a crack yet." He danced backward a few steps. "Much as it pains me to abandon the Marquis of Queensberry, I fear something less sportsman-like is required." He spun into a straight-legged kick. Charlie groaned. Schmidt sighed. "Not even that. Oh, well." He looked left and right. "No one would happen to have a baseball bat handy, would they? I thought not. Ah, me, I suppose I simply must try harder."

Turning in preparation for a second kick, he caught sight of Sam. Sam shook his head, giving Schmidt a hard look. He was happy the mercenary wore dark glasses because he genuinely did not want to meet his eyes.

"No?" Schmidt asked. "And why not?"

Sam could barely hear him over the boom box. "Can you turn that thing down?"

"Reluctantly. *Le Prophete.* Meyerbeer. Rousing good

stuff from the days when grand opera was truly grand. Still, if you insist . . . " He bent from the waist, lowering the sound. "There, does that make you happy?"

Sam knew he was about to take a risk—never a pleasant thought. Schmidt was almost out of control. Sam had to assert his authority now; if he didn't, he'd have no authority left. "The only thing that will make me happy is getting my hands on Whirlwind. McKenzie's just a sideshow."

"On the contrary, Samuel. Charles is an annoying pest who has thwarted me one time too often. It is my intention to recompense him for the irritation he has caused me. I believe that much is due me."

"Oh, to hell with that. We have bigger fish to fry. Just Glock him and be done with it."

Schmidt stepped close. Sam managed not to flinch, although it wasn't easy. "I have taken casualties this morning, Samuel. A price is owed. I do not desire to deprive my men of vengeance's simple pleasures."

If Sam backed off now, Schmidt would never obey him again. "I'm not paying you to amuse your people. I'm paying you to catch a Russian spy. The more time we waste here, the worse are our odds."

"Three points." Schmidt raised a finger. "One, Mr. Maximilian Henkes of DefCon Enterprises is paying me, Samuel, not you." The second finger shot up, "Two, the time is not wasted. No investment in morale is wasted." Three fingers like a trident, "Three, she will not escape. I know where she is going, exactly where she is going, and I shall be waiting for her when she arrives."

Taken aback, Sam blurted, "Charlie talked?"

"Of course not." He glanced at McKenzie, limp and propped by two of his soldiers. "You'd never talk, would you, Charles?"

Charlie managed to whisper something. Sam thought it might have been *fuck you.*

"You see, Charles and I are members of the same profession, scholars of the same school. As he was able to read the signs, so was I. Being, I acknowledge, more deductive than I, he reached his conclusions more swiftly. Nonetheless, we both arrived at the same answer, didn't we, Charles? Come now, man, don't look at me like that, you know how it upsets me. All you need do—your voice being alarmingly weak—is nod yes or no. Your deduction was that she would run for San Francisco, for the Russian *rezidentura.* That was her first full-time duty station, the American city she knows best. Confess, Charles, I am correct, am I not? Be a good boy, a single nod is all it takes." He leaned close to Charlie, lifting his prisoner's chin with a finger. "Ah, Charles, in your weakened condition your face betrays you. Try though you might to disguise it, I can readily see that you know I am right. That must hurt, mustn't it? Indeed, I suspect that it hurts a bit more than anything I have done to you thus far. Well, fear not, old friend, I have something planned to take your mind off Miss Kolodenkova, and all the entertainment she shortly will provide."

Charlie writhed, finding somewhere deep inside himself a reservoir of strength. He almost managed to shake himself loose of his captors. Sam almost felt sorry for him.

"By the way, Charles, did I mention your cat's-paw, the *late* Mr. Conroy?" Charlie groaned. "Yes, that hurts too, doesn't it—the knowledge that you and you alone are responsible for putting him in harm's way. You miscalculated—dear, dear—and someone I suspect you liked paid the price. Although you may take comfort in the fact that I gave him a quick death, I want to assure you that he suffered beforehand."

At last Charlie managed to speak, his voice faltering. "I wanted to get through this job with as little bloodshed as possible. That just changed."

"With respect, Charles, your circumstances are such that your threats ring hollow." Schmidt called over his shoulder, "Mr. Keough, do you have your drill handy?"

A potbellied, bowlegged man answered, "Aye, Mr. Black and Mr. Decker at your service, sir."

"Charles, have you ever wondered what a power drill might feel like as it pierced your belly and churned your entrails? I would guess not, not until now."

Blood misting from his lips, Charlie snarled, "Baloney. You know . . . you and Sam *both* know the kind of shitstorm that gets unleashed if anything happens to me."

Schmidt laughed. It was the most artificial laugh Sam had ever heard. "Your insurance policy? Your precious data vault? Those videos you've hidden on the Internet, a deadman's brake to protect them? Sorry, Charles, but during the wee hours of the morning a computer gentleman known to you, a Mr. Sledgehammer by name, unearthed your secret storage place in a hacker's hideaway quite ridiculously called the Underground Empire—dot.com, of course. Now your files are gone, Charles, all gone. As is Mr. Sledgehammer. Before departing this veil of tears, he conveyed your password to one of my associates. Odysseus, it is. I give you that password so that you may have absolute confidence in the truth of what I say. You've no protection left at all, and when you die—it will take approximately an hour— your secrets die with you. Then my good friend Samuel may rest easy in his sleep." Schmidt flicked his hand, "You two, pin him down by the shoulders. You other two, hold his legs. Mr. Keough, you are free to indulge yourself. However, I would be obliged if you kept him alive and scream-

ing for as long as possible. Yes? Then get to it. There's a
good lad."

Keough knelt beside Charlie. Sam tried to look away but
could not. The Irishman tightened the drill bit with a chuck
key, placing the point against Charlie's left ankle. "I believe
I'll start here, and work me way up. We'll stop at a few
beauty spots along the way, as befits the kind of cunt who'd
shoot me mates in the bollocks."

Schmidt laughed that laugh of his again. "Charles, if you
have any last words, now would be the time to speak them."

PART THREE

Charlie's Epitaph

She was not one of those limited creatures who are swept clean by a gust of wrath and left placid and smiling after its passing. She could store her anger in those caverns of eternity which open into every soul, and which are filled with rage and violence until the time comes when they may be stored into wisdom and love; for, in the genesis of life, love is at the beginning and the end of things.

—James Stephens

9

Memories Are Made of This

Most of the corpses had been coloreds, only a few white mercenaries like Schmidt.

What was supposed to be a simple coup had gone terribly wrong, and the carnage was absolute. He alone survived. A mortar blast had hurled him into unconsciousness. When he awoke beneath a blackened schoolhouse wall, his fellow mercenaries were no longer near.

They were, in fact, farther than he wished to travel.

He was only eighteen, his first time in battle. The sight of his dead comrades sickened him. Half of them, almost half, had not died cleanly in combat. Men fallen in honorable battle are not found stretched out in rows with their throats gaping and their testicles in their mouths. The enemy had taken them alive, killed them playfully, desecrated them in death.

He took no shame in terror. If they got their hands on him, he would die as horribly.

Nearby he heard their joking and jubilant laughter. The smoke of a plundered village concealed him from their eyes. Belly-crawling among the bodies, he bathed his uniform in the blood of others, and from a dead man's mouth took . . . he took . . . it made him vomit, but he forced himself. Then he lay frozen in an outdoor abattoir as the victors strutted past, kicking carrion out of simple joy.

He prayed. Dusk was not far. If he lived past sunset, darkness would conceal his escape. He asked God to speed the night.

The chuckling black butchers moved on. Johan Schmidt tried not to weep.

Time passed. A minute? An hour? He did not know. It was still daylight, although tending toward evening when he heard the crunch of boot heels on broken glass, two men coming near . . . stopping . . . standing where he lay.

Cold metal kissed his neck. His bladder released itself. A hammer clicked back. His bowels emptied. He did not want to die, although he felt he could die for disgrace.

"Kid, you're out of your league." An American voice, not kindly, not forgiving.

"Got yerself a live one there, Charlie?" The second voice was improbably accented, a Texan's twangy tones, the sort of cowboy hero Schmidt once cheered during Saturday matinees.

"This fish is too small to keep, Jack. I'm going to throw him back."

Beneath prescription sunglasses no one had seen fit to steal, Schmidt opened his eyes. The man squatting over him was tall, broad-shouldered, sandy-haired. Unlike the other one, the Texan, he wore no American Army insignia.

"Whut? You the Christmas fairy? Gonna give this sprat a present?" Silver maple leaves on his lapels, the Texan was a colonel. The patch on his BDU sleeve proclaimed him a member of the elite Special Operations Group. Schmidt blinked in astonishment. This colonel, this Colonel Jack, had the longest pair of incisors he'd ever seen in a human mouth.

"What's your name, son?" The one called Charlie eased the hammer of his .45 automatic down. Schmidt almost fainted with relief.

"Schmidt. Johan Schmidt." His mouth was dry. The words did not come easily.

"I'm Charlie McKenzie, Johan, and I've got some advice for you. If you're trying to play dead, don't let snot bubble out of your nose."

Schmidt blinked back tears.

"A second piece of advice: go home to your mama. You're a loser, Johan Schmidt, a born loser, and you weren't cut out to be a fighting man." The American holstered his gun, and, together with Colonel Jack, loped away.

That was the first time Johan Schmidt promised himself that, given the opportunity, he would kill this man named McKenzie.

The second time was in Russia, two years after the collapse of the Soviet Union. Schmidt, now a rising star in the mercenary firmament, was under contract to pick up a package just north of Novosibirsk, special delivery for a client in Pakistan.

He'd traveled light, five men on the team—low profile, no luggage to speak of, in and out quickly, a speedy mission, a speedier getaway.

It was a trap. The Spetsnaz was waiting, combat-hardened veterans of the Afghan war, each and every one. Schmidt's party didn't have a chance. Five soldiers facing fifty assault rifles never do.

The interrogation had been . . . difficult. Yes, that was the word. But he'd accepted his punishment stoically, knowing that he and his men were worth more alive than dead. After all, this was the new Russia, entrepreneurship supplanting socialism, and whatever could be sold at a profit would be sold more or less intact.

Comfortable in the knowledge that he would be allowed to live, he'd given them the information they wanted. The beating they administered was mere ritual, a custom of the trade, neither ardent nor imaginative. Eventually they tired of it, leaving him roped to a chair in the traditional darkened room.

He'd been sleeping when the light snapped on. He recognized the voice instantly. "Well, I'll be damned. You again. Didn't listen to me the first time, did you?"

McKenzie.

The light was bright. He barely opened his eyes, the lids thin slits to sharpen vision damaged—ancient history—by an explosion in a country church.

This time the American was in Spetsnaz battle dress, midnight blue fatigues, a heavy Czech pistol buckled around his waist. Schmidt hated him, and he let it show.

"Sonny boy, I know exactly what you're thinking, and you're absolutely right. I've got an informer. Is he in your organization? Is he in Pakistan? Sorry, chum, you're never going to know. All you're going to know is that when some clown tries to hijack ten kilos of weapons-grade plutonium, I'm going to stop him. If that means cutting a deal with the Russians, then I'll cut the deal. But I don't think I have to explain that to you, because I can see you've already figured it out. And, I can see something else. It's written on your face clear as day. Want to know what it is? I'll tell you. It's a single word: loser. Yup, that's what your ugly mug proclaims, Johan Schmidt. You were born a loser, you've lived a loser, and it's only because you are a lucky loser that you aren't a dead loser right now. Go back to South Africa, boy. Once you get there, stay there. Because, as God is my witness, you are never going to make anything of yourself in this business."

Johan Schmidt spoke his vow aloud then, "I'm going to kill you." McKenzie laughed, and left the room. Silently,

Schmidt added a prayer to his harsh deity: send this man my way again. Please, God, do this for me.

God granted the wish.

Afghanistan, 2001. His mission was to escort an aging Saudi prince—one of al-Qaeda's moneybag boys—from the ruins of Kandahar to safety in Iran. It was about three in the morning when the prince's chest exploded. A mocking voice echoed across the plains. "Schmidt! Hey, Johan Schmidt, you dumb Dutchman! Boy, you are *such* a loser!"

Johan's reply was a shouted death threat and a hail of blind gunfire. McKenzie laughed an obscene insult.

It had, therefore, felt most agreeable to beat Charles to a pulp. Johan was sorry he had to stop—although, truth to tell, he knew the greater pleasure would come from watching a hated adversary die in ingenious pain.

"If you have any last words, now would be the time to speak them."

"I do. Put some decent music on your ghetto blaster. I mean Meyerbeer? Jesus! Try to show a little class, you loser."

Sam watched Schmidt uneasily. He wasn't a man, not human at all, just a pale waxworks statue, no spark of life in his frozen features. He sat like a crash test dummy, an inch of space between his back and the upholstery. He might as well have been stuffed and mounted.

Sam didn't try to talk to him. The roar of helicopter blades would drown out his voice. Besides, the only thing they had to speak about was Charlie, and Sam couldn't have borne that.

Goddamnit, two years earlier, if things had gone the way they should have—no muss, no fuss—everyone would have gone home happy. The president would have gotten what he wanted (even though, technically speaking, he didn't *know* he wanted it). And Sam would have received a discreet pat on the back for making a sound, albeit illegal, decision.

However, things had not gone the way they should have. Sam had made . . . well . . . an honest mistake. It could have happened to anyone. In fact, if you looked at it in the right way, he was as much a victim of circumstances as Charlie.

Charlie, the president will back you one hundred and ten percent, full presidential immunity guaranteed. You have my word, you have his. But you've got to move now, right goddamned now because the bastard's on his way home to his camels. Shit, Charlie, he's already headed for JFK International.

No one less than his pissant nation's UN ambassador had personally greeted the just exonerated Kahlid Hassan on the courtroom steps. The ambassador laid on a chartered Airbus to ferry the Islamic avenger from the den of the Great Satan back to the safety of his tents and flocks—and offered Hassan the Heroic his very own chauffeured limousine to ferry the acquitted (but guilty as hell) terrorist to the plane.

Charlie hit the road. He knew what he was looking for: a Lincoln stretch limo with "DLP" diplomatic license plates.

He found it on the Van Wyck Expressway.

Traffic was light at ten thirty on a Thursday evening. Charlie sped by his target. Once past, he wrenched the wheel, downshifted to first, jerked on the emergency brake, and floored the accelerator.

He blocked two out of three lanes. Works every time.

The limo screeched to a halt.

Charlie was already out of his car with a Heckler & Koch street sweeper in his hands, and no mercy in his heart. After noisily emptying a brace of forty-round magazines through the limo's windshield, he tossed two fragmentation grenades onto the front seat.

Charlie's motto: any job worth doing is worth doing well.

The police were quick to the scene. But not, of course, quick enough. Charlie had serenely driven south to the next exit, wheeled through Queens until he reached a suitably ripe neighborhood, and then abandoned his Agency-issued Crown Victoria with the keys in the ignition. New York being the place it is, the car was in the nearest chop shop in less than thirty minutes. And because there's always a market for quality auto parts, it was in itty-bitty pieces an hour after that.

Charlie hadn't even bothered to wipe his fingerprints off the wheel. He should have gotten away clean.

Too bad about the civilian with the digital camera on the seat next to him. Too bad about the photographs. Too bad about news commentators and the media mob, mad dogs each and every one, may they rot in hell.

Also too bad about the Dutch ambassador being on the Van Wyck driving toward JFK while Kahlid Hassan was headed for the Newark Airport via the Lincoln Tunnel.

An intelligence breakdown, misinformation, an honest error. Sorry you blew away the wrong man, Charlie. Honest to God, you have my deepest sympathies. But you have to understand, I'm sure you understand, that you can't blame me, it was just one of those things, not my fault, hell, shit happens.

What about my presidential immunity?

Problem. A significant problem. It's election season. The press is in an uproar. Our asshole allies are bitching about how light your sentence was. Half the Senate is screaming "cover-up!" The president can't help, Charlie. If he tries, the voters will think he was involved. We can't let that happen, you know we can't. Our hands are tied. You understand, don't you?

Nope.

Well, both of them knew it would end badly. One of them would be down and bleeding, and the other one no longer vengeful or even especially angry—just anxious to get it over, and be done with it.

Such was Sam's impatient frame of mind when Schmidt asked for Charlie's last words, and Charlie, predictably, replied with an insult, "Try to show a little class, you loser."

Schmidt chopped his hand down, hissing "Do it!" to the man with the drill.

"Hang on, I've some last words for Sammy boy." His voice was weak. Nonetheless every syllable was all too clear. "Hey, birdbrain, according to Schmidt, one of his pet psychopaths destroyed my data vault. *One* of my data vaults. *One* of ten. Sam, it is with the greatest pleasure I convey to you the fact that there are nine more left."

Sonofabitch!

Charlie knew where he was. Sort of.

He'd been there before. Sort of.

Principal evidence: pleasant pink clouds wafting through his mind.

Further evidence: the sounds—hushed voices mostly, hushed in a way that they were nowhere else; in the background, the electrical chatter of gizmos measuring heart beat, brain activity, blood pressure, and breath. Then you had the smells. You never forgot the smells: the odor of a place scrubbed beyond ordinary cleanliness, scrubbed until only a faint chemical scent pervaded disinfected sheets, sterilized vinyl mattress pads, and the sanitized blue-green uniforms hovering at the foot of your bed.

Somebody had stuck an IV needle in his arm.

Somebody had doped him to the gills.

Jesus, I hate hospitals.

He managed to open his eyes. A guy in the inevitable

white jacket was whispering to a short, plump nurse. Charlie murmured, "I know you," although moving his numbed lips wasn't easy.

The white jacket guy turned. Stethoscope in his pocket. Naturally. "Welcome back to the waking world, Mr. McKenzie."

I've heard that line a dozen times. They must teach 'em it in medical school. He recognized that face, grasped dimly for its identity. He was ... *who?* ... a doctor, but what the hell was he called. "You're the one with two first names, right? My son's friend?"

"David Howard." *Sure. How'd I forget? Medium build, old acne scars, mid-forties, one of those people whose age is tough to guess. It's the smile that does it. You can't read a guy with a good smile.* "Nurse, make a note. The patient seems cognitively alert."

"Wrong word." Charlie's w's were coming out as B's—a little problem with his tongue. "Should be 'cognizably.'"

"The word should be 'irascibly,' but I can't put that in a medical file." *Scott interned under him a decade ago. Big Kahuna on the Rez. Married a Navajo woman. Fine physician by all accounts. Also ... also what? I'm forgetting something, something important. God, I hate that.* "Mr. McKenzie, you'll be pleased to know that none of your bones are broken—pretty amazing given the shellacking you took. No critical internal damage either, at least none we've been able to find, although some of your organs are badly bruised. Of course we'll want to run more tests."

Also a pilot. Goddamnit, he's also a pilot! "What the hell are you doing here?"

"Trying to mend a cranky old coot who doesn't seem to appreciate my services."

He never stops smiling. That's good in a doc. "You're supposed to be in that crap airplane of yours. You're supposed to be—"

"Nurse, would you give us some privacy? Yes, please close the door behind you. I'll call when I need you." He placed his hand around Charlie's wrist, taking the pulse. "Calm down, Charlie. For crying out loud, your heart rate's above a hundred and twenty, and I bet your blood pressure's off the charts. For a man who's just coming up from sedation—"

I'm fading. Back to dreamland. No! Damnit, no! I have to stay awake! "Where's Irina? Why aren't you flying her to safety?"

The doctor took three halting steps backward, pointing at his left leg. It was immobilized in a walking cast. "I figured I shouldn't try to fly with a busted wing. But don't worry about your lady friend. Your son's flown my bird before."

My son? Scott? Oh, Christ! Coldly and suddenly, Charlie was alert. "What did you say?"

"Scott flew your friend out of here. That was nine, maybe ten hours ago. They're in California by now."

Charlie remembered every curse word he knew. None of them would do any good. *Goddamnit! I promised Mary, swore to her on my honor, that none of the kids, none of them, would ever get involved in one of my messes. And now Scott's up to his ears in it. Dear Jesus, what have I done?* "Tell me," he whispered, "tell me everything that happened."

The doctor shrugged. "Not much to tell. Scott and I were waiting for you at the airstrip. She—you said she was called Irina—showed up right on schedule. She said you were in hot water and to get some law down to Mitchell Canyon. We could hear gunfire in the distance. Scott figured you were holding the shooters off—or was he wrong about that? No? Okay, then I made the right decision. I told Scott I'd call the Navajo police while he got that gal to safety. So he took my plane, and they were off the ground before I limped to the hangar and found the phone. Half hour later the cops showed up. They went out to the canyon rim. They came back with you. By the way, once you're up to it, they'll have some questions to ask you."

"Any word from Scott? Has he called?"

Howard shook his head. Charlie recognized it as a melancholy shake, the gesture of a worried man. "Nope. Before he left he told me he wouldn't risk using the phone. I didn't ask why. Long time ago he said . . . well . . . he said his father was one of those folks nobody should ask questions about because . . . " His voice faded into a sigh. "Hey, you know, I'm a doctor. So I know better than to smoke. But I sure could use a cigarette right now."

"Indulge yourself."

"The nurses would have a shit fit. I can wait."

"I can't." Charlie shifted his weight, trying to roll his legs off the edge of the bed. *Oh, hell! I can't feel my feet! They've shot me full of enough dope to knock out an elephant.*

David gave Charlie a slow look. "With all due respect, climbing out of that bed would be a monumentally damfool stunt."

"With all due respect, doc, I'm getting out of here or I'll die trying."

"It's a possibility."

Betrayed by his own body, Charlie slumped back, weaker than before. "How long before the drugs wear off?"

"Six or seven hours. If I don't order another needle stuck in your butt."

"Only if you want your other leg broken." He could feel slumber creeping toward him, soft narcotic peace, an irresistible urge to shut his eyes and find comfort in oblivion. *No way!* Clawing at the mattress, he tried to pull himself upright.

The doctor hobbled to the bedside, his smile still strong, no artifice in it. "Charlie, Charlie, Charlie. Look, you've taken one hell of a pummeling. Want to know how bad? Every Sunday morning I have a dozen patients in the trauma room. Saturday night they drive down to Gallup, get ripped, get ugly, get into fights. Big-time bar fights. The kind where a room full of mean drunks kick the shit out of you with steel-capped pointy-toed boots. And Charlie, you look like you've been in three of those fights in a row."

He was holding on to wakefulness as hard as he could. He wasn't sure he could hold on much longer. "You said I'm okay."

"What I said is I haven't found any life-threatening trauma. Yet. More tests, old man, and maybe I'll find something different."

"Write this down on your little clipboard. 'Patient declined further treatment. Patient demanded immediate discharge.' Then call that nurse, and get me a release form to sign. If I die, I don't want you catching hell for it."

"Charlie, there's nothing you can do. Scott's gone. It's almost nighttime and I don't—"

He was slipping. *Damn, damn, damn.* His mind was shutting down, and there was nothing he could do about it. "They'll kill her. They'll kill Scott too. Those guys. The ones who beat me up. I've got 'til noon tomorrow to stop them. No one else can. No one else will."

David Howard laid the back of his hand across Charlie's forehead. He started to speak, then paused to collect his thoughts. Charlie dug his fingernails into his thighs, hoping pain would keep him awake. He could barely feel his own touch, even though he was gouging hard enough to draw blood.

The doctor leaned down. "I'm not giving you stimulants.

Not in your condition. Well, maybe some coffee. That's the most I'll risk. And I will listen to what you have to say. If Scotty's in trouble, I'll let you out of the hospital. I guess I don't have much choice. But first, I need to make sure you're . . . you're . . . Charlie? Charlie? Can you hear me?"

I do.

By the power vested in me, I now pronounce you man and wife. You may kiss the bride.

Mary, I gotta say, waking up next to you is the sweetest thing that ever happened to me.

C'mere. I'll show you something sweeter.

Charlie, do you know, having a grandson makes me feel mighty fine.

Pleased to be of service.

Next time you should have a daughter. Daughters are pretty darned good, too.

Mary and I will see what can be arranged.

Uh, different subject, Charlie. Well, the same subject, really. Olivia and I . . . well, we've been talking things over. We want to set up a trust. For our grandson, I mean.

Don't. Too much money—

Yup, I know. God knows, I know. Being rich as Croesus isn't all it's cracked up to be. Money makes everything too easy. Unless you're careful, you lose life's zing.

That's one problem I've never had. Easy, I mean.

Bet you've never had a problem with the zing, either.

Not since Mary came along.

Dad would never take a vacation in Africa. Every animal under the sun makes him sneeze.

To be denied the company of cats. God, Mary, is there a worse fate?

Hey, what about being denied me!

Your husband just put his foot in his mouth. I offer you a kiss by way of apology.

Take your foot out first.

Wiseass.

Mmmmm . . .

And you are very welcome. You know, Mary, my whole life I've wanted to do this: sit in a canvas chair, watch the sun set over the Serengeti, sip a cold drink, kiss my best girl, and . . . hey, where are you going?

There's something I've always wanted to do in the Serengeti, too. And I think we ought to do it in our tent.

Two grandsons and a granddaughter. Don't know why I feel so proud. You and Mary did all the work.

Mary, I'd say. I just happened to be in the neighborhood.

The thing is, Charlie—and I hate to bring this up again—but life isn't getting any cheaper. You've got three kids now, and a government salary doesn't go very far. I want you to think about coming into my company. It would be a good fit, and the pay is a whole lot better.

Paychecks aren't the only thing in life.

I'm thinking about your children. About my grandchildren.

Oddly enough, so am I.

What is it, Charlie?

A check from your father. A damned big check. In point of fact, a whopper.

I told him not to do that. Just send it back.

You sure?

Unless you think it can buy more happiness than we have.

Never happen.

Give it to me, Charlie. I'll write him a note. It will be better coming from me than from you.

It's a graduation present, Charlie.

We've had this discussion before.

I'm putting my grandson through medical school. And you're going to live with it because you don't have a choice.

Like hell.

Oh, Charlie, give up. Who do you think I'm doing this for? You? Scott? Nope, I'm doing it for myself. Seeing Scott through the best school in America is a present I'm giving myself. Indulge me. I'm getting on in life. Don't deny an old man with only a few years left to him the pleasures that remain.

You are an astonishingly creative liar.

It takes one to know one.

Tell you what, let's leave it up to Mary.

Nice try, but I already cleared it with my daughter.

I've lost this one, haven't I?

Yup. Try to be gracious about it.

How do I look bald, Charlie?

As beautiful as ever. More beautiful.

They say it will grow back. Once the chemotherapy is over, my hair will come back.

I don't give a good goddamn about your hair. Just get better, okay?

Mr. McKenzie, I regret telling you this, but your petition for compassionate parole has been denied.

My wife is dying.

Sir, I wrote the strongest recommendation I could. The parole board endorsed it. Seven votes for, none against. Washington overruled us. That's unprecedented. In all my years in the penal system, I've never seen anything like it. If there is something else I can do . . . well, Mr. McKenzie, you would have my wholehearted support.

She doesn't have long left. There'll be a funeral soon. See if they'll let me attend. Even if I have to go in handcuffs, I want to be there.

Hi, sweetheart. I brought you some flowers. Big damned bouquet. It's got all sorts of stuff in it. Roses, carnations, mignonettes, mums, and a whole bunch more. Wish you could see it. You loved . . . love flowers. Next to the kids and the cats, and maybe me, flowers were closest to your heart. Are closest to your heart. Here, let me put them next to the stone. Maybe you can smell them. I hope so. You'll get a fresh bouquet every week. I've set that up with the people who run this joint. Don't worry about the cost. Your dad is helping with the bills. And I'll be by too—pretty much every day, I suppose. I don't have anywhere else to go. Besides, there's no place I'd rather be, no place I ever wanted to be,

than with you. We can talk. We've still got a lot to talk about.
All the stuff we never got around to saying, and especially
the stuff I could never bring myself to say. Oh, damnit,
Mary, I love you so much, and you always deserved a better
guy than me.

REM, doctor. He's dreaming now. The sedative is wearing off.
*Give him until morning before waking him up. He's not
young anymore, and he's got a lot of healing to do.*

Live oak, old olive, and liquidambar shaded suburban
Livermore's streets from the thirsty sun of a California afternoon. Irina drove cautiously beneath blue shadows.

Had she not known the address, one of dozens memorized
for emergency use, she wouldn't have given the house a second glance.

Think Russian, she ordered herself. *I must begin to think
in Russian. I am going home, and should no longer think in
English.*

Within minutes she'd be safe in an ordinary-looking house
on an ordinary-looking street, the first stop on the underground railway that would carry her, triumphant, to victory.

The house was just ahead, to the right. She slowed, studying it.

Think Russian.

Kvartira-lovushka— middle-class simplicity in wood and
stone: blue-grey with white trim, a picture window and half-
drawn curtains, a small front yard surrounded by a low
hedge, a chocolate-colored door with no windowpanes.
George and Sue might live there, or Alice and Mike. Their

last names would be Jones or Ford or Smith, because only single-syllable Americans would live in a dwelling such as this.

So the house appeared. Appearances are deceiving.

Kvartira-lovushka. Translation: mousetrap.

The lady of the house would speak English more naturally than Irina. The week before, or the month before, or whenever the mouse met her, she would have sounded like the girl next door, although she'd look much better than that.

Inside, the mouse would find comfortingly familiar furniture. From Sears, perhaps, or Levitz. Nothing flashy, nothing out of the ordinary. Mice felt safe in such surroundings. That was the point.

Well, yes, the mouse might be a little nervous about the husband. However, Sue or Alice told him there was nothing to worry about. During those long phone calls, or the exchange of e-mail messages that began so innocuously, but later became less so, she complained of her spouse's busy travel schedule, later turning complaints into hints, and, after all, it would be so easy to visit her on a quiet, suburban afternoon.

Komprometiruyushchikh materialakh.

A video camera behind the bedroom mirror, and another in the lighting fixture above. A microphone concealed beneath the nightstand. Tape decks in the attic. Two agents sweating at the monitors, exchanging the usual jests as the mouse took the bait.

Komprometiruyushchikh materialakh: compromising materials.

They called such women little birds; "swallows" to be specific. You earned the job title by going to a very special school. For male officers one of the perks of serving with

KGB, now FSB, was to be practice subjects for that school's students.

Better still, homework.

Swallows. Many jokes were made about the word. In Russian or in English, the puns were much the same. Men laughed. Women did not.

Irina's skin was clammy cold. Memory is a knife in every human heart; remembered betrayal pierces deepest.

No! No introspection, no reflection, no reflection on a past that could not be changed! She must, absolutely must, focus her full concentration on the only thing that mattered: escape.

Eyes flicking left, Irina drove past the house.

Brosovyy signal? Nyet.

If the mousetrap was in use, a signal would be visible— something as plain and innocuous as the house itself. Here, the town of Livermore, home of America's largest nuclear weapons laboratory, that signal was a tricycle near the front steps.

No tricycle, no danger. The house had not been compromised. She could enter freely. And she, in possession of the Whirlwind computer disk, would have won.

Although, of course, Charlie would have lost.

Irrelevant! The fate of a defeated foe is irrelevant! And, curse me, I must stop thinking in English!

Not daring to use the telephone, the occupant of this simple suburban home would send a runner to the San Francisco *Rezidentura,* an hour's drive west. Shortly thereafter, an anonymous car would be dispatched together with a full *garderob operativnyy,* an entirely new disguise. She'd be spirited out of the country, first to Canada, then on to Moscow.

Then, at last, she would have won her father's respect. For what little the respect of such a man might be worth.

She braked to a halt at the corner, looking left and right for traffic. Good citizen, careful driver, she switched on her right turn signal. *Drive three blocks,* she told herself, slipping back into English unaware, *and leave the car. They will not find it soon, although when they do, Scott will take the blame.*

Unfortunate but necessary blame.

Four hours earlier Charlie's son had rented her an aquamarine Toyota at the Chico airport. Understanding that her license and credit cards were compromised, Scott had gotten the car under his own name. He asked no questions, said nothing except that he believed his father would approve.

Giving her the keys, he smiled. At that moment he did not merely look like a young Charlie, he *was* Charlie. She kissed him, and he didn't understand why.

Neither did she.

Turning right, eyes watchful of her rearview mirror, she thought about her mad flight from Arizona. A small plane of erratic performance. A broken radio and primitive navigational systems. Nearly seven hundred bumpy miles at a hundred and twenty miles an hour; three refueling stops; the sickening closeness of treetops as an antique engine groaned over the Sierras; Lake Tahoe distant indigo ink; a long slow glide down the mountains' western slope; Sacramento and its wide river; then farm country, nut orchards, a hot brown landscape, and a small college town.

She and Charlie's son had taken rooms at a Best Western. They paid cash, paid in advance. She still had the money Charlie had given her, although that, her wallet, and her father's pistol were all she had.

She bought toiletries and a change of clothes at a shopping mall. As she shopped, she laughed, Scott made her laugh, he so much resembled his father in word, and attitude, and appearance.

Dinner was delightful. It was just like being with Charlie.

Ah, there. After the next block, anonymous as all the blocks before, the neighborhood changed. Slightly lower on the social scale, its houses had a weary look, tired people with soul-killing jobs. More cars lined the curb. She could slot her rented Toyota between an unwashed Buick and a brown station wagon of indeterminate make.

Park. Lock. Take the keys. Walk to the mousetrap.

And heave a sigh of relief because it would be all over, and she would have nothing more to worry about.

Except that I must worry about Charlie. Scott did not think it safe to call—not to call his doctor friend at the clinic, not to call his sister . . . what is her name? . . . Carly. Perhaps I should find a phone. I passed a gasoline station a few miles back. Surely they will have a pay phone. But, no, the lines will be monitored, of that I may be certain, for if I were in command, it is the first order I would issue.

She noticed she was thinking in English again. She decided to think in Russian later.

I believe I should circle the block. Just to be safe.

How strange to worry about Charlie. He was merely an enemy who had been overcome. There was no debt between them, no bond, no reason why she should think of him at all. His fate was immaterial, was it not?

I promised I would come to him again. Why did I say that?

Because he trusted her. Because he put her safety ahead of his own. Because he gave her a computer disk with which she might purchase her life.

With which he might have purchased his own.

She almost missed the stop sign. Slamming on her brakes,

she jolted to a halt. A shouting woman with a baby carriage stood at the curb. Irina accelerated away.

They might kill him. That man, that Schmidt, hates Charlie. In the hotel, in the Hilton, they said . . . he said . . . he promised to kill him.

And Charlie mocked him. At risk to his own life, he mocked him to save me.

Why did he do that?

Does there have to be a "why"? For a man like Charlie, perhaps there never is. Perhaps the only "why" is because he is who he is, and cannot be otherwise.

She could see him, oh, that infuriating grin, as he stood on Mitch Conroy's porch with a bag of Big Macs in his hand. He was still smiling when she chained him to the sink, more amused than worried, and although he was her enemy he was, well, charming. No charm, though, when he faced down Schmidt, one man against ten in a motel lobby, no weapon in his hand, but armament more powerful—bravery that lions might envy. And then . . . and then . . . he knew about her father, knowing far more than he said. He knew the worst, she was sure of it, although he was too good a man to speak a truth he surely had deduced. So shrewd, he knew it all, but kept it silently locked within him. Instead he spoke of sailboats, bad enough, and somewhere deep within she understood that he would spare her that other thing, and was grateful to him for that.

He made her smile. Out of simple goodness, he made her smile, and what man had ever done that? His story, so sweet, a fable of a fairy-tale paradise, a peaceful little village called San Carlos, did such a place exist? Would such a warrior as Charlie lay down his shield and sword, and retire there, no ambition greater than the comfort of cats?

Oh, Charlie, Charlie, do you think I did not know what

you did? Do you think I did not see you drop sleeping pills into my drink? I took them willingly, Charlie, I took all your baits because I thought myself more cunning than you, and was always thinking one step ahead of you. But you were not fooled, were you? I cannot fool you. Nor can you fool me. We share the same mind, Charlie, are the same person. And do you know, I have never felt closer to any human being than I feel to you, and how could I have left you behind?

Her jaw was clenched painfully tight. She had never thought she'd want any man's love. Now that she did, she found the emotion unexpectedly sad.

I have won no victory. I only have been given it, a gift from someone who never was my enemy.

The medal they would pin on her would not be hers, for she had not earned it. She would stand in uniform on a podium with ribboned officers, a parade of tribute on the field below. After a speech acclaiming achievements that belonged to another, the guest of honor would rise from his seat to affix a medallion to her blouse. Ceremony demanded it. The proper forms must be observed. It was not enough that they give her an award; they would insist that it be presented to her by he who made her what she was, a loyal and faithful servant of the state, a daughter who was as much credit to her fatherland as she was to her father. In dress blue uniform and bright brass buttons, he would step forward.

A cold kiss on either cheek.

And a salute. A salute! He would salute her not because he honored her but because, at long last, she had become what he wanted her to be. She had become no different from him.

Bruised and aching, Charlie slammed down the notebook computer's screen, switching the wretched, balky machine off. The only portable that David Howard, he of the egregiously underfunded Indian Health Service, had been able to scrape up was as slow as molasses and as user-friendly as . . . Charlie snarled . . . as Bill Gates.

The best that could be said was that it got the job done—barely—downloading the documents Israeli experts had sent via the less-than-high-speed lines of the Navajo Phone Company, Inc., another egregiously underfunded operation.

It took until eleven A.M. Mountain time for him to retrieve the last of the files. Just as the final document dripped byte by tedious byte into his computer, the blue Citation charter jet landed—if "landed" was the right word. "Controlled crash" would be a better description. Putting a private jet down on a stubby dirt runway in the middle of a cow pasture was, at best, an iffy proposition. Getting off the ground again was more so. The damned thing actually dropped below Mitchell Canyon's rim during its quote-takeoff-unquote and Charlie found himself remembering prayers he'd thought he'd forgotten.

However, the pilot earned his pay (all cash, and a lot of it). A little more than an hour and a half later, Charlie deplaned at the San Francisco general aviation terminal.

In a vengeful mood.

During the flight, he'd studied all the files his Mossad friends had sent him. Everything had come together. Almost everything. There was only one open question: the pricetag.

The rest of the puzzle was no puzzle at all. Dr. Sangin Wing, head of research for DefCon Enterprises and the brains behind Whirlwind, had gone to a scientific conference in Tokyo, February third through February seventh, just another tax-deductible scholarly boondoggle, a bunch of eggheads from India, England, Germany, Norway, Singapore, and—uh-huh—China, sitting around, chewing the fat. Such conferences were one of the scientific world's few perks, excuses for hard-working researchers to spend a couple of days away from the lab. Hundreds of them were held every year. There was nothing unusual about DefCon subsidizing Wing's attendance . . .

. . . nothing except that on February the seventh Dr. Wing didn't show up for the panel discussion he was supposed to moderate.

Neither did the gentleman from China.

According to their hotel receipts, both had checked out two days earlier, and, hey, what a coincidence, the day they disappeared was the same day the People's Republic announced that Wing's son had been arrested for espionage.

The kid was bait. Daddy bit.

Wing did what the boys in Beijing expected him to do— made a beeline for China in the company of an ever-so-sympathetic fellow scientist, a benevolent and friendly guy from his own profession who claimed to have high-level contacts.

Which, no doubt, he did, mainly because he moonlighted for the Chinese Ministry for External Calm. A.K.A.: the spook shop.

It was all there, the whole story, in the travel records the Mossad had shipped to Charlie. He could read it as if it was printed in big bold type: "Oh, Dr. Wing, my esteemed colleague, I am sure this is an unfortunate bureaucratic error. Happily, my cousin Chan is placed highly in the civil service. I am confident that if we—you and I together—explain the situation to him . . ."

Yeah, sure.

And so Wing scampered off to China, and the interrogators were licking their chops. They might not know precisely what kind of research Wing did, but they sure as hell knew it was defense-related. That much was in the public record.

The stuff that wasn't in the public record would be what they wanted.

Legally the Reds had every right to squeeze it out of him. Wing was born a Chinese citizen. Under international law, they had absolute sovereignty over him. They could have, and should have, wrung him dry.

But behold: rather than tossing him in their deepest dungeon for "intense interrogation," two days later the Chinese government apologetically set him free. *Here's a guy who has the most valuable secrets imaginable locked in his pointy little head,* thought Charlie, *and nobody tried to pry them out. Instead, unbelievably, they let him go.*

Unless they didn't let him go.

Unless they sold him.

So who was the buyer? Easy answer: a certain fat-assed national security advisor who boasted of being in charge of *both* Whirlwind *and* Chinese diplomacy. Sam was directly accountable for the well-being of the scientist he'd personally appointed to lead the Whirlwind project, and, most conveniently, was in daily contact with China's highest officials.

Sam, you insect, you did a deal with them. What did you promise those scum to get Wing back? Dropping tariffs maybe? Letting them import restricted technologies? Or did you offer to share Whirlwind with them? I wouldn't put it past you. Whatever they asked for, that's what they got. And when I find out what it was . . .

Would he get his presidential pardon? You betchya, and it wasn't going to bear the signature of President Sam.

Although—this was odd, this was a new thought—exoneration was no longer his top priority. His first, and if necessary, *only* priority, was getting a young woman named Irina Kolodenkova to safety.

Assuming she wasn't already under the protection of the Russian legation.

Bad karma, that. He was sure, damned sure, he'd won her over. But then he'd been sure Schmidt's men wouldn't shoot him. He'd been sure he could provoke Sam into losing both his temper and discretion. He'd been sure Mitch Conroy wouldn't be harmed. He'd been sure, he'd been sure, he'd been goddamned cocksure too many times in his life.

And now he was sure that a Russian spy in possession of a priceless secret would abandon her own side, come over to his.

Pick one from column A or one from column B: (A) Irina goes home to Moscow with that disk. Or, (B) Johan Schmidt gets his hands on her. If it comes down to that, do I honestly know which I'll choose?

Hell, yes, I do.

Entering San Francisco's general aviation terminal, favoring a wobbly leg, Charlie chewed his lip. No choice, he had no choice. The only way out of this mess was to retrieve the disk and spirit Irina out of harm's way. Sam's noon deadline had expired. Irina was an open contract with a price on her head. He had to find her, damnit, had to. Obligation, duty, commitment, call it what you will, she was his responsibility, and there was no one else to protect her.

Only problem: he didn't know how.

However, he did know that, for starters, he had to make a phone call.

His cell phones were long gone, lost in a war bag hurled into a canyon along with two fine handguns, plenty of ammo, and all the greenbacks he hadn't been able to stuff in his money belt. Doc Howard was leading a search party to find the bag, and as far as Charlie was concerned, he could spend every penny he found upgrading his clinic.

Not that money was important at this present time. The only important thing was a Russian girl, a girl good enough to be Mary's daughter—good enough to be Mary's twin, goddamn it—and the rest of the world could go to hell because he was going to bail her out, and that was that.

Charlie glared around the small general aviation terminal. No surprise: a couple of dozen expensive suits loafed around, briefcases in one hand, mobile phones in the other. The private jet business had boomed after the destruction of the World Trade Center. No chief executive could afford the two or three hours it took to check onto Continental, American, Delta, or any of the other passenger carriers. Everyone who was anyone flew charter.

He spotted a kiosk near the end of the terminal, four pay phones next to a newsstand. Not much privacy. If he was overheard, he would be in serious trouble.

But then he was in serious trouble anyway. Calling a foreign spymaster from a civilian telephone—eavesdroppers on every line—couldn't make his situation any worse.

Pumping four quarters into a slot, he dialed a number no honest American should have known. A guttural voice answered. Charlie cut him off at the first syllable. "Mikhail, this is Charlie McKenzie, listen close—"

"Charlie! Is good to hear you! But also is not so good. Some people, Charlie, some people they say they got a problem with you."

Hellfire and damnation, Sam and Claude have gotten to him first. "Yeah, well, I've got a problem with them too."

"They solve problems for keeps, Charlie. You watch your back, okay?" He was a big guy, Mikhail was, broad shouldered, with a barrel chest. He less spoke than boomed like a kettle drum.

"Always. Look, Mikhail, I don't have time for polite chitchat—"

"From what I hear, you got no time at all. Charlie, I give you some good advice: wherever you are, go somewhere else." He'd been a first-rate enemy, one of the best, always honorable. Charlie thought of him as a friend. God knows, once the Soviet Union had collapsed, they'd gone out drinking often enough.

"I will, but first I have to talk to you about one of your agents—"

"This would be Kolodenkova. She is not my agent anymore. This is made very clear to me. Mikhail, they say, if she knocks, you don't open the door. Persona non grata. Stripped of her citizenship. A woman without a country. I got a personal call, Charlie, personal. Straight from the Kremlin. The big boss himself. Somebody in Washington leans on him pretty hard. So he leans on me pretty hard too. He leans on me about Kolodenkova. Then he leans on me about you." There was a note of sadness in that last sentence. "You know what I'm saying, Charlie?"

Charlie knew. "If I contact you, you have to . . . well . . . "

"I already have, Charlie. This is what you call 'deep shit,' no? They put the bridge on my phone last night. Soon as I hear your voice, I hit the switch. Sorry, Charlie, I am very sorry. But you know how it is." Mikhail was going to crack open a vodka bottle as soon as Charlie hung up. He knew the man, and knew that one bottle wouldn't be enough.

"No problem. We're still friends. Someday we'll have a drink and laugh about this."

"Maybe instead I toast your memory. Unless you get under cover pretty soon, this becomes highly probable, my friend."

"I'm outta here. But one last question, Mikhail. Has she contacted you? Has Irina Kolodenkova contacted anyone at the *Rezidentura?*"

"No, Charlie. On this you have my solemn word. Now hang up. Hang up and run. People are coming for you."

All of a sudden, Charlie felt good. Indeed, he felt downright great! Bruises and aches notwithstanding, he broke into the broadest of smiles, pride and laughter and, yeah, all that cocksure vainglory in his voice, "Wrong, Mikhail. They aren't coming for me. I'm coming for them!"

At first, the words didn't register. Sam heard them but did not grasp their implication. The military policeman standing in the open hatch of his plane said, "Are you sure he's expecting you, sir?" Sam, lounging exhausted in his seat, a badly needed single-malt scotch in his hand, didn't react. Why should he? Schmidt had finally decided that he was more of a liability than an asset, and left him behind. Sam stormed into the general aviation terminal, phoned Travis AFB, and waited impatiently until an early-model Gulfstream V (with fresh clothes, by God, he'd insisted on that) trundled up to the boarding area. No one except the president and a couple of jet jockeys knew he was in San Francisco. So, to repeat, why should he have been concerned that persons unknown were standing at his jet's hatch, telling the guard they had a meeting with the national security advisor?

It wasn't until he heard the answer to the guard's polite question that he belatedly understood what was happening. "If he isn't expecting me, he's dumber than I thought."

He sprang to his feet. He didn't have time to shout for help. Besides, Charlie had a gun.

Two guns, actually. Only one of them was aimed at Sam.

The other was burrowed behind the left ear of a badly frightened MP.

Sam wasn't quite sure what happened next. It was over too quickly, and besides, he was, let's face it, scared shitless. The only thing he could remember was sitting frozen in his seat, thinking, *For a damned old dinosaur, that fucker moves a lot faster than you'd expect.*

Somewhere along the way, the MP wound up chained to a seat with his own handcuffs. Sam's second bodyguard, who'd been in the bathroom, seemed to be out cold on the floor. And there was someone else in the cabin, a younger someone, and who the hell was he?

Whoever he was, he closed the plane's hatch when the ground crew gave the signal. Or maybe he'd closed it when the pilot's voice came over the squawk box with some bullshit about civilian safety procedures being mandatory on government flights.

Whatever.

The sequence of events really didn't matter. All that mattered was the plane was taxiing on the runway, and Charlie was inches away from his face, eating an apple. He had a big knife, Charlie did, and he whisked thick wet, wedges out of the fruit with every flick of his wrist.

Juice splashed on Sam's fresh shirt. He didn't complain. Odds were it would be the wrong thing to do.

Meanwhile Charlie's partner had opened the plane's first-aid kit and was putting a dressing on an unconscious bodyguard's forehead. *Shit! A doctor! He's Charlie's son! Little bastard even looks like his old man. Now I've got two of them in my face.*

Charlie was saying something. Sam hadn't been listening. He shook his head and mumbled, "I didn't quite catch that, Charlie."

Charlie held that big goddamned knife in front of his eyes, flicking it back and forth so that Sam could see how sharp it was. *Johan Schmidt sharp, psychopath sharp, fuck me, I put both those headcases on the payroll.* "What I said, Sam, is that time's short, and so's my patience. Either you answer my questions, or I will start cutting pieces off of you. And Sam . . . " He paused. Sam didn't like the glint in his eye.

"What?" He doubted that he'd like the answer either.

"I can cut 'em off faster than my son can sew 'em back on."

No shit, Sam believed him. Little more than twenty-four hours earlier, the prick had heard Sam order Schmidt to kill him. Now—unless he was very, very careful—it was pay-back time. "There's no need for threats, Charlie. I'll tell you whatever you want."

"Where's Irina?"

"Don't know."

"Wrong answer."

Charlie's hand suddenly was over Sam's mouth, and that cold, cold blade was lightly sawing at his left ear. *Jesus fuck!* Sam tried to scream. Charlie's hand muffled the cry. Sam twisted and pulled away. Charlie held him fast. And all the while, the cocksucker was smiling, because he really and truly was enjoying this. "One more time, Sam. One last time. Where. Is. Irina?"

Sam could barely breathe. Everything around him was speckled yellow and red. He was going to die, goddamnit, die in an Air Force VIP jet, and there was nothing—

"Speak to me, Sam. I am beaten and bruised and full of pain. My mood is poor, and even the saints in heaven would not blame me for hurting you more than you can believe."

"Honest to God, I don't know! If I did, I'd tell you! You know that!"

"You get one sentence to make me believe you."

"She didn't come. We staked out the Russians, Schmidt staked out the Russians, and she didn't come. Then Schmidt got a phone call. Someone reported that Kolodenkova called your home, left a message on your answering machine. Jesus! Don't hurt me! Please, I'm telling the truth!"

"Five sentences. Put a premium on conciseness, Sam, or there will be consequences."

Consequences? There will be consequences? He said that earlier. When? Was it only four days ago?

"Next question, Sam. What was the message?"

"Something about you being her saint. Saint Charlie, she said you were Saint Charlie."

The dangerous old fuck's eyes flashed. Was there some hidden meaning in what that bitch had said? If so, Sam didn't get it. And neither had Johan, that was for goddamned sure.

"Where's Schmidt and his trained gorillas?"

"Can you take that knife away from my ear? It hurts."

"No."

Fuck you, man, just fuck you! Four days of non-stop needling, acid sarcasm, withering insults, and insufferable arrogance—and that, babycakes, was all she wrote. Sam had had enough, more than enough, and *fuck you, fuck you, fuck you.* All at once he was over the edge, off the deep end, blood in the water, rage that murder wouldn't begin to appease, the border of the nation called Berserk far behind, and he was in a place where he couldn't care, didn't care, and he'd *kill you, kill you, kill you and drink your fucking blood!*

"Schmidt, Sam? Answer my question or what I do to you will be one hell of a lot nastier than what he did to me. And, Sam," Charlie dropped his voice low and intimate, "what he did was pretty damned nasty."

Meat, McKenzie, you are raw meat on the butcher's

*counter. I will cut you up and eat your fucking liver. You're
dead now, do you know that? Dead! I'm getting through this
alive and in one piece, but you, you cocksucker, are going to
be bite-sized goblets on my dinner plate!*

Damn it felt good. It would feel even better if he said it,
no, roared it as loud as he could. It was hard to resist, almost
impossible. The only thing that stopped him was Charlie's
knife—that and the look in his eye. "He left some watchers,"
Sam said. It was difficult to voice those words; the other
words were screaming to be heard. "I mean at the Russian
residence. Then he headed south. Schmidt and his people.
He dropped me off at the airport on the way. That's the
whole story, that's all there is."

"There had better be more. Look, meathead, my son
Scott . . . " He nodded at the young doctor, so, yes, Sam had
been right, he was Charlie's son, cut from the same cloth,
and the little shit was going down like his dad. *I'll have the
rotten fuck's kid killed first. Schmidt'll unwind his entrails.
And you'll get to watch, Charlie, oh, yes, you'll get to watch
it all.* " . . . tried to tail Irina. I never taught him any trade-
craft. She shook him off in five minutes. So he drove straight
here. He knows my style; he guessed I'd show up in a chartered plane. He was watching for me when you arrived. Together with a convoy of monster trucks, he said. Plug-uglies
driving each and every one. . . . "

The pilot's voice came over the loudspeaker: "Gentlemen,
we are number one for takeoff. Please make sure your seat-
belts are tightly fastened around your waist, your tray tables
are up, and any loose items are stowed safely beneath the
seat in front of you."

*The pilot. He's got a gun. Air Force officer. Bound to have
a gun. Come back here, you dumb bastard, come back here
and kneecap this cocksucker. Then leave the rest to me.*

Charlie raised his voice. " . . . From what Irina told him the night before, Scott figured those guys were the source of all her woes—hers and mine both. They booted your fat ass out on to the tarmac, and he's been watching you ever since. When he saw you climb aboard this fine aircraft, he came and found me. Bad luck for you, Sam. I was getting ready to hightail it out of Dodge. If Scott hadn't spotted you, if he hadn't had an eye out for me, you'd be able to spend what's left of your life with two ears, all your fingers—"

Out of the plane. Say ten thousand feet. You can breathe at that altitude, Charlie, and you'll scream all the way down. Where is that fucking pilot? "Be careful with that damned knife! We're taking off! What if we hit turbulence?"

"Like you say, shit happens. Now tell me where Schmidt is."

He bellowed. No more soft-spoken voice. That was beyond his power. It was hard enough saying what he was supposed to say rather than what he wanted to say. "Headed for the coast, you fuck! Said he's deploying his men all up and down the Pacific to watch the marinas! Thinks she's going to try to steal a sailboat! Cocksucker, Jesus! Put away that knife!"

The plane jolted off the ground, Sam felt a trickle of blood run down his neck, and he wanted to howl like a wounded animal. Instead he tried to tell it all, and tell it true. "On the plane out here, he read her father's file. The same file I sent you. Ow, you motherfucker, be careful! He kept looking at those pictures. The ones you saw. He said he thought she had a thing for boats—had an issue with boats. Said she was going to grab one and sail solo down to Baja. Goddamn you, McKenzie, stop it!"

Charlie pursed his lips. Sam felt the knife lift from his ear. He tried to sigh, couldn't manage it, his lungs were puffing like a locomotive. Hyperventilation. Blood pressure sky high. Old hormones flooding his bloodstream. He could take him on, he could take him on and beat him to a bloody pulp. If only the old sonofabitch didn't have that knife. . . .

"Sam, you'd better not be lying."

"Truth, Charlie. Every fucking word." And it was. He shouldn't have let it out, he should have used the truth as a bargaining chip, but, you know, he really didn't give a shit.

"Dad . . . ?" It was the kid. He even sounded like his fucking old man.

"Put a bandage on this worm, Scott."

"Is this Schmidt guy right, dad? Is Irina going to try to take a boat to Mexico?"

"I doubt it. However Johan has drawn a very unfortunate inference. Irina *is* headed for the sea. She *will* be near sailboats. And yeah, she does have a . . . well, 'issue' is probably the right word . . . with sailboats. Also with older guys—hell, with men in general."

Sam didn't understand a word of it. *Calling Dr. Freud, calling Dr. Freud.*

"You're wrong, dad. We talked last night, talked a lot. She told me all about what her father did, and she told me she's gotten over it. I believe her. I think she's . . . well, she's the most together woman I've ever met."

The kid's got a thing for that Russian cunt. Same as his bastard old man. Good. Once Schmidt gets her, we'll dissect her in front of your eyes, you cocksuckers, conduct an amateur autopsy, vivisection while you watch, and I'll wash your ugly faces in her blood!

"Dad, how can we find her? The California coast has to be nine hundred miles long."

Wetting his lips, Charlie answered hesitantly. "I can make a guess. Let's hope it's the right one."

You prick, you know it will be right. You're reading her

mind, or doing whatever voodoo you always do, and I'm going to sit here very quietly, and if I'm lucky you won't read my mind because if you did . . .

"Will Schmidt guess the same?"

"Maybe." Charlie blew between his teeth. "He's smart enough. Best we can do is get to her before he does."

Two knives, a matched set, Charlie sonofabitch McKenzie held one in each hand. Fingers clenched, knuckles white, Sam gripped his armrests.

Resignation in his voice, Charlie said, "Which means another major felony. Damnit, Scott, I never wanted you involved in this."

"There's no place I'd rather be." *Same fucking smile, the both of them smile like goddamned werewolves.*

"Sam, I've got some good news for you and some bad news." *Now what?* "The good news is that I can't handcuff you to your seat because I need all four sets of manacles those MPs were carrying." *What's the motherfucker mean?* "The bad news is that I can't let you out of that chair."

Sam almost saw it coming. He almost began to move out of the way. He almost—but not quite—was fast enough.

Charlie's two knifes stabbed down, pinioning Sam's hands to the armrests.

The shock was so great that Sam couldn't scream. At least not for a while.

10

Saint Charles

Friday, July 24.
1530 Hours Pacific Time

HOLLY STREET EXIT—SAN CARLOS

An hour and a half before Sam began to scream, Schmidt—
a few miles south of the San Francisco airport—spotted the
sign. *But of course,* he thought. *San Carlos. Saint Charles.
How obvious.*

If memory served, Saint Charles was a reformer, and
therefore a pest. Schmidt had seen monuments to him in Milan. *Ah, Milan! A wretched city, but a fine opera house.*

Swinging his Mercedes M-Class SUV onto the exit ramp,
he murmured an order at his scout. "Keep your eyes open.
Kolodenkova may be closer than I imagined." Milksnake, a
Yemenite Sunni, and not the brightest star in the mercenary
sky, cocked a Beeman air pistol modified to fire tranquilizer
darts.

Schmidt wondered if he'd misjudged Kolodenkova's
plans. Perhaps she did not intend to make her escape by sea;
perhaps her sad little message to "Saint Charlie" conveyed a
secret meaning: *meet me in San Carlos.*

But no, a quick tour persuaded him otherwise. It was just another American suburban purgatory: a strip mall here and there, shabby taco shops, too many gas stations, motels that likely did more daytime than nighttime business—there was no focus to the place, no obvious location for a runaway spy to hide. Kolodenkova was elsewhere. She was, as he originally hypothesized, fleeing for the water.

But then again . . .

A fresh thought. He snapped his fingers. "Milksnake, do you know how to use my laptop computer's GPS?" The idiot was attempting to clear the Beeman. "Just fire the dart into the floor mat. Never attempt to decock an air gun."

"Yes, suh." The Yemenite's accent was thick, and his command of English was barely adequate. Schmidt would not entirely miss the man if he shot himself in the foot.

The pistol, quite powerful for its kind, recoiled as Milksnake discharged it. "I well-trained on de Global Bositionin' System." Like many Arabs, Milksnake couldn't pronounce the letter *P*. It came out as *B* instead.

"Let us hope so. Search the database for towns named Saint Charles." Better safe than sorry, Schmidt spelled it for him.

Milksnake opened Schmidt's sleek Sony featherweight computer like it was a jewel box. Schmidt swung back toward the freeway as the man maladroitly pecked on the keyboard. Some long moments passed before he had an answer. "Five Yankee Sain' Charles."

"Any in California?"

"No. Louisiana an'—"

Impatiently, Schmidt snapped, "Try San Carlos."

Milksnake moved his lips as he typed, whispering each letter. Schmidt felt himself becoming immoderately annoyed. "Got me two here. Dis town we leavin'. Other one's called

San Carlos do Cabo." He pronounced it "Dew-Cabew."

Schmidt didn't bother to correct him. *Do Cabo. Of the cape. On the cape. In other words, on the water.* "Pull up the map, Milksnake. Tell me where this interestingly named metropolis might be found."

"Uh, lemme . . . no dat's not right . . . uh, you gotta do dis. Uh, yeah. Got it. It's . . . how you say . . . long ways away, south on da California coast, north of dis blace called San Lewis Obiss—"

"San Luis Obispo. Milksnake, you really must work on your pronunciation. Is there an airport nearby?"

"Lemme try this key . . . San Louie O-Biz-Bo be da nearest. Sixty mile. San Carlos, she's a little blace. Bobulation is tree fifteen hundred, I mean tree hundred and fifteen. Combuter says no motels or nutin'."

"Fishing village," Schmidt mused. "What driving time does the computer predict?"

"More 'an tree hours."

Schmidt weighed his odds. Kolodenkova had called McKenzie's daughter just around two in the afternoon. No surprise, the Federal Bureau of Ineptitude's phone tappers had not had time to pinpoint her location. The most they'd been able to ascertain was that she was in the 650 area code—somewhere between San Francisco and San Jose, a distance of roughly fifty miles.

It had taken him thirty minutes to assemble a convoy, another thirty to reach the airport, and an irksome ten-minute detour to deposit Samuel at the airport. Assuming she was at 650's southern boundary when she called, under the worst of circumstances, she had a ninety-mile lead.

Overtaking her would be difficult, although not impossible. But wouldn't it be faster to return to the airport, fly to

San Luis Obispo, and drive to the flyspeck coastal town to which Kolodenkova might—or might not—be running?

Schmidt calculated the travel time: *Twenty minutes to the general aviation terminal. A half hour to get flight clearance, and quite possibly more. Another twenty minutes taxiing on the runway. Forty-some minutes flying time followed by another hour on country roads. Just shy of three hours if I'm lucky, considerably longer if I am not.*

He'd keep to the highway—it would be as fast, possibly faster. Besides, there was no guarantee his prey was on her way to San Carlos do Cabo. She just as easily might be running for any one of the thirty-plus marinas between San Francisco and San Diego.

I have no desire, he reflected, *to be trapped in an airplane, thirty thousand feet and three hundred miles from the woman when one of my teams locates her.*

When, not if.

Make no mistake: they would find her. A dozen truckloads of men were speeding down the coast from San Francisco. Another two dozen were sweeping up from the south. Soldiers would be peeling off at every marina and boat basin along the way. Kolodenkova was in a vise.

"Milksnake, you said the computer estimates our driving time is more than three hours. How much more?"

"Tree hours and twelve minutes, she say."

"Oh, I believe we can do better than that." Johan Schmidt hammered the accelerator to the floor.

"Oakland Approach, this is five-seven-juliet-november-bravo. We have a problem."

"57JNB, is this a mayday?"

"Negative, Oakland," Scott McKenzie said, credibly imitating the laconic tones of a veteran Air Force pilot as he lied to the San Francisco Bay Area's Air Traffic Control center. "Just an intermittent indicator on my landing gear."

Charlie hated it, hated every bit of it. Scott had no role in this. He should have run for cover as he'd been ordered. Instead—as anxious about Irina as his old man, and as bullheaded—he'd followed Charlie onto Sam's Gulfstream. Now, goddamnit, he was up to his neck in all the trouble in the world.

"57JNB, hold at flight level two-two-zero; repeat: twenty-two thousand feet. I'm clearing a runway for you at SFO," an affably unflappable voice, another routine day in one of the nation's busiest air spaces, don't worry, Captain, we have these little hiccups all the time.

"No need, Oakland. My computer is telling me it's a sensor problem."

"Computers can be wrong." A slow drawl, peaceful and calming.

"True, but pilots get the blame. Especially when there's a VIP passenger on board."

"According to your Air Force designation, he's a level three, a real heavyweight. Okay, 57JNB, you've got my attention. What's your suggestion?"

"I want to show my bigwig how the best of the best handle things."

"Negative on that. I won't have any cowboy stunts in my airspace."

"I don't do the Wild West. Look, Oakland, I'm turning over the Pacific north of Santa Cruz. I'll make a descent into Monterey, take a low pass over the runway with my wheels lowered. If I've got landing gear trouble, the tower will see it."

The moment of truth, Charlie thought, *either ATC buys*

this fairy tale or somebody's going to start scrambling fighter planes.

The controller paused, mulling the proposal over before agreeing, "Sounds reasonable. I'm handing you off to Monterey Approach, 57JNB. If you're damaged, I want you back up here. We've got more and better emergency crews and equipment."

"Roger that, Oakland Center."

"Good luck, cowboy."

Charlie let himself breathe again. Scott blotted his forehead with a handkerchief. The plane's pilot, sitting in handcuffs on the flight deck floor, said (not for the first time), "You two are going to jail." No threat, just a simple statement of fact.

The copilot, a major also frowning in handcuffs, added, "The nine-eleven laws will put you in front of a military tribunal; jail is the most lenient verdict you'll get."

Charlie corrected him, "Verdicts are the decision of the jury. Sentences are what the judge hands out."

"With a military tribunal there isn't a whole lot of difference."

"Point taken." Charlie glanced back into the cabin. Sam, white with pain, was still pinned to his seat. "Scott, can you see the Monterey airport yet?"

"Look for the green and white flashing light," the pilot drawled. *These guys,* Charlie thought, *are the most imperturbable guys in the world. I guess if you spend your life driving thirty tons of iron at supersonic speeds, nothing scares you.*

"I know that," Scott shot back.

The pilot sighed. "You two fruitcakes—do you have a story, or is this just a joy ride?"

Charlie thumbed his automatic's safety. "You're doing

that pretty well, Colonel. Most people wouldn't have noticed you're about two feet closer to the controls than you were five minutes ago. Too bad I'm not most people. Scoot your butt back into that corner unless you want me to get riled." The pilot complied. "Stay put from now on, okay?"

"I'll be the prosecution's lead witness."

"Not if you try something stupid again."

"Dad, I see the airport."

Wincing at the pain clawing his ribs, Charlie bent forward. "Take it slow and easy, Scott. Do it like a professional would."

Scott nodded crisply. Charlie couldn't help being proud. His son knew how to fly puddle-jumper prop planes. Handling an infinitely more complex twin-engine jet required qualifications he simply did not have. However, he was doing fine—at least as far as Charlie could see.

Of course he had a little help. The copilot, encouraged by a pistol tickling his neck, answered Scott's every question. On the other hand, the copilot, like the plane's captain, wanted nothing more than to get the aircraft down safely. That was always a pilot's first priority. Unfortunately his second, in this particular case, would be to put Charlie and his son behind bars for the rest of their natural lives.

If I can get Irina, if I can get that damned computer disk back, we've got a chance. If Schmidt finds her first, then Scott's going to be a jailbird just like his father. Goddamn goddamn, goddamn!

"Monterey Tower, this is 57JNB. Has Oakland Center briefed you on my situation?"

A woman's voice, laid back tones, full of quiet confidence, not the least hint of worry. "Affirmative, 57JNB. You're cleared for descent." She pronounced it "dee-scent," same as every other aviator in America.

"Where's the landing gear on this thing?"

"It's the lever marked to look like a little tire," the copilot muttered, "right next to the—"

"Got it," Scott said.

Charlie heard the whir of the hydraulic system, a hatch opening, the undercarriage lowering. He felt a modest, but nonetheless perceptible, deceleration. Unnoticeable on a big commercial jet, lowering the wheels altered the smaller plane's aerodynamics. Scott kicked the throttle up to compensate. The additional power wasn't enough; an artificially feminine computer voice complained, "Sink rate! Sink rate!"

"Goose it," instructed the copilot. "And get your nose up. Okay, now work the flaps . . . " The computer went silent. " . . . and keep your airspeed at a hundred and ten knots. A twin-engine jet isn't a Piper Cub. This plane can *land* at one of those puppy's top speed. Look, prior to touchdown be sure to arm your spoilers and deflectors. Then as soon as you land, power up—"

"We're not landing," Charlie snapped.

"You will sometime."

"I stand corrected. Thank you."

He peered out the windshield. Out to sea—ten miles he guessed—a sullen concrete wall spanned the ocean. *Massive fog bank. Half mile high. Runs as far south as the eye can see.* What lay ahead of the airplane was a different story. The coastal landscape was verdant green, emerald green, greener than a green bottle. The air had become a delicate golden haze, late afternoon fog condensing over water, ethereal mist filling the sky. Each minute water droplet caught light from the lowering sun, tiny prisms refracting the fires of descending angels. Charlie flew through heaven.

The Heads Up Display isn't a problem, Charlie thought. *That's a surprise. I always figured a HUD system projecting all that data on the windshield would be distracting. But instead you barely notice it.*

"57JNB, I have visual."

"I'm coming in at eight hundred feet. Give me a status on my landing gear."

"Pull into a right turn over the runway, put yourself in a circle around the tower."

"The indicator just cleared, Monterey. I think we're fine."

"Just follow my instructions, 57JNB."

"Roger, ma'am. You're the boss."

Charlie was amazed at the speed of it. As many times as he had flown, he had never flown like this—standing in a cockpit, looking out the windscreen of a jet on its descent above, over, beyond an airport, and it was all in the blink of an eye.

"57JNB, your gear appears to be down. Circle around, make another pass, raising your wheels on the approach."

"On my way, Monterey. To repeat, my indicator's cleared. I'd say the computer was right—nothing but a sensor glitch."

"They'll do that."

The sea below the plane was slate. Scott banked before turning out again into the startling glory of the Pacific sun.

Another rocketing flight over a small airport, and the encouraging voice of a ground controller, "You're A-OK, 57JNB."

"Thanks for your help, Monterey. I'm going back to my flight plan."

"Next time stop by to visit. We've got good eats in this town."

"You've got a deal . . . Hang on, Monterey . . . What . . . yes, sir. Certainly, sir . . . Monterey, I've got a request from my VIP passenger. He'd like a quick tour of Big Sur. With your permission, we'll head south from here before vectoring back east."

Charlie whispered a prayer. This was the second phase of his hastily improvised plan. Success or failure hinged on the Monterey controller's response.

"I'll give you an affirmative on that. We're still VFR—better than a thousand-foot ceiling with three miles horizontal visibility. Stay below eighteen thousand feet. There's a lot of traffic at higher altitudes, not a good place for the tourist trade."

Whew!

"I'm going to give my passenger a thrill. One thousand feet, the scenic route. Then I'll start my turn at San Carlos do Cabo, if that meets your approval."

"If your level three is happy, I'm happy. You're cleared to proceed as requested. But you're going to need to switch to IFR south of here. Repeat, that's Instrument Flight Rules, Captain. Meteorology reports everything is socked in below Big Sur. And be careful when you make your turn, there's restricted airspace down that way, missile range out of Vandenberg, and you don't want to drift into it."

"I read you."

"If your indicator acts up again, don't even think about coming back this way. That fog is rolling in here too, and this time of year it moves faster than you'd believe."

"Roger that, Monterey. Five-seven-juliett-november-bravo out."

Charlie could already see the Big Sur coast—stippled orange, a fractured wall of rusted rock, waves exploding at the feet of fortress cliffs. It stretched eighty miles, a handful of villages clinging to the sides of a highway that washed out every year or two. There was no place to hide. If Irina was on that road, Route 1, he'd see her. Or at least he'd see an

aquamarine Toyota Camry and pray to God that she was behind the wheel.

If she wasn't . . .

*I got it wrong. She didn't mean she was running for San
Carlos. Or worse, she did, and she's already arrived, and
there's no way I'll know because the whole damned coast
down there is fogged in. Then what the hell do I do?*

"Okay, dad, what do we do next?"

Schmidt was down on the flatlands now, driving a te-
diously tame road. Big Sur, ah, that was more to his liking: a
rollercoaster highway of fishhook curves, saw-toothed cliffs,
death just over the guardrail—a place where a man could
test his mettle, determining with gratifying exactitude the
extent of his competence under the unbelieving eyes of
happy holidayers in their station wagons, insufferably arrogant bicyclists, shocked commercial travelers, all those
placid sheep gaping as he wove among them, and more than
one of them timidly skittered onto the shoulder, fierce mortality foremost in their domesticated minds.

And the sea. The sea!

Those waves crashed with such almighty power that the
spume hurled itself hundreds of feet high, speckling his
M-Class's windshield, blinding him for the barest few seconds while he savored the audible fright of soldiers who
should have been braver. It was a moment to remember, a
memory to relish.

The posted speed limit had been fifty miles an hour. Johan's heart rate remained constant, even when his speedometer ticked over the hundred mark, and if a man could not
command his own body, what hope had he of commanding
warriors?

True, he had a good tool for the mission. The Mercedes M-Class handled well, although it was no Gelandewagen, merely the sort of vehicle driven by simpleton civilians who thought manliness could be purchased with 3 percent APR financing. Nonetheless, its German parentage showed, superb engineering, and he'd never doubted its performance for a moment—just as he had never doubted his own.

At the moment *Samson and Delilah* provided him with background music, the chorus hailing Dagon's rebirth as blind Samson was led to the temple. It was glorious, a melody most suitable for a triumphal victory march.

When triumph came his way, he might play it again.

However, he'd begin celebrating success with that famous bacchanal, the orchestra *en forte*, hot orgiastic rites, these being an appropriate accompaniment for what would be, in the end, a blood sacrifice.

Presuming a suitable burnt offering could be found.

An open question, that. Kolodenkova was as elusive as ever. Schmidt's armed and efficient troopers had taken up position at virtually every marina from San Diego to San Francisco. The result: no sighting, not the least hint of her whereabouts. For the moment, she was off the radar.

But nothing to worry about. Everyone knew what to look for. A four-door Toyota Camry from Budget Rent A Car. An odious aqua in color. California license 34RCB684.

A gentleman named Scott T. McKenzie had rented an Intrepid from Hertz the night before, rented it in distant Chico, California. The following morning, he'd also rented the Camry.

Two cars, one renter? A renter with an Arizona driver's license, who signed himself "Doctor"? It was Charles's whelp, Schmidt was certain—all the more so because a Piper Cub registered to an Indian Health Service physician was parked on the tarmac at Chico's small airport.

How helpful that information would have been if he'd known it earlier. But of course, federal bureaucrats are slow to correlate the data they download each day from credit card companies, car rental agencies, airlines, and all the rest. Moreover, while there was a watch-list posting for Charles McKenzie, unfortunately there was none for his son. It was, Schmidt allowed, an understandable oversight—although nevertheless nettlesome.

Still, he reflected, he need not be overly concerned. He had solid ID on the girl's car. And, within—he glanced at his dashboard clock—a half hour, no marina would be without a full complement of watchmen.

Including the last, and most remote: tiny San Carlos do Cabo.

Would she be there? Schmidt's intuition told him she could be nowhere else. His men were patrolling the length of the coast, each and every one of them on the lookout for a blue-green Camry driven by a woman. Indeed, they had intercepted a few. Happily there'd been only one embarrassment—a minor incident of the sort that could be assuaged with cash. Just another expense to be added to the invoice he would submit . . . when? . . . certainly no later than tomorrow morning. Whereupon Samuel, or rather his proxy, Maximilian Henkes, DefCon Enterprises' chief executive, would proffer full payment.

"Dagon se révèle! La flamme nouvelle," sang the chorus. The God awakes; the fire is reborn. Schmidt tapped his fingers in beat with the tune.

"What's our position and ETA, Milksnake?"

The Yemenite blinked, momentarily baffled by the acronym for estimated time of arrival. "Tree-boint-six miles from de turnoff. Den eleven-boint-one to de village."

"Just to verify: there is no other access to San Carlos except for that one road, correct?"

"Yes, suh."

"A roach motel," Schmidt whispered, speaking only to himself. He tilted his head over his shoulder, "Pit Viper, I'm dropping you a couple of klicks from the turnoff. I want you to take up position near the access road. Stay out of sight. Have your weapon cocked and locked, but don't show it unless you have to."

"Should I stop traffic, sir?"

"Negative as regards anyone going in. Should you see Kolodenkova driving toward town, let her pass. Vehicles coming out are a different story. If you spot an aquamarine Camry, destroy its tires. Don't worry whether she's the driver, just open fire. In the event you inadvertently ventilate an honest citizen's Goodyears—well, we'll deal with it later. Anyone else who's leaving the town—let them pass unless it's a lone woman. Every woman on her own is to be intercepted and interrogated. Am I understood? Good. One more thing: I want you in constant radio contact with me. Apprise me of anything and everything you observe."

"Yes, sir," Pit Viper replied. Schmidt heard the satisfying snap of a rifle magazine being slapped home. *A much more professional soldier than Milksnake. Formerly of the French Foreign Legion, I believe, a fine training ground for gentlemen of our calling.*

"You other three back there, Bushmaster, Python, and Krait—the facilities at San Carlos should be in our favor, an open field of fire. I expect little more than a parking lot and a single walkway down to the boat slips. A town of San Carlos's size is unlikely to offer much in the way of amenities—no concession stands, no workshop, I'd be surprised if there's as much as a ship's chandlery. I imagine there'll be a chain-link fence along the waterline, separating the slips from the land. It probably will be topped with razor wire, even though grand theft sailboat is not an oft-committed crime. The gate will be locked, but the lock will be a joke. If Kolodenkova has a set of picks, she'll be through it in thirty seconds. If not—well, she's been trained how to clear taller fences than anything she'll find in a flyspeck fishing village."

"Turnoff ahead, suh," said Milksnake.

"I see it." San Carlos Do Cabo. 11 M. POP: 318. Schmidt remembered an old soldier's complaint: *It isn't the end of the world, but you can see it from here.* He flicked on his right turn signal, braking down to thirty-five miles per hour. Could an M-Class corner at that speed? He was looking forward to finding out.

Disappointingly, the top-heavy four-wheeler skidded precariously as it turned. The result tested Schmidt's competence as a driver, but, of course, he passed the test, and there was little surprise in that.

"Do you have to do that, sir?" complained Bushmaster. *Americans,* Schmidt thought. *They are born whiners.*

"As a matter of fact, yes."

The terrain flanking San Carlos's shabby little two-lane access road was tabletop flat farmland furrowed with rows of some low plant, artichoke perhaps, Schmidt was not certain. In the distance, workmen in faded clothing and straw hats stooped at their labors—Mexicans, he supposed, part of the underpaid illegal army that made California's agriculture the world's wealthiest. *Hard labor for low wages. A pity. I could train those men, make something of them, and with guns in their hands they'd earn more in an hour—*

Bushmaster exclaimed, "Shit! The whole world's disappeared!"

Schmidt narrowed his eyes. Less than a mile ahead the road vanished, melting into a fog bank like a snowcapped castle wall.

"De-DA de-DA," Bushmaster mouthed the theme music from *The Twilight Zone*. "You are traveling to a different dimension, a dimension of—"

"Bushmaster," Schmidt snapped irritably, "zip your lip."

He braked to a halt near a stand of eucalyptus and a drainage ditch filled with Scottish thistle, their purple crowns the only gaiety in a banal landscape.

"Pit Viper, these trees are as good a cover as anything else. Take up your position."

"I'm on it, sir."

The Mercedes' rear door opened, then shut.

Schmidt glanced out the window. Pit Viper, black and slender, was screwing his earpiece into place. "Radio check."

"I read you loud and clear, Cobra."

"Report every five minutes. Even if there's nothing to report, I want to hear your voice."

"Yes, sir." The mercenary brought his rifle to port arms and trotted into the trees. Swinging back onto the road, Johan Schmidt switched on his headlights and drove into steel wool fog. *Another four miles to go. Will she be there? Of course she will. There's no other place she can be.*

"**M**ake another pass up Highway One," Charlie ordered.

"It won't do any good, dad. We've been as far south as San Luis and almost back to Monterey. She's not on that road."

Charlie scanned the coast highway with his binoculars—or rather with the pilot's. You could find a set in every cockpit in every aircraft in the world. These were Nikon ten-powers—

adequate, but not as sharp as the Leicas he'd lost in Mitchell Canyon.

Down below a black Mercedes M-Class turned onto an access road. Charlie was pretty sure he'd marked out that particular intersection before. "Scott, is that the way to San Carlos?"

"Should be. Why, do you see something?"

"Guy in an SUV took the corner one hell of a lot faster than he should have."

The copilot shook his head, "At this altitude and speed, you can't judge what's going on at ground level."

"It's Schmidt. I can smell him." *I'm right. I know I'm right. Don't ask me how, I just know.* He was as confident as he'd ever been—unnervingly so. Irina was somewhere in San Carlos. Schmidt was right behind her. And he, *damn me!*, was stuck in an airplane sixty miles from the nearest airport. "Take this thing in low over the town. As low as you dare. If Schmidt thinks she's there, and if I think she's there, then, by God, that's where she is!"

"Sir, with respect . . . " the copilot again. About fifteen minutes earlier he'd started pretending that he was on Charlie's side. Charlie played along. He figured he'd get better information that way. " . . . you've got zero ceiling and zero visibility over the coast. Nobody's seeing anything."

"Maybe we'll get lucky."

"Again with respect, those are words no one in my business wants to hear."

"Mine's the opposite. Scott, take this thing down. Treetop level if you can manage it."

Both the pilot and the copilot simultaneously shouted, "No!" Charlie cocked an eyebrow. The pilot, senior man, spoke urgently. "This is a jet, mister, a jet! Do you know how a jet works? You've got two big turbos powering this aircraft. They suck air in at the front, and blast it out at the

back. Basically this plane is a flying vacuum cleaner with
seven tons of thrust! Get low enough, and those engines will
suck branches off of trees, shingles off of roofs, and livestock out of pastures. You do not, repeat, do not barnstorm in
a jet aircraft!"

"Suggestions?" Charlie growled.

"To see what's at ground level in zero/zero weather? Get
out and walk."

"Thank you very much, but I think we'll try it my way.
Scott, take us in."

*And if I find her, then what do I do? How do I get to her?
How do I get that disk back? How do I keep my son out of
jail? Oh, God, give me some answers here!*

From what Schmidt could see—*precious little in this
fog*—the word "village" was too wide a word for San Carlos
do Cabo, consisting as it did of a laughably small commercial district and a scant few blocks of brightly painted Victorian gingerbread homes.

Downtown, such as it was, was no more than two cafe-
style restaurants, a no-name general store, a Texaco gas station, and a handful of civic buildings—a cinder-block
schoolhouse, a town hall, a medical clinic, a fire house, but
(for which he was duly grateful) no police station, at least
none that Schmidt could see.

Where the devil is the marina? he asked himself.

The Mercedes crept forward, high beams giving him fifteen yards' visibility, and often less than that.

Spooky. Schmidt did not care for that trite adjective, although it seemed peculiarly appropriate for the place. There
was not another vehicle on the road. Nor a pedestrian on the
street. But for a handful of parked cars, their bodies slick

with condensation, the town might well have been abandoned. The Twilight Zone indeed.

West, due west, on the main street of a tiny township. Soon enough he'd reach the Pacific. Once on the coast, surely he'd find—

> SAN CARLOS DO CABO
> MARINA PARKING
> NO CAMPING
> DEPOSIT $5.00 DAY FEE AT GUARD HOUSE

He smiled, lips as thin as a nail file.

The guard was gone for the evening, his shack empty. A miserable half dozen vehicles were scattered around the parking lot. Four of them were hard working pickups, probably commercial fishermen's trucks. The fifth was an ancient TransAm, vintage 1977, as much Bondo as metal, a once-prideful muscle car come to bad times and low company.

The sixth, of course, was an aquamarine Toyota Camry, California license 34RCB684.

Did he feel relieved? No, not at all. His confidence had never wavered, at least not seriously. Nor was self-doubt a sentiment with which he was acquainted. He'd found her as he'd known he would. If he sensed a frisson of pride—*a glow, actually*—it was merely the anticipation of a profitable mission drawing to its predestined conclusion.

He parked the M-Class near Kolodenkova's rented car. "Python, trot back to the guard kiosk at the entrance and take up position inside. In the unlikely event a visitor comes along, send him away. Tell him the parking lot is off-limits because there's been a toxic spill or something. Use your imagination."

Python was the biggest trooper in the team, a *Sayeret*

Matkal Israeli who, if Schmidt's memory served, had once been a decorated hero in his homeland. His face was broken rock, his eyes impassive obsidian. No civilian interloper would question the word of a man who looked so much like what he was: a proven killer.

"Yes, sir." Python rolled out of the car, falling into a crouch. Seasoned soldier that he was, he swept the parking lot with his rifle before running, bent at the waist, toward the guard shack.

Schmidt put his hand on the door latch, then thought better of it. Milksnake, sitting in the passenger seat, was, like Johan himself, slender of frame. Although darker skinned than his superior officer, in the fog, at a distance, he might be mistaken for someone whom he was not.

Better safe than sorry. "Milksnake, those sunglasses in your shirt pocket—do me a service and put them on."

"Uh . . . why dat, suh?"

"Because I ordered you to."

"Yes, suh."

The corner of Schmidt's lip twitched, almost a smile. "Thank you. Now jog over to that Camry, put your hand on the hood, and tell me if it's still warm. If you think yourself up to it, give me your best estimate as to how long it has been parked there."

The Yemenite answered with a hesitant nod. He suspected something, but was insufficiently quick-witted to deduce what.

"Don't forget your weapon."

Milksnake slid out of the Mercedes. Instead of employing the routine precautionary measures expected of every trooper, he merely walked—did not even trot—to Kolodenkova's car. Once there, he strolled quite idly around it before placing the back of his hand over the engine. "She not warm. She hot." At a distance of four yards his thickly accented voice sounded muffled, as though he was talking through a handkerchief. *No echo,* Schmidt thought, *no reverberation. The fog blankets both sight and sound.* "Uh . . . dere's no . . . how you say? . . . de wet stuff, you know, no dew on her. Dis car been here only—"

Milksnake's blood dewed—which was the right word—the Camry's hood. Hushed by fog, the gunshot's report sounded faint, distant, and who could tell from what direction it came?

Schmidt took joy in the moment. An element of challenge made every victory sweeter.

Scott's head twitched left. "What the hell was that?"

"A rooftop," Charlie whispered hollowly.

"Jesus, dad! We were below it!"

The computer's robot voice bleated, "Ground proximity. Danger. Ground proximity." *Bitching Betty,* Charlie thought, *that's what the copilot called the annunciator system. Come on, Betty, tell me something I don't know.*

The copilot, not as calm as he had been, tried to sound relaxed. "Sir, you are going to hit a house, a hospital, a school. You're going to crash, and when you do, you're going to kill a lot of innocent people. I don't think you want to do that, sir. I really don't think you want to do that at all."

The pure hell of it was that even at treetop altitude Charlie barely could see the ground. Only patches of green every now and then, shrubs and grass. Maybe the hint of a road. The rest was dirty cotton, choking fog above and below and all around the plane.

"She's down there. I have to find her. I don't have a choice."

"Sir, you don't know she's down there. You made that clear earlier. You only think she *may* be."

More hell: sunset was near. Such light as there was, was low and fading. Scott had flown west before turning back toward San Carlos, descending so low over the Pacific that they could see milky waves. The sun was near the horizon, a watery brightness in the fog, and it seemed to Charlie that he could see it inch lower toward the fall of night.

"You're wrong. I know. I know for certain."

"You can't."

"I can and do! Damnit, don't you see?" *I'm shouting. Can't stop myself.* "I know her like I know myself! Her mind is as much in mine as mine is in hers! She's the same as me, and I'm the same as her, and there's not a bit of difference between the two of us!"

Well, hell, that sounded certifiably insane. What kind of nuttiness was he going to spew out next? *Actually, I'm her guardian angel. Yeah, God hisownself has assigned me personal responsibility. Pleased to meet you, I'm Saint Charlie of the seraphim.*

"Dad?" Scott asked, sounding worried. "Are you all right?"

No, I'm nutty as a fruitcake. He started to reply, suddenly couldn't, felt the breath sucked from his lungs, wanted to fall limp to the cockpit floor. Doc Howard's painkillers were wearing off. An express train of unalloyed agony roared up his leg, through his stomach, next station stop: the brain. Crystalline and pure, he'd never known hurt that hurt like this. His vision blanked, and for a dizzy moment he truly feared he'd fainted.

But he held. His old man's old body held, and after a moment it passed, and he was back to where he'd been. Pulling himself straight, praying that no one noticed, he bit back a groan. "Okay, look . . . I mean, look . . . " He took a deep breath before continuing softly, almost in reminiscence.

"Not so long ago Death gave your mother his black rose. There wasn't a goddamned thing I could do about it. Nothing. It was totally beyond my power to influence. Do you know what that felt like? What it felt like for a guy like me? I never met a problem I couldn't finagle my way around or bull my way through. Not ever. Me, I'm the guy who gets the job done. One way or another, that's what I do, and I do it very well." He wiped a hand across his clammy forehead. "Only not that time. That time I was impotent. All I could do was wait helplessly for the end. Do you understand how I felt, Scott? Do you understand, Major? Colonel?"

The two officers exchanged glances.

"I failed my wife. That's what it felt like. It felt like there had to be something I *could* have done. The thought that there might have been will haunt me 'til the day I die. No way in hell am I letting it happen this time because this time there *is* something I can do, and I'll fight to get it done as long as I have a breath left in my body, and ten minutes after I stop breathing I'll still be fighting. Have you got that, Major? Colonel, do you read me? At the moment, that girl down there in San Carlos is what my life is about—the only thing it's about—so just shut to hell up and let me get on with my job."

The copilot gave him a psychiatric ward look. "I think I understand, sir."

"I doubt it."

"Whether I do or I don't isn't the issue. The issue is whether or not you want to live long enough to help your lady friend. Or would you prefer to die?"

"Maybe later. Not just now."

"Then," the major shouted, "I respectfully recommend that your son get—this—GODDAMNED—PLANE—INTO—THE—SKY!"

He's losing it. Any minute now and all that Right Stuff *ve-*

*neer is going to flake right off of him, and he's going to go
postal.* "Take her up a bit, Scott."

The copilot blew a breath between tightly compressed
teeth. "What I don't understand is what you hope to accomplish. Even if you spot her—and in this weather the odds of
that are nil—the nearest airport is sixty miles away."

*The man has a point. Damn me, but he has a point. I still
haven't got a clue as to what to do.* "Signal her. At a minimum I can let her know I'm here. Wiggle the wings or something. Somehow or another tell her to get out of that town,
get back to the highway. We could land on Route 1, couldn't
we? If she knows I've come for her, we could touch down
and—"

Total disgust: "That is such an exceptionally bad idea."

He's right. "Traffic. Yeah." The coastal road was packed.
High summer, and vacationers taking the scenic drive up
and down Big Sur—cars, vans, campers, you name it, it was
rolling on Route 1, daddy driving, and mommy pointing the
camcorder at everything that looked interesting. "Okay,
Major, I'm open to suggestions. There's a young woman in
that village who is in deadly danger. As of noon today,
there's a price on her head and a lot of people wanting to
collect. If I . . . if *we* don't extract her, she will be killed. I
repeat: killed. It is a certainty. Equally certain, she will be
tortured in ways you don't want to know about. If I told
you, you'd puke. The thugs who are after her want information, and cutting it out of her is just one of the ways they'll
get their jollies. So, Major—and you too, Colonel—give
me some ideas. Help me out here. Do that, and you have
my word, once I get that young woman out of trouble, I'll
surrender."

"I wish I could believe that, sir."

Charlie laid his hand on the copilot's shoulder—a gentle

squeeze of sincerity, then words calculated to convince: "You can. On my honor, as soon as she's safe, the cuffs come off you. I'll lay down my gun. You can tie me up and turn me in. Hell, you can shoot me where I stand. I honestly don't care. Just as long as we save that lady's life, I don't give a good goddamn about anything else."

Well, that was a lie. He gave a good goddamn about much more than Irina. Top priority: seeing to it that his son wasn't punished for his father's misdeeds. Then too, there was a computer disk that could not be allowed out of the country. Add to that Sam, still pinioned to his seat; Charlie wanted the truth, and if he had to carve it out with a knife, well, it wouldn't be the first time.

Plus Schmidt. His bill was overdue. It was time to collect.

Surrender? In your dreams, Major!

"You have my word," he lied piously, "as soon as we get Irina to safety, I'm your prisoner."

Some men were rattled when they saw a comrade take a bullet. Those men were weaker men than Johan Schmidt. Calm and collected, he whispered into his radio, "Pit Viper, do you read me?"

"Roger, Cobra. What's your status?"

"Kolodenkova is in my ops zone. Pass the word up and down the line. I want all units converging on this town."

"Nearest squad's an hour away, sir."

"I am aware of that. Tell them to move as briskly as they can."

"Will do."

Schmidt peered into, but not through, a maddening fog. Where was she? Hard to tell. He'd parked to the left of her Camry. Milksnake exited the Mercedes's passenger side, cir-

cled the Toyota, and had been standing to its right when—
nice shooting, young miss—she'd switched off his lights.
Odds were, she was somewhere in a one-hundred-and-
eighty-degree arc beginning at the Camry's front bumper,
and ending at its rear. She couldn't be to his left. His M-
Class would have blocked her line of fire. Nor, now that he
thought about it, was she behind him. There was nothing
there but the flat expanse of a parking lot under Python's
surveillance—and if Python had seen her, he most certainly
would have opened fire.

"Python, Milksnake is down. Did you happen to see a gun
flash a few seconds ago?"

No answer.

"I repeat. Python, did you observe a muzzle flash?"

Something's not right. A warrior's instinct, a chilly tickle
along the spine, the stuff of which goose bumps are made.
You didn't know what was wrong. You only knew danger
was near. That's when your testicles tightened up.

Schmidt slid down in his seat. "Python, I asked you a
question."

He fingered the radio from its cradle, clipping it to his
belt. Raising his right hand, index finger stretched, he drew
two circles in the air, first pointing to a fog-shrouded picnic
bench, second to a fire-charred driftwood log a dozen yards
away. The Mercedes rear door snicked open; Bushmaster
and Krait slid to the ground, preparing to dash for cover.

"Python, please respond."

He slipped his pistol into his belt—a Beretta U22 Neos
with an extended barrel. It would give him the accuracy he
wanted, nail-driving accuracy, but not the knock-over power
he needed. Carrying low-caliber weapons on this mission
had been a mistake. Thank Samuel for that.

"Python?"

Pumping his fist three times, Schmidt whispered, "Go!" Bent low, two mercenaries darted into a broken field run. As they did, he threw open his own door, rolled prone on wet asphalt, snaking out of sight beneath the Mercedes.

He listened.

Listening was an art. What you could not see, you might hear. All he desired was a single telltale footstep on wet pavement. Instead he heard . . .

. . . a dispute of seagulls, birds bobbing in the marina's water . . .

. . . the cowbell clang of loose boat fittings blown in a rising wind . . .

. . . snapping signal flags hung from a pretentious yachtsman's mast . . .

. . . a woman's voice, almost musical, crooning from his radio. "Hello. You must be Johan Schmidt."

Well now, that's an unwelcome surprise. "Where's Python?"

"A big man? Not so good-looking? Is this the one you call Python?"

"Yes."

"You will not be speaking to him again."

No longer a tingling down his backbone, but rather a skeletal finger drawing its nail from his neck to his buttocks. "Pit Viper, I need you here. I need you now."

"Sir, I must be four miles from your position—"

"On the double, Pit Viper. You know I don't like repeating orders."

"I'm on it, sir."

"Mr. Schmidt, he will not get here fast enough, I think."

Good voice. She probably sings well. A mezzo, I should say. "You would be Irina Kolodenkova, would you not?" His mind raced, sifting alternatives, choosing the psychological weapons he needed rather badly at this particular moment.

"I am she."

Paul Linebarger, 1954. *Psychological Warfare.* The definitive text. Rule one: use courtesy to unbalance your enemy. "Irina . . . I may call you Irina, may I not? . . . I have all the time in the world."

"There were five of you in your car. Now three remain. It took me only a minute. I think the rest of you will not take much longer."

The guard shack! How clever. She was hiding inside. When Python entered . . . what did she use? . . . a knife, perhaps, although a handgun pressed against the chest produces a sufficiently muffled report that I would not have heard it, not in this fog. And then . . . why then, when Milksnake stepped out on recon, she had a sweet shot from a concealed position.

Belly-crawling toward the Mercedes' rear axle, he spoke softly and politely, "I know it is trite of me to say this, Irina, but in all candor things will go better for you if you surrender now." The kiosk was twelve yards away, Python's lower legs slack through its open door. *She's long gone. Once she had Python's radio, once she saw us ducking for cover, she darted off somewhere. Where? Anywhere. Step a few paces back in the fog, and you're invisible. Right now she's out there circling. Ah, but circling in which direction?*

"Surrendering when you have your opponent where you want him—this is poor practice, is it not?"

Artificial. Her English is a little too perfect. She doesn't use contractions. That's a flaw—although not one I can use to my advantage.

"I hope you won't hold this against me, but you're being foolish. I . . . we . . . my men and I have tracked you down, Irina. You thought you were running for a place where we couldn't find you. But instead, we were right behind you, knew exactly where you were going. We've been a step ahead—"

"You have made a mistake, Mr. Schmidt."

He didn't like the way she said that. It sounded as if she thought she was the one in control here. He'd need to disabuse her of that fallacy. "Oh?" he asked sharply.

"You have come to the place where I wanted you. You have come as I planned. Everything you have done has been anticipated. You behaved as I wanted you to, doing what I knew you would."

"That's absurd." *She's taunting me, trying to prick my temper. Well, child, two can play that game.*

"Do you think that I am so simple a little girl as to have left a clue to my whereabouts on Charlie's answering machine? If so, you insult me. I said what I said for your benefit, Mr. Schmidt, not Charlie's. I chose the words Saint Charles quite carefully. It was rather subtle of me, do you not think? A phrase that might be innocent, or might contain a hidden meaning—did you not feel quite proud of yourself when you deciphered it, Mr. Schmidt? Did you not say: ah-ha, now I have her?"

Was she really so cunning? Or was she merely improvising?

"You think yourself the hunter. This is not correct, Mr. Schmidt. You are the hunted."

"57JNB, this is San Luis Obispo Control. I want an explanation of your shenanigans, and I want it now!" *That,* thought Charlie, *is one air controller who definitely is* not *cool, calm and collected.*

"San Luis," Scott replied, slow and easy, "my apologies. I've got an aunt in San Carlos and was just doing a flyby to say hello."

The controller's voice evidenced neither belief nor patience. "Bullshit! The coast is socked in. Pea soup fog."

"So I've noticed."

"57JNB, either you *will* give me an explanation or I *will* scramble a Marine Corps intercept."

"Well, it's like this—"

"My radar shows you turning over the Pacific. Your altitude is . . . good God, man! What the hell is going on up there?"

"I can explain—"

"Explain it to the marines, Captain. I just hit the red button."

Oh, hell! There'll be no sweet-talking our way out of this.

"But—"

"But me no buts. Barnstorming at unsafe altitudes in IMC conditions near restricted airspace—you're in deep shit, buddy. You're going to a military base under F-15 Eagle escort. Now get that plane up above the weather pronto."

"I don't think I want to do that, San Luis."

"Your alternative is an AIM-120 up the tailpipe."

"They can't see me in the fog, I'll be—"

Charlie lunged for the microphone. His son had made a fatal mistake. An AIM-120 was a fire-and-forget air-to-air missile. Initially guided by inertial data from the aircraft that launched it, once it was in range of its target, its onboard radar kicked in. Visibility was not an issue. The pilot didn't have to see his foe, didn't have to get closer than forty-six miles before *bang, you're dead!* The air traffic controller would know that—and, therefore, know he was not talking to the Air Force colonel who was designated as captain of this aircraft.

"You're not the pilot!" the ground controller hissed. "You're a fucking hijacker!"

Charlie, hoping for the best but expecting the worst, answered, "Technically speaking 'commandeer' would be a more accurate—"

The man in the control tower wouldn't let him finish the sentence. Charlie couldn't blame him. "Okay, Mohammed, or Osama, or whatever the hell your name is, kiss your raghead butt good-bye."

I have to play my high cards. Correction, high card. Singular. "Check my flight designation. I'm carrying a level-three passenger. The White House national security advisor is aboard this plane."

"If you knew your ass from your elbow, you'd know the president inked an executive order—even if the hijacked plane is Air Force One with him aboard, you and your kind get blown out of the sky. No more World Trade Centers, asshole!"

Charlie gave the copilot a questioning look. The major nodded. "Standing orders. Either you put this plane down now or someone is going to put it down in pieces."

"San Luis, call off those interceptors. I can explain this."

"Don't waste your breath. You're on your way to hell, and I'm one proud American to be sending you there."

"How long?" Charlie asked the pilot.

"They'll be wheels up in under five minutes. Even if they're coming out of Camp Pendelton, it will only take ten or fifteen minutes to get in range. An AIM-120 clocks Mach four. A minute after the pilot fires, forty-five pounds of high explosive are going to detonate on this aircraft's fuselage. Mister, you've got two choices. One is surrender. The other is die."

There's a third choice. There's always an alternative. And, God help me, I know what it is. Faking it every step of the way, he forced himself to sound calm. "How much fuel does this plane burn in five minutes?"

The captain's answer was more reflex than anything else. "At fifty-seven pounds a minute, two hundred and eighty-five pounds. Why?"

Charlie had been eyeing the controls, marking out buttons and levers and switches that looked . . . interesting. He bent forward, his index finger brushing a touch-screen panel. He cursored down, then tapped Enter. Bitching Betty began squawking, "Fuel loss. Fuel loss."

Of all the sins on my soul, dumping jet fuel over the Pacific Ocean may be the one I most regret.

Smiling, showing his teeth, he put his face close to the copilot's. Very softly, very sincerely, he whispered, "When the gauge shows four hundred pounds, I'm unlocking your handcuffs and giving you control of this plane. You won't have enough juice to get to an airport. You'll barely have enough to land. By which time, by God, you had better have come up with a solution to my problem. Because if you don't then you—and I—and all of us—are going to die together."

Utter disbelief: "You're crazy!"

"In my profession we call this 'forcing a resolution.' Major, either we are going to flame out at two hundred knots, or you are going to figure out how to help me. There is no middle ground." Bitching Betty bleated again, "Fuel loss! Fuel loss!" Charlie showed his teeth. "And how the hell do you turn off that damned annunciator. If it doesn't shut up, I'm going to shoot it."

"Sir, uncuff me now."

The major's face—a little pale, a little sweaty—told Charlie all he needed to know: he'd won. "Nope. We've still got twelve hundred pounds to go."

"I'll do what you say. Just . . . damnit, sir, you have my word."

"I trust no one who has a choice."

"The switch there, the yellow one, upper right. It's marked EVS."

"And what might that stand for?"

"Enhanced Vision System. Real-time infrared, I can see . . . we can see what's down there."

Well now, that calls for a stern rebuke. Charlie nudged him behind the ear with the pistol. "Sonny boy, you've been holding out on me. That makes me grumpy. Believe me, you don't want me grumpy. So if you've got any other little secrets up your sleeve, now would be a real good time to speak up."

"Fuel loss! Fuel loss!"

The copilot swallowed hard. "Your son's been drifting."

Charlie didn't like the sound of that. "Explicate."

"Just take the cuffs off me. I'll tell you everything."

With throaty menace: "You're going to tell me everything anyway, aren't you?" *Oh, yes,* he thought, *that was nicely done. It takes a lot to put one of these Air Force boys into a panic. This one's getting close.*

Scott hit the EVS switch. The plane's Heads Up Display projected a quivering electronic horizon across the windshield, the empty Pacific seen—or more likely inferred—by infrared detectors. Charlie was taken aback; he'd expected the computer image to be pale green, a color too often seen through a night scope; instead it was red-orange, the hue of hot work, and he didn't like the implication.

The copilot spoke rapidly. "I've been watching the Flight Management System display, sir. Your son . . . Scott's a good enough pilot, but he's flying this plane like it's a single-engine prop job—navigating off compass headings, not the FMS. We've got strong westerlies off the ocean—enough to nudge us a little off course. Unless you understand the HUD readouts you don't even notice."

Scott had completed his turn inland. Charlie glanced up at the infrared display. Still a flatline horizon. No sign of the jagged coast. The Gulfstream's technology was impressive, but it wasn't magic; nothing could see through a fog as thick as this. "What's our position? Our *real* position."

"Twenty nautical miles off shore and zero-point-eight miles north of your target area. Sir, please quit dumping fuel."

Tempting. At least it would shut up that blasted computer. "Scott, you're part of this." *Damnit all!* "What do you think?"

"Keep dumping, dad. There must be a dozen ways the major can get the upper hand. He could put the plane into a spin or—"

The copilot shouted, "A spin! A passenger jet! Holy Christ! Do you think I'm as crazy as you are?"

"Adjust your course, son. Aim her a little south, just like the man said. Major, you're not taking the helm until the both of us have no alternatives left."

Bitching Betty's complaint had changed. Now the computer warned, "Low fuel. Danger. Low fuel."

Wiggling backward, trading hand signals with Bushmaster and Krait, Schmidt tallied up all the facts he knew about Irina Kolodenkova, and all that he had deduced. On balance, he concluded, it was enough to tip the scales.

She's too poised, too self-contained. I believe a little attitude adjustment is called for. "Irina, what did you think about that rodeo rider, Mitch Conroy?"

No static, no interference, the radios worked fine in the fog. "Why do you ask?"

Schmidt's lightweight tropical slacks and shirt were soaked wet and cold—colder still with a stiff breeze off the ocean. He pressed a numb finger down on his transmit button. "Because I killed him. With a knife. It was delightful."

Her inflection was unchanged—distant and polite. "Charlie will hurt you for that."

Well, that didn't work. "Charles is not going to be hurting anyone. I beat him until he looked like grape jelly."

"That only would have made him angry." Mockery in her words.

He was moving slowly—low profile, silent, damp clothing turned grey, camouflage on the parking lot's asphalt. She'd never see him. Nor would she see Bushmaster and Krait, both of whom were, like him, belly-crawling toward the marina fence. That was the safest place. With their backs to the water, they'd be able to cover the entire field of operations: Bushmaster to his right with a rifle pointing at two o'clock, Krait on the left aiming at ten o' clock; and he himself in the center, high noon. "On the contrary. When I beat a man, I make sure he knows he's beaten. The objective is not physical pain, it's psychological pain. Humiliate your opponent, and you unman him."

"Charlie is more of a man than you shall ever be."

She was out there somewhere, somewhere in the fog, stealthily making her way toward him. Fine, let her be the hunter. The ignorant woman didn't have enough sense to know that she was merely saving him the trouble of stalking her. Nonetheless, he gnawed his lip.

"That was a rather obvious ruse, young lady." He knew himself to be a humorless man; still he tried to imitate an amused tone of voice. "The sort of offensive ploy Charles would assay—a tiny prick from a small needle to goad your opponent. You've learned something from him, haven't you?"

"Everything, Mr. Schmidt. I have learned everything from Charlie."

Schmidt snorted derisively—although, truth to tell, unnerving her was proving more difficult than he'd anticipated. She was, he supposed, a bit stronger than he had expected. "I'd like to ask you something about your ingenious lie. With your permission, of course."

"What lie would that be?"

"That you laid a trail, that you lured me into coming to San Carlos. That is the lie to which I refer."

"Are you so vain that you cannot admit that I—as Charlie would say—have outfoxed you?"

Another annoying gibe. He tightened his jaw. *You'll pay for that piece of arrogance.* "Nonsense. You came here to steal a boat, a sailboat to be precise."

Her laughter was cold, inhuman—perhaps even frightening, he supposed. For a moment it actually discomfited him. But, of course, she was only acting.

"To steal a boat? What ever for, you foolish man?"

Nettled by this inexperienced neophyte *with no field expertise whatsoever, a raw recruit wet behind the ears,* this mere girl talking down at him, he shot back. "To escape, of course. To escape to Mexico. Then make your way home to Russia."

She laughed again. "You are so silly. I do not wish to return to Russia. I wish only to kill you. Then I am done with killing. Forever."

You do not laugh at me, girl. You do not call me silly. All you do is beg for mercy.

He was on a graveled path now, the fence a few yards in front of him. San Carlos was so law-abiding a village that the authorities did not bother to string razor wire along the fence's top, nor even barbed wire. Pathetic, really, it was no deterrent at all.

"Well, that's good. I mean it's good that you have no plans for going home. If you try, they'll turn you away. You see, they've stripped you of your citizenship."

"This makes me happy. This lifts a burden from me."

"The American government had words with Moscow—words at the highest levels. You can't go home because you don't have a home. You are an exile, expelled in disgrace."

"I thank you for informing me of this."

Infuriating. Everything that should disconcert her has the opposite effect. Schmidt wiped fog dew from his glasses while he evaluated his options. What to say next? How to shake her too perfect equilibrium? He gave thought to the matter, a chess player considering both the move he must make next and the moves that would follow. *Strike as hard as I can—strike straight at this annoying young woman's heart—that's the best strategy now.*

"What about the disgrace, Irina? You've shamed your father's good name. How will he take the news?"

"My father is a *kibini-matt.*"

Schmidt surprised himself by wincing at this, the most scathing of Russian obscenities.

The Kolodenkova girl continued: "I do not care what my father thinks. When we are little children, then we try to please our parents. Now I am a grown-up. In these past four days, Mr. Schmidt, I have become an adult. The only person whom I must please is myself."

Schmidt shook his head like an angry bull. Kolodenkova should have been furious—rushing to silence him, and therefore rushing into his gun sights. Instead she was behaving like a professional, *as much of a professional as me. All right, girl, let's see the stuff you're really made of.*

"You came here for a boat. Don't deny it. Your father never trusted you—"

"Oh, Mr. Schmidt, you also are a *kibini-matt*."

He'd kill her for that. Well, he'd kill her anyway. All that would be different would be the art of it.

A rattle of gunfire. Seven pop-pop-pops in a row. They came from the left, distant, the reports muffled beneath a blanket of fog. Krait glanced toward Schmidt, shaking his head. Bushmaster too signaled negative, no target in sight. What had she been shooting at? Certainly not Pit Viper; he'd not had time to run this far.

She used a rifle, small caliber, stolen from the late Python. There's no doubt of that. And she emptied a full magazine. But she wasn't firing at us. If she was, I would have heard the ricochet. What is *her game?*

He flipped to his side, peering at the tiny marina—thirty boat slips, three rows of ten, each slip twelve feet wide and separated by a narrow boardwalk. Most of them were occupied by small sailboats, none larger than thirty feet. Their masts were a dead forest in the fog. Some of their cockpits were covered with blue tarpaulins. A few slips were occupied by rusty trawlers, commercial fishers bobbing on an incoming tide. The sea cat-lapped at the shore, soapsud waves on dirty sand. In the far distance a foghorn sounded, its light unseen in thick cloud billowing inland on a freezing wind. Did something move out there, out at the farthest, almost invisible end of the dock? Was that a man standing . . .

Kolodenkova!

He threw his rifle to his shoulder, sighting through its Mil-spec scope. He'd already begun to caress the trigger when he recognized his target for what it was: no man, no woman, merely a gas pump located, as all marine gas pumps were, at the distant end of the upwind dock. The fog swirled; for a moment he saw it sharply before another eddy of dirty grey hid it from sight.

Something about that pump . . . Something wrong . . . Instinct again, not knowledge, and all the more unsettling for that.

Peering blindly through his scope, he thought of evil. There was malice in this fog, a hostility that transcended natural phenomenon. The weather had become his enemy. He hated it and wished to kill it.

Superstition. Old Kafir women telling ghost stories around an open fire, and jackals whining in the dark. Am I afraid? If so, it is only a tale I tell myself. My enemies are foul weather and a frail woman. Not even a child would be afraid of that!

As angry at his momentary weakness as he was at her, he taunted, "You missed, Irina. Do you wish to try again? If you do, you're going to need to get closer."

"I am closer than you think."

Was that possible? Had the girl somehow managed to outflank them? Was she out in the marina, hidden on some pleasure craft, slowly making her way from boat to boat, creeping up on him from behind? Schmidt wiped a hand across his brow.

Sweat? Has this doomed child so frightened me that I am sweating?

The coast was a fractal orange outline on the Heads Up Display. An ambiguous geometry that might have been a parking lot, a baseball field, a cow pasture, lay directly behind shapes that were more regular, three long rectangles, each with rows of right-angled catwalks. It was the marina, and they were closing on it fast.

Charlie would see what was going on at ground level, although what he'd see would be encrypted abstraction, the Gulfstream's infrared vision system detecting what the human eye could not.

"Can't you get lower?" he growled.

The copilot, now flying the Gulfstream, replied tightly, "The technical term for lower is 'under water.' "

The major had a sense of humor. Charlie found that encouraging.

"Dad, I think those are cars." Scott was still in the pilot's seat, still resting his hands on the yoke. He could seize control of the plane in a second.

Yeah, he thought, *cars. How many? Seven. Are any of them Toyota Camrys? Who the hell can tell?*

"I'm going to bank now. I don't want to come in over the marina. I could clip a mast, and the engine blowback might—"

"Screw the boats!" *I need the best view I can get. This is my only shot.*

"Trust me, sir. You don't want me sucking a mainsail off one of those sloops."

Charlie gave it a moment's thought. "Okay, Major. We'll do it your way. You know the consequences if it doesn't work."

The copilot nodded.

The contours of two dozen boats sharpened, leaf-shaped hulls glowing orange, masts that wavered not of their own accord, but electrically as infrared detectors strained to pick out their silhouettes through blinding fog.

"Can you turn up that infrared so that it will detect body heat?"

"We've got first-generation EVS on this craft. It's cranked as high as it will go."

A seemingly infinite parallelogram disappeared to the east. *That would be Main Street. The town's on either side of it.* Cubes and polygons, flickering pyramids on their tops, houses and roofs seen by pure energy, were interpolated by a computer that Charlie wished was much more powerful than it seemed to be.

The plane could not be more than four hundred feet above ground. Yet nothing, not a goddamned thing, could be seen by the human eye. Only the technology saw, and it did not see with sufficient clarity to pinpoint a lone woman in danger of her life.

Charlie was not certain whether he should pray or curse.

I'm powerless. Neither deed nor word will have the least influence. I'm impotent, and for the second *damned time in my entire life there's not a thing I can do.*

"Look sharp, sir, we're coming in."

A thunder where silence should have been, an elephant trumpeting in the mist, Johan Schmidt flinched at the unexpected howl of hot metal hurling through the mist.

A jet. Insanely low. We must be near an airbase. No one but a military pilot would dare fly in this weather.

"Charlie is here, Mr. Schmidt. He is coming for you." Her voice was girlish, high-pitched and mocking—one more debit on a ledger that must be cleared.

"Drivel." He shook his frigid fingers, rubbed his hands together, rolled his muscles to stretch out the stiffness. The Alaska current ran just offshore; fog had lowered the temperature to fifty degrees; the wind-chill factor brought it lower than that. And he, in summer poplin, felt his teeth chatter at the cold.

"What will Charlie do when he finds you? Nothing nice, I think." Spiteful irony in facetious tones that had become quite unbearable.

She's feinting, a fencer's gambit to trick me into lowering my defenses. Me? Are you so full of yourself as to try to trick me? Enough games, girl, I have had enough! Johan Schmidt launched his attack. "Tell me more about your father, Irina."

Her accent became flat and guarded. "He is unworthy of discussion." *No spite in your voice now, is there, girly?*

"Ah, but he is. He's why you're here."

"I am here to kill you."

Keep it up, just keep it up. All you do is make it worse for yourself. "I mean 'here' in the broader sense of the word. I mean he is why you joined the FSB."

"I am not so infantile."

You're trying to hide from the issue. I intend to rub your face in it. "Your father encouraged you."

"I believe I know what you will say next, Mr. Schmidt."

Oh no you don't. "And what would that be?"

"That my father expected me to become a swallow, a spy who uses sex to steal secrets. Am I correct, Mr. Schmidt? This is where you hoped to lead this conversation?"

God damn this woman!

"You will further say that he wrote a letter to my commander endorsing such an assignment. Perhaps you have access to intelligence sources. Perhaps you have read this letter. Perhaps you believe that a father who proposes prostitution for his daughter's career scars her for life. Perhaps you even believe that reminding me of my humiliation will cause me to break down in tears like a helpless child. If such is your expectation, you will be disappointed. I am neither a child, nor am I helpless. Do you understand why that is so? If you were half the man Charlie is, you would."

Schmidt roared, "I'm twice the man he is!"

"You said I shall disgrace my father, Mr. Schmidt. Think of that. Think, and then ask yourself if this is not the justice that is owed him."

"Sir?" A harsh whisper, Krait off to his right. Why wasn't the soldier using hand signals? Schmidt put a finger to his lips. Krait shook his head. Leaving his station, he slithered toward Schmidt. "Sir, do you smell something?"

Schmidt felt like slapping him. Kolodenkova could be outflanking them through the sector that Krait was assigned to guard. "Get back on your post, soldier!"

"It's gasoline, sir. I smell gasoline."

Well of course he smelled gasoline. Every boat in this marina carried an engine of some sort or another. Fuel spills were common. After all, you couldn't put a sailboat in the water without a motor, usually one from Atomic Engines Inc. if memory served, because . . .

The gasoline pump. The one at the end of the upwind dock . . .

"If you were as wise as Charlie, you would know that any woman having been shamed in such a manner can never be shamed again. Do you know how strong my father's betrayal made me, Mr. Schmidt? Charlie does. You shall learn. Quite soon, I think."

He was searching through the rifle sight, trying to find a gas pump lost in rolling fog, and, yes, he could smell the fumes, and yes the stench was stronger than it should be.

. . . the upwind dock. Strong gusts blowing inland. A rising tide.

"Mr. Schmidt, it shall be the last lesson you learn."

Could she have done it? Had McKenzie put his own iron into her heart?

"Sir! Look!"

Fireworks, a rocket in a silver arc, white actinic fire in high parabola, its origin somewhere to the left, its terminus twenty yards behind Johan Schmidt.

Twenty yards into the marina, twenty yards over the water.

Hissing high above him, bright as a strobe but unflickering, it trailed shining smoke behind.

"Flare gun! What's she trying to do, signal that airplane that just flew over?"

Without warning, the wind stiffened, swirling the fog aside. Through his scope, Schmidt saw seven bullet holes in the gas pump's base, seven urine-colored streams of fuel spitting down into the sea. Those shots, those shots minutes earlier—she hadn't been shooting at him. She hadn't been shooting at any of them. The pump was her target. Out of sight, invisible in impenetrable fog, she'd brazenly walked to the edge of the fence line, calmly stood waiting for a few seconds of clear seeing, and coolly emptied Python's rifle into a bright red Texaco pump, not missing a single shot.

The wind, the tide, were washing fuel in. Had washed it in. Small waves were spilling it on the sand. The entire marina was awash with it, every boat hull and every piling— each soaked with creosote, a torch in its own right—coated with gasoline.

The conflagration would be beyond comprehension.

Who would have thought she had it in her?

So fearless, she had crept to another place of concealment, waiting to taste the scent of hell upon an evening breeze—waiting with a flare gun stolen from the guard kiosk. A serpent of patience, she radioed Schmidt, distracting him while his back was ten paces from a bomb primed for detonation.

Ice water in her veins. I would never have believed it.

Then, careful in plan and conscientious in execution, she had aimed her flare out over the harbor, stroking a trigger, and Schmidt had not sensed the least change in her serene and self-possessed tone of voice.

A woman one might almost admire.

Goddess of death, she waited tranquilly for flaming magnesium to caress the sea—and for the eruption of an inferno that would burn Schmidt off the face of this world and into another.

"Run!" He shouted to Bushmaster and Krait, "Run, you fools!"

He himself made it ten yards before he heard the first shot. The bullet sent Krait rolling in puddles, his blood spraying as he tumbled. He flapped his arms like a wounded seagull, but made no sound, said no word.

Bushmaster was noisier. He died, as such men do, not whispering needed prayers, but screaming the conventional obscenities. Fuck, motherfuck, cunt, cocksucker . . . all of that. Schmidt was used to it, had seen and heard it many times, and hoped that when the time came he had sufficient self-discipline to recite the Lord's Prayer.

He was more than thirty yards from the fence when the blast came, and with it an unimaginable tempest of fire and flame and the roaring of demons boiling up from hell.

A hot typhoon threw him off balance, whirling him like a drunken dervish as two bullets cut the air on either side, and his feet slipped out from under him as a third bullet percussed toward where his chest should be.

Then he saw her.

She was fumbling in her pockets for ammunition, an empty Tokarev in her hand.

Vulnerable at last.

The major was going to make a second pass over the marina, and that was that, and if Irina was down below she'd understand, get in her car and drive straight out of town, and straight into Charlie's waiting arms.

He'd be waiting for her because the jet jockey was as

crazy as he was. Crazier maybe. He was going to put the plane down on San Carlos's preposterously narrow access road.

He said he could do it. The moment they'd broken out of the fog bank, soaring over open farmlands, he'd said the road was wide enough. Maybe. There wouldn't be any traffic. Maybe. And besides, landing a Gulfstream only took about three thousand feet of runway, roadway, black asphalt, call it what you will.

Maybe.

Risky? Yeah. So what? The only thing that mattered was going in so low that Irina knew no one in the world could be in that plane except Charles McKenzie, Esquire. Who the hell else did you expect to be blind-as-a-bat barnstorming in a hijacked jet?

She'd know it was him. She was too damned smart not to.

Charlie stared out the cockpit window. The setting sun painted the sky with light from angels' eyes. And beneath it . . . *oh, hell* . . . the fog bank. Only cloud, it looked like a granite mountain, ground level to twenty-five hundred feet. It was hard, damned hard, to keep control of your guts while you were flying straight at it, a hundred and twenty knots, trying to convince yourself that it was only mist, not the solid rock it looked to be.

And Charlie flying blind was once again in its nowhere heart.

Pale light, dusk light, grey emptiness beyond time and space. There was only a hint as to where the setting sun was, dawn in Japan, nightfall in California, just a milky glow that flickered like—

"Sonofabitch!" Charlie shouted, "that's not the sun! It's a beacon! Irina has lit a fire beacon!"

The copilot leaned forward. "Impossible. You couldn't see a

bonfire through this soup. At sunset the light does strange . . . "
then very softly, " . . . oh, God."

"What?" Charlie asked urgently. He bent over the man's
shoulder. Blinding pain exploded in his battered ribs, his vision blanked, and for a moment he found himself less
breathing than gasping. He shook his head clear, straining to
get a closer look at what he knew, no doubt in his mind, was
Irina's signal.

"Jesus wept! That's no signal. It's . . . it's an inferno . . . it
must be burning five stories high!"

Fear pierced him with such shocking swiftness that he
might scream. "The town? Is the town on fire?"

"No. We're almost over the town. Christ, it's the marina!
Look at the EVS! The whole thing's blazing!"

No time for thinking, no time to puzzle out what was happening, Charlie had no time left at all. "Land this thing."

"What!?"

Pistol against the major's neck, he didn't want to do it this
way, but if he had to, he would, "I. Said. Land. The. Fucking.
Plane."

"No way!"

"Scott, take control."

The major jerked. "No! Jesus! Your son can't handle this,
it's way beyond—"

Very calmly, very softly: "Then you do it."

The answer: whispered capitulation. "Shit."

Two hundred feet above ground level, Charlie stared at
the infrared EVS display. San Carlos was a chunky grid, the
main street arrow-straight through its center, and dead on toward the marina. How far was it from the last building in
town to the marina turnoff? *Well now, I'd say that might be a
half mile. Sure as hell isn't three thousand feet.*

Landing gear lowered. Flaps full up. The throttle feathered back. The copilot held the yoke with white knuckles, a death grip if Charlie had ever seen one. "This is hairy. Oh, yes, yes, yes. Instruments only. Zero/zero. Residential area, civilian road. *Wet* civilian road. Smart pilots do not do this sort of thing. Son of a bitch, that's a car! Jesus God, oh, Jesus God! Are we still alive? Okay, this is it. I'm doing this. I can do this. Brace yourself. We may go in the drink. Christ, they'll promote me if I pull this off. I love you, mom. Hail Mary, full of grace, the Lord is with thee . . . "

Charlie felt the road before he saw it. Wheels hissed, water streaming beneath tires. The plane was on the ground, rolling fast, but by God, it was down safe, and that was half the battle.

Twenty-five tons of aerodynamic iron rocketed down a country lane. Charlie watched the flickering passing of fence posts, grassy bunkers, drainage ditches choked with pussy willows, century-old eucalyptus tall and gnarled and dripping moisture, and the Gulfstream's wingtips whisked against their leaves. A car, headlights on high beam, braked hard in a driveway, and he caught a glimpse of shock and almighty disbelief.

One tree limb hanging over the road, one motorist in either lane, one stray cow, one anything, and this, dear God, is a winged hearse.

" . . . blessed art thou among women . . . " Braking so hard that the plane's nose tilted sickeningly, the major was a copilot on autopilot. Years of training and experience commanded his every move. He didn't think about what he was doing but simply did what his exquisitely honed reflexes knew was right. Two engines changed pitch as the Gulfstream's squat switch automatically deployed the spoilers. Simultaneously, deflectors like enormous clamshells closed behind the engine vents, channelling two turbines' thrust ahead rather than behind the plane. Now throttle up—seven thousand tons of blistering thrust blown forward to slow the

Gulfstream. Brakes applied, hands hard on the control yoke, eyes scanning the infrared display for the merest hint of an obstacle. Ground speed declining. " . . . and blessed is the fruit of thy womb, Jesus . . . " Ninety miles an hour, eighty-five, eighty, and something different displayed on the EVS, a change in the outlines, infrared blurred beyond interpretation by a towering fire, and, in the wink of an eye, electronic blindness, the sensors unable to adapt to a light too bright for any computer to make sense of.

" . . . Holy Mary, mother of God, pray for *oh HELL!*"

Silhouetted against a wall of flame, unmistakable in outline, the fully recognizable shadow of a human being. A man was running on the roadway. He whirled and saw exploding from the fog behind him a jet plane moving at—Charlie glanced at the Heads Up Display—seventy-four miles an hour, and the poor bastard was a deer in the headlights, no time to move out of the way, roadkill on the highway, and another death on Charlie's conscience.

No, not on my conscience. Die, you son of a whore!

He was one of Schmidt's punks, and he was lifting his weapon. Before its butt touched his shoulder, he took wing and flew.

Engines reversed. How many tons of thrust did the major say this thing puts out?

He wasn't dead. That was the horrifying thing. He was alive and, for the moment, in good health. With his mouth open in a silent scream, he spun up high, higher than Charlie would have believed. Once, decades earlier, Charlie had seen a pedestrian struck by a speeding car. It had been in Bangkok, and Charlie just happened to be at the intersection when it happened. Some poor Thailander got hit head-on, and up he went, just like this, but Charlie knew he was dead by then. He'd been hit hard enough to kill, and probably died without knowing he was dead.

Not this time.

Schmidt's flunky, whoever he was, knew exactly what was going on, and knew it long enough to know how his life would end: thrown through the air like a ragdoll, slammed down on asphalt with his back snapped and his neck broken, and his limbs like shattered twigs. He slid. His body slid. What transpired with his soul could only be guessed. As the plane raced forward, a corpse skidded limply in front of it, and the one was faster than the other, and there was nothing the pilot could do about it.

The bump was barely noticeable.

Thirty miles an hour, and Charlie could see everything that was to be seen. The heat of a monstrous conflagration boiled away the fog. What had been a marina was hell now come to a quiet seaside village.

The major braked furiously, prayers forgotten, curses under his breath, and it wasn't quite enough because the plane's momentum was going to take it straight past the end of the road, over a low drop, and into a wall of flame.

He twisted hard on the steering harness. Kicking up muddy divots, the Gulfstream's left wing plowed wet earth as it skidded into a sharp left turn, and skidded more because its wheels were just oversized rollers, no powertrain driving them, and an aircraft does not, repeat, does not handle like an automobile.

Newton's laws of physics hurled the plane toward the ocean. A pair of BMW Rolls-Royce engines propelled it toward the parking lot. The Gulfstream slid sideways to a full stop, and an Air Force pilot, reflexively, not thoughtfully, retracted his deflectors and powered down his engines to standby while murmuring, "Thank you, God, thank you, thank you."

Charlie laid a hand on the major's shoulder. "You're the best, flyboy. I owe you one. If you ever need a hand, just give me a thumbs-up. That's all it'll take. Thumbs-up and I'm there for you. Understand?"

The major twitched a nod, and kept on praying. Charlie understood. He felt like praying himself.

Instead, he turned and left the cockpit. Seconds later he had a Browning nine millimeter in his right hand, and Sam's throat in his left. "If I don't get what I want, I'll kill you. Hold on to that thought."

Sam tried to spit. Charlie slapped him.

When he pulled the knives out, Sam shrieked. Charlie didn't especially care. Wrenching a bloody hand up behind Sam's back, Charlie hustled him to the plane's door. "Tell me about the cover-up, Sam, tell me about Whirlwind."

"Fuck you," a predictable answer. Charlie thumbed back his Browning's hammer. Sam snarled at the click.

"You paid off the Chinese, slimeboy. You bought Sangin Wing back from them. Come on, let's hear it. What was the price?"

"Nothing! Not one fucking cent!"

He threw Sam face forward against the bulkhead. Jerking the hatch open with one hand, using the other to screw his pistol barrel into Sam's neck, "Pay attention, bonehead, if I don't get the truth, I'm painting this plane with your blood."

"You dumb dipshit," Sam roared in brute rage. "It *is* the truth. Don't you get it, asshole?" No question, Charlie had finally gotten what he wanted—a man so maniacally enraged that he couldn't control himself, couldn't keep from speaking honestly. "I didn't pay them, they paid me."

Charlie blinked at the words. It was true, had to be true, and it explained everything he hadn't understood. "You'd better clarify that, Sam."

It all came out in a single rush. "Campaign money! Squeaky clean cash! To get me elected!"

It made sense, God, did it make sense. He'd been wrong all along, misreading the evidence, off on a wild-goose chase, and he cursed himself for not even thinking about how obviously the puzzle pieces fitted together.

"After a lifetime in this business, I thought I knew everything there is to know about how low a man can sink. But you, Sam . . . you've taught me something new. I do not thank you for it."

"Live and learn, asshole."

The hatch gaped wide, searing heat gusting into the cabin. The marina had become a furnace, burning off the fog, illuminating the parking lot with lurid hell-light. Charlie thought it a landscape by Hieronymus Bosch, night and crimson cloud over the Pacific, red fire on the water, two dozen boats boiling in an inferno so hot that their fiberglass hulls melted like wax, and their proud masts sagged limply in the heat, sails unfurling in flame, sheeted fire fluttering, the shores of Hades and these all were Charon's ferryboats. Odysseus had come at last to the Isle of the Dead.

"Tell me," Charlie whispered because he was incapable of shouting. "Tell me what they get for their money?"

Sam sneered. "Their own man in the White House! Jesus, do I have to draw you a picture?"

No, Sam did not have to draw a picture. "A free hand in Asia?"

"Christ, yes!"

"They'll invade Taiwan. Overrun Vietnam. Occupy Singapore."

"So what? The voters won't give a shit."

Charlie would have given a lot to wipe the smug sneer off Sam's face. "Domestic cooperation, too, I suppose?"

"Whatever they want. Technology transfer, trade preference, denial of asylum to dissidents. Plus they want me to shut up the human rights loons and Free Tibet nuts. Bunch of dumb-ass actors, so who cares?"

I do. Me and everyone who hears what you're saying straight into my digital recorder. "And what does your boss have to say about it, Sam? Or does he even know?"

"If he does know, he doesn't give a flying fuck. It won't happen on his watch."

Not on yours, either. Charlie threw him out the hatch. It wasn't far, eight feet maybe. When he hit the pavement Sam exploded in monstrous obscenity.

Doubling over, Charlie gripped the hatchway with both hands, swung down, and dropped. He landed hard enough to wake up all the tortured places Schmidt had left him with the day before. The stitches in his leg popped with an audible snap, blood warm as urine ran down his thigh, he felt like barbed wire was being pulled through his veins. Dizzy with pain and fighting to remain conscious, he hissed, "Up!" as he jerked Sam under the arm. Charlie wasn't angry anymore. He was beyond anger now, moved on to a harsher place. "You worthless piece of shit, you've been on their payroll since the president put you in charge of Chinese diplomatic relations."

"Longer than that, shithead. The Chinese and I, we're old friends."

Pushing his resistant prisoner toward the rear of the plane, Charlie hissed, "Explain to me why I shouldn't kill you on the spot."

"Don't you get it, McKenzie? I'm going to be president, and when I am—"

"I don't want a pardon, Sam. I don't need a pardon. Forget about it."

"Already have. My point, my point, you sanctimonious

dickhead, is that I've done what no diplomat dreamt possible. I've put China on our side. When I'm president, they'll be our closest ally. When they fucked up and arrested Wing's son—"

Charlie was stunned at how wrong he'd gotten it, how wrong he'd been every step of the way. Less speaking to Sam than to himself, he whispered, "You're saying arresting the Wing kid really *was* a bureaucratic mistake?"

"Of course it was! Christ, you still don't see it, do you? You're old, Charlie, way too old. Back in your salad days you worked it out in a New York minute."

"Worked what out?"

"Wing and I, we're on the same team. The winning team."

Hell, Charlie thought, *you're right: I should have known that the moment that DefCon guy, Henkes, told me you recommended Wing for the job. So, yeah, Sam, yeah, I'm over the hill, should be put out to pasture, another burnt-out case. But not until I finish this, Sam, not until I settle things with you and your pet pit bull.*

"You amoral sonofabitch, you're the Chinese's hired whore, bought and sold, and what's good for this nation and all it stands for just doesn't mean a thing to you."

Sam exploded. "Want to know what means something to me? Sitting in the big chair, the buck stops here, numero uno, President of the United States, most powerful man in the world! That's the only thing that matters! It's all that counts. The rest is bullshit. The game, Charlie, the fucking game is about winning, and that is all the game is about."

Rounding the Gulfstream's tail section, Charlie answered, "Game over, Sam. Game over."

"Indeed it is," said Johan Schmidt.

Red by firelight, he stood atop a rusted TransAm using Irina for his shield.

She was unconscious, slumped in his grasp, he with his

hand twisted in her long hair, holding her bleeding head against his shoulder. Bright blood, fresh blood flowed freely; Charlie prayed it was only a scalp wound.

Fifty feet away and five feet above the ground, Schmidt twisted the muzzle of a long-barreled pistol into Irina's rib cage. Charlie recognized it for a target gun, high tech, infallibly accurate. He ducked behind Sam, a shield of his own.

Opening his mouth, Schmidt made a show of obscenely lolling his tongue before licking the blood from Irina's forehead. He smacked his lips, and leered, "Yum, yum."

Johan, now would be a very good time for you to be dead.

"Charles, my load is .22 caliber wadcutters. Pathetically weak, I know. But point blank they'll eviscerate her. If you so much as aim at me, I will put a minimum of three slugs into her."

Mute in a circle of flickering light, the two of them held their hostages. Charlie was beneath the Gulfstream's tail, Schmidt a few yards in front of the right engine pod. Both were in the open, both vulnerable, no place to hide, each a fine target for the other's marksmanship.

Mexican standoff. If I try to nail him, I'll hit Irina. If he shoots at me, he has to kill Sam first.

The marina burned, fire roaring, boats groaning in the flames. The Gulfstream's engines, still on standby, hummed low, the wind from their turbines passing over Charlie's head. Fog surrounded the parking lot but did not encroach. Scorching heat drove it back, and this open square of asphalt had become a gladiators' arena illuminated by a mighty burning.

I win, Charlie told himself. *All I have to do is persuade Schmidt of that little fact.*

"Johan, put down your gun. You know I'm holding the high cards here."

"Not so, Charles. I have a queen. You have a jack. Or rather a jackass."

Spittle flew from Sam's lips, "For fuck's sake, Johan, do something!"

Charlie kicked Sam's leg. Sam tried to pull away. Charlie wrenched him back, a wave of agony rippling through his muscles at the effort.

"Wrong, Johan. Sam's the most important guy in your world—the customer who pays your bills. You aren't going to let anything happen to him."

"How astute of you, Charles. You are quite correct, professional ethics demand that no client comes to harm."

"Then let Irina go. Give it up, and let her go."

"Sadly for you, my client—that is to say the man who signed the contract for my services and is therefore obliged to pay my duly submitted invoice—is Mr. Maximilian Henkes, Chief Executive Officer of DefCon Enterprises." Schmidt's hand moved too fast for the eye to see. It was a damned good shot, straight through Sam's left eye and into the brain. Charlie knew Sam was dead, knew Schmidt didn't have to take a second shot, and Sam's deadweight was dragging him down.

Schmidt burrowed his gun back into Irina's chest. Charlie followed Sam to the ground, painfully taking cover behind such little protection as the man's corpse offered.

"Practice makes perfect," Schmidt coldly lectured. "Even the lowly wadcutter is lethal in the hands of a trained professional. Do try to bear that in mind."

Prone behind Sam's limp corpse, Charlie spoke a single word: "Why?"

"Why what? Oh, you mean Samuel? I should have thought that was self-evident. You see, Charles, you see, the thing is this: as long as that irritating little fat boy was alive, you were safe. He would never permit me to do what I want to do so very, very badly. Those incriminating videos you have hidden on the Internet saw to that. But behold! Such a simple and, I frankly admit, pleasing solution: no Samuel, no problem."

I can do it. If you could put a slug in Sam's head, I can put a slug in yours.

"Charles, Charles, do not point that thing at me. My finger is tight upon the trigger. In the unlikely event that you hit me, in death my reflexes will tighten it. Moreover, I am an exceptionally disciplined man. Even if I were dying, I believe I would manage to pump more than a single killing round into this delectable creature."

One shot. It has to take him straight through the skull. If only I can stop my hands from shaking. If only I can get my eyes to focus. If only I can forget how goddamn much I hurt.

"You know you might be able to hit me. Indeed, it is not beyond the realm of possibility that you could kill me. But I assure you, Charles, if you do, you kill two people, not one."

Damnit, if only you were a little taller. Little bastard, half your ugly head is hidden behind Irina's.

"If you want her to live, if the idea of her placing a bouquet on your grave consoles you, then you'd best put down your pistol." He tilted his head, then said brightly, "Listen! Oh, do you hear? Is that not the sound of fire engines? The brave firefighters of this pathetic town are on their way, sirens blaring. Well, now, that puts the punctuation mark on our negotiation. As soon as the fire truck arrives, I will kill this woman. You have my solemn vow. I have no alternative. And then you and I may take our chances, *mano a mano,* as it were, gunfight at the OK Corral. Perhaps I will be the victor. Perhaps you will—presuming your definition of victory is being alive when Kolodenkova is dead."

If I had a rifle, I could do it. No problem. A handgun . . .

hell, the best shot group I ever managed with a factory gun had a two-inch spread.

"Time is running out, Charles. Lay down your weapon and I will release this young woman. Continue to brandish your pistol—an old Browning Hi-Power, is it not?—and her fate is sealed."

He's going to do it. He's going to pull that trigger. And me . . . oh, hell, I can't even see straight.

"Last chance, Charles, last dance. Throw away that quaint antiquity. Then rise to your feet like a good boy, and I will see to the formalities."

Charlie hurled the gun over his shoulder.

"Tell me, Charles, what words do you wish inscribed on your tombstone. I will arrange for the engraving. My treat."

Charlie growled, "He was better than his enemies."

"A good epitaph, albeit untrue. But then so many of them are." Irina jerked like a puppet as he fired two rounds into her chest. "Mission accomplished. My goodness, that felt good." As a child discarding an unwanted toy, he flung her away. She tumbled limply to the ground, her shirt ripe red as she rolled lifeless beneath the Gulfstream's wing.

Dear God, send me to hell. I want to be waiting when he arrives.

"You cannot know how much pleasure the expression on your face gives me. Now be so kind as to stand up. If you've got the starch for it."

There's nothing to do now but die proud. Choking back nausea, Charlie pressed his hands against wet asphalt.

Out of the corner of his eye he caught sight of a pale face in the Gulfstream's cockpit window. The major. The copilot. He was goggle-eyed and mouthing words that Charlie could not hear.

What the hell, he thought, *it's worth a try. Anything is worth a try.* He lifted his hands, fists balled, thumbs pointed to the sky. *Thumbs-up, flyboy. Come on, think about it. I'm giving you the thumbs-up.*

The copilot's expression was blank. He didn't understand Charlie's message. That's life.

Death, actually.

Charlie began to rise. His body didn't seem to be working right, all his muscles watery and aching. He cocked a knee, groaning at the pain. The breeze sounded stiffer, a whistling of winds stronger than ordinary coastal gusts. Schmidt's damp shirt flapped around his narrow hips, untucked by what seemed to be a sudden gale.

Not the wind. That sound's mechanical. The rumble Charlie heard wasn't hard weather unexpectedly storming off the sea. It was closer, localized, emanating from a single place. The place in question was not far above him.

Schmidt had struck another theatrical pose, his pistol above his head in a two-handed grip, a master marksman lowering his sights to the bull's-eye. It seemed, however—it seemed to Charlie—that he was fighting with the gun, not quite able to pull it down, wrestling against some power that pulled it upward.

The roar of tidal waves and runaway trains, a pocket hurricane over Charlie's head. The noise was unbearable. Charlie dropped prone, his fingers in his ears.

Schmidt's sunglasses flew from his face. His eyes were wide and round and brown and unfocused, a cow's eyes, rolling with myopic terror in the face of thunder and lightning. The Gulfstream's jet engine, powering up, sucked the pistol from his hand. He tried to leap down from his perch atop the TransAm, but could not. He could not move, and—evident from the fury on his face—he could not escape.

Seven tons of thrust, the man said. He called it a flying vacuum cleaner. It can suck roofs off houses and livestock—

Schmidt shrieked. Loud though fourteen thousand pounds of jet power might be, Schmidt's rage was louder. "Fuck, shit!" he screamed, rising into the air. For just a moment, he hovered, floating in a sort of stillness as if weighed in the hand of a judging God.

Judgement rendered, he disappeared with shocking swiftness.

The engine's pitch changed, an abrupt grinding sound, and by the time the copilot switched the engine off, Johan Schmidt was neither meat nor morsel, but only a sewer stench that turned Charlie's stomach.

Charlie glanced up at the cockpit window. The major was there, and maybe he was smiling. Maybe not. In either case, he'd gotten the message: *If you ever need a hand, just give me a thumbs-up. That's all it'll take. Thumbs-up and I'm there for you.*

He forced himself erect, limping toward Irina. He would not, would *not, not, not*, look over his shoulder to see what had been blown out of the engine's exhaust port. He looked only at a girl still breathing, although not breathing much. There was nothing that could be done for her. Charlie had seen enough death and more than enough. He knew where life's borderline lay, knew that she was on its other side.

A single vein throbbed in his neck. All else was frozen, not the least evidence of a bone-breaking struggle within.

Mankiller. Assassin. Avenging angel. He'd mastered the art of smothering his emotions, and he'd never needed it more than he did now.

No mercy, no prisoners, the war he waged against himself ended in seconds, reason triumphant because he was who he was, and only could be true to himself.

Ice not man, he bent over Irina, she beneath the Gulf-stream's wing, untouched by the turbine vortex that had devoured Schmidt. The computer disk, the Whirlwind disk, was in her breast pocket.

He'd failed her. He would not fail his son. Tears would have to wait. He had a job to do. Two jobs, really. One was seeing to it that his son did not follow his father to prison. The other was killing Dr. Sangin Wing.

Nothing personal. Charlie just needed to kill someone at this present time. A Chinese spy would be as satisfactory as anyone else he could name.

He lifted the Whirlwind disk from Irina's pocket, slipping it into his own. He might have kissed her then, but stopped himself. If he did that, it would be the end, and he'd still be by her side when the law came.

He saw Scott jump from the plane, medical kit in hand.

Waste of time. The girl had stopped breathing. She wasn't Irina anymore. She was just a dead thing. Charlie stood and walked away.

Schmidt had left the keys in his Mercedes M-Class's ignition. *Fidelio* played softly on the stereo: *Oh namenlosen Freude,* oh unnameable joy.

Not hardly. Charlie switched it off.

He pulled out of the parking lot, passing a fire truck—siren wailing, lights flashing—as he turned onto the highway.

Somewhere down the road he'd abandon the Mercedes and steal a different vehicle. Somewhere farther on he'd get his leg stitched up again. Then he'd arrange a meeting with one of the Sledgehammer's friends—someone who could unlock the contents of an encrypted disk. It would be expensive. He didn't mind. Buying Scott his freedom was the best use to which the money could be put.

And after that?

Dr. Wing, of course. Quick and clean because he'd take no pleasure in it, and would be no happier once it was done.

Then what?

He could give himself up, he supposed. Or he could kill himself. That would save everyone a lot of trouble.

He wasn't sure which was the better choice. He'd make up his mind later.

EPILOGUE

THE FALL OF THE FOLLOWING YEAR

Injustice is relatively easy to bear; what stings is justice.

—H. L. Mencken

Most of the packing boxes were full. Tomorrow the movers would come. If the trucking company was to be believed, two weeks after that the McKenzie household's possessions would arrive at a ranch with a fine ocean view, not far from the village of San Carlos do Cabo.

Sitting among the crates, Charlie typed a last letter to his wife.

He'd been writing her less often these past months. Life was changing—had changed. He was moving on. Mary understood. She was moving on too.

He was so concentrated on perfecting every word and phrase that he did not hear the footsteps behind him. Despite five months' pregnancy and a beach-ball belly, she moved like a cat, and startled him with a kiss.

He laughed, "Hey, you can do better than pecking my cheek, can't you?"

"Of course I can. You will stand up now, please."

He took her in his arms and it was maybe the best and

most loving kiss he'd ever had—well, except for Mary's—
and Charlie McKenzie felt forty years younger.

"I am the luckiest woman in the world."

Charlie drew his finger across her forehead, tracing the
thin white scar that she would always bear. "In more ways
than one," he frowned, remembering a day of fire and fog;
remembering the sight of his son in his rearview mirror; remembering how futile he thought Scott's pounding on her
chest was, and how useless he knew a Gulfstream's emergency medical kit would be.

But the San Carlos fire department rushed her to the town
clinic, and she was still alive when the gurney rolled into
ER. After fourteen hours of surgery, Scott collapsed. By
then the danger was over, and, in any event, a surgical team
from San Luis Obispo was on the scene.

There'd been only one hero that day, only one. Charlie
was damned proud of him.

Prouder still of Irina, cradling in her womb another
McKenzie who, in four months' time, would begin life in
San Carlos, a village where the child's mother had—in a
very real sense—begun hers.

Now he looked deep into her eyes, savoring the memory
of a perfect kiss, just the one he wanted, packed with all the
affection in the world, and none of sex. *Thank God she's
over it. Me too.*

Scott came into the room. "Dad, will you *please* stop hitting on my wife."

Irina looked sternly over her shoulder at her husband. "Be
careful, you. You can be replaced easily, I think."

Cocking an eyebrow, Scott folded his arms. Charlie
winked at him. Keeping his distance from Irina during the
months she'd been under Scott's full-time care had been a

struggle. He rationed his visits, stopping by rarely, just often enough to give the two of them a nudge in the right direction. It hadn't been much of a challenge. Scott had fallen for her more or less the first time he laid eyes on her. Nor did it take long for Irina, smart girl . . . *damnit, woman . . .* that she was, to see Scott for what he'd always been, a considerably upgraded version of his old man—Charlie: Release 2.0.

Yeah, sure, he knew she still loved him. Always would. But now he was—as maybe he had been all along—a proxy for the good father she'd never had. Nothing wrong with that. Plenty right. It felt fine too, felt a hell of a lot better than taking advantage of a beautiful young woman in the springtime of her life, saddling her with an over-the-hill codger more than twice her age.

He admired his upright behavior, and regretted it only slightly.

Irina knew exactly what he'd done. He'd never fooled her. He never would. From now on, for the rest of her life, she need not ask herself what was right and what was wrong. *The only question I must ask is: What would Charlie do?*

She watched his handsome face turn from affection to dismay as Carly—thunder and lightning in her eyes—stalked through the door, her two thoroughly cowed children in tow. Jason wore short pants, a blue blazer, and a red striped tie. Molly was adorned in a frock whose expense had made Irina blanch—until she heard what Carly had paid for her own summery, ever-so-Washingtonian ensemble: hat, gloves, and all.

"Dad!" The voice of doom. "You're not meeting the president dressed like that!"

Charlie in grey twill cavalry slacks and a collarless cobalt

Walking Man shirt, growled, "As a matter of fact, I am." *Oh, Charlie, you have used the wrong tone of voice, I think.*

"I wasn't asking a question. I was stating a fact."

Irina looked at him with sympathy. He was going to lose, and knew it. Heaving a theatrical sigh, he tried to wheedle a compromise: "Sport coat, white shirt, no tie."

"Tie."

"No tie."

"Tie!" She shook her index finger at him, as lethal a weapon as Irina had ever seen. *"My* children are *not* appearing in front of *every* news camera in America with their grandfather looking like . . . like . . . " Sputtering with anger, she was unable to finish her sentence with the insult it required.

"Okay, okay," Charlie yielded, although not gracefully. "The one from Thailand, the one made of four-hundred-year-old silk. When he hands me the pardon, I'll have the satisfaction of knowing my neckwear is more expensive than his."

Victorious, Carly marched out of the room.

Irina caught a glimpse of herself, a reflection in a window. She was not as fashionably dressed as Carly, wore no jewelry but for a simple gold band, wore no makeup at all. Someday perhaps, some special day, she would surprise Charlie and don the jewels he'd pressed on her, gold and gems made all the more precious because, he'd said, his wife had instructed him to give them to her. With a Gioconda smile, she linked arms with her father-in-law. "The American people are not so smart, I think."

"Oh, yes, they are," Charlie retorted, hugging her close. "There's not a voter in this country who doesn't recognize a professionally staged photo op when he sees one. And there's not a voter who believes the story Washington has been feeding them. Our citizens may not always know what the truth is, but they'll spot a lie every time."

Lie, hell, Charlie thought, *it was a whopper of positively epic proportions.* The spin doctors had concocted a cock-and-bull story about the Dutch ambassador being gunned down on the Van Wyck Expressway by members of a terrorist conspiracy. A baloney sandwich to be sure, with extra baloney on top—at the Agency's behest, Deputy Operations Director Charles McKenzie, that patriotic paragon, heroically allowed himself to be unjustly accused and imprisoned, thus luring the forces of evil into a false sense of security. Nonetheless the intrepid McKenzie (ably assisted by Federal Officers Participating In A Multi-Agency Task Force ferchristsake), was on the case.

Said case culminating in the hijacking of the national security advisor's plane, and we mourn the memory of a loyal public servant who sacrificed his life so that the nation's enemies could be brought to justice.

There were enough loose bodies, a few of which looked credibly Mideastern, strewn around San Carlos to lend a minimum amount of believability to the fairy tale.

Said fairy tale being improvised under pressure, by the way, because Charlie had secreted the full contents of the Whirlwind disk out on the Internet. Extra added attraction: Sam's wholly damning confessions, every word of them, including a sentence that the White House devoutly wished no voter to hear: *If he does know, he doesn't give a flying fuck. It won't happen on his watch.*

Charlie only wished he could have seen the president's face when the downloaded recordings had arrived at the White House—accompanied by an e-mail itemizing in excruciating detail the media companies that would receive memorable recordings of Sam spilling his guts.

Unless certain terms and conditions were met.

Immunity for Scott, political asylum and citizenship for Irina, a pardon and apology for Charlie himself—stuff like that. Charlie asked for a lot.

In the end he got it all, every damned thing, and he'd expected no less.

A Secret Service agent popped his head through the door. "I just got a heads-up. Marine Corps One will be touching down on your lawn in three, that's three, minutes."

"Dad—" Carly was back, brandishing shirt, tie, and jacket like implements of mass destruction.

Good-naturedly, Charlie changed clothes. Irina tweaked his tie knot while Carly, bearing a tool kit that every mother carries, put a photogenic part in his hair.

Charlie grinned at his daughter. Even though she didn't smile back, he knew she was happy—in fact, downright ecstatic. A rural California village would be a good place to raise Jason and Molly. Her disgraced father was suddenly a national hero. And (ask me no questions, I'll tell you no lies) she had a bank account that meant no more scrimping along on inadequate alimony checks. Moreover, she'd hit it off with Irina. That was a blessing. Living in the same house with two warring women was a bullet Charlie devoutly wished to duck. Besides, once the unnamed new McKenzie was born, Irina planned to pursue her doctorate at the University of California. Carly had volunteered that she wouldn't mind having a Ph.D. after her name—unstated footnote: promising matrimonial candidates were as likely to be found among the ranks of post-doctoral scholars as anywhere else.

Well, the ranch house Charlie had bought was big enough for all of them. Scott had set up shop at the San Carlos clinic, his brother was applying for a tenure-track professorship an hour's drive south, and Charlie himself had more or less decided that breeding pedigreed Maine Coon cats would be a fine way to spend his retirement years.

It would be a good retirement, comfortably subsidized not only by the money he'd extorted out of Sam a year earlier, but also by his reinstated Agency pension and the check for three and a half years' back pay the *new* director of Central Intelligence was obliged to present him in just a few minutes' time.

They walked out onto the porch, all six of them. Jason whined that he needed to go to the bathroom. Carly clipped him behind the ear. Molly smiled, as a sister always will when a brother is punished.

Irina put her left arm around Charlie's waist, her right around her husband's. Marine Corps One hovered over the lawn, cameras rolling as it gently landed. Then the cameramen—there must have been thirty out there—panned slowly toward the house, focusing their lenses on a hero and his family waiting to greet the president of the Unitewd States.

Charlie turned around and unloosened his belt.

By his side, a sharply indrawn breath and a murderous whisper: "Dad! Don't you *dare!*"

Out of the corner of his mouth, Charlie answered sweetly, "Of course not, darling. My behavior shall be as though I am the veritable angel of the Lord." To which he added silently, *And smiting sinners is my job. . . .*

THANKS TO:

The sturdy souls who read and mercilessly criticized my early drafts: Avner, Earl, Janice, Mary, Pete, and Terry.

Ellen, Robert, and Scott at Trident Media who offered especially insightful advice.

Editor Marjorie Braman and copy editor Bill Harris for their intelligence, patience, and peerless judgement.

And special gratitude to Jack Francis and Gib Hoxie who advised me on matter aeronautical and nautical. Any errors are my fault, not theirs.

A final word: neither San Carlos do Cabo nor Mitchell Canyon appear on any map. Both locations are composites. However, intrepid explorers can visit Three Turkeys; I recommend it, although there is no IHS clinic there.

—*JRG*
NOVEMBER 2003

GET $250 OFF

Name (Please Print)

Address   Apt. No.

City   State   Zip

E-Mail Address

See Following Page For Terms & Conditions.

For booking form and complete information

go to <u>www.AuthorsAtSea.com</u> or call **1-877-ADV-NTGE**

GCRA 0805

Carnival Pride℠
April 2 - 9, 2006.

7 Day Exotic Mexican Riviera Itinerary

DAY	PORT	ARRIVE	DEPART
Sun	Los Angeles/Long Beach, CA		4:00 P.M.
Mon	"Book Lover's" Day at Sea		
Tue	"Book Lover's" Day at Sea		
Wed	Puerto Vallarta, Mexico	8:00 A.M.	10:00 P.M.
Thu	Mazatlan, Mexico	9:00 A.M.	6:00 P.M.
Fri	Cabo San Lucas, Mexico	7:00 A.M.	4:00 P.M.
Sat	"Book Lover's" Day at Sea		
Sun	Los Angeles/Long Beach, CA	9:00 A.M.	

ports of call subject to weather conditions

TERMS AND CONDITIONS

PAYMENT SCHEDULE:
50% due upon booking
Full and final payment due by February 10, 2006

Acceptable forms of payment are Visa, MasterCard, American Express, Discover and checks. The cardholder must be one of the passengers traveling. A fee of $25 will apply for all returned checks. Check payments must be made payable to **Advantage International, LLC and sent to: Advantage International, LLC, 195 North Harbor Drive, Suite 4206, Chicago, IL 60601**

CHANGE/CANCELLATION:
Notice of change/cancellation must be made in writing to Advantage International, LLC.

Change:
Changes in cabin category may be requested and can result in increased rate and penalties. A name change is permitted 60 days or more prior to departure and will incur a penalty of $50 per name change. Deviation from the group schedule and package is a cancellation.

Cancellation:

181 days or more prior to departure	$250 per person
121 - 180 days or more prior to departure	50% of the package price
120 - 61 days prior to departure	75% of the package price
60 days or less prior to departure	100% of the package price (nonrefundable)

US and Canadian citizens are required to present a valid passport or the original birth certificate and state issued photo ID (drivers license). All other nationalities must contact the consulate of the various ports that are visited for verification of documentation.

<u>We strongly recommend trip cancellation insurance!</u>

For complete details call 1-877-ADV-NTGE or visit www.AuthorsAtSea.com

---

For booking form and complete information
go to <u>www.AuthorsAtSea.com</u> or call 1-877-ADV-NTGE

Complete coupon and booking form and mail both to:
Advantage International, LLC,
195 North Harbor Drive, Suite 4206, Chicago, IL 60601